RAVES FOR THE NOVELS OF CHRISTINE DORSEY

My Savage Heart

"*My Savage Heart* will leave readers breathless and eagerly anticipating the remaining novels in this new trilogy. Ms. Dorsey has created another incredible hero and a wonderful love story."

—Romantic Times

"As always, Christine Dorsey can be counted on to give us a tale full of adventure and romance. *My Savage Heart* is a poignantly written, emotion-packed read that will touch your heart. Her full-bodied characters and well-written storyline will have you engrossed from the first page to the very last."

—Affaire de Coeur

Sea of Temptation

"In *Sea of Temptation*, the sensational conclusion to her outstanding Charleston Trilogy, Christine Dorsey demonstrates why she is one of the most talented authors of the genre today: strong, unforgettable characters, rousing adventures, and history combine to create "keepers.""

—Romantic Times

"Ms. Dorsey's hero and heroine are both strong-willed individuals and their misunderstandings add some very funny situations to this action-packed historical. On the other hand, their fiery passion will send your temperature rising. An outstanding conclusion to a fascinating series on the Blackstones."

—Rendezvous

Sea of Desire

"Christine Dorsey has written a tale of passion, adventure, and love that is impossible to put down. Her heroine is feisty and her hero will leave you breathless. *Sea of Desire* is a book you shouldn't miss and will need some space on your keeper shelf. It is marvelous!"

—Affaire de Coeur

"Blazing passion, nonstop adventure, and a "be-still-my-beating-heart" hero are just a few of the highlights of this captivating second novel in Ms. Dorsey's Charleston Trilogy. *Sea of Desire* is not to be missed!"

—Romantic Times

PIRATE'S SURRENDER

"We spent nearly a month alone together on our island," Anne said.

"A fact I hope you've the sense to keep to yourself."

Anne lowered her lashes. "I haven't told anyone here, no." Raising her eyes, she caught Jamie's gaze. "But that doesn't mean it didn't happen."

"Ye'd be best off forgetting it did."

"I can't."

Her simple declaration seemed to splinter Jamie's resolve. Reaching out, he gave in to temptation and grasped Anne's shoulders. She felt warm and soft beneath the simple dark bodice. "Ye are making a mistake, Annie Cornwall. One you'll live to regret."

"I know we're no longer on our island," Anne whispered. "We have other things to consider now besides ourselves. But for this one night, can't we just pretend nothing else exists?"

She stepped into his embrace then, smiling when his arms tightened around her.

"Ye know I want ye."

But she could still sense his resistance. "And I want you." Standing on tiptoe, Anne brushed a string of kisses along Jamie's chiseled jaw. His eyes closed, the gold-tipped lashes fanning his cheekbones, and his body quickened.

"Ah, Annie, I can't resist ye." His open mouth melded with hers.

And Anne was lost.

Taylor-made Romance from Zebra Books

WHISPERED KISSES   (0-8217-5454-8, $5.99/$6.99)
Beautiful Texas heiress Laura Leigh Webster never imagined
that her biggest worry on her African safari would be the handsome Jace Elliot, her tour guide. Laura's guardian, Lord Chad-
wick Hamilton, warns her of Jace's dangerous past; she simply
cannot resist the lure of his strong arms and the passion of his
Whispered Kisses.

KISS OF THE NIGHT WIND   (0-8217-5279-0, $5.99/$6.99)
Carrie Sue Strover thought she was leaving trouble behind her
when she deserted her brother's outlaw gang to live her life as
schoolmarm Carolyn Starns. On her journey, her stagecoach
was attacked and she was rescued by handsome T.J. Rogue. T.J.
plots to have Carrie lead him to her brother's cohorts who mur-
dered his family. T.J., however, soon succumbs to the beautiful
runaway's charms and loving caresses.

FORTUNE'S FLAMES   (0-8217-5450-5, $5.99/$6.99)
Impatient to begin her journey back home to New Orleans,
beautiful Maren James was furious when Captain Hawk delayed
the voyage by searching for stowaways. Impatience gave way
to uncontrollable desire once the handsome captain searched
her cabin. He was looking for illegal passengers; what he found
was wild passion with a woman he knew was unlike all those
he had known before!

PASSIONS WILD AND FREE   (0-8217-5275-8, $5.99/$6.99)
After seeing her family and home destroyed by the cruel and
hateful Epson gang, Randee Hollis swore revenge. She knew
she found the perfect man to help her—gunslinger Marsh
Logan. Not only strong and brave, Marsh had the ebony hair
and light blue eyes to make Randee forget her hate and seek
the love and passion that only he could give her.

*Available wherever paperbacks are sold, or order direct from the
Publisher. Send cover price plus 50¢ per copy for mailing and
handling to Penguin USA, P.O. Box 999, c/o Dept. 17109,
Bergenfield, NJ 07621. Residents of New York and Tennessee
must include sales tax. DO NOT SEND CASH.*

CHRISTINE DORSEY

MY SEASWEPT HEART

ZEBRA BOOKS
KENSINGTON PUBLISHING CORP.

For Anne . . . sisters are forever.
And as always for Chip.

ZEBRA BOOKS are published by

Kensington Publishing Corp.
850 Third Avenue
New York, NY 10022

Zebra and the Z logo Reg. U.S. Pat. & TM Off.

Second Printing: August 1996

Printed in the United States of America

The majority have the right to act and conclude the rest.
—John Locke

Every man has a vote in affairs of moment.
—Pirate's Articles of Agreement

London
June 1746

Trying to stanch the overwhelming fear was like keeping warm in the damp, vermin-infested dungeon.

Impossible.

James MacQuaid huddled knees to chest as shivers of cold and terror wracked his thin frame. He would fill out to become a brawny man, at least that's what his stepmother had assured him. But she was wrong. There was no time left for the promise of broad shoulders and muscled arms to transform him.

Within a fortnight he would be dead.

Jamie let his head fall back against the moisture-bleeding stones of his cell. It wasn't supposed to end like this. By now he was to be riding into London astride a mighty stallion amid joyous huzzahs and cheering multitudes. He would be a hero, adored by the masses for his help in restoring the rightful king to his throne.

Closing his eyes, Jamie let the fantasy flow through him like warm honey. The flowers strewn in his path, the smiling faces of pretty maidens eager for a kiss from the handsome crusader. He would be hailed as one of Prince Charles Edward Stuart's lieutenants. One of the intrepid souls who'd risked all to see the rightful heir proclaimed king.

The deep echoing sound of voices outside his cell pierced the gossamer dream. The throngs disappeared, the cheers drifted to nothingness like the mist lifting over Culloden. Revealing the dead and twisted bodies of his compatriots, lying on the rain swept plain. The agonizing screams of prisoners as they were slaughtered by the Duke of Cumberland's soldiers.

As his cell door swung open with a groaning protest, reality crashed over Jamie like waves over the rocks of the Heberdes. There was no more glorious revolution. Prince Charles was defeated, his once mighty army in ruins, the prince himself . . . Rumors were rampant. He was dead, said some. Others spoke of his escape garbed as a woman. Still others bragged that he would return to fight again another day.

But it would be too late for Jamie. He was captured and tried. Found guilty of the heinous crime of believing in a lost cause. And sentenced to hang.

Lifting his arm, he squinted toward the light shining into his dark cell. Jamie couldn't tell who stood behind the lantern till he spoke. Then tears of joy . . . of hope burned his eyes.

"Father." His voice was rusty from disuse.

" 'Tis a fine mess you've gotten yourself into this time, James. A fine mess."

Jamie scrambled to his feet, but his limbs were as out of practice as his tongue. He waited for the light to move closer, his shoulders drooping when it didn't.

"I warned you of this, James. Do you recall?"

"Yes, sir."

"I told you to put aside your foolish beliefs in that pompous pretender to the throne." There was a hesitation. "You do remember my words, don't you?"

"Aye." Jamie remembered them well. His father's harangue. His own fevered speech in defense of his actions. Leaving.

Jamie cleared his throat. He didn't want to talk of this. He hadn't seen any of his family since he left home to join the Highland army near Manchester. "How is Margaret, and Logan?"

"You're a fine one to ask such questions. 'Tis no thanks to you that they are safe."

"I'd never do anything to harm them," Jamie protested. "Never."

"You think your stepmother didn't cry when you left? Do you think your brother, Logan, won't suffer for your stupidity? But you didn't care."

"I cared. I care." He loved his stepmother in a way he never thought possible when his father first brought her home. She formed a buffer between Jamie and his stern father that had been missing since his own mother died. "Is she coming to see me?"

"Are you mad? That's it, isn't it? You're as mad as your mother was. Margaret wants nothing more to do with you, nor do I. I came to London to try and convince the authorities that I've disowned you. That your foolish deeds were your own and not mine." He lowered the lantern so Jamie could see his scowling face, the features almost demonic in the fractured light. "Lost causes are for fools."

Then he turned, punctuating his words with the metallic clang of the cell door as it closed behind him.

Chapter One

New Providence
July 1762

"I ain't sure ye should be goin' in there, Mistress Anne."

"Nonsense, Israel." Anne Cornwell chose to ignore the burly ruffian entering the Shark's Tooth Tavern. And the loud, raucous laughter that spewed through the door when he opened it. If she thought about what she was going to do for too long, Anne would have to agree with her friend. And she didn't have that option. Sucking in a breath of air heavy with the smell of tar and brine and rotting garbage Anne raised her chin. "I shall be fine."

"Hell, I'll go talk to the bastard. I've been in enough of these dives to know me way around."

"That's very kind of you, Israel. However, we decided I should plead our case with him."

Anne didn't take her eyes off the tavern door to see Israel's reaction, but she could hear him shuffling his feet and grumbling to himself. And she could imagine him pulling on his scraggly beard as he chewed on the pipe stem that never seemed to leave his mouth.

"Your uncle ain't gonna like this," he finally said and Anne could only shrug.

"You're right of course, but then he shan't find out about it." Anne did slant a look his way now and her expression spoke of all the reasons Israel wouldn't snitch on her to Richard Cornwall. Top on the list was the fact that Israel had sailed her to New Providence in the first place.

With a sigh Anne straightened her shoulders, and patted the dark hair neatly pinned beneath her cap. "We decided this was the only way. And heavens knows something must be done."

"You decided, 'tis more the truth," Israel mumbled and Anne tilted her head in acknowledgment. For though Israel was the one who first suggested James MacQuaid might be able to help them, it was Anne who came up with this plan to tell the captain of their plight.

Which she had best be doing. Anne touched the old man's ragged sleeve. "You're sure he's in there?"

"Followed him here meself while ye was rentin' your lodgin' from the Widow Perkins."

"Good. I shall look for a tall man with light hair."

"Aye, big he is, and with golden ringlets any fine lady would envy."

Anne started across the muddy street, rolling her eyes and wondering how the infamous Captain MacQuaid would view Israel's description.

"Don't be forgettin' what I told ye," Israel started his reminder at a yell, then quickly lowered his voice when a passing sailor looked his way.

"I shan't." Anne patted the side of her skirts. Beneath

the plain petticoats she cold feel the pistol nestled in her pocket. The solid feel bolstered her confidence, until she felt a hand clasp around her arm. With a stifled scream she jerked around. "Heaven's, Israel, are you trying to scare me to death?"

"Just remember to fire it only as a signal. Don't go tryin' to kill no one."

"Of course I won't." Anne patted his arm again. Mustering her courage she stepped into the puddle of light from the swinging lantern over the tavern door. Her last words before she reached for the latch were tossed over her shoulder. "Don't fret so."

Stepping inside the Shark's Tooth was like entering another world. Anne imagined hell might be something like this. Loud and boisterous, the air heavy with smoke and odors she couldn't begin to identify. She stood a moment, back pressed to the door's splintery wood and looked about her. Her eyes burned and she squinted, trying to find the man she sought.

The golden-haired Captain James MacQauid.

Anne peered around the crowded room, thankful no one apparently noticed her yet. They were all too busy doing Lord knew what. Drinking and yelling and wenching, she revised as each individual scenario came into focus. Anne swallowed down her revulsion. Before she entered this den of iniquity she feared she would be the only women inside. Now she wished she were.

For the other females were obviously loose women, lost souls who strutted about with their breasts bared, hoping to attract the attention of the equally immoral men.

Anne shook her head and forced her attention back to the problem at hand. She needed to find the captain of the *Lost Cause.*

"What have we here?" A beefy hand clasped about her arm and Anne leaned away from the wretched stench of the man's breath.

She could make her voice ring with authority—a vice she usually eschewed. But now Anne put forth her best effort. "Unhand me."

Unfortunately the brute didn't appear to understand or respond to authority. He merely laughed, throwing his massive head back and sending forth gusts of his disgusting breath. And all the while he kept her upper arm manacled in his grip.

When he recovered sufficiently from his mirth to wipe a filthy hand across his streaming eyes he yanked her toward him. Anne found herself pressed against the wide girth of his flabby body.

Screaming for help would do no good. If anyone could even hear her in this cornucopia of sound, she doubted they would be inclined to give her assistance.

The only person who would try was crouched in the shadows outside, and he'd never hear her.

"Now, sweet wench, hows about a kiss for old Stymie? Leastways we'll start with a kiss."

His slobbery lips descended and Anne wriggled to get her arm free. Just as his hot breath burned her face she managed to squeeze her hand up between their bodies. The slap of her palm against his cheek seemed to ring in her ears. Or maybe it was only the tightening of his arm that encircled her back making it seem that way. She could hardly get her breath. But she could see the angry sneer on his face.

"That t'weren't nice, ye bitch. Ol' Stymie is gonna have to teach ye ta—"

"I've come to see Captain MacQauid!" Anne wasn't

sure what made her say that, but she was glad she did. Stymie's reaction was immediate. He let her go as if she were suddenly too hot to hold. Anne stumbled backward managing to catch hold of the rum-sticky rung of a chair before she fell.

"Well, now, why didn't ye say ye was one of Jamie's wenches?" He grabbed a tankard off the nearest table, a move that provoked the old man sitting there, and took a healthy gulp. "I ain't one to interfere with Jamie's pleasures." He plopped the mug down, spilling brownish liquid over the sides. "Ain't never had to," he finished, then shrugged off the hands of the drink's owner and turned away.

"A moment, please," Anne called, taking only a small backward step when he twisted his burly head around toward her. "Where is he? Where can I find Captain MacQuaid?"

His response could best be described as a grunt, but he pointed toward the back corner before he took a swipe at the grizzled sailor who still clung to his elbow.

Anne didn't stop to notice how that altercation ended. She wended her way in the direction the bully indicated, keeping her head down and her eyes averted. Biting her lip to suppress an angry tongue-lashing, Anne did her best to ignore the offensive slap that landed on her bottom. Luckily whoever touched her didn't repeat it or grab her.

The back table was long and littered with dirty tankards. A candle stub flickered in hot tallow giving off just enough light for Anne to see a huge blackamoor, naked to the waist and a stiff-lipped man dressed in a black waistcoat and jacket, with a whiter stock than she expected to see inside this establishment. There was another man seated between them, but he was mostly hidden by the two "ladies" who had attached themselves to him.

But Anne paid him little heed. She addressed her remarks to the stone-faced gentleman who wore a powdered wig. "Do I have the pleasure of addressing Captain MacQuid?"

"Who'd be wanting to know?"

Her manners seemed ill spent in this place, conferring with these people, but Anne nevertheless tried to remember them. The person to whom she spoke focused his one good eye straight ahead, not choosing to look at her, while the blackamoor stared her way. The third man hadn't paused in his quest to roam the entire length of one of his friend's thighs. His other hand, large and surprisingly well-shaped and clean rested on the buttocks of the woman nestled between his legs, her bosom pressed into his face. She didn't even have the decency to muffle her moans.

Shifting her weight and trying not to squirm, Anne introduced herself to the black-garbed man. But it was the blackamoor who spoke.

"I'd be leaving this place if I was you, Mistress Cornwall."

His voice was deep and almost kind, despite the rows of fierce-looking tattoos that crisscrossed his sweat-slick countenance.

Anne swallowed. "Thank you for your concern, sir. However, I traveled a great distance to converse with Captain MacQuaid. So if you would kindly—"

"Suppose the good captain does not wish to take part in this conversation?" This from the man devouring the woman's nearly exposed breasts. His words were slurred by a bit of Scottish brogue, and more than a touch of drink. But though his movements had stopped, he'd yet to look up. Nor had the man in black glanced her way. Only the blackamoor stared at her.

Anne focused on each man in turn, then returned her gaze to the one in the center. "I doubt the term 'good' is ofttimes used to describe Captain MacQuaid. However, I should hope he has the decency to at least acknowledge my presence and tell me himself whether or not he wishes to speak with me."

The head jerked up, a tumble of golden hair fell forward and Anne found her gaze locked to one of bloodshot blue-green eyes. Both women voiced displeasure as he motioned for them to leave. The buxom serving girl who scurried from between his legs gave Anne a scowl as she pushed past. Her breasts strained against the flimsy linen. They were also pink and wet from his mouth. When she caught Anne staring her tongue came out to moisten her lips. "Don't be selfish with him, girly. There be plenty of Jamie to go 'round."

This brought a titter of laughter from the other woman and when Anne, red-faced, turned back toward the man, a grin came from him.

Now that the women were gone, he shoved his chair back, balancing it on two legs and took his time to peruse Anne from head to toe. The look he gave her made fresh blood race to shade her cheeks. Still Anne refused to turn away. Though she assumed he found her lacking compared to the two tavern wenches, it made no difference at all to her. Her plainly cut gown was serviceable, and certainly not meant to attract attention.

She cleared her throat, when he refused to cease his perusal. "Are you indeed Captain MacQuaid?"

He seemed to consider the question a moment, then

pushed forward, landing the front chair legs on the floor with a bang. "Aye." He leaned bare elbows on the table. "And why is such as you wanting to know?"

Anne still stood on the opposite side of the table from the three men, none of whom had the decency to stand or offer her a seat. This Captain MacQuiad wasn't anything like she'd expected. He seemed much younger than she would have thought, though in the dim light, it was hard to distinguish his age. And, of course, he was ruder. She took a step forward. "I've come to ask your help."

Well, if nothing else this remark gained the attention of the one-eyed man. He twisted his head to turn the full focus of his pale blue orb on her.

The man whose assistance she sought merely threw his head back and laughed, a deep booming sound that was nearly as unsettling as his stare. When he stopped, it was to again let his gaze drift over her.

"Have you any idea what manner of sea captain I am?"

"You're a pirate," Anne responded without pausing to consider the consequences.

"Aye, 'tis the truth. A freebooting buccaneer who doesn't go about doing good deeds for sweet young things such as yourself." His expression changed. His eyelids lowered. "Unless, of course . . ." he said, then paused. "What manner of payment did ye have in mind?"

"I had thought you might be persuaded out of the goodness of your heart."

This brought a spat of fresh laughter, which even the blackamoor joined.

"A pirate doesn't have a heart, Mistress Cornwall. You best remember that."

"I shall attempt to do so." Anne flattened her palms on the scarred tabletop. This wasn't going at all as she'd envisioned, but if she could only tell him. "If you would give me but a moment, sir, to explain what has happened." She leaned forward, forging ahead before he could say otherwise. "Our island was raided, ravished really, by—"

"Penitence from God!"

Anne stood up in shock. It was the one-eyed man in black who spoke, yelled actually, and he now looked at her, his expression bright with righteous indignation.

"Now, Deacon." The captain's hand clasped his shoulder. "I doubt the lass has done anything to bring the wrath of God tumbling down upon her." One brow, dark like the whiskers covering his lower face, lifted. "Have ye now?"

"No!" Anne turned her attention back toward the captain, though she was uneasily aware of the man he called Deacon. "And I doubt anyone would liken Willet d'Porteau with God."

"The Frenchie," the blackamoor said, then shared a look with his captain that Anne didn't understand.

But the very mention of the name seemed to sober the captain. His chest, barely covered by a linen shirt open to the waist, expanded as he sucked in a breath. Then he leaned back and steepled his fingers. "Count yourself lucky that you can stand here before me if Frenchie d'Porteau attacked your island."

Her voice was somber. "Some cannot."

Anne thought she saw a flicker of sympathy cross those blue-green eyes before he reached for his tankard. After a long gulp he lowered it to the table with a slam.

" 'Tis no business of mine what the Frenchman does."

"I thought him your enemy."

His eyes narrowed. "Where would you hear such as that?"

Anne shrugged. "It's not difficult to know." Actually it was Israel who told her. "The two men hate each other. A long-standing blood feud." Israel said those words one afternoon as they sat on the beach. Anne, thinking as she always did of the destruction and pain caused by d'Porteau mused aloud that her uncle's settlement needed a savior. Someone strong enough to go up against Willet d'Porteau and his crew.

Her first reaction was shock when Israel suggested a pirate might be that savior. "I can't imagine what is in your head. Pirates are the bane of our existence."

The old man only shrugged. "Some folk say takes an angel to fight the devil," he said, taking his knife from the thong about his waist and tossing it blade first into the sand. "I say it takes a stronger devil."

As it was Israel convinced Anne that Captain James MacQuaid was more fallen angel than devil, and she'd believed him . . . until now.

The captain leaned forward till she could smell his musky scent. " 'Tis your time you're wasting."

"It's mine to waste."

"Aye, but mine is not." He lifted his tankard in dismissal, seeming surprised to find her still standing on the opposite side of the table when he lowered it. "Be gone with ye now, wench. I'm sorry for your troubles but they're not mine."

"But if you'd only listen." Hope gave way to despair. "He came to our island and stole and killed." Anne swallowed, unable to say what else he'd done. "He took my cousin and he swore he'd be back. He swore it on my uncle's blood." Anne realized her voice had risen and several of the tavern's disreputable patrons were watching her. She forced herself to calm down.

He stared at her a moment and again she thought, hoped, she saw a flicker of sympathy. When he spoke his voice was firm. "I suggest you leave your island."

"We cannot. Our homes are there. And Libertia means everything to my uncle."

"Then 'tis a matter of taking your chances with the Frenchman."

Finding no satisfaction in the captain's words, Anne turned to the blackamoor, then the man called Deacon. Neither met her eye. The captain was bolder, but his expression was one of annoyance. A more feeble-hearted female might have retreated, but Anne had been through too much, feared too much, for such tactics.

"If you would only listen to me—"

"I've heard enough."

"You've heard nothing!" Anne's nostrils flared in anger. "I'd thought you might care a bit because of what you named your ship," she said in disgust.

"The *Lost Cause*?" His brow arched. " 'Tis a name meant to remind me of that basest of all human frailties. 'Tis not that I champion lost causes. I loathe them, and the fools who perpetuate them."

There was nothing to do but leave. Anne turned on her heel, but his voice stopped her before she could take a step.

"Mistress Cornwall." His grin was sly when she faced him. "Perhaps we shall meet again, and I can show you there is more than one way for a captain to be good."

His laughter followed her as she made her way through the loud throng of drunken sailors. Even smelling as foul as it did, the outside air was a relief after the smoke-filled inside. Anne took a deep breath, gasping when someone grabbed at her.

"Israel, my heavens, you gave me a fright." Anne clasped her fingers to the base of her throat, annoyed to see that her hand shook.

"No more than you gave me. Do ye know how long you were in there?"

"Not exactly." Anne took Israel's arm, and pulled him away from the tavern door."

"I was just about to come in after ye."

"It would have done no good."

"Ye found him then."

"I did."

"And, will he go after d'Porteau?"

"Not at the present, no." Anne brushed aside a wisp of brown hair the trade winds blew into her face. "He wasn't very willing to listen."

Israel settled onto an overturned barrel. "Well, I suppose that be it then."

"What? Oh, I'm not ready to give up on him yet."

"But ye said." Israel paused and shook his head. "Ye don't know Captain MacQuaid. He's a stubborn one. If he won't listen—"

"Then he'll simply have to see for himself." Anne rushed on before her friend could argue. "He'll like my uncle, I'm sure of it. And once he sees Libertia himself, understands what Uncle Richard is trying to do . . . Don't you see, it's the only way."

"I ain't sayin' he wouldn't be impressed. But if he don't want to go, there ain't no way we can force him. It ain't as if ye can kidnap him."

Anne slowly lifted her head. "But, Israel, that's exactly what we're going to do."

* * *

"He's the devil's curse."

"That he is, Deacon. That he is." Jamie called out to the barmaid to refill his tankard.

"The girl doesn't stand a chance against him."

Jamie scowled at his chief gunner. The black man didn't appear intimidated. "She is not our problem, Keena." He leaned back against the wall. "Besides, she's a comely enough lass. The Frenchman likes beautiful women."

"She will lose her beauty quickly."

"Hell and damnation, Keena, what 'twould you have me do? If her island is in danger, she damn well better get off the island." Jamie folded his arms across an impressive chest. "What was the likes of her doing here anyway?"

"Appeared to me she was asking for help," Keena said and earned himself another dark scowl from his captain.

"Let her set sail for England or somewhere. She's too much the lady for these parts." A smile played around his mouth. "Though she has a sharp enough tongue, I wouldn't be surprised if it cut the Frenchman to ribbons if they ever cross paths again."

Keena didn't seem to appreciate his joke and Deacon sat sober as you please, so Jamie was forced to laugh at the witticism alone. That is until Polly appeared with a tray full of ale and bodice that barely contained her straining breasts. She deposited the tankards on the table, making certain to give each man his just view, then settled with a squirm onto Jamie's lap.

"Now, Polly, 'tisn't nice to be tempting the Deacon so," Jamie said with a laugh.

"I only give him a peek at what he's missin'," she cooed

into his ear. "But ye know, don't ye, Jamie?" Her work-rough hand slipped between their bodies and busily stroked the front of the captain's breeches.

"Aye." Jamie sucked in his breath. "Now, Polly, all I was wanting was a bit of brew."

"Don't be foolin' with me, Jamie MacQuaid. Ye think I can't feel you all swollen up and stiff as a mainmast?"

"And whose wouldn't be, with the most experienced hands on the island working their wonders." Jamie wrapped his fingers about her wrist, bringing those wonders to a stop.

"I can do better with my mouth, Jamie," she breathed, rubbing her breasts against his hair-roughened chest. The billowy bodice lost its hold on her flesh and one large, brown nipple popped out. Polly glanced down, then wet her narrow lips with her equally narrow tongue. "As you well know."

"That I do, Polly. That I do." He gave her rump a squeeze as he lifted her off his lap. "Be a good lass, though, and run along for now."

Polly turned back toward Jamie, not bothering to cover herself. "I'll be 'round later, Jamie." She brushed her breast against Deacon as she strutted away.

"Spawn of the devil," Deacon said, his good eye staring straight ahead.

"She's not so bad," Jamie said, though at the moment he shared his quartermaster's distaste for the barmaid. There was no denying the woman, despite her expertise in the French way of making love was coarse and dirty. But then he'd never thought too much about it till now. Till he compared her with the woman who'd come into the Shark's Tooth looking for him.

And he wasn't about to tell Polly or anyone else that the

ache in his breeches was ignited not by the experienced barmaid, but by thoughts of that slim, sharp-tongued wench.

He was drinking too much. Familiar as he was with the gradual blurring of his senses—and the dull ache in his head—Jamie couldn't think of a good reason to stop. Keena was matching him tankard for tankard, but the damn African seemed as sober as when they entered the tavern.

"I've the blood of kings running through my veins," he said once when Jamie questioned him about his capacity for drink. As if that somehow accounted for his sobriety. Jamie snorted now, remembering the conversation. Keena certainly didn't resemble a king when the *Lost Cause* picked him up off the coast of Trinidad. He looked starved and bloody and nearly drowned.

"It's time we leave this den if inequity."

Jamie peered at Deacon through red-rimmed eyes. "What's the hurry? The problem is you need something to drink." Jamie slid his own tankard across the table, spilling much of the contents in the process. Not surprisingly Deacon pushed the pewter mug back.

"Deacon is right, Captain. We should return to the ship."

"Who in the hell was in charge here?" Jamie stared from one to the other. In the part of his mind that still functioned, he knew his companions were right. But he didn't feel like leaving. Something had sabotaged the high mood he was in when he entered the harbor at New Providence, his vessel's hold full to overflowing with riches. "More like someone," he mumbled, only to shake his head when Keena questioned what he said.

"You two go on with ye. I'll be staying a bit longer."

"Captain, I don't think—"

"And ye don't have to now, do ye?" Jamie spotted Polly across the crowded room. "I've a certain lady I can't go disappointing." Jamie slapped his palms onto the tabletop. "But you both be off. I don't think even Mistress Polly will be wanting to service all three of us tonight."

He'd argued for them to leave, but as soon as his men were gone, Jamie wished he hadn't. Contrary to what he told them he had no interest in visiting Polly's smelly room upstairs.

He had no interest in doing much of anything.

" 'Tis the drink," he murmured, then glanced up, thankful no one was near enough to hear him talking to himself. Not that anyone would say anything. He evoked enough fear, even among the scurvy lot inside the Shark's Tooth to ensure his privacy.

Damn his blood, he didn't want privacy. Jamie stumbled to his feet. He didn't want to think, and he didn't want to wrestle Polly between the sheets. Pushing aside anyone who crossed his path, Jamie made his way to the door.

The night air was soft, a caress after the hours of languishing inside. Jamie took a deep breath, and pushed his fingers back through his tangle of hair. He wasn't sober, but he wasn't as drunk as he'd earlier thought, either. Certainly not drunk enough to block out memories.

"Hell and damnation." Jamie took an unsteady step toward the pier, then another. Something had stirred a flood of recollections in him . . . and he knew exactly what, or who it was.

Mistress Anne Cornwall.

With her delicate features and brassy tongue.

There was a time he would have leaped at the opportunity to assist a gentlewoman. But that was before, when *he* was a gentleman. When his conscience burned with the passion of righteousness.

When he was a fool.

That was what his father called him. His last words to him. "Lost causes are for fools."

Jamie had thought of those prophetic words often while he sat in the squalor of his cell, awaiting the hangman's noose. Knowing his father would lift not a finger to help him.

God, he could shut his eyes and be back there again. The stench. The damp cold. The fear.

Jamie took a deep breath, leaning his back against a palm tree. He needed to remember who he was. Where he was. This was New Providence and he was free. And if the hangman ever caught him it would be to pay for sins well earned.

"Where are your friends?"

Jamie jerked his head around at the sound of the voice, as soft and gentle as the breeze off the bay. "Well now, if it isn't Mistress Cornwall." He peered into the shadows to see if she was alone. "What are you about this night? Hoping to solicit help for your cause?"

"I've given up on that . . . for tonight." Anne took a step closer. He was taller than she imagined when she saw him sitting. Over a head taller than she even while leaning against the tree.

"Oh?" Jamie lifted a brow. "So why are you here?"

Anne moved again till she was close enough to touch him if she chose, to smell him. "I wished to . . . to . . . She didn't know how to say it but she hoped he could read her wishes in her movements.

He did nothing. Though she could barely make out his

features in the dim light, Anne imagined his expression was one of amusement. Seduction was not an art she practiced. Straightening her shoulders Anne decided to force herself to attempt some of the things she'd seen in the tavern.

But before she could his arms wrapped around her and she was yanked against his hard, hot body. She didn't expect anything so overpowering, so consuming, and without considering her plan she opened her mouth to scream. That's when his head lowered and he caught her in a devouring kiss.

His tongue invaded her mouth and she tasted ale and something else, darker and more erotic than anything she'd ever known before. He was a pirate, crude and coarse, and she should have been revulsed by his touch, by his taste. Yet even as Anne pushed against the hot skin of his chest, trying to separate them, part of her wondered at the way he made her feel. The tingle in her toes. The weakness of her knees.

"No, please." Anne angled her mouth away from his and tried to ignore the lips that now blazed a trail down the side of her neck. "Please stop. Stop!" Her tone held unmistakable panic.

Her words seemed to penetrate and he paused. Anne could feel the ragged gusts of his breath along the length of her jaw. Unbidden came the vision of the barmaid's breasts where he'd kissed them, red and wet, and Anne's own nipples, pressed against his naked chest seemed to swell with the memory.

And then he let her go. His arms dropped to his side and he leaned back again against the palm. "What 'tis it you want from me, wench?"

Anne sucked in air and tried to calm her racing heart.

"The same that you want. It's just that there's no privacy here." Anne swallowed. "I have a room on Bay Street. If we could go there . . ."

Anne couldn't even finish saying what would happen if he accompanied her there. Everything she said sounded so false to her ears. But somehow he believed her lies. At least he appeared to. With a bow worthy of the finest gentleman he offered his arm.

Neither spoke during the short walk down the side street. All was dark when they reached the room she had let. It was on the ground level of Widow Perkin's house, and Anne cautioned the captain to be quiet as they entered through the front door. He seemed to find nothing about her request unusual and managed to follow her to the small room without bumping into anything.

Once inside Anne struck the flint, lighting a candle and placed it on the table by the bed. She tried to keep her hands steady, but it was nearly impossible as she moved under the pirate captain's steady gaze. She knew he watched her, could feel the heat of his stare, but it wasn't until she glanced up meeting his eyes that she knew their intensity.

"I . . . this is it," she said, feeling foolish and utterly unprepared for what she must do.

"So I see." His stare didn't waver, even when he folded his arms across his chest.

Anne tried a smile, then reached for the decanter beside the candle. "Would you care for something to drink? I've a fine Mader—"

"Nay, nothing."

Disappointment and fear coursed through her body, though Anne tried not to show either. But when he spoke she couldn't help her nervous jump.

"I must admit to a bit of surprise."

"How so?" Anne stood awkwardly, wondering what to do next. Unlike on the street outside of the tavern the captain didn't seem in any hurry.

"I expected . . ." His brow arched. "An impassioned plea for my help."

"Is that what you wish? For if it is I can . . ." Anne's voice trailed off as he stepped forward.

" 'Tis not my desire."

Anne's heart pounded. "I thought not. You already made your position very clear."

"Aye." Jamie reached out to hook her chin with the tip of his finger, lifting her face toward his. " 'Tis still the question of why you asked me here."

Without looking down Anne reached for the laces of her bodice. He said nothing as she tugged on the bow with trembling fingers. His hand covered hers as the top of her corset yawned open. The heat of his palm warmed the curve of her flesh.

"Why are you doing this?" His words were as breathless as she felt.

Anne swallowed. "You find my desires surprising? What of that woman . . . those women in the tavern?"

"Ye are not like them."

"You are so certain?" Anne slowly pulled her hand from beneath his. Now there was nothing between him and the swell of her breast. She prepared herself to bear the repulsion, surprised when it didn't come. With her fingers she reached out, touching the hot skin at the base of his neck. "Perhaps all women are alike when it comes to you, Jamie MacQuaid."

She expected the kiss, but not the fire that shot through her body. It left her unaware that he'd lifted one breast from her corset until the exquisite torture of his thumb became near unbearable.

"Please." Anne pushed against him with the flat of her palm. His head lifted but his hand continued to circle the puckered tip of her nipple until she pointed toward the glass decanter. "I'm nearly parched. Some wine . . . please."

She sank onto the bed when he reached for the bottle. There were two glasses beside the wine and she nearly wept with relief when he splashed amber liquid in both of them. The first he handed to her, the second he drank as greedily as she wished to drink hers.

But she didn't.

Before Anne could worry that he would notice he was on the bed beside her. She shoved the still full glass onto the table as he pushed her back onto pillow. His mouth covered her as easily as his body. The kiss was deep and searing and before it was over, Anne wasn't certain which of them had been drugged.

Chapter Two

Why was he still awake? Not only awake but seemingly as fit . . . and amorous as before he gulped down the laudanum-laced wine. If the sedative had any effect upon him, Anne had yet to see it.

"Please, Captain . . ." Anne managed to turn her mouth away from his passionate kiss.

"Please what? And don't ye think you can call me Jamie?" He wet the delicate underside of her jaw with the tip of his tongue. She tasted . . . smelled sweeter than any woman he could remember.

Please what indeed. Anne wriggled under his weight, trying to think of something, anything to say. Her skin tingled wherever he touched her. And fighting him, fighting the temptation to stop fighting, was becoming more difficult with each passing moment.

She jerked when his hand clasped her bared breast. And that's when she felt it. It was large, long, and very hard and it pressed into her hip. "Captain . . . I mean Jamie." Anne barely recognized the breathless quality of her voice.

"Aye?" He lifted his head and looked down at her with

eyes now grown dark with passion. His thumb never paused from its erotic arousal of her nipple.

"Your pistols," Anne managed to get out before she bit her bottom lip to suppress a moan. She couldn't believe the way he made her feel. So different from the revulsion d'Porteau stirred.

Thoughts of that hated of all demons cooled Anne's blood. She pushed against the captain's chest. "Your pistols are hurting me. Please remove them."

It took a moment for her request to pierce the fog settling over his mind. Jamie shook his head at his own stupidity and rolled to the side, planting his feet as firmly as he could on the rocking deck.

No, floor. He wasn't on the *Lost Cause* being tossed about by the savage winds of a hurricane, though, by God, it felt as if he were. Jamie lurched to his feet, yanking one, then the other of his guns from the leather strap crossing his chest. He laid them both as carefully as he could on the bedside table, annoyed with himself when he bumped the wine decanter. If not for the woman . . . Jamie searched his brain . . . ah yes, Anne Cornwall. If not for beautiful Annie's quick movements the bottle would have shattered to the floor.

"Perhaps you should have some more wine."

Jamie watched as she poured the amber liquid into his glass. The motion of shaking his head now caused a wave of dizziness to swamp over him. "Think . . . I've drunk . . . too much already." He knew exactly what he wanted to taste and it wasn't in the glass.

His hand reached out to touch the extended tip of her breast, and closed instead over something smooth and cold. The glass. Had he asked for it? Whatever, it seemed to stand between him and the sweet oblivion of Anne. With one jerky motion, Jamie gulped down the drink.

The crystal shattered onto the floor, but Jamie didn't notice. He propelled himself forward, falling onto the bed on top of Anne. His mouth settled over hers, open and hungry. His hands fumbled with her skirts and petticoat, surging higher when he felt the soft warmth of her leg.

As his mind slowed and reality faded, his desires burned hotter. He couldn't get enough of her. He couldn't get her quickly enough. She wriggled and writhed beneath him, inciting his already explosive passions.

He yanked at her skirts, pushing and prodding to untangle them from her twisting legs. When his palm covered her mound she bucked and he wasted no time slipping his finger through the tangle of curls. She was hot and moist. Inviting beyond reason.

Jamie could bear it no more. He didn't know which would explode first: his head or the swollen flesh that throbbed against his breeches. His fingers left the scalding heat of her body to fumble with the front flap of his breeches, but returned when he couldn't master the buttons. Wild with a torture like he'd never known before Jamie jerked, dragging his mouth down her body.

Her thigh beckoned and he tasted her sweet flesh, devouring it as he skimmed higher toward his goal. His hands spread her legs. His tongue blazed toward her waiting womanhood. He burned. He desired. He . . ."

"Stop. Oh please stop." Anne grew hoarse from her strangled pleas. She shoved at his shoulders, her fingers digging into his sweat-slick skin, and only then noticed that he had stopped.

Completely.

His burnished gold head lay cradled between her thighs and she could feel the flutter of his breath fanning her tight curls. But he no longer teased with his mouth or moved at all for that matter.

"Jamie. Captain MacQuaid?" Anne's voice was ragged as she lifted her head. She could see nothing over the bunched-up fabric of her gown.

She listened but there was no answer, just the sound of soft snores.

Even when she called his name louder he didn't respond.

Letting out her pent-up breath Anne flopped back onto the pillow. He had succumbed just in time. Actually, she admitted to herself, he hadn't passed out in time at all. She'd been touched and kissed and . . . Anne pushed all that from her mind as she rolled to the side, pulling her leg from beneath his head. This was not the time to think of what he did. What she'd let him do. Or the way he'd made her feel.

Her hair was down around her shoulders, her skirts were a rumpled mess and her bodice . . . Anne shook her head as she pulled the linen over her exposed breast and retied the laces. She was finger combing her hair when she heard the first light rapping on the windowpane. Before she could pull back the curtain Israel was pounding.

"Cease what you're about, Israel." Anne shoved the casement open "It is not impossible to wake Mistress Perkins." The landlady was nearly deaf, but there was no need to take any more chances than they must.

"Sorry, Mistress Anne, but I's a wondering what was takin' ye so long."

A good question to be sure, but one Anne didn't wish

to answer. "Come around to the door. He's asleep, but I don't know for how long."

"Aye and the laudanum will keep him dreamin' sweet dreams till mornin'."

"Yes, well, let us hope so." Considering the difficulty with which he fell asleep, Anne wasn't convinced. She stared down at the captain, sprawled on her bed and wondered that he could could seem so benign. Even with his hair disheveled and a day's growth of whiskers darkening his square jaw he appeared almost innocent. Like the fallen angel Israel described.

But she was allowing foolishness to color her thinking. James MacQuaid was a pirate. He might be useful to her . . . to Libertia if he wished, but he was a pirate nonetheless.

After scooping the wooden hairpins off the pillow she thrust them through her skirt pocket and turned to open the door.

Israel's eyes were knowing when they first met hers.

" 'Tis sure, I am, whatever he tried to do ye took care of it since ye didn't call for me help. Am I right, girl?"

Anne lifted her chin. "Yes. Now how do you propose we get him to the pier?"

There seemed only one way. Pushing and pulling and shoving and grunting the two of them managed to take the pirate captain out of the house and load him onto a wheelbarrow. From there the task was easier until they reached the dock. Then it was more hard work.

"He must weigh near fifteen stone."

"At least." Anne fell back onto the small sloop's seat and looked down at the captain sprawled on the bottom. She didn't think she'd ever been so tired. Out on the bay morning was painting the horizon a pale pewter and they still had a three-hour sail to home. Pushing to her feet Anne helped Israel maneuver the sloop out of the harbor, picking up a quickening breeze that snapped the sail smartly.

"Have ye thought about what you're gonna tell yer uncle?" Israel leaned against the tiller, his long, grizzled hair streaming behind him like a banner.

"The truth." Anne squinted up at the elderly man. "He won't accept anything less."

He seemed to ponder that a moment, finally showing his agreement with a curt nod. "I reckon that's fair. But there be truths . . . and then there be truths."

Anne shook her head and chuckled. Israel had a way of thinking that she found amusing, and often agreed with. He wasn't one of her uncle's settlement, but had lived on the island for many years prior to their coming. As a matter of fact no one knew exactly who or what Israel was. But Anne had her theories. Israel certainly knew a lot about sailing. And pirates.

Israel was always helping the small group of settlers that lived on Libertia. He seemed especially fond of Anne— said he liked her spirit, but even for her he would not reveal his past.

Anne studied her friend for a minute. "I think we have to convince Uncle Richard that d'Porteau's threat is real. And that we need to do something about it."

"He still ain't likely to look kindly on this here little undertakin' of ours." Israel's dark eyes rolled toward the man who lay snoring on the bottom of the boat.

He was right, of course, but . . . "What else was I to do? *I* couldn't convince Captain MacQuaid to come to our assistance. Uncle Richard is much more persuasive than I."

"If'n he be in the mood."

Anne sighed. Though her arguments seemed sound when voiced to Israel, she knew that made little difference. Making her uncle understand reality was becoming increasingly difficult. And over the years it had become Anne's responsibility. As time had passed and his dream of a utopian society unfolded, he became more and more idealistic and less realistic.

And then there were the memory lapses, which seemed to be worse since d'Porteau's raid on Libertia.

"He has to understand what will happen," she said as much to assure herself as Israel. But his response wasn't what she wished.

"Which he is ye talkin' 'bout?" the old man asked, motioning with his head toward the pirate who starting to stir, showing every sign of waking up.

"I thought you said he would sleep till we reached the island." Anne slid off her seat to get a better look.

"Said I thought he would." Israel squinted into the rising sun. "Should be there soon."

"But it won't be soon enough, I fear." Anne sidled up beside the captain, staring into his face. She was in that position, her breath held, when his eyes slitted open.

His initial expression registered bewilderment, then a smile tilted one side of his mouth. "Ah, Annie," he mumbled before licking his lips. His lids drifted shut, fanning his cheeks with the longest lashes Anne had ever seen on a man. They were a dark auburn with gold tips and Anne thought herself the silliest of creatures to notice such a thing. She was turning to rise, congratulating herself that he'd gone back to sleep when his eyes popped open again.

This time he pushed up on one elbow, grabbing his head with the other hand. "Where in the hell am I?" His gaze swept over the small sloop before locking with Anne's.

She met his stare but words escaped her until she felt the bite of his fingers about her arm. That's when she realized she should never have moved so close to him. The pressure increased till Anne sucked in her breath.

"I asked you a question, Mistress Cornwall."

"And she'll be answering it the moment ye let her loose . . . Captain."

Jamie twisted around toward the source of the voice, Anne Cornwall in tow. His head hurt like hell, even worse when he moved, and somehow or another he was sailing on the high seas. That much he could tell. But he hadn't the foggiest recollection how that circumstance came about. And shocking as that was, Jamie was in for another surprise when his eyes focused on the man standing by the tiller. Not only was he aiming a pistol toward Jamie—one of his own or he was sadly mistaken—but he looked hauntingly familiar.

Jamie's eyes narrowed. "Israel, is that you?"

"One in the same, Cap'n."

Jamie gave a sharp laugh. "Expected you'd be picking the devil's pocket by now."

"Reckon that's what most folk thought."

"You know this man?" Anne's question was directed toward Israel, but it was Jamie who answered.

"Israel and I go back a long way. He once sailed on the *Lost Cause.*"

Even though she'd long suspected Israel of having a less than exemplary past, Anne's mouth dropped open. "You really were a pirate?"

Neither man answered as they stared at each other.

It was Israel who broke the silence. "Cap'n, I suggest ye be lettin' the girl go."

"Annie's all right, and will be as long as we turn this tub about and head for New Providence."

"Ye seem to be forgettin', Cap'n, who's got the pistol." Israel moved the muzzle in a lazy arc.

"True enough."

"Good 'a ye to see it me way. Now if'n you'd just be loosenin' yer grip."

Looking first at Anne, then back to the grizzled old pirate, Jamie complied, not surprised when she scurried away. "What's this about, Israel? Revenge for what happened all those years ago?"

Now, Cap'n, I ain't out to kill ye, though at first when I stood there onshore watching the *Lost Cause* sail away leavin' me stranded, the thought kept me goin'."

"Understandable."

"There was times, I dreamed of your cursed mug staring up at me blank-eyed while flames danced about your head." Israel laughed and to Anne's surprise so did the captain.

"So if not revenge, then what?"

"Ye talked with Mistress Cornwall. Ye should know."

Jamie searched his foggy brain for what they'd discussed. "D'Porteau?"

"Aye."

"But what has he to do with you?"

Israel settled back against the side. "The low-down bastard don't deserve to live." His whiskered jaw locked about his pipe with an air of finality as if to announce that nothing else need be said.

Jamie didn't buy that. He wanted answers and he wanted them now. But most of all he wanted to turn this sloop around and head back to New Providence. He shifted his weight toward the tiller, settling back when Israel cocked the pistol. The old blackguard wasn't as decrepit as he seemed. At least he appeared quite capable of pulling the trigger and blowing a whole the size of a small island through Jamie.

He decided to change tactics, wishing his head didn't feel like it was full of good Scottish wool. Jamie turned his attention toward Anne Cornwall who was studying him, her expression suspicious. "And just what do ye hope to accomplish with this kidnapping?"

"It isn't a kidnapping." Anne ignored the arch of his brow. "I simply thought it would behoove you to meet my uncle."

"Ah." Jamie's finger followed the curve of his whiskered chin. "This . . . ." His hand spread to indicate the sloop and surrounding ocean. "This nonkidnapping is just by way of an introduction." His voice grew deeper. "An introduction I want no part of."

Crossing her arms Anne met his stare. "You have no say in the matter."

"True enough, Annie. For the time being." His lids lowered and Jamie leaned toward her. "But I shan't always be at your beck and call, my lady."

"Sit yourself back, b'for I forget it was you who saved me life."

This revelation was enough to make Jamie twist toward the older man. "What foolishness are ye speakin' there, old man? I never did a thing for you, certainly not saving your miserable life."

Israel didn't seem to take offense at the captain's denials. "I knows what I knows," he said, then waved his hand toward the east. "There be Libertia."

Jamie's gaze followed and he saw the island for the first time. It was like so many other oasis of land that spotted the sapphire-blue sea, the interior mountainous and green with vegetation, rimmed by blinding white coral sand. It wasn't until they sailed into the protected harbor where the waters turned a clear turquoise that Jamie noticed anything to recommend this over any of a hundred other islands.

There was a dock, made of wood and sturdy, stretching out into the water perhaps a hundred rods. Beyond that were several warehouses smaller, but equal in structure to any he'd seen near the wharf on New Providence.

Beyond these buildings were more, a small village of them, all nearly the same in size and shape.

"That's the town," Anne said as she watched him squint into the sun, his hand thrown up to shade his eyes. "It was larger but your friend d'Porteau burned more than half the homes."

His gaze jerked about to meet hers. "He's not a friend."

"Well, he might as well be." Crossing her arms Anne twisted back to look toward the fast-approaching island, her chin set at a defiant angle.

"Now, girl, we decided to let your uncle do the persuading since you couldn't." Israel's remark had both Anne and the captain staring at him.

"There will be no persuading," Jamie assured him. "I'll be setting sail back to New Providence before the sun climbs much higher and if you're very lucky I won't be hanging the both of ye up by your toes." Jamie folded his arms in a parody of his female captor's stance and set his jaw. Neither of them, not Israel, nor Mistress Anne Cornwall knew who they were dealing with.

By the time the small sloop was tied to the dock a group

of several men were rushing toward the beach. Anne recognized her uncle, following close on the heels of Mort Tatum, who must have been the island's lookout for the morning. And Matthew Baxter. Matthew and Mort were carrying two of the few muskets they'd been able to hide from d'Porteau. Climbing out of the boat Anne hurried to meet them.

"My goodness, child!" Richard Cornwall grabbed his niece's shoulders. "Are you all right?" His eyes searched hers. "We didn't know what had become of you."

"Yes, Uncle. I'm fine. Truly I am. I didn't mean to cause you any alarm."

Richard's hand touched the top of her head. "But you see you have worried me. You should have known that a reasonable uncle would."

" 'Twas mostly me doin', Your Lordship." Israel stepped forward and Jamie took the opportunity to latch onto the pistol . . . his pistol, swinging casually from the old pirate's hand. To Jamie's amazement, Israel just let it go without a struggle. "I talked her into goin' over to New Providence and lookin' up some p—some fellow seaman I knowed."

Richard's eyes moved from scanning Anne's face to rest briefly on Israel, then opened wide as they settled on Jamie. He opened his mouth to speak, but before he could, Anne had regained his attention.

"It's not true what Israel says. I take full responsibility for what occurred. You see—"

"Perhaps it would be an excellent idea if you explained, then." Richard spoke to Anne but he watched the tall, broad-shouldered stranger, as did the other members of the council. They'd been in the middle of a planning meeting when Mort ran in yelling about a sloop entering Libertia's natural harbor.

"Well . . ." Anne straightened her shoulders. "I thought . . . that is—"

"A wee bit of privacy might make this easier." Jamie stepped forward, not surprised when several of the men behind Anne's uncle cringed back. He seemed to have that effect on people and truthfully he usually considered it helpful. As he did now.

Anne's uncle seemed to spring to life, dragging his fingers back through his thinning hair. "Of course, of course," he said with a wave of his hand. "Come right this way." Taking his niece's arm he led the way up the beach, apparently expecting the others to fall in behind.

Israel motioned for Jamie to proceed, and he quickly returned the favor, not wishing the wily old bastard access to his back. The others who followed, forming a tiny procession didn't concern him much, even if one of them made a point of rubbing his hand over the stock of a dilapidated musket.

When they reached the front of a small but neat cottage, Richard Cornwall paused, ushering Anne, and the two seafarers inside and motioning for the others to return to their chores.

"I don't think you should be in there without me," Mort Tatum announced, spreading his legs. "I never did trust that Israel fellow, and his friend doesn't seem any better."

"Now, Mort, I'm sure he's perfectly respectable."

"Did you see the size of him? And his garb? Forswear, Richard, the man has all the markings of a pirate."

From inside the small parlor the three occupants could hear all that was said outside perfectly well. Anne slanted a look toward Captain MacQuaid, surprised to see him grin at Mort's words. Her own lips thinned and she hustled the others toward chairs, turning in time to meet her uncle when he stepped into the front room. He shut the door behind him, holding up his hand when Anne tried to begin her explanation.

"I think since we waited this long a few more minutes will not hurt." He crossed to the table, lifting a bottle of deep red liquid. "Gentlemen, would you care for some refreshment? Our guest might be surprised to learn that we made the wine ourselves from grapes grown right here on Libertia." He handed a glass to Jamie, who took it with a small bow.

"Uncle Richard, this is Captain James MacQuaid." Anne stepped forward. If everyone intended to be polite—and the pirate did seem to be making an effort despite his insistence on the sloop to the contrary—she might as well introduce them. "And this is my uncle, the founder and inspiration behind Libertia, Richard Cornwall."

"Now, Anne, as usual you give me too much credit. Everyone is equally important on our island." He handed wine to Israel. "It is the creed by which we live."

Anne said nothing but watched the pirate captain as did everyone else in the room as he tasted the wine. She wondered if he thought at all of the wine she'd given him in New Providence. Fortunately, he seemed not to recollect that as he sipped the fragrant liquid. With a nod he acknowledged the flavor and Richard let out a breath.

"We're proud of our little wine, sir."

"As you should be." Jamie took another drink, then set the glass on the small table beside his chair. Though the furnishings in the room were few, they were well made and clean. He leaned forward. "I imagine you wonder why I've come here."

"Actually we receive quite a few visitors who are interested in our colony." Richard settled into a chair. "Granted, Anne does not often sail out recruiting them, but I suppose there is always a first time." Leaning back, Richard took a deep breath, steepling his fingers. "What aspect of Libertia interests you, Captain MacQuaid?"

"Well, I—"

"No, let me guess. You are a sea captain, I assume?"

"Aye." More or less, Jamie added silently.

"Then unless you plan to settle here . . ." Richard paused long enough for Jamie to shake his head. "I thought not. You don't appear the settling type." Richard's smile softened his words. "Then I imagine it is trade with the island that has brought you here."

"Actually—"

"We have quite a bit to offer, Captain. Besides this fine wine, we grow sugarcane and are trying our hand at indigo. Granted, we are still small, however I have every hope that our colony will grow as more and more people hear of our grand experiment."

"And as long as d'Porteau leaves us in peace," Anne interjected.

"Now, Anne, don't go worrying the good captain here with talk of that one. He is not worth thinking of."

"Uncle Richard, he and his men killed several of our citizens, they burned our houses and fields. They took Arthur."

Richard slowly shook his head. His forehead creased and the excitement left his eyes. He looked first at Anne, then Jamie. "Yes," he said slowly. "I do believe my niece is correct." But he looked strangely like a man agreeing because he thought he should.

Was Anne Cornwall fantasizing about d'Porteau's attack? Jamie didn't think so. She was too passionate about her cause. But then why didn't her uncle share her feelings. He appeared more excited by his wine, than the fact that a pirate had ravished his island. And what was more amazing was that his niece didn't pursue the subject. She merely guided the conversation back toward the philosophy of the island, a subject her uncle could clearly discuss at length.

He spoke of John Locke and his Law of Nature, and how the government of Libertia was modeled after the philosopher's doctrines. "We are a democracy here on Libertia," he said proudly. "Every man has a vote in what occurs. Whether we plant sugar, or . . ." His face regained the puzzled expression of moments before. But quickly, almost before anyone noticed the pause, Anne said, "Indigo."

"Yes, yes, that's it, indigo."

On and on he went, yet Jamie found he admired the old man despite his zeal and long-windedness. Finally, Anne interrupted with a suggestion that her uncle needed to rest.

"Yes, yes," he agreed. "Unfortunately the body grows weaker as age claims it," he said to Jamie. "But a short rest and I'll be as good as new. You are staying with us awhile, aren't you?"

"Nay."

"Yes."

Jamie and Anne spoke simultaneously, turning to stare at each other as they did.

Jamie was the first to look away. "I fear I've business elsewhere that must be attended," he said with a bow toward the older man.

"Nothing that can't be postponed till tomorrow, I'm sure," Anne countered, only to receive the full force of his glare.

"Uncle Richard." Anne stood, rushing forward to fall on her knees in front of his chair. If she didn't do something and do it quickly the captain would leave. She hadn't missed the pistol stuck in his breeches. There was nothing keeping him from taking the sloop and returning to New Providence. Nothing but his gracious attitude toward her uncle. And Anne wasn't above using that courtesy against him.

"We must protect ourselves from d'Porteau. That's why I brought Captain MacQuaid to the island. He can help us . . . if he will."

"Now just wait a damn minute." Jamie stopped, shocked by the guilt he felt in speaking his mind in the only way he knew to do it. What was it about Richard Cornwall that made him feel ashamed of his profanity? Lowering his voice, Jamie continued. "I thought I made it clear to you Mistress Cornwall that I am not going to fight your battles for you."

"But I thought—"

"What, that I'd see this island and be struck with an overwhelming desire to throw down my life for it?"

"Of course not," Anne insisted, though that was pretty much what she hoped might happen. Oh, not that he'd throw down his life, but that he would want to help. Everyone loved and admired her uncle. Everyone. Even Israel. It was merely one of those facts of life that Anne had learned to accept like the sun rising and the trade winds blowing.

But Captain MacQuaid wasn't giving himself a chance to appreciate her uncle's fine qualities. To understand what he was trying to do here. He was simply standing there glaring down at her, his green eyes blazing.

"Don't look at me as if I've disappointed ye. It wasn't my idea to come here, and don't ye forget it, Annie. If not for the drugged wine I'd be—"

"It isn't necessary to tell us where you'd be." She knew what he'd been doing before the sleeping potion took effect. And so did he.

"Drugged wine." Richard's expression registered bewilderment. "What do you mean by that, Captain MacQuaid?"

He'd said too much and he wasn't even drunk. Jamie clamped his mouth shut, wishing he didn't let his lips move faster than his brain. Sure and he was angry with the wench for doping his drink and bringing him here, but he could understand desperation. Lord knew he could understand that. Not that he planned to do anything about hers. But he didn't mean to spill his guts to the old man either. Except now it was too late.

Jamie shifted from one foot to the other. "I suppose you'll be having to ask your niece that."

Anne could feel all eyes shift toward her.

"Well, Anne, what is the good captain talking about?" Richard asked.

Good captain indeed! "He's referring to the means I employed to bring him to Libertia." She sucked in her breath. "I spiked his wine so he'd fall asleep."

"Anne, my goodness. Why ever did you do that? Reason, dear, is the way we deal with reasonable men."

"Yes, well, Captain MacQuaid is not a reasonable man."

"Annie." Richard shook his head slowly. "You shouldn't—"

"He's not, Uncle Richard. He's a pirate."

Chapter Three

The announcement didn't seem to faze the old gentleman in the least. To be honest, Jamie wasn't sure he understood what his niece told him. He had the oddest desire to sit Richard Cornwall down and explain the realities of life to him. But of course he didn't. Richard Cornwall's problems were of no more concern to him than his niece's.

He bid Richard a good rest, but the older man seemed to have forgotten his desire for a nap. And then though Anne protested, he insisted upon showing his guest around the colony.

To his chagrin Jamie accepted the invitation. But he planned to make it a short tour, and then he was sailing for New Providence.

"Remember, Cap'n, I've got me eye on ye." Israel sidled up beside him, patting a pistol he'd thrust into the waistband of his pants. Indicating it was more than his eye he'd aim Jamie's way if he didn't watch himself.

Jamie only scowled, deciding not to point out that he had his own gun, then forced his attention back to Anne Cornwall. What did Israel think, that he planned to grab the girl and her uncle and hurl them into the sea? He might be a pirate but he wasn't an uncivilized scoundrel. Well, perhaps he was a scoundrel, but he prided himself on not harming innocent people. And Richard Cornwall seemed a complete innocent. But his niece sure the hell wasn't. Mayhap he *would* toss her to the sharks if given the opportunity.

Jamie caught Anne's eye as she explained the workings of the sugar mill. She ignored his glare as she led the way inside a stifling hot building where the thump thump of the water-powered roller near drowned out her voice. But Jamie wasn't interested in how the wheels squeezed the dark brown liquid from the ratoon cane. And he didn't think Anne really cared about telling him.

"Everyone who is able takes their turn in the sugar works," she said as they stepped outside into the blinding sunlight. "It's part of the philosophy of—"

"Even you?" Jamie arched his brow in mock disbelief. He had noticed that unlike the sugar plantations in Jamaica and the other islands he visited, this one lacked slave labor. At least the slaves who came from Africa. But he assumed the workers were indentured.

"Oh, yes, yes, Annie takes her turn with the sugarcane. She's quite adept at judging when the syrup is tempered. Though I feel her greatest gift lies in managing the plantation."

"I imagine that *would* be her forte."

Ignoring the jibe and smug expression on the pirate's face, Anne led the way toward the edge of a clearing. She paused before a mass of charred boards. "This," she said with a flourish of her hand, "is the warehouse where we store the sugar cones. At least it's what is left of it after d'Porteau's visit."

Jamie said nothing, just stared at the destruction . . . senseless destruction.

"Nasty man that Frenchman," Richard said with a shake of his head. And then as if he suddenly remembered something pleasant the older man's countenance brightened. "Have you been a student of John Locke for long, Captain MacQuaid? I find his view on the government fascinating, don't you?" Richard took Jamie's arm and led him back toward the village.

The helpless expression the pirate threw over his shoulder toward her would have been amusing if the circumstances were different. She was in no mood to come to his aid, though as her uncle rambled on about the merits of Locke's theories, it was obvious Jamie MacQuaid had no earthly idea how to respond.

"I think perhaps the captain would enjoy a tour of the fields," Anne said as she moved between the two men.

"Oh, of course, whatever was I thinking? Certainly you wish to explore all of Libertia before deciding to bring your shipload of settlers here."

"Settlers . . . ?" Jamie's eyes cut toward Anne.

"There is always room on our island for those who wish to join our grand experiment." Richard's smile was indulgent. "Go see for yourself the paradise of Libertia, then please join me for tea." He clasped Jamie's shoulder. "I shall endeavor to find Arthur. You would get on with my son very well."

"Let me find him, Uncle Richard." Anne stepped forward, clasping the two frail hands in hers. "I think you should rest a bit. You remember what Doctor Phillips said."

"Ah yes. The ban of aging. Resting when there is so much to be done." Despite his words the older man, leaning heavily on his cane, started off toward the row of cabins.

"T'z still behind ye, Cap'n, so don't go gettin' any ideas."

Glancing behind him Jamie saw that Israel's fingers were wrapped around the gun butt. "Do ye think I couldn't overpower you before that gun cleared your breeches if I had a mind to?"

"Well, now, you can try it, Cap'n, but I wouldn't recommend it."

"Israel, we haven't time to wrangle. I wish to show the captain the havoc his fellow pirate wreaked on the sugar fields." Without a backward glance Anne set out on the path that led toward the jungle. It wasn't until she heard Israel's voice that she realized the pirate failed to follow. "What is it?"

Jamie stood arms folded over his bare chest, chin set defiantly. "I have no intention of seeing fields of any kind. Nor do I plan to prolong this charade. If you don't wish to see this *friend* of yours broken like a twig, you will find a way for me to return to New Providence, now."

"I see." Anne struck a pose mirroring his. "It was my understanding you were interested in Libertia."

"Interested!" Jamie let out a bark of laughter. "Ye have to have more brass than the whole British navy. Whatever gave ye such an idea?"

"Well, you listened to Uncle Richard and—"

"I listened to your uncle out of respect." Jamie held up his hand to keep her from interrupting. "And aye, despicable pirate though I am, I do not spit in the face of all authority." His gaze held hers. "No matter how grievously I've been treated."

She knew he meant the drugged wine and kidnapping.

Of course that's what he meant. But when he looked at her like that, his wicked green eyes narrowed, Anne couldn't help thinking of the things he was doing to her before he fell asleep. Anne shook her head to dispel that notion. "I naturally assumed once you saw for yourself—"

"You were wrong, Annie."

His use of her name like that and the lift of his mouth beneath that dark beard was more than she could take. "You're no better than d'Porteau." Anne's hands were on her hips now as she glared at him across the narrow expanse separating them.

"I never claimed to be." He was, of course. Jamie considered himself vastly superior to the Frenchman in just about every way that mattered. But it was obvious this overbearing woman didn't think so, and he wasn't about to argue the differences.

Especially when she seemed in no mood to listen. Jamie watched as she stamped down the path and then whirled about to face him. "Then there is nothing else to say." She glanced toward Israel who stood, his bandy legs spread, the pistol gripped in his hand. "Please take him down to the pier. He can take the sloop." She sighed. "Might as well give it to this pirate as have d'Porteau kill someone over it."

"Yer letting him go, just like that?" Israel's good eye was wide with astonishment.

"What else can I do?"

Jamie had never seen someone change so completely. Moments ago he would have thought nothing would ever defeat her. She was nearly throwing off sparks as she faced him. But now her features were a study in failure. He liked her better looking as if she could single-handedly over-power the British admiralty.

"Your uncle is expecting me for tea," Jamie heard himself say. " 'Twouldn't do to disappoint him."

"That's quite all right. I shall give him your regrets."

"No one is giving him my regrets." Jamie straightened till he loomed over her. "I shall speak with Mr. Cornwall myself."

She didn't back away. "Very well, if you insist."

And he did. Jamie would be hanged for a sinner before he'd let a slip of a girl tell him what to do. It wasn't until they were all seated on the wide veranda of her uncle's cottage that Jamie began to wonder why he'd insisted upon taking tea.

Her uncle was more confused than ever. Just when she wanted him to expound upon the devastation d'Porteau did to Libertia he seemed to remember none of it. It probably didn't matter. Anne doubted MacQuaid would be likely to offer his aid regardless. She didn't really know why she was prolonging this. Perhaps if she petitioned the governor of Grand Bahama again or—

"Anne, are you listening?"

"Oh yes, Uncle Richard."

"Then will you tell me where he is?"

"Where who is?" Anne felt heated color tinge her cheeks and took a sip of tea.

"Arthur. I haven't seen him all day."

The bottom fell out of Anne's stomach, though she should have expected as much. How could her uncle not remember what happened to the island? To the settle-ment he worked so hard to build. Not that he always seemed oblivious to the tragedy. There were times when he sat in his room pouring over his books as if he might find the answers there. "What went wrong?" he would ask. And Anne could barely stand to witness the melancholy in his eyes.

Now she chose what she'd begun to think of as the coward's way. Dabbing her lips slowly she shook her head. "Arthur is busy. Perhaps he can join us later."

But this time her fabrication didn't calm her uncle. Instead his brow wrinkled and it was almost as if he was viewing the raid again through eyes that saw too much. He gripped Anne's arm, his fingers pressing into the soft skin beneath her ruffled sleeve.

"We must do something," he screeched. "They're burning everything. Can't you see them, Annie? They're killing . . ." Richard jumped to his feet. "God, what are they doing?"

Without thinking Jamie pushed out of his chair. His arm circled the old man's shoulders by the time Anne pressed a tumbler of dark liquid to his lips.

"Drink, Uncle Richard," she coaxed. "Yes, that's it. Everything will be all right." Her eyes flashed to Jamie's. "I promise."

"But they took my boy. They took Arthur."

"He'll come back. You'll see. Just a little more," she said, tilting the glass higher. "There now." Anne wiped his mouth, then turned toward Israel, not surprised to see him right behind her.

" 'Pears to me 'tis time for a rest, wouldn't ye say, Master Richard?" As Jamie stepped aside the wiry expirate slid his shoulder under Richard's and led him toward the door. Anne rushed to open it and through the wedge Jamie saw a bedstead and chest. As soon as Anne, Israel, and Richard, who by this time could barely walk on his own, were through the opening the door shut and

Jamie fell back into his chair. His hands were sweating and he took a gulp of tea wishing it were something stronger.

Richard Cornwall was mad.

There was little doubt of that. Jamie took another drink and tried not to let those memories of his mother slide into place. But he wasn't able to block them out. He was five when she left so there were few things he remembered clearly. Except the screaming. And the mad look in her eyes. Jamie blinked and lurched to his feet when Anne reentered the room.

She pressed a finger to her lips, then led the way outside. Jamie filled his lungs with fragrant moist air.

"Now do you understand why d'Porteau must be found?" Anne said when they'd walked a short distance from the cottage.

"I understand that your uncle would be better off in Bedlam."

"Don't say that!" Anne turned on him with a vengeance, her fists pounding against the hard muscles of his chest.

At first too shocked to do anything Jamie let her anger run its course, only pulling her against him when her blows became no more than ineffectual thumps. She rested in his embrace only a moment before pulling away and quickly scrubbing at her tear-streaked face.

"He isn't crazed. Not really," she insisted. "Until the Frenchman came there were only certain times when his mind failed. . . ." Her voice trailed off, was stronger when she continued. "He was fine until the pirate came. Just fine. And he'll be that way again if I can only find Arthur. And if we no longer have to worry about that . . ." Anne turned away abruptly.

When she looked back at him her expression was composed. The late-afternoon sun caught the coppery highlights in her brown hair. "You've seen what d'Porteau did. You dislike him yourself. Why can't you and your crew go after him?"

"Because I'm not some damn crusader. And whatever gave you the impression I am is beyond me."

"It was Israel." Anne wiped her hands down the panels of her skirt.

"Israel?" Jamie laughed. "He has no reason to think me other than a scoundrel such as himself."

"Perhaps, but he feels otherwise." Her head cocked to the side. "Do you recall the last time you saw him?"

"Aye. He was standing knee-deep in the surf, arms flailing, howling his head off. And blasting me to the devil, I may add."

Anne couldn't help smiling. She could just imagine Israel doing such. "Well, blast you though he may have, apparently Israel thinks you have a compassionate nature."

Compassionate nature? What the hell was the chit rambling on about? He was a pirate, for God's sake! "I've a notion your uncle isn't the only one on this island going mad. I'm beginning to think you all are." Ignoring the flash of anger that crossed her face, Jamie turned and strode down the path toward the dock. This entire incident was like a crazy dream, a nightmare that he was escaping. As far as he knew Israel was still with the crazed uncle. But the way he felt now, he didn't care.

If there was anyone on the wharf foolish enough to attempt to stop him from taking the sloop, he'd rue the day he crossed Jamie MacQuaid.

"Stop. Oh, will you stop!"

Jamie wheeled on her when she grabbed his arm. Feet planted wide in the sandy soil, arms on hips he faced her. She should be intimidated. Few men could face Jamie when he allowed his demons free reign and not cower. But she faced him square. He was certain the breathless quality in her voice was a result of chasing him, not fear. He was beginning to think he was right. Everyone on the island was insane.

"It angered you to be called compassionate?" she asked, her tone one of surprise . . . and possibly a touch of amusement.

"I'm a pirate, by God, not some crusading fop."

"You think I don't know that?" Anne shot back.

"Aye, 'tis possible ye have your doubts." Jamie's eyes narrowed. "Else why would you find yourself alone, and defenseless?" He watched her features soften, then the breath expand her chest as she realized their isolation. Around them wind-trimmed pines and thick undergrowth isolated the bend in the path.

Jamie stepped closer. "Mayhaps ye think me too compassionate to take what I want? What was offered so enticingly before?"

Without waiting for a response Jamie reached out. His fingers speared through her hair, framing her face, and sending the lacy cap and wooden pins showering to the ground. Her only protest was a muffled, "No," as his mouth swooped down on hers.

His lips were hard, punishing. The tongue he thrust into her mouth ignored her futile attempts to stop him. He took; he plundered. He showed her what it was like to deal with him; deal with him without the advantage of drugging potions and cocked pistols aimed at his heart.

His kiss was relentless. His hands curved round her

head, angling her mouth toward his. And he took. Took all that he could and still he wanted more. She aroused him from the first moment he set eyes on her, standing before him, scared but defiant. He wanted her then. And the ache she caused in his groin only intensified when she took him to her room. And nothing, not the drugged sleep nor the vinegar of her tongue had cooled his ardor.

She squirmed beneath his hands, the movements only fueling his passions. By God she saw him as some golden-haired crusader she could bend and twist to her liking. He would show her differently. He would show her who would bend and twist.

His hands forged down, tangles of dark curls trailing along as he followed the line of her neck, the rounded curves of her shoulders. She fought him, but he was larger than she, stronger. And the force of desire heated his blood.

With one arm he yanked her against him, hard to unbearably soft. His other hand swept down the swell of her buttocks, pressing her tighter to his throbbing flesh.

Stunned.

From the moment he lurched toward her Anne was stunned to inaction. She didn't expected this, had begun to think of him as less than the pirate he was. How very foolish of her. Now she couldn't stop his onslaught. His arms were like iron bands, binding her, drawing her to him. And his hands were everywhere on her body.

She wriggled but it did no good, tried to kick but his powerful legs seemed to surround her, tangling with her skirts and keeping her from squirming away.

And his mouth. His lips seemed to shape hers, demanding that she move them in tempo with his. Anne tried to think what to do, but she couldn't seem to focus. Her skin tingled and she felt an odd heavy sensation in her stomach. Her head was heavy and when his lips left hers to burn a path down her neck, she couldn't seem to keep from swaying back, exposing more of her skin to the heat of his tongue.

She felt drugged and euphoric.

His golden head dipped lower, branding the rounded flesh above her bodice. He nipped, then soothed and Anne thought her knees would lose their power to hold her upright. His very breath, whispering across her moist skin entranced her. She was melting away, caught in a swirling eddy of she knew not what. Falling deeper and deeper until his words sliced through the fog.

"This. . . ." Jamie caught the laces of her gown between his teeth and tugged, ". . . 'tis what a pirate does to his women."

He was a pirate. No better than the one who'd come before him. Anne stiffened as memories of the other filled her mind. His foul scent, the bitter taste of blood as the press of his mouth split her lip.

"Stop."

The word meant little to Jamie and wouldn't have brought an abrupt halt to his ravaging of her breast if not for the accompanying bite of cold steel against his ribs. His hands dropped to his side and with an expression of disbelief on his face, he stepped back.

She looked wild and wanton. Her dark hair flowed about her shoulders and the lips he found so fascinating from the start were rosy red and wet. If it weren't for the knife poised in her hand Jamie would have lowered her to the sandy path and taken her on the spot.

But the knife *was* there. And when he glanced down toward the burning on his side, he realized the crimson on the blade was his own blood. She'd sliced through his shirt and skin leaving a jagged tear that oozed and was beginning to hurt like hell.

"Damn your eyes, woman! Look what you've done."

Anne held the knife higher as he stepped forward. "And I'll do a lot worse if you dare touch me again." Her jab, though striking nothing but air, brought him to a halt.

His stare pierced through her as he sucked in air, then he shook his head and to Anne's surprise began to laugh. "Good God, lass, you're a strange one." With one hand he balled up a section of shirt, bunching the cotton to his wound, attempting to staunch the flow of blood. He twisted to watch his own progress for a moment seemingly oblivious to Anne and the knife she held.

But when he glanced back, his gaze riveting with hers, she knew he hadn't forgotten her presence or the shameful way she acted.

" 'Tis some experience I've had in pleasing wenches, Mistress Anne. And by all accounts you seemed to be enjoying yourself mightily."

Anne lifted her chin, and tried to steady her hand. "I wonder how many other women have fooled you such."

"Fooled?"

The arch of his brow made Anne grip the bone handle tighter. She swallowed. "I have no interest in your inflated ego or anything else about you other than your ability to defeat d'Porteau."

His grin revealed strong white teeth. "And I think it's a liar you are. We both have an interest in the other that has nothing to do with that scoundrel d'Porteau. Who by the by, I have no intention of fighting."

"Are you afraid of him?" Anne's own brows arched in question.

Anger shot through his body, and Jamie opened his mouth to protest any cowardice on his part. But a certain light in her eyes gave him pause. He'd seen the same expression when she tricked him into having tea with her uncle. The woman might have the eyes of an angel but her mind ran as sharp as a charlatan's.

Now she stood waiting for his answer looking as innocent as you please despite the love-tousled state of her clothing and hair.

She waited for him to angrily deny any fear. To even be willing to prove his bravery by doing her bidding. Well, the wind would blow ice and snow upon this tiny island before he would let her trick him again.

"Afraid?" Jamie asked as if pondering the meaning of the word. "Well, I suppose it's a foolish man who doesn't fear the possibility of death." Her crestfallen expression made him grin. "But it's a man with no sense at all who risks death with no thought of reward. And," he added, lifting his blood-smeared hand when she started to speak, " 'tis not rewards of the spirit that interest me."

"You are a rogue."

Jamie bowed despite the pain in his wound. "Captain Jamie MacQuaid, rogue, pirate, and blackguard, at your service . . . but not literally, of course." Jamie gently pulled the sodden shirt from his side, scowling when he saw again the damage she did. Luckily the blade only pierced his skin. He didn't think there was any harm done to his innards. But he wasn't a man who enjoyed pain and he imagined Anne Cornwall would be remembered for some time as the woman who caused him considerable.

Jamie turned, his boot heel digging into the sand, then glanced over his shoulder. "I assume ye aren't one to stab a man in the back?"

"No matter how despicable I find him?" He could almost believe she might if given the chance, but she shook her head. "You're no good to me dead."

"I, Mistress Cornwall, shall be no good to you at all." Deciding he'd seen the last of her Jamie started down the path, determined that nothing would stop him from quitting this island. But then she said the one thing that could.

"I shall give you my jewels to capture d'Porteau for me."

Jamie stopped in his tracks, tossing a look over his shoulder that made her retreat a step. "Ye have jewels?"

"Yes. A ruby brooch, and pearls. Also a diamond necklace and matching ear bobs." She raised her chin. "They were my mother's."

Turning abruptly Jamie retraced his steps. "What is to stop me from simply taking them from you? That's what pirates do, you know."

"Do you think I haven't thought of that?" Her arm was tiring from holding out the knife, and Anne decided it afforded her precious little protection if he chose to disarm her. Carefully, as Israel had taught her she resheathed the knife, fitting it through the slit in her skirt. When she looked up the pirate watched her, an amused expression on his face.

"They are hidden," Anne said, for she wished to return his attention to the matter at hand. "Where you shall never find them."

"I see." Jamie stood a moment, arms akimbo looking first at her, then at the surrounding jungle.

"There are jewels, worth a great deal of money, I assure you. It's my inheritance. When Uncle Richard took me in after the death of my parents he swore never to touch the jewels, and he hasn't."

"Not even for his grand experiment?"

"Libertia has been self-sufficient almost from the onset." Her gaze lowered. "At least it was before d'Porteau."

Jamie stepped forward. "Now let me see if I undersand—"

"Hold it right there, Cap'n." Israel yanked out the pistol, aiming it at Jamie as he came skidding to a halt. He was out of breath from running. "It suddenly accord ta me that I'd let you alone with . . . Lord a'mighty, what happened ta ye, girl?" Israel's horrified gaze flew from Anne to Jamie. "And ye, Cap'n, is bleedin' like a stuck pig."

"Really?" Jamie glanced down, then grinned. "A lover's spat I wager."

"It was nothing of the sort. I simply had need of gaining Captain MacQuaid's attention."

"And I assure ye she got it. As a matter of fact, there seems little need for pistol pointing where Mistress Cornwall is concerned."

"He's right, Israel." Anne motioned for him to lower the gun. "Actually I believe the good captain and I were on the verge of reaching an understanding. Is that not true?"

"Let us say, ye'd gained my attention." Jamie leaned forward. "But then jewels usually do."

"Jewels?" Israel turned on Anne. "Ye told him about the jewels?"

"It was unavoidable." Anne leveled a look at the old man. "I offered to pay the captain and his crew to go after d'Porteau."

"But the jewels are—"

"All I have, yes, I know, Israel. But the captain is a

shrewd man and will not risk his glorious life for mere good works alone."

Israel scratched at his nearly bald pallet. "So's ye promised him the loot."

"Yes, I have." Anne's heart sank at the bewildered expression on Israel's face. This wasn't going to work if Captain MacQuaid suspected the truth. He wasn't a stupid man . . . unfortunately. "How is Uncle Richard?"

Israel stopped clawing at his head. "Sleepin' like a babe. I still don't understand about—"

"And really there is no need for you to." Anne took Israel's arm and headed him back toward the village. "Please check on my uncle. I shall be along soon."

When she turned back toward the pirate he was shaking his head. "Mistress Cornwall, I'm beginning to think there be no jewels."

"You doubt my word?"

"Aye, Annie. You've given me reason to doubt more than your word."

"Fine." Anne tossed her head. "Then I shall find someone else willing to risk a fortnight for them."

"Nay." Jamie was upon her before she knew what he was about. His fingers locked about her wrist as she fumbled for the knife. "I shall find d'Porteau and bring him to Libertia, but I'll be wanting more than jewels for my trouble."

Anne's heart pounded beneath the silk of her bodice. She tried to keep her voice steady. "But I have nothing else."

"Oh, but you do, Annie. You do indeed." With a jerk he had her arm bent behind her back, folded into his embrace.

Her breasts flattened against his chest. She was frightened, yet did her best not to show it, to show him. Even when his mouth lowered to cover hers she held herself still.

"Aye, ye have much more to give, lass, and when I return I shall demand payment in full."

"I have no idea what you mean."

His laugh sent chills down her spine. "I think ye do. We need to finish what was started in New Providence." He kissed her once more, quickly and hard, then stepped away. "Do we have an agreement, then?"

"Yes." Anne couldn't believe it was her voice agreeing to his demand. But his grin confirmed that he heard her. "Yes, whatever you say, just bring back d'Porteau and Arthur."

"Whatever ye say," he repeated her words, then took off toward the dock.

Chapter Four

"Some of them aren't real happy 'bout this, Cap'n."

Jamie turned, eyes narrowed against the Caribbean sun that rose like a golden orb on the horizon. "As I recall a vote was taken."

"And barely won," the blackamore countered.

Wind snapped in the sails, sending the fifty-ton sloop, *Lost Cause,* dancing across the waves toward San Palma, a string of keys to the east. D'Porteau was known to favor the waters there for his raiding. And for the most part, Jamie had steered clear of the area.

Now Jamie spread his legs against the sway of his vessel. "And what of ye, Keena? Do ye have doubts about my leadership?" His whisker-covered jaw jutted forward defiantly.

But it was obvious the chief gunner was not one to be easily intimidated. The grin that split his fierce countenance shone white against his ebony skin. "Most all the time," he quipped. "But I follow you anyway."

Jamie's expression lightened until he grinned as well. "That says little to recommend your judgment."

"Or my intelligence, for that matter."

Jamie's burst of laughter was lost on the stiff breeze. He took a deep breath, then leaned forward bracing his forearms on the scared wood railing. "Will they cause trouble, do ye think?"

Keena shook his head. "Nay. Not for the moment."

Their eyes met. "You're telling me we should find d'Porteau with all due haste."

Keena's naked shoulders lifted. "Stymie and Cunningham aren't likely to wait long before raising a ruckus."

Jamie slapped the rail with his palms as he pushed away. "They'll be singing a different tune when we sail back to Libertia to claim the jewels."

"If you say so."

"What am I hearing?" Jamie's brow arched. "Could it be that Stymie and Cunningham are not alone in making a bit of mischief?"

"I say what I think to your face, Cap'n."

"Then say it and be done."

The blackamoor looked him square in the eye. " 'Tis bad business what we're about."

Jamie met the stare soberly for a moment, then threw back his head with laughter. "Have ye been sacrificing chickens again, and listening to their squawks? Or mayhaps 'twas the design the blood made as it dripped from the wrung neck. 'Twas that what made ye decide we shouldn't seek the Frenchie?"

When Keena said nothing Jamie knew he'd gone too far. The blackamoor took his heathen religion as seriously as Jamie took his lack of one. And it wasn't like Jamie to belittle his beliefs. But damnation he was tired of trying to convince this band of bloodthirsty pirates that going after d'Porteau was a good idea. In the back of his mind perhaps he was beginning to doubt it himself.

"Hell and damnation." Jamie slapped the rail again. "Admittedly I was rather deep in me cups, but if memory serves, ye were the main one bellyaching about what the Frenchman would do to the lass."

Keena still said nothing and Jamie grunted his displeasure. "Fine. Ye can glue your lips shut for all I care. 'Tis no concern of mine." Jamie started across the quarterdeck. "I'll be below catching up on me sleep."

Nearly to the ladder, Jamie paused when he heard Keena's softly spoken warning. "I'd watch my back if I was you, Cap'n."

Jamie nodded once in acknowledgment, then bypassing the steps leaped onto the main deck. Stepping over several sailors sleeping on deck, their snores gurgling in their throats, Jamie worked his way to the hatch, Keena's warning ringing in his ear.

So Stymie and Cunningham were doing more than arguing against chasing d'Porteau. He wasn't surprised. They were a nasty pair whom he'd toss from the ship if he could. Well, let them rant and rave. The pair of them hadn't the brain power of a flea. They weren't about to harm him. He was Captain Jamie MacQuaid and he'd lived through a hell of a lot more than two disgruntled half-wits.

But Jamie didn't feel very invincible as he climbed belowdecks. He hadn't slept more than a few hours in three days. Not since he was drugged. Jamie shook his head. Damn him for the pirate he was, Anne Cornwall had brass to do such a thing. A wench after his own heart . . . if he had one, Jamie quickly reminded himself.

No, it wasn't his heart the lass seemed to have a stranglehold on. Jamie snorted as he made his way down the passage. There'd been an ache in his loins since he first saw her. That was a wonder in itself, for she didn't have the look of a woman who usually made a man smack his lips and drool.

Well, whatever, he'd be rid of the itch as soon as he took d'Porteau back to Libertia, for having Annie Cornwall was part of the bargain he intended to keep . . . was part of the bargain he'd relish keeping.

As Jamie reached for his cabin door latch a sound caught his attention. He glanced around and scowled in disgust. "What the hell are ye doing, lad?" Jamie's nose wrinkled at the stench, only partly hidden by the odors of bilge and tar. "Me God, boy, don't ye have the sense to empty your stomach over the rail?"

"I . . . I . . ." Trying to stand erect only brought a fresh onslaught of heaves . . . these blessedly dry.

"Get yourself to your hammock, lad." Jamie opened his cabin door, then turned back. "And when your stomach settles get back and clean up this mess." With that he kicked the portal shut. He trounced the clothing and charts that littered the floor as he walked to his bunk. It, too, was piled with his belongings, and with one swipe he cleared it. Without bothering to remove his boots Jamie stretched out his long frame. Minutes later he was snoring softly and dreaming of a firm young body and eyes the color of warm whiskey.

Anne shut her eyes and tried to breathe deeply. But the nausea still clawed at her stomach, forcing her to bend at the waist and gag. How was it that she became so ill as soon as the *Lost Cause* set sail? She'd been aboard other vessels. She and Israel sailed the small sloop often and her insides never threatened to wring themselves out. And when she came to Libertia . . . True, she'd been much younger, but she didn't recall feeling as she did now.

Perhaps it was just the idea of being aboard a pirate ship. Or being so disgustingly dirty. Anne glanced down at her shirt and britches. Filthy was the best way to describe them. But then she decided dirt was the best camouflage she could find, other than her men's clothing.

And she certainly wanted to keep her identity hidden. Just her luck she chose the passageway in front of Captain MacQuaid's cabin to get sick in.

But one good thing. He hadn't recognized her. No, he saw what he wished to see. A scrawny lad who couldn't keep his victuals down. Anne smiled despite her discomfort. But her expression sobered as another wave of sickness made her break out in a cold sweat. Leaning against the splintery bulwark, too weak to go looking for her hammock, Anne wondered how wise she'd been to come aboard. It had seemed the perfect plan while on Libertia. She didn't trust the pirate, so she'd keep a wary eye on him. And there was also the problem of the jewels she'd promised him. Jewels she didn't have. But how was she going to watch him when she couldn't take her eyes off the pitching deck?

A pounding woke Jamie and he leaped from the bunk before he even opened his eyes. When he did he could see the late-afternoon sun streaming through the salt-encrusted panes of the transom windows.

"Cap'n." A pirate named Roger poked his fat body through the door. He was out of breath and Jamie had to prod him with a "What in the hell is it?" before he continued. "Ship off the starboard bow."

"Is it d'Porteau?" Jamie strapped on his cutlass and jammed a pistol into the leather sash across his chest.

"Deacon don't know for sure. But he says she looks French by her cut."

Before Roger had finished, Jamie was past him into the passageway heading for the hatch. The main deck was alive with activity. Powder monkeys, the boys who carried the powder and shot to the cannons were scurrying around. Keena was doling out weapons, muskets, and cutlasses to the men.

Deacon stood on the quarterdeck and he handed Jamie the spyglass after he bounded up the ladder.

"Over there, Cap'n."

Jamie pointed the glass in the direction Deacon indicated, though by now he could see the ship. " 'Tisn't the *French Whore.*" Jamie shrugged his shoulders. "So unless d'Porteau is sailing a different boat these days, it looks as if we have ourselves an innocent French merchantman." When Jamie looked around he was grinning. "Since the French and English are warring as usual, 'twould seem our duty as fine upstanding Englishmen to relieve the good captain of his cargo?"

"Even though ye be a Scot by birth?"

Jamie laughed. "Especially then."

The chaos was frightening.

Men ran about, loading guns and flashing swords. So much of it reminded Anne of the day d'Porteau raided Libertia. It was a day she feared would burn in her memory forever.

Anne pressed her back against the foremast and shut her eyes wishing the sights and sounds would go away.

Her lids flew open when something was shoved hard at her stomach. Reflex had her grabbing the wooden canister.

"Look lively, boy! This ain't no time ta be dreamin' of your momma's teat," a gruff voice yelled.

Using her knee to keep the heavy barrel from slipping, Anne looked around the deck, trying to decide what to do with it.

"Over here." Anne glanced up to see a boy of perhaps ten motioning to her with spindly arms. "Is ye deaf?" he yelled when she continued as if rooted to the spot.

"No, my hearing is perfectly fine," she said as she made her way across the sand-strewn deck to where the boy stood.

"That there is langrage. Scrap metal," he explained when Anne said nothing. "It chews up rope and canvas good."

"I see."

He looked at her askance, his coppery brows beetled. "Ye talk strange."

"Do I? I mean . . ." Anne glanced nervously about her. "I ain't never been in a battle before."

The boy spit on his hands, then rubbed them together. "Didn't need to tell me that. Thought you was gonna shit your pants over there."

"I was not." Throw up perhaps, but certainly not that.

"No need to get yourself in a twit. Happens to everyone their first time." He leaned a bony elbow on the cannon by his side. "Ye can put that down here. Probably won't be needing it anyways. Don't expect yonder boat will put up much of a wrangle."

Anne glanced out over the ever-narrowing expanse of

cobalt-blue water that separated the two ships. "How can you be sure?"

"Ain't. But I've seen enough 'a this to know most of them captains don't care a fig about their cargo. Losin' one here or there makes no difference ta them as long as they've plenty of salt pork to fill their bellies and a soft pillow for their heads."

"So?" Anne pressed into the space beside the cannon and turned to look out to sea as the captain strode by.

"So," the boy repeated looking at her as if she knew nothing. "We give them a warnin' and they give up."

"Sounds simple enough."

" 'Tis." the boy smiled showing a gap where his front teeth should be and stuck out his hand. "Name's Joe. What's yours?"

"Anne . . . dy. Andy." To Anne's relief Joe didn't seem to notice her near slip. She grabbed his hand and shook it, then almost jumped overboard as a loud boom shook the sloop.

"That would be the warnin'," Joe said.

By now a burly pirate with no shirt and blousy-striped breeches stood by the cannon. He held a long pole that Joe explained was a rammer. And he waited as the captain called over to the brig, now within hailing distance. Anne looked up to where he stood on the quarterdeck. He yelled again and this time he was answered in a heavy French accent.

"You have the pleasure of surrendering your cargo to Captain Jamie MacQuaid and his crew, or of visiting the bottom of the sea. Which shall it be?"

There was a pause and then a wild cheer on board the *Lost Cause* as the French fleur-de-lis fluttered slowly down the yardarm.

"Now there's work ta be done," Joe said as he gave Anne's arm a friendly punch. "But don't fret, there'll be an extra ration of grog this night."

Which was hardly wonderful news as far as Anne was concerned, she thought later. She sat in a *V* of deck between a barrel and an untidy tangle of rope. Joe wedged himself in beside her and after giving her a friendly grin downed a healthy gulp of liquid from a dented tin cup.

"Told ye 'twouldn't be so bad."

Anne sipped the grog, trying not to make a face and nodded. What Joe called not too bad had involved shimmying across the ropes that tangled the *Lost Cause* to the French vessel it captured and tossing kegs of salt pork over her shoulders. She ached in places that had never whispered a complaint before, even when she took her turn in the sugar works. Stretching out her legs she had such a strong longing for a soft bed with clean sheets that she considered . . . and just as quickly rejected, the idea of marching toward the cluster of pirates reveling on the quarterdeck.

The captain was there, along with the blackamoor and the one he called Deacon. Several others lounged about, but she didn't know their names as yet. What would they think . . . what would the captain think . . . if she joined their midst and tore off the knit cap that concealed her hair and itched her neck? Would they offer her a place to sleep other that any spot on the crowded deck she could find?

Probably not, unless she was sprawled beneath Jamie MacQuaid in the captain's cabin. And she had no intention of doing that.

"Weren't much of a fight today," Joe said, bringing

Anne's attention back to the boy. He took another drink and belched. Then with a satisfied smile on his thin, freckled face leaned back against the rope. "But I guess that ain't too bad."

"I imagine not."

His chuckle was swift in coming. "Ye sure does talk funny."

Sinking her neck down lower in the ragged wool jacket Anne went silent. Why couldn't she remember to keep her voice low? But Joe's next words made her realize it wasn't her voice she needed to watch.

"Ye had schoolin'?"

"Some," Anne answered truthfully. "But it weren't for me."

"Yea, I know." Joe lifted his head toward the scatter of stars overhead. "This be the life for me, too. No one ta be tellin' ye to do this or that. Plenty ta eat." His tone changed. "And no booted toe kickin' at ye."

"Booted toe?" Anne sat up straighter, but in the light of the dripping candles stuck into the timbers, she could see the guarded expression on Joe's face.

He laughed again, that short gruff sound she'd learned to recognize after spending most of the day in his company. "Me old man was quick with a kick."

"Your father kicked you?"

"Not more'n I could handle," Joe said with a bravado thin enough to shatter. He stuck his chin out. "Don't need to worry 'bout him none. Left 'em soon as I got me the chance."

"I'm glad." Anne took another drink from her cracked cup. The liquid, strong as it was, did little to wash away the foul taste of Joe's story. She knew there were evil people, of course. Willet d'Porteau and his crew. Jamie

MacQuaid might fit into that mold, too, but a father? That was too frightening to imagine. Her own had been as kind and gentle as his brother, Richard. Like her guardian, Henry was a scholar, a man who read and explained and lived for his books. He had never spoken a harsh word to her let alone physically harmed her.

"Won't find much 'a that on the *Lost Cause*, though."

"Much of what, beatings?" Anne's thoughts had been yanked to the painful day she learned her parents had perished at sea, so it took her a moment to realize what the boy meant.

"Aye." Joe drained his cup. "Cap'n Jamie don't hold with none."

" 'Tis good to hear."

Joe nodded, then twisted his head toward the sailors who sprawled near the main mast. They sang a song Anne didn't recognize and could barely understand. But it was loud and judging from the accompaniment of snickers and guffaws, bawdy. Catching only the occasional word was enough to pinken Anne's cheeks despite what she'd gotten used to from Israel.

When Joe looked back at Anne he scrunched up and leaned his bony elbows on equally bony knees. "Being more experienced and all I think I should warn ye."

"About what?"

"Some a' them ain't as kindhearted as the cap'n."

Kindhearted? She hardly thought that a fair description of Jamie MacQuaid, but since Joe seemed so sincere about his advice she kept her council and shifted to hear him better.

His voice dropped to a whisper even though there was no one within hearing distance. "Stay clear 'a Stymie."

"Stymie?" She'd heard that name before. "What does he do?"

Joe pulled back as if his father had caught up with him and delivered one of his kicks. "Just stay clear." He looked at her, his eyes narrowed and Anne wondered if he could see beyond her disguise. And if he did what she would do. But he only shrugged before settling back, his head pillowed by the rope.

"He ain't likely to fancy ye none as dirty as ye be."

Dirty? Anne's gaze skimmed over the group, none of whom appeared much cleaner than she and felt a pang of resentment. Which was quickly squelched. Heaven knew she didn't want any of the pirates to fancy her anyway. And staying away from all of them was her plan.

A plan that over the next few days proved difficult.

The *Lost Cause* was a single-masted sloop, sharp of hull and swift of sail . . . and crowded. There was hardly a square rod of unused space, and the men who sailed her seemed forever falling over one another. Anne would turn around and there would be one of the pirates lounging about on the deck, feet propped on a stack of canvas. And belowdecks was worse. There was little room, no privacy and keeping her gender a secret was a problem.

Joe was always about. For all his rough ways he was a pleasant companion, but Anne ached to yank off her cap and give her hair a good washing. But washing didn't seem to be of prime concern to anyone on board.

Nor was straightening or keeping the ship's decks in order. Anne was filling the fire buckets, one of the few tasks she'd been given, when she turned to stare into the pockmarked face of the man Joe warned her about. He startled her so that she jerked, spilling briny water down the side of her breeches and splattering his.

With a movement so quick she couldn't avoid him the pirate grabbed her arm. "Watch what you're about, boy, else you'll be feelin the rough of me palm across your bottom."

The voice. Anne recognized it instantly as belonging to the man who'd grabbed her in the tavern on New Providence. It had been so dark and she was single-mindedly searching for Captain MacQuaid that she didn't get a good look at him. But she knew him now from the distinctive timbre and sneer of his words.

And she wondered if he would have the same epiphany of recognition. Sweat streamed down her shoulders pooling in the small of her back before soaking into her woolen pants. The jacket she wore to disguise her form only made her hotter as it seemed to attract the Caribbean sun and trap the heat against her skin.

He leaned forward, narrowing his eyes and baring his yellow-stained teeth and Anne forced her voice as low as she could.

"Sorry, sir," she managed, not faking the quiver of fear in her voice.

"Sorry, is ye?" His fingers tightened. "Well now mayhap you'd like ta feel me hand on yer backside."

"Nay." Wriggling was useless but Anne couldn't help trying. His smell, his touch, everything about him was making her nauseas.

"Spunk," he said, his free hand latching onto her other arm. "I like that in me boys." With one violent shake he stilled Anne's struggles. Her neck jerked back and she stared up at him, her eyes wide. "What's yer name, boy? I ain't seen ye before."

Anne tried to swallow but her mouth felt as if it were filled with sand, and that feeling, too familiar since d'Porteau's raid was making her stomach churn. "Andy," she finally managed to mumble.

"Well, Andy, is it." Stymie licked his thick lips and his hands worked up and down Anne's sleeves. "Looks like ye and me needs ta get better—"

"Stymie!"

The word cracked like a whip across the windswept deck. Anne twisted her head to see the captain standing less than a rod away. His feet were spread and his arms were crossed. And his face, darkened by whiskers, was stern. Beside him, his expression one of worry, was Joe.

It took Stymie longer to acknowledge the call, though his hands stopped their crawling. His lips spread in a sneer and he flexed his shoulders as his fingers loosened. Then slowly he turned to face Jamie MacQuaid.

"What ye be wantin', Cap'n?"

Anne didn't think she'd ever heard the title spoken with more disdain. The two men stared at each other and Anne could almost feel the hatred ricocheting between them. She stumbled back a step, tripping over the fire bucket. It tipped over, spilling water that soaked quickly into the wide plank deck. Neither man seemed to notice.

Jamie took his measure of Stymie, wishing he could simply leap over the barrel separating them and grind his fist into the curled lip and evil pig eyes. To have it out once and for all was what he wanted. But there were too many who sided with Stymie, too many who waited for something just like this to start a bloody brawl. And dammit, if that happened, Jamie couldn't be sure who would end up captain.

So he forced himself to grin. "Just wondering if ye plan to help with the mainmast. Winds picking up."

"Ye given me an order, Cap'n?"

"Aye." Jamie kept his expression pleasant though his stare didn't waver. "As I recall 'twas issued a bit ago."

For what seemed minutes Stymie said nothing. The only sounds were the winds stretching the canvas taut. Then he shook his head, spilling clumped hair over his shoulder. "Well now, Cap'n, I do recall ye sayin' something 'bout that sail." He flexed his shoulders. " 'Course that was before this boy here spilt seawater all over me." He flashed a look around at Anne. "Oughta do something 'bout that, Cap'n."

Jamie just nodded, which could have meant he would or simply that he heard the complaint. He wasn't about to elaborate. Especially when Stymie ambled past him, close enough so that he could smell his foul odor. But he headed for the shrouds, swinging into them without a backward glance.

"He isn't going to leave it be, Cap'n."

"I think you're right about that, Keena." Jamie turned to smile at his head gunner, not surprised to see him standing slightly behind him, Deacon at his shoulder.

"What are you planning to do about him?"

"I haven't a clue." Looking back, Jamie touched Joe's shoulder. "You did good to come to me."

"Aye, Cap'n." Joe nearly beamed, then hastily grabbed up his own bucket and scurried away when Jamie motioned for him to get back to work.

"You're not going to hold him off forever, Cap'n." Deacon squinted his good eye toward the sails. "You know the talk among the men same as I do."

" 'Tis nothing but a lot of wind."

The eye fixed on Jamie. "If you believed that Stymie'd be nursing a cutlass wound by now instead of frolicking over the sails."

"His being up in the shrouds proves he isn't ready to make his move." Jamie turned and headed for the hatch. They already discussed this every way but under and he knew how Deacon and Keena felt. Hell, it was the same as him. But that didn't mean there was a thing he could do about it now.

"Remember what I said about watching your back."

Jamie paused when he heard Keena, then went below.

He wanted to see her.

Anne leaned back against the bulwark and tried to calm her breathing. What in heaven's name did Captain MacQuaid want with Andy? She settled the rope-handled bucket on the decking and tried to think it through.

Joe had come over to her minutes before while she sat in her little wedge of space eating some god-awful concoction that one of the pirates had served up. At first she swore she couldn't gag down a bite of the vessel's fare, but after a few days hunger won out and she was actually wolfing it down.

She'd stopped chewing when Joe spoke.

"Who wants to see me?"

"Cap'n MacQuaid. He said I should find ye and send ye down to his cabin."

She swallowed. "Why?"

"Didn't say." Joe filched a bite of meat from her trencher. "But I wouldn't dawdle."

So she'd passed her plate to Joe and crawled out of her corner. When she was near the hatch Joe yelled that she was to take a bucket of water with her.

So here she stood . . . wondering.

Had he recognized her?

Though that seemed as likely a reason as any, Anne didn't think he would wait this long to call her down if he had. And she hadn't seen him since the incident with Stymie this morning.

Anne crossed her arms, hugging herself around the middle. Just thinking of that dreadful Stymie gave her gooseflesh. Oh, why couldn't they find d'Porteau?

But that didn't solve her immediate problem. She would just have to keep the hat low and hope the captain saw what he wanted to see.

Anne tugged the knit brim over her forehead and picked up the bucket. Her first knock was tentative and obviously couldn't be heard over the singing inside. It was a tune she didn't know and different from anything she'd heard before on the ship. The words were lyrical, and hauntingly sad. And they were sung in a rich, deep voice that held her entranced. Anne listened, her fisted hand raised to knock again, but unwilling to break the spell by pounding harder. And then she realized what she was doing and hit the paneled wood with as much force as she could.

The song stopped and the pirate captain growled "What?" with such annoyance that she almost dropped the bucket and ran.

Instead she swallowed and spoke as low as she could. " 'Tis Andy, Captain."

"Come on then," came the command and slumping her shoulders Anne lifted the latch and pushed open the door. She didn't see him at first, but when she did, Anne's mouth gaped open.

The captain was naked as the day he was born.

Chapter Five

"Ah good, lad, you've brought more water." Jamie scrunched around trying to get comfortable in the small, curved tub. It was a tight squeeze and his chin nearly rested on his jutting knees. "Pour it on me if you'd be so kind, Master Andy. I might as well be takin' a bath in a puddle as trying to clean up in this wee bit of water."

The heavy rope bit into her curled fingers as Anne shifted from one foot to the other. "You want me to . . ." Anne realized her voice was even higher than usual and paused to clear her throat.

The captain didn't seem to notice anything but the lack of speed with which "Andy" obeyed his command. "Come on now, boy, I've a need to rinse the soap away."

He was right about that. Anne could smell the strong scent of lye and his wide, sun-bronzed shoulders were covered with a film of flaky dried bubbles. But to pour the contents of the pail over him would mean moving closer to him. As it was, though, she could imagine he wore nothing below the waist and since he was folded into the tub, she couldn't exactly see anything.

Other than his naked chest, that was. But then with his

penchant of going about barely clothed, with no jacket and his shirt blowing open in the wind, she'd seen that much of him before. Which she would just as soon not, Anne reminded herself. Though she seemed to have a difficult time keeping her gaze from straying to the broad expanse of hair-covered skin whenever she saw him. As always it intrigued her how the hair on his head was so much lighter than that on his chin and chest. The triangle of curls that arrowed down below the rim of the tub seemed almost coppery when wet. The—

"Hell and damnation, lad. Pour the water."

The growled order jolted Anne from her deep contemplation of his body. She jerked the bucket up and advanced on him, determined to do this thing and be gone. The last thing she noticed before she hefted the bucket was the look of astonishment that crossed his face.

And then she upended the pail, splashing seawater down over his head.

"What the—" Cold, salty liquid spewed over his face, stinging his eyes and riveting down his cheeks. Jamie sputtered and spat, knuckling his eyelids, and shaking his head so that diamond droplets of water flew in all directions.

Too shocked by his reaction to do more than stand her ground, Anne's clothing absorbed a splattering of water. When he squinted up at her she returned his stare, then realizing her mistake lowered her lashes.

"Is it your desire to drown me, lad?" Jamie shivered, then wiped at his face again. "And would it have hurt ye to warn me that the water was cold?"

"I . . . No one told me . . ." Anne began but now that she thought back on Joe's instructions, he'd said to fetch a pail of heated water from the galley. Apparently she'd been so overwrought by the summons to the captain's cabin that she forgot that small part of the order.

Thinking that Joe might join her on the receiving end of the captain's wrath, Anne cleared her throat. "Mayhap heating the water was mentioned."

"Well, that be a relief to know." Jamie forked his fingers back through his hair, skimming it away from his face. "Hand me that towel yonder," he said, still blinking his eyes against the salt water.

"The towel?" Anne felt like an idiot for repeating his words but now that she was close to the tub most of his secrets were revealed. And she couldn't seem to keep her eyes off him. Water lapped around his hips, swirled about the tight dark curls between his muscular thighs and floated an odd mushroom-shaped appendage. At least she assumed it was an appendage. Whatever, she'd never seen such a thing before and was busy watching it bob and sway among the soap bubbles when he surprised her by pushing to his feet.

It was attached all right. Now it hung thick and long between his legs, and Anne realized what it must be. She also realized she was a lot closer to him than she should be. He might have trouble seeing with the salt stinging his eyes, but after grabbing the linen towel himself he was busy scrubbing it over his face.

While she could, Anne backed up to the door, pressing her spine against the splintery wood.

After rubbing his face and hair, the pirate wrapped the scrap of fabric about his narrow waist, then turned to face her. She couldn't tell whether he planned to chastise her or laugh. Then his lips twitched and it was an amused chuckle that she heard. "Well, I suppose that rinsed me off as well as anything." He padded toward a small looking glass nailed to a timber by the windows, leaving watery footprints as he went.

As he studied his face in the glass, angling it first one way, then another, Anne took a good look at his cabin. It was as messy and unorganized as the rest of the ship. Clothes, and boots, books and rolled charts were everywhere: on the decking, piled on the one chair and covering the desk so that she couldn't tell for certain if the piece of furniture truly did serve that purpose.

The room was as unkempt as the captain.

That thought made her eyes roam toward him. He stood now, his back toward her, hands fisted on narrow hips, his legs spread. Only the water-soaked piece of fabric covered him, and that molded to him as if a second skin. Anne forced her gaze higher, trying to keep her mind on how disheveled he was. His hair hung in burnished-gold clumps over his shoulders, all attempts at keeping the wavy locks in a queue gone.

He turned then, his whiskered jaw jutting out. "I think I could use a shave. Have ye ever given one?"

"Me?" Her voice was little more than a squeak. "Nay." Anne shook her head violently.

The captain shrugged those wide shoulders, the motion slipping the precarious tuck of toweling. " 'Twas just a thought." Retracing his steps to the tub he bent over, fishing in the water until he pulled out a congealed slime of soap. Grinning as if it were a hunk of gold he rubbed it between his hands and then worked the lather into his whiskers.

When the lower half of his face was coated in a gray film he dumped a small bag on his pillow, the one bare spot on the bed, and sorted through until he found a razor. That, too, he seemed to view as a prize before scuffling back to the mirror and proceeding to shave.

Anne watched all this with a speculative eye, wondering if she were dismissed and what the captain wanted her for in the first place. For the better part of five minutes the only sounds were the lap of waves against the hull, the creak of timbers, and the scrape of razor against chin. Just when Anne decided that she would simply open the door and slip into the passageway he spoke.

"What made ye decide to join our crew, Andy?"

The question was so unexpected Anne couldn't think of an answer. She hemmed. She hawed. She caught his eye as he stared at her in the looking glass.

"There must have been a reason, for a lad your age to go on account. Since we didn't pull you off another vessel, I just wondered what it was."

"Adventure," Anne blurted out and saw the captain nod. He was shaving his cheek and twisted his mouth to the side.

"Adventure, eh. Well, there's plenty of that to be sure." His upper lip was next, and Jamie said nothing more until that was free of soap and whiskers. "But then there be times when a pirate ship isn't the safest place." He paused and turned, half of his face still covered in bubbles, to face Anne. "Like this afternoon."

Anne swallowed. "I'm not afraid of a bully."

The pirate grinned, then resumed his shaving. "Well said, but perhaps a bit foolhardy. There are bullies it's wise to fear. And to stay clear of."

As Joe had told her. Anne shrugged her shoulders inside the too-large coat. "I do my best."

"I'm sure ye do, lad. But if your best ever isn't enough, I want ye to let me know." Satisfied with the reflection staring back at him, Jamie walked to the tub, bent over and rinsed away the remaining soap. He reached for the towel around his waist to dry his face but before he could unfasten it something was thrust into his hand. He looked down at one of his shirts offered by Andy. With a shrug he wiped at his cheeks and chin.

When he glanced up Anne couldn't help staring. Without his layer of whiskers the pirate was, well, handsome . . . almost beautiful. She'd known there was a certain appeal about him. But this! His cheekbones were strong, his nose straight, and the mouth . . . Unhidden by the fringe of whiskers, it was wide and sensual.

"Are ye understanding what I'm saying to ye, lad?"

"What? Ah . . . er . . . aye. Stay away from Stymie," Anne finally managed to blunder out. He had a cleft in his chin that she forced herself to ignore as she averted her eyes.

"Be ye all right, lad?" Jamie tossed the damp shirt over his shoulder and approached the boy, stopping only when he cringed away, turning his head and looking as if he wanted to meld with the bulwark.

Jamie lifted his hand to touch the filthy knit cap covering his head, thinking better of it when he heard the whimper. "I'll not hurt ye, lad." Jamie waited for him to glance up and when he didn't, retraced his steps. It was obvious the poor boy was terrified. And after Stymie's advances this day, he probably had a right to be.

Jamie took a deep breath wishing he could rid his ship of Stymie and his cohorts . . . knowing he couldn't. "Be off with ye then," he said as he started looking for a clean pair of breeches. "But keep your guard up."

Not giving him a chance to rescind his order, Anne scurried out the door. She rushed forward along the passageway without paying attention to where she was, hurrying past the ladder leading above deck. Something skittered in front of her. She recognized the rodent's squeak, but it was too dark to see much. On either side of her were shelves jammed with rope. Though the air was dank and chilled, sweat rolled down her back and between her breasts.

The sloop rolled and Anne's stomach did the same, sending her lurching forward. It had been days since she was bothered by the seasickness and she hoped she'd felt the last of it. But apparently the pressure of being so close to Captain MacQuaid did more than give her trembling hands.

Anne stayed below for as long as she thought she could. It was dark, and she had no way to know the time. And though she had hunger pangs, food wasn't something she wished for now with her stomach acting up. Especially not the kind of swill served up on the *Lost Cause*.

Crunched up beside a coil of damp rope, her chin resting on her raised knees, Anne imagined what it would be like if she took over the galley. A little organization would go a long way toward making the finished product more appetizing.

From there her mind wandered to the captain's quarters. Such a mess she'd never seen. If he simply spent a few minutes . . . perhaps it would take more than a *few* minutes . . . cleaning and putting away his things, there would be much less clutter. He could run the ship more efficiently.

Tucking her chin she rubbed an itch on her nose with her woolen-covered knee. When she lifted her head again a smile curved her lips. What was she doing trying to plan ways for a pirate to manage his ship better? Well, if it helped him catch d'Porteau she supposed it would be all right.

With a sigh Anne settled her head onto the rope. The next thing she knew she heard sounds coming as if from far away. It was like a dream but when she opened her eyes, she could still hear them. By the feel of her neck when she tried to straighten it she'd been asleep for some time. She was stiff and chilled to the bone, glad for once that she wore a heavy jacket and woolen cap.

Anne blinked, looking around and trying to remember where she was and why. And how she could get back up on deck. She'd been so upset after she left the captain's cabin that she hadn't really watched where she was going. And now it was black as pitch around her.

But she could still hear the voices, a mere mumbling off behind her so she carefully slid off the grated shelf where she sat. Her shoes sloshed in some bilge water and she cringed as it seeped through the leather and oozed around her toes. Oh, she would be so glad to be off this floating torture chamber.

Using her hands to guide her she moved along the gangway toward the voices. They were getting louder and she was tempted to call out, but something kept her from it. She wasn't sure what. Anne finally decided it was the darkness making her feel so spooky. After all, she intended to show herself when she reached whoever was talking.

At least she thought she would. But when Anne crept around a corner, piled high with barrels and saw the men sitting around the single candle she changed her mind. Holding her breath she sidled back into the shadows and pressed against the bulwark.

She could hear them more plainly now, though they were mumbling and obviously trying to keep their voices down. She didn't know all their names, only Stymie's, but she'd seen most of them on the ship and she knew instinctively to steer clear of them. Her glance at the cluster was so brief she didn't know exactly how many men there were but she guessed there to be nearly a dozen. And right now they seemed to be arguing about something.

"I say we do it now."

"Aye, now it is," Anne heard several more agree. It sounded as if the majority would win, in true Locke tradition, whatever they were discussing until she heard the voice of the dissenter.

Stymie.

"And how are we to get the weapons?" The question sounded logical enough. It was the tone that made the skin on Anne's neck seem to crawl.

"From the guardhouse," one answered logically, to be joined by a chorus of support.

"Aye, we'll break down the blasted door and help ourselves."

"And how many of us will get ourselves killed in the process?" The chilling voice of reason pierced the rowdy cheers. "I've no desire to go up against the cap'n, and get me head blown off."

"Yea, we noticed."

This was followed by enough snickers that Anne knew the pirates were remembering Stymie's reaction this morning. Anne was close to smiling herself when a loud bang made her gasp. Flattening herself against the boards, she waited, deathly still, half expecting to be discovered, only to realize the noise had nothing to do with her. Stymie apparently took exception to being the butt of mirth and slammed something down.

Whatever it was it effectively quieted the group. The

silence seemed to permeate the hold, making the pounding in her chest sound deafening. Just when she thought she would burst if she didn't take a breath, Stymie spoke.

"Any man here who thinks he can take on the cap'n will die like the fool he is." He sniffed and Anne could imagine him lifting his burly shoulders. "But there be more than one way to be rid of 'em."

Anne wrapped her arms about her waist.

"But when? How?"

Anne leaned her ear closer to the crack between the barrels.

"Leave the when and how ta me. But know 'twill be soon." There was the grating sound of wood against wood, and Anne shrunk back as small as she could. "Now get along, the lot 'a ye, 'fore Cap'n MacQuaid comes lookin' ta tuck ye into yer beds with a lullaby."

This brought a chorus of chortles, amid the shuffling of feet and cracking of bones too long settled on damp wood. The light slowly faded and Anne silently slid her back down the bulwark until she hit the decking. She'd heard enough to know that Captain MacQuaid and her mission were in grave danger.

The question was, what should she do about it? Surely the captain knew Stymie didn't like him. The expression on the man's face this morning was clear enough for even an idiot to read. And she didn't think Jamie MaQuaid was an idiot.

Then why did he keep Stymie and the others among his crew?

Of course he didn't know about their plot of mutiny. Only she was privy to that information.

Just in case one of the conspirators had stayed to make certain no one overheard their plans, Anne made herself count slowly to one hundred. She peeked out around the kegs, thankful no one was there, then cautiously made her way out of the hold. Once in the passageway she blinked her eyes against the glare of the stubby candle smoking in its iron holder. After glancing around she rushed toward the hatch.

"Aw, Momma, let me sleep a bit more," Joe mumbled, then jerked awake the whites of his eyes wide in the moonglow. "Stymie?"

"No, it's Andy." Anne whispered. She reached out and touched the boy's arm, sorry she hadn't taken more care with waking him. He trembled beneath her fingers.

When he moved over she squeezed into the space they shared between the extra cordage and some torn sails.

"I didn't mean to frighten you."

"Didn't," he lied before scrunching back down and resting his check on folded hands. "Just startled me, s'all." His lids closed.

"Joe, wait. Don't go back to sleep. I have to talk to you."

One eye opened. "Where ye been? Looked for ye at supper."

"That's not important." Anne pushed up and looked about nervously. Several pirates were on deck, the mid-watch, but they didn't seem to be paying her any mind. But she wasn't taking any chances. Anne lowered her voice. "I need for you to do something for me."

"What?"

Joe obviously wasn't as sensitive to the need for secrecy. Anne pressed her finger to his lips. "I want you to tell the captain something."

Joe wriggled down onto his blanket. "Ask me in the mornin'."

"No." Anne shook his skinny arm. "You have to do it now."

Joe's eyes popped open again. "Ye mean ye want me to go below and wake 'em up? Wake up Cap'n Mac-Quaid?"

"Exactly."

"He'd have me hide, for sure."

"No, no, he won't. Listen . . ." Since the boy showed no signs of sitting up, Anne lay down beside him. "There's a plot afoot to take over the ship." She had to clamp her hand over Joe's mouth when he whooped his surprise. "Will you be quiet?"

Rising on her elbows, Anne checked to see if the outburst sparked anyone's attention. The sailor closest to them appeared to have drifted off to sleep. Anne could only hope d'Porteau's vessel didn't break the horizon during his watch.

Joe was wide awake now, sitting and full of questions. But at least he kept his voice low. "Who told ye? What is they gonna do? 'Tis Stymie, isn't it?"

Now it was Anne's turn to open her eyes in surprise. "What makes you think that?"

Joe's shrug didn't seem careless. "He's a bad 'un."

Anne could only nod in agreement. "And you're right. He's one of them. Actually, I believe he's their leader."

"Who else?"

"Truthfully, I don't know. Perhaps, I'd recognize their voices. . . ." Anne bit her lower lip. "But I can't be sure. Anyway." She brushed aside that problem with a sweep of her hand. "I think the captain should know."

"Well, why don't ye tell him?"

Why didn't she indeed? Anne had a perfectly logical reason, but she didn't think she could share it with Joe. She didn't know how he'd take an admission that she was really a female, and needed to keep her distance from Captain MacQuaid lest he recognize her.

"I just can't, is all." Anne sucked in her breath. "You've known him longer than I. He's more likely to believe you."

Joe seemed to find that explanation acceptable for he bent forward. "So tell me," was all he said.

"When do ye think they'll try it?" Joe asked when Anne finished running through most of the details. She didn't tell him that she ran from the captain's cabin to hide in the afterhold.

"I told you I don't know." Anne paused. "They don't know. But it could be anytime. And I think the captain should be made aware of this."

Joe rubbed his jaw. In the moonlight he looked older than his ten years. "I better go tell 'em."

Though her muscles cried for rest Anne couldn't settle down after Joe scurried off in the darkness. She wriggled this way and that, trying to get comfortable, even though she was too nervous to sleep.

Would the captain believe Joe? Would he know what to do? Anne sighed and stretched out her legs. Wearing breeches gave her welcome freedom of movement, but she'd sacrifice it all for a bath and a night on a down-filled mattress.

That was the thought in her head when Joe plopped down beside her. Anne jerked onto her knees facing him. "Well, what did he say?"

"Before or after he striped me back with his whip?"

Anne's lips thinned. "You look none the worse for wear

to me. And come to think of it, I don't believe Captain MacQuaid even has a whip."

"Maybe he don't, but he sure threatened to use one on me when I first went poundin' on his door."

"Simply a reaction to being awakened, I'm sure." Anne sidled closer. "You did tell him, didn't you?"

"Aye. But I think it were a waste 'a me time." Joe gave Anne a none to gentle shove and sprawled out on the deck. "He didn't seem ta set much store by it."

"What? You mean he didn't believe you?"

Joe shrugged off the hand on his arm. "Oh, he didn't doubt me none. Just acted as if it weren't no big deal. Said there's always malcon . . . malcon . . ."

"Malcontents," Anne supplied without thinking.

"Aye, that's what he said. There's always them on a ship who wants ta take over, but it weren't nothin' to worry 'bout." With that he turned over, showing Anne his back and growling, "Go ta sleep and leave me be," when Anne tried to roust him.

Frustrated, Anne slumped back against the coiled rope. What was she to do now? She hadn't eavesdropped on a group of grumblers who planned to do nothing about their grievances. They were serious, especially Stymie, about a mutiny. They planned to get rid of Captain Mac-Quaid. And even if Anne didn't need him to find d'Porteau and Arthur, she couldn't imagine being on board the sloop with Stymie in charge. It was bad enough just trying to stay out of his way.

Perhaps she'd simply go to the captain herself and convince him the threat was real. Except how many times could she be around him and hope that he didn't recognize her? She'd been lucky so far. Deciding there was nothing more to be done tonight, Anne settled down on her blanket and fell asleep.

The next morning dawned as bright as the Caribbean sun and early for Anne who slept but a few hours. She stretched, noticing that she was alone in the little alcove of space and went in search of Joe. She found him aft, leaning against the windlass, crunching on a biscuit.

"Thought ye was gonna sleep the day away," he said, barely glancing her way, but reaching in his pocket and offering her a biscuit.

Anne took it and with an inward shrug jammed it into her jaw and broke off a bite. She already learned these delicacies were not easily broken by front teeth. "I was tired," she said around her food. With a yawn she slid down beside the boy. "What are you doing?"

"Keepin' watch."

Anne followed his gaze. First in view came Stymie sitting on his hunches with three other men. They were playing a game, each tossing a knife into a circle and seeing who came closer to hitting a piece of sailing. So far none had succeeded.

Beyond them, on the quarterdeck, stood the captain. He was leaning against the rail, looking out to sea, his back toward Anne and Joe . . . and Stymie.

"I figure, if the cap'n won't watch out for hisself, then I'll have to do it."

Anne turned toward the boy, her eyes wide. "Then you're not mad about last night?"

"Nay." Joe grinned. "I just ain't me best when someone wakes me."

Anne smiled back, then her expression sobered. "I better talk to Captain MacQuaid. Perhaps he'll listen to me."

"Doubt it." Joe took another bite of his breakfast. "But go ahead and try if'n ye like. I'm tellin' ye he just ain't scared of Stymie."

By the end of the day Anne was thinking Joe's assessment was correct. The two kept their watch over the captain every time they weren't called upon to do anything . . . and on this boat that was nearly all the time. Captain MacQuaid went about his duties and a considerable amount of rest time, with seemingly not a care in the world.

Stymie appeared equally at ease.

No hint of a mutiny.

"Ye think ye could 'ave been wrong?"

"No. I know what I heard."

Still she wondered as the sky darkened on another day at sea. A day with no sign of d'Porteau, a stomach that never really felt calm, and watching the captain and his adversary do nothing. Wondered not if she heard correctly, but what she was thinking when she stowed aboard in the first place. Why she even asked Captain MacQuaid for his assistance.

Anne lay on the deck watching the stars appear, waiting for Joe to return. He'd gone below to use the head, still apparently not suspicious that Anne never went at the same time. At least that much of pretending to be a boy wasn't difficult. Actually none of it had been too bad; she probably wouldn't even worry about fooling Jamie Mac-Quaid if he hadn't known her as a woman.

Desired her as a woman.

Anne sat up, disgusted with herself for thinking of that. So he'd kissed her. Knowing him, he probably went after anything in petticoats. She tried to suppress a giggle as she folded her hands beneath her head. What would the captain think when he discovered she'd been on board all along? She'd tell him after this was all over. When they captured d'Porteau and found Arthur, then she'd yank off her cap and wipe the dirt off her face. A smile curved her lips. She couldn't wait to see his expression.

Anne realized she fell asleep thinking about the captain when she awoke, her body humming. "Oh my heavens." She sat up, wiping trembling hands across her brow. She'd been dreaming, but it seemed so real. The captain was lying beside her doing things to her with his hands and mouth and she hadn't been able to resist . . . hadn't wanted to resist.

Anne tried to push those thoughts from her mind. She found the pirate captain repulsive. She did. Anne leaned back against the rope . . . and realized Joe wasn't there. Unless he came and went while she slept, he'd been at the head way too long.

Anne pushed to her feet, stretching and taking a look around. All seemed calm enough. The *Lost Cause* lolled about on a peaceful sea, what wind there was, filling her sails and taking her skimming into the night.

There seemed to be even fewer pirates on watch tonight. Deciding if she could fool the pirate in the light she could certainly do as much to the blackamoor in the dark, Anne climbed the ladder to the quarterdeck where he stood at the wheel. He didn't seem to recognize her, but he hadn't seen Joe either.

Nor had any of the other men on watch. Gathering her nerve, and deciding when she found him, she'd tell him what she thought of the scare he gave her, Anne climbed through the hatch.

The few lanterns swaying overhead on the berth deck gave off little light. But enough for Anne to know that Joe wasn't among the men lucky enough to have space for a hammock on the crowded boat.

From there she went down the port aft gangway. She knew better than to try the captain's door. And wandering beyond only led her to the dark, dank hole where she'd heard Stymie and his friends. She didn't want to go in there again but something drew her. Something she couldn't explain.

She could hear the rats scurrying about, and the bilge water dripping. Sweat broke out across her upper lip as she moved further along the cable tiers. When she stopped and looked around, unable to see anything in the darkness, Anne called herself a fool for coming in here. Nothing was to be gained by roaming around in the bowels of the ship. Joe was probably on deck asleep by now and she was—

The sound was little more than a whimper, at first too near the call of vermin for her to notice. But it kept up, a low keening that tore at her heart.

"Joe?" Her first call was tentative. "Joe, is that you?"

Anne climbed onto a grated shelf, moving toward the whimper. By now her eyes had adjusted to the darkness and she could make out shapes, but it didn't keep her from banging her knee into a timber.

"Joe. Answer me." The sound was louder now and she pulled herself onto another coil of rope in time to hear him call out in pain.

"Oh dear Lord, Joe!"

Chapter Six

"He's a spawn of the devil."

Jamie rolled his eyes heavenward, then lifted his hand, palm out when Deacon leveled his stare toward him. "I'm not disputing your words, Deacon. Really I'm not." Pushing his chair back on two legs, Jamie rested his own, booted feet, crossed, on his desk, knocking a log book onto the deck in the process. He merely shrugged. "Unfortunately he appears to be our devil for the moment."

"Does that mean you will do nothing about this plot?" This from Keena who sat on the bunk in Jamie's cabin.

Stretching back, Jamie grimaced. "Are we not giving Stymie too much credit? A plot seems a wee bit more than he can handle."

"The boy heard him. You said so yourself."

" 'Tis true, I did," Jamie allowed. "But now that I think on it, Joe didn't seem to have some of his facts straight. He couldn't tell me where he was, or where Stymie was for that matter."

"Didn't you question the boy?"

"Of course I did . . . some. Hell, he woke me up, for God's sake. Sorry, Deacon," Jamie added when he saw his quartermaster's expression. Cursing was one thing, in Deacon's mind. Taking the Lord's name in vain was something else entirely.

"Perhaps we should talk to him again."

"Talk to him all ye wish." Shifting his weight, Jamie sent the two front chair legs banging to the floor. "Don't misunderstand me. I'd be the first to admit that Stymie wants to be captain. Hell, he'd kill me for the privilege and be glad of it. But hatching a plot isn't for the likes of him."

"It would take a deposed prince to do that, eh, Cap'n?"

Jamie let the barb pass. "It would take someone a wee bit smarter than Stymie."

"Perhaps." Keena folded his fingers. "But I do not believe you give that man enough credit."

Jamie looked from the blackamoor to Deacon. "Would ye mind standing still? Your constant pacing is making me uneasy." When the black-garbed man stopped in mid-stride to face him, Jamie's expression was contrite. "If you both think there be something to this . . ." He shrugged. "Perhaps I should speak with the lad again. Though if Stymie wants the *Lost Cause* so dearly, I do not know why he doesn't just challenge me for it."

"And risk fighting you? Besides, he knows better than to put anything to a vote. No matter how much the crew grumbles about chasin' d'Porteau all over the Caribbean, they won't kick you out."

"Grumbles?" Jamie leaned his elbows on the cluttered desk. "Hell, they should be singing me praises. Diamonds and rubies are worth more than we can take from a half-dozen worm-infested merchantmen." Glancing up Jamie caught the look that passed between Keena and

Deacon. His eyes narrowed. "What in the hell is goin' on here? Tell me what ye be thinking."

Deacon went and flopped down on the window seat, his arms crossed, his expression blank, leaving it for Keena to receive Jamie's stare. He shrugged his powerful, dark shoulders. "We wonder how much the woman had to do with your decision to pursue d'Porteau."

"The woman?" Jamie knew exactly what woman they meant.

"In the Shark's Tooth. She *was* a comely wench."

"And God know's you're susceptible to the breed." This from Deacon, who turned back to contemplate the inky sea after delivering the line.

Jamie twisted back in his chair. "Let me be sure I'm hearing this right. Ye think I'm chasing down the Frenchman because I'm lusting after some lass?"

"Now, Cap'n, we didn't say—"

"Aye, ye did. You think I'd risk the *Lost Cause* on a roll in the hay."

"There is no need to—"

Jamie never discovered what Keena was planning to say for at that moment someone pounded on the door. Before he could ask who was there, the portal burst open. The lad, Andy, rushed in, filthy as ever, his face a mask of panic.

"What in the hell—"

"He's hurt!" Anne tried to catch her breath. "Hurt badly, I fear." Without thinking she grabbed the captain's arm. "Come on." Her yank didn't budge him, but he did stand, though he didn't seem inclined to follow.

"Who's hurt? Lad, you'll have to be more—"

"Joe." Anne swallowed and spoke as calmly as she could. But she had to leave him to get help and she hated for him to be alone. "He's been beat up down in the cable tier." Before she could finish the words the captain was out the door, his two officers on his heels. Anne followed as quickly as she could, running into Keena's back when he paused to grab a lantern off its hook.

"Over here. Bring the light."

Anne pushed around the blackamoor and Deacon and climbed to where the captain crouched beside Joe. In the wavering puddle of light she saw Jamie glance up. Their eyes met, hers questioning, his unreadable. Then he scooped up Joe and sloshed through the water toward the entrance.

Anne did her best to keep up, running along behind as the captain retraced his steps to his cabin. Stepping aside he allowed Anne to open the door and then waited while she swept clothes from his bunk. Then he lowered Joe to the mattress.

"Fetch Big Will." He tossed the words over his shoulder before brushing the boy's hair off his face. Both eyes were shut, one swollen and discolored. And there were cuts on his cheeks and around his mouth. He wasn't making any noise now.

"Is he going to be all right?" Anne knelt beside the bunk, clutching Joe's hand. She could see the rhythmic motion of his chest, but wished he'd open his eyes.

"Doesn't look too bad." Jamie touched the kneeling boy's shoulder. Andy obviously cared very much about his friend. "Be a good lad, and bring some water. Go on with you now."

Anne hesitated only a moment, then pushed to her feet. The captain had a tin pitcher full of what appeared to be fresh water. Anne stuck her finger in and tasted it to be sure. Finding a clean towel was more difficult. She finally had to settle for one that wasn't filthy.

By the time she returned to the bunk the captain was sitting back on his heels staring at Joe. One look at the captain's face and she dropped onto the floor beside the bunk. "What is it?"

Jamie shook his head. "Just these bruises. Can't imagine why anyone would do this. Here now, hand me the pitcher."

The wet linen pressed to his forehead woke Joe. He moaned and opened one eye, grimacing with pain when the captain touched the towel to his cut.

"Who did this to ye, lad?"

The question made Joe shut his eye. With a whimper he turned his head.

"Tell the captain, Joe. Who hurt you?"

"He'll kill me if I do," came the tearful response. "He done said he would."

"No one is going to hurt you, lad. I'll see to that." The words sounded hollow to Jamie even as he said them. He hadn't kept someone from hurting Joe this time.

"You have to tell Captain MacQuaid, Joe. It's the only way to bring the culprit to justice." Anne gently reached up and ran her finger along the boy's jaw. "We can't let him get away with this, Joe. It wouldn't be right."

She thought he would tell her. Leaning low, Anne listened intently as his mouth opened, but before he could speak the door pounded open and Big Will burst in.

"Who does ve have hurt in here?" he demanded in a heavily accented voice. He was a big man, taller than the captain even, with a shaved head and light blue eyes that seemed lost in his moon-round face. It was more than his size and the scar across his forehead that made him frightening. He was one of the many pirates that Anne did her best to avoid.

But now she couldn't avoid him. He blustered over to Joe and she suddenly knew how a mother hen felt when one of her chicks was threatened. Anne had the strongest desire to throw herself across young Joe and protect him with her life. How could someone so large and boistrous do anything but hurt poor, beaten Joe?

"I don't think—" she began, but was pushed aside before she could finish.

"Come on, lad. Let Big Will have a look."

There didn't seem much she could do, since Big Will was already having his look. Anne stayed as close as she could, keeping an eye on what the pirate was doing, but he appeared to be doing no harm. His large hands seemed almost gently as they skimmed over Joe's body.

"Don't worry so."

Anne glanced around to see the captain staring at her. She pulled the knitted hat lower.

"Big Will studied medicine in Prussia. 'Tis lucky we are that he joined our merry group."

"Ha!" Big Will opened a wooden chest and fingered through the jars and vials, his sausagelike fingers finally finding what he sought. "Luck had nothin' to do with it, as you vell know. Get the boy a drink of something."

It was Keena who produced a mug. Big Will added a few drops from the jar, then lifted Joe's shoulders and commanded him to drink.

"That should let him sleep for a vhile." Big Will stood and stretched his arms. "The boy vill be all right." He pulled a small pot from the case. "A bit ov this on his cuts vill help them heal."

"Good. Now, lad, just tell us where Joe's hammock is and we'll—"

"He doesn't have a hammock," Anne said. "He sleeps on deck, as I do."

Captain MacQuaid seemed bewildered by this and glanced toward Keena who shrugged his shoulders. "We've a full crew. Not enough space for all the men."

"He could stay here." Anne lifted her chin, before remembering her disguise. "It seems like a comfortable enough bed."

"It is," the captain assured her. "And 'tis mine." He met her stare, then shrugged. "Ah, let the lad use it for a bit."

"Vonderful, Captain." Big Will slapped Jamie on the back, hard enough to knock him forward. "Now, I could use a drink."

While Keena poured a generous serving into another mug, Anne settled on the bunk beside Joe. He looked up at her, his gray eyes already showing the effects of the sleeping potion he received.

"Just rest now, Joe. There's nothing to worry—" Anne gasped when he reached up and locked his fingers about her hand.

"Andy," he said, a hitch in his voice. "Stay clear of Stymie."

"Is he the one who beat you?" It was hardly a surprising revelation, but when Anne watched Joe close his eyes and nod, rage boiled within her.

She pushed to her feet, whirling around to face the four men, three of whom now had mugs in their hands. "It was Stymie who did this."

"Did Joe tell ye that?"

"Yes." Anne paused. "Well, aren't you going to do something about it?"

They all stopped drinking and looked at her. But only one stepped forward, eyes narrowed and staring at her as if there was a hint of recognition. Too late Anne realized she was not acting like a humble cabin boy.

He moved closer.

Anne dropped her lashes.

"Vouldn't surprise me none if it vas Stymie. He's a mean one."

"I doubt 'twould surprise any of us," Jamie said, but he didn't take his eyes off the boy standing before him.

And with each step he took he came closer until Anne could feel the sweat bead on her upper lip.

"I should be getting on deck," she mumbled and turned toward the door. But before she could move Captain MacQuaid's hand surrounded her upper arm.

"Leaving us so soon . . . Andy, is it? Aren't you interested in giving any more orders?"

Anne swallowed. "Ain't in me place to be givin' orders, sir. Reckon that's for the cap'n to do."

"Is it now?"

"Aye." He was pulling her closer, until she could smell the musky scent of his skin. Anne tried to keep her head down, but he hooked her chin, jerking it up with his thumb. Recognition sparked in his blue-green eyes when they met hers. She knew that he knew.

Anne squirmed, but it did no good. His grip was iron tight. "Let me go, Cap'n."

"Aw, come on, Cap'n, the boy didn't mean nothin' by it. He's just vorried 'bout his friend."

"Is that it, Andy? Are ye worried about your friend?"

"Yes, yes, I am." Anne tried to dig in her heels as he started dragging her toward the door.

"Cap'n, where are you takin' the boy?" Keena stepped in front of the door, but one look at his friend's face and he stepped aside.

Before anyone else could say a word, Anne and the captain were in the passageway. He grabbed a lantern with one hand and shoved her into a small cubbyhole of a room with the other.

Anne lifted her arm against the glare as he held the light up to her face. She didn't even resist when he yanked off her hat. A tangle of curls spilled down about her shoulders.

Though he knew before, the unrefutable proof of her hair was more than he could handle. He speared five fingers through his own hair, loosening the thong of leather holding it back.

"I can't believe this." He looked away, and then back, as if thinking his eyes deceived him. "What in the hell are ye doing here?" Anne opened her mouth to explain, but he kept talking. "You're a woman, for God's sake. On a pirate ship." He paced a step to the door, then back. "Who else knows of this, my God, I'll cut out the liver of any of my crew who helped ye."

"No one knows."

"What? What did ye say?" Now both hands were in his hair as he continued to stride back and forth.

"I said no one knows. No one helped me."

He stopped then and looked at her, his eyes narrowed. On the floor, where he'd dropped it, the lantern sent a tapestry of shadow and light dancing over his handsome features. Anne could only stand her ground and hope for the best.

"Ye fooled the entire crew?" He sounded skeptical, until his jaw dropped and he shook his head. "Hell, ye fooled me, sure enough. And I've . . ." What? Kissed you? Dreamed about you? Somehow Jamie didn't think saying either was appropriate. He leaned back, finding the door with his spine and sliding down the length until he sat knees bent on the floor.

"Why did you do it, Anne? Why did ye dress like that and come aboard?" When she didn't answer, he tilted his head. "Didn't think ye could trust me?"

"Trust had nothing to do with it." Anne shifted. She shouldn't, of course, but he made her feel guilty for doing what she did. For heaven's sake he was a pirate. It wasn't as if he followed rules. Why should he act disappointed that she hadn't.

She lifted her chin. "I wanted to be there when you caught d'Porteau."

"You wanted . . ." He started to repeat her contention, and began laughing instead. "Are ye mad?" He pushed to his feet. "Hell, of course ye are. Look at ye." He advanced until he loomed over her. "You're filthy. I should think a gentlewoman would have more pride than to cover herself with—" His finger skimmed her cheek. "What is this anyway?"

"Grease and tar."

He wiped a black smear down the front of her coat. "I don't imagine this will do much for your complexion."

Anne knocked his hand away when it lingered near her breast. "I'm not concerned about my skin."

"Nay, I don't imagine ye are." Jamie let air out through his mouth. Now that he took a good look at her he couldn't imagine how he hadn't recognized her the moment he saw her. Forget that her face was darkened with grime and her hair covered. Those eyes alone should have given her away. And the way she moved.

Jamie looked away before he did something he might regret. Even dressed as she was she excited him. The sooner he was rid of her the better.

"Well, ye shan't be getting your wish." He leaned back, crossing his arms. "I'll not have a woman on board, nor will I expose ye to danger during a sea battle. Under full sail we should reach New Providence in a few days. From there ye can get passage to Libertia."

"But I thought we were going to San Palma?"

"We were. But we shall lose over a sennight delivering ye somewhere safe."

"I do not wish to be safe."

"That much Mistress Cornwall is evident."

"And I refuse to be put ashore."

"Ye refuse?" Jamie's voice boomed. "Ye refuse. Who do ye think ye are to refuse me anything?"

She wouldn't be intimidated. She wouldn't. "I'm the person who hired you. The person who will pay you to find d'Porteau."

"I'm a pirate. Not a hireling."

"Nonetheless, I did hire you." The expression on his face kept her from continuing that argument. She reached out toward him. "I see no harm in letting me stay aboard."

"Obviously. However, I do."

"What?" Anne grabbed his arm when he turned away. "I've been on the *Lost Cause* nearly a sennight and I've come to no harm."

"Are you forgetting yesterday morning? Stymie?"

Anne was silent a moment. Then, "You must do something about him."

His eyes wide, Jamie could only stare at her.

"Well you must. After what he did to Joe, he deserves to be punished. It's impossible not to agree." Anne hesitated. "Why are you shaking your head . . . and laughing?"

Leaning back against the door, Jamie effectively put space between them. " 'Tis ye, Mistress Cornwall, and your penchant for giving orders. Even dressed as ye are." He lifted a warning finger when she tried to interrupt. "Caught on my ship, ye still insist upon telling others what they should do."

Anne lifted her chin. "You intend to let him get away with what he did to that poor boy?"

"Nay!" Jamie pushed off the wall and stalked toward her. "I intend to do what I must. But if memory serves 'twas not Stymie's transgressions we were discussing, but yours." He continued before she had a chance to speak. "Until we make New Providence ye shall remain in my cabin, is that understood?" He didn't wait for her acknowledgment, but turned toward the door. Her quiet words stopped him from lifting the latch.

"I shall tell them I'm a woman."

"What?" His eyes sliced through her as he looked around.

Despite the fierce expression on his face, Anne swallowed and forced herself to continue. "I know a bit about pirate behavior."

"As well you should, after living as one for nearly a sennight."

"I knew before. Israel told me."

"Ah, Israel. As poor as an excuse for a sailor, let alone a pirate as I ever saw. I suppose he put ye up to this . . . this masquerade?"

"Israel knows nothing about it."

Jamie's brow arched. "And ye expect me to believe that?"

"I expect you to believe your crew would disapprove of you bringing a woman aboard for your own pleasure. According to Israel, it is a rule not lightly broken."

He stared at her long and hard. "I did not do that."

Their gazes locked. "But unless you allow me to stay on the *Lost Cause,* I shall tell them you did."

His smile was slow in coming. "I don't think that would be a good idea, Mistress Cornwall."

It was Anne's turn to cross her arms and lift her brows. "And why not?"

"I doubt anyone would believe ye." His eyes hardened as they traveled from her disheveled hair to the tip of her salt-encrusted shoes. "Though I've been known to take my pleasure where I may, 'tis doubtful anyone would credit I've sunk this low."

Anne couldn't stop the color that rose to brighten her cheeks. She told herself it bloomed of anger, but knew it to be more than that. Her jaw tightened. "We shall see what they believe."

He cocked his head. "Is this to be a battle of will, then? Yours against mine?"

"If it must." Anne let out her breath, then reached around him for the latch. His hand firmly pressed to hers made her stop.

They stood close and Anne could feel the heat from his body, feel his anger as he tried to control it. Finally, unable to help herself, she looked up. His expression was not at all what she expected. She couldn't put a name to what she saw in his eyes, but it frightened her nearly as much as his rage.

"Don't ye know what they would do to ye? They're pirates, for God's sake."

"As are you."

"Aye, and lucky ye are to be standing rather than flat on your back with your . . ." He hesitated. "Breeches about your ankles."

"But I thought you said they wouldn't believe you'd sunk so l—"

"The hell with what I said." Jamie slammed his palm against the door. She was the most exasperating woman he'd ever encountered. And it irked the hell out of him that she was also the smartest. And the one he couldn't stop thinking of burying himself in. "You can't tell them you're a woman. I wouldn't be able to stop them." He cupped her shoulders. "Do you understand what I'm saying to you, Annie? I couldn't stop them."

All she could do was nod.

"Now." Jamie let out his breath, then leaned over to scoop up the knitted cap. "I want ye to be putting this back on, and keeping it on. Until we reach New Providence ye're to stay in my cabin. Talk to no one. See no one."

He pulled the hat down over her head, tucking curls underneath as he went. When he finished Jamie used his thumbs to tilt her face up toward his. She was disguised just as before, hair covered, skin blackened, and he wondered again how he could have mistaken her for a boy.

Without realizing what he was going to do, Jamie bent forward. Her lips were as soft as before, and after the initial shock, as receptive. He kissed her until they were both breathless, then forced himself to back away. Then he opened the door, grabbed up the lantern and pulled her into the passageway.

Joe was the only one in his cabin when they returned, and he was deep into a drugged sleep. Anne checked on him while the captain brushed an assortment of clothing and books from the top of a sea chest, then lifted the lid. He pulled out a blanket and handed it to Anne.

"I suggest ye get some sleep," was all he said before retrieving his pistol from his desk and leaving. As she slumped down on the side of the bunk Anne heard the key twist in the lock.

"I'm not going back to Libertia," she whispered. "Not until d'Porteau is defeated."

It was a blessing Jamie didn't hear her defiance, for he was boiling with rage. More furious than he could remember being in years. What in the hell was he to do now?

His step quickened as he headed toward the ladder. With jerky motions he attacked the rungs, his head, then shoulders bursting through the open hatch. The first deep breath of salt air seemed to sting his lungs, open and clear his mind.

But still the question persisted. What should he do?

Agreeing to hunt down d'Porteau was a mistake. That much was evident to him. It was an error in judgment . . . one he'd known from the start. One made more of lust than reason no matter how much he might protest to Keena and Deacon. Jamie strode across the deck, zigzagging to pick his way through the snoring bodies littering his way. He hadn't realized how crowded the *Lost Cause* was. Something else to take care of, he mused, not at all pleased by the prospect.

He wondered for a moment if he could blame this

particular dilemma on Anne Cornwall, deciding with a grimace he couldn't. But near everything else . . . near everything else.

His pursuit of the Frenchman. Hell, he was confident the world in general, the Caribbean in particular, would be better off without d'Porteau. But it wasn't his place to accomplish that feat. He wasn't the blasted admiralty, but a not-so-honest pirate drifting about on the sea.

At least he was until Mistress Anne came along, with her warm-whiskey eyes and vinegar-laced tongue. Jamie leaned against the rail, staring out through the web of ratlines. Above him the sails sang their ode to freedom, below the wide expanse of sea carried him where he might go. Jamie took another deep breath.

No restraints.

No tangles or intrigues.

For someone whose only desire in life was to avoid anything of the sort, he was twisted up pretty tight. So tight he had to do something. Tossing Anne Cornwall over the side wasn't an option, no matter how attractive it might seem. Which left him with doing something about the myriad problems she created.

Stymie.

Giving the devil his due, Jamie knew Anne hadn't started the problem with Stymie. He was a low-life bully who had caused trouble ever since joining the crew. What he did to Joe made him sick. But—

Jamie sucked in his breath. There was no "but." Someone needed to do something. And that someone was him.

Still, he didn't have to like it.

Jamie reached for the pistol he stuck in his waistband. Lifting it out he squinted, checking the prime in the weak light from the moon. Satisfied, he made his way back toward the hatch.

The berth deck was packed, the smell of unwashed bodies strong enough to overpower the stench of bilge water and tar. Most of the lanterns burned so low, sputtering in the melted tallow that little light spewed forth. But Jamie managed to spot Stymie.

His hammock slung near the passageway, a prime location if one was to be found, was separated by uncharacteristic space from its neighbor. Even in sleep Stymie welded enough power to have his wishes carried out.

Except in this case, it made Jamie's task easier.

Silently he wended his way until he stood directly beside the sprawled man whose legs and arms flopped over the canvas bedding like excess roping. The metal against metal cocking of the pistol sounded loud to Jamie's ears, but apparently he was the only one to hear, for no one else seemed to stir. Least of all Stymie.

It wasn't until the cold barrel pressed into the rolled skin of his neck that the snoring stopped and his eyes popped open.

"What the hell . . . ?" He snorted and tried to turn his head, jerking to a stop when the muzzle dug deeper. "What's this 'bout, Cap'n?" His voice was strained.

"It's about Joe and your fist, ye son of a bitch."

"I don't know what—"

"Save it, Stymie. Now get up. And be real careful about it."

Stymie shifted, then slowed his movements when the pistol gouged under his chin. "Yer makin' a big mistake, Cap'n."

"Won't be the first."

"Aye." The bulgy eyes narrowed. "But 'twill be yer last."

Chapter Seven

"What in the hell are ye doing?"

Anne jerked her head around when she heard the captain's bellow. She'd been so absorbed in her task she hadn't noticed the key turn in the lock. He stood in the doorway, hands on hips, feet spread, looking as disheveled as his cabin had. Anne wondered if he ever took the time to fasten his shirt or wear a jacket. She knew he owned several fine suits of clothing. Anne skimmed her fingers over the deep green silk waistcoat she held, trying to imagine it buttoned up to cover the wide expanse of sun-bronzed skin. She couldn't.

"Ye heard me, An . . ." Jamie's gaze darted to Joe squatting on the floor beside a stack of books, then back to Anne. "Dy," he finished. "Andy." Taking another step into his cabin, Jamie slammed the door behind him with more vehemence than sense. Damnation, the woman had him flustered, and him in his own cabin, on his own damn ship.

"We was just straightenin' yer cabin some, Cap'n. Didn't mean no harm." It was Joe who spoke. Joe with his face still grotesquely swollen from contact with Stymie's fist. He pushed to his feet, the one eye he could open, wide with fear, and Jamie felt like a beast for yelling.

Without thinking to keep his hand light, Jamie reached for the lad's shoulder, pulling away quickly when Joe flinched. " 'Tis all right, Joe." Jamie took the log book he clutched and tossed it haphazardly onto the pile at his feet. The leather-bound volume slid off the stack to land on the decking.

Jamie thought he noted an expression of disapproval on Anne's dirty face, but it couldn't have been stronger than the one registered on his as he looked her way. But his countenance softened as he glanced back to Joe. "If ye be feeling up to it, a trip above deck might be just the thing."

"Captain, I don't think he should—"

He turned on her so quickly she nearly dropped the waistcoat. She did clamp her mouth shut.

"I don't recall asking your advice, Andy. Nor will I tolerate it." He'd frightened the boy again and for that Jamie was sorry. "Go on with ye, Joe. Get a breath of air. But no working or climbing the ratlines, do ye hear?"

"Aye, Cap'n." The boy chewed at his lower lip, hesitating with his hand on the latch. He seemed to gather his nerve, blurting out his request before he lost it again. "Can Andy come with me then?"

"Not at the moment. But Keena is there waiting for ye." Reaching around him, Jamie opened the door, surprised when Joe still hung back.

"Ye ain't gonna hurt him none, is ye, Cap'n? We didn't mean any harm."

"I'll not be hurting anyone, Joe. Now run along."

This time when the lock tumbled in place it was from the inside. Anne watched the pirate's movements, trying to keep herself calm. When he turned to face her it became more difficult.

"You really shouldn't have sent him on deck. If Stymie—"

"Stymie's locked in the hold."

"Oh." Anne pressed her lips together.

"Oh?" Jamie's brow lifted. " 'Tis all ye have to say, Mistress Anne? Just 'oh'?"

"What do you wish me to say?" Anne folded the waistcoat and laid it on top his sea chest.

"I wasn't aware my wishes were ever considered when ye spoke your mind, Annie." Jamie strode further into the cabin, kicking aside the pile of books on the floor. They tumbled with a thud. "Hell, I'd say it was obvious my wishes were never considered, period."

She refused to back up, in part because there was only so much space in the cramped cabin. There was nowhere to go. So Anne did the only thing she could. Straightening her shoulders, she faced him. "If you're trying to frighten me—"

His sharp, mirthless laugh cut off her words. "Frighten ye, Annie? Is that what ye think I'm trying to do? If that were possible, I'd have done it the first time I laid eyes on ye." Stopping just before he was close enough to touch her, Jamie planted his fists firmly on his hips, in case he were too tempted to wrap his hands about her neck.

She didn't like him standing this near. He was so tall she had to lift her chin to look him in the eye. And there was something intangible about him when he was close. Some attraction that seemed to tug at her. Anne couldn't tell if it was the scent of his skin or the heat that seemed to radiate from him. Whatever, she found it disconcerting and she didn't like it.

But he didn't seem inclined to increase the space between them. If anything he narrowed it, by leaning forward on the balls of his feet. "Now explain if ye will, what in the hell you're doing to my cabin."

"Straightening it."

"Ah. So that's what ye call it?"

His tone was infuriating. If she thought it would do any good Anne would push against him, flatten her hands in the burnished hair covering his chest and shove. But she was no match for him physically. Instead she stared him straight in the eye. "I thought you might prefer not to live like a wild boar." Watching his reaction to her words was almost as satisfying as forcing him away.

His eyes narrowed until they were little more than slits and his nostrils flared. "I do not live like an animal."

Anne merely shrugged.

"And ye be a fine one to talk, covered with filth as ye are."

"It's part of my disguise," Anne countered quickly. She hated being dirty.

"Well, it didn't work very well." He did move away from her now, turning and walking toward the bank of windows. Anne followed.

"You didn't recognize me."

"Once given a decent look I did." Jamie glanced over his shoulder.

"Decent look, indeed." Anne tossed her head. "I brought water for your bath, poured it over your head and you still didn't know who I was." She knew she'd said more than she should when he slowly turned to face her, a grin spread across his face.

"Ah, that's right. I'd forgotten the lad who helped me with my bath."

"I didn't help you." Anne crossed her arms, wishing he didn't make her feel so uncomfortable.

"Really?" His brows arched. "To my way of thinking, we each got ourselves a good look."

"You're depraved."

"Of course I am. Pirates are supposed to be depraved. Or didn't ye know that when ye made your decision to become a lad and go on account?"

Anne didn't feel that worthy of comment, so she simply bundled her arms more tightly. A fact that made the captain shake his head.

"I wanted ye to know we're headed back toward New Providence." Jamie raised his hand when she opened her mouth to protest. "Ye have no say in it. Till we arrive you're to stay down here."

"Locked in your cabin?"

"If need be." He walked to the door and turned to face her. "I won't have anyone else discovering Andy's secret." After saying that he left. But she didn't hear the lock click so he must have decided it wasn't necessary in order to keep her below.

Anne imagined he was right. As much as she'd like a breath of fresh air her deception would be easier this way. With a shrug she returned to her task of straightening the captain's cabin.

She couldn't understand how he could live like this, so completely unorganized. How did he ever find anything? Anne sorted through the books and charts first, piling them neatly on his desk. The number of books surprised her, as well as the diversity of subject matter. If he read them, and she wasn't at all sure he did, he wasn't as ignorant of the world as she first thought.

There were novels by Milton, Spencer, and Dryden, as

well as Payne's *Observation On Gardening*. Several books on history littered his bunk. One, Clarendon's *History of the Rebellion*, underneath. Some were bound in leather, others were quite plain. But when she'd gathered them all, Anne realized the pirate had himself a fairly extensive library.

"No doubt, every single book is stolen," she mused as she wiped the back of her hand across her forehead. It was warm, too warm for a coat and wool cap, but she couldn't be sure no one would come to the captain's cabin, so she kept them on. She didn't even wash the dirt from her face, though she was sorely tempted. Anne's eyes darted to the dented pewter pitcher and bowl on the crudely made table. For all the pirate captain's slovenliness he did keep himself fairly clean.

Unable to resist any longer, Anne placed a book on navigation on the pile and walked toward the cracked bit of looking glass nailed to a timber. Standing on tiptoe she was just able to see the top half of her face, dirt streaked, and barely visible beneath the low pulled knit hat.

Her eyes clamped shut. She would simply have to wait to get clean again. With a sigh she turned and surveyed the cabin. Meanwhile, there was plenty for her to do.

He was avoiding his cabin.

Jamie leaned forward, his arms resting on the cracked and splintered railing and watched the moon send slivers of silvery light to dance across the ebony sea. Above him stars twinkled. The night, soft and sweet as only the Caribbean could offer was its own excuse to linger. And normally Jamie needed no other.

But for some reason his short acquaintance with Anne Cornwall, turbulent as it was, defied rationalizing. And forced him to be more honest with himself. It wasn't the beauty of the night that kept him above deck, it was the woman in his cabin.

"The men are not happy."

Jamie jerked around toward the man who spoke, a puzzled expression on his face. "A good evening to ye, too, Deacon."

"Make light of it if ye must, but the talk is not good."

Shrugging, Jamie turned back to contemplate the sea. The breeze was freshening. He could feel it on his face, hear it in the snap of the sails. "What has them vexed now? I thought they might be more agreeable without their leader."

"Is that why ye have Stymie chained in the hold?"

His head tilted around. "Ye heard about that did ye?"

"Every man on board the *Lost Cause* has heard of it, Cap'n. Did ye think to keep such a thing a secret?"

Jamie thought about it a moment. "Nay, but I hoped his disappearance would give the crew a puzzle to fuss over."

"Ye should have tossed him to the sharks."

"Why, Deacon, ye surprise me. Such bloodthirsty talk coming from a man of the cloth." Jamie took a deep breath. Humor was lost on Deacon. "Haven't ye been after me to do something about him? 'Tis all ye and Keena speak of."

Deacon aimed his good eye at Jamie. "He shall cause ye trouble, Jamie MacQuaid. Mark me words."

The hairs on the back of Jamie's neck stood up and it had naught to do with the breeze. "Ye know I hate it when ye prophesise like that."

" 'Tis fear that my words are true."

"One time, Deacon. 'Tis only that one time in Barbados that I recall ye foretelling the future." Jamie turned to face him. "That does not an Old Testament prophet make."

" 'Tis blasphemy ye speak."

Letting his head fall back, Jamie took a deep breath, letting the tangy sea air fill his lungs. "What would ye have me do, Deacon? And don't say throw him overboard."

"What did ye have in mind to do with him?"

"Bring him before the crew. 'Tis the usual way we deal with crimes against a fellow seaman."

"But Stymie isn't the usual pirate and ye knows it."

"He's a loudmouthed bully and no more." Leaning forward he laced his fingers together to keep from making a fist. "Except that he finds an odd fascination in pounding on those weaker than himself."

"How is Joe?"

"Better" Jamie glanced up, a grin twinkling his eyes. "Asleep in Stymie's hammock at present."

"And the other boy?"

The grin faded. "Below in my cabin, learning the proper way to speak to a captain."

Anne sat on the edge of the bunk mentally listing what needed done on the morrow. She'd managed to sort the books, arranging them by subject, which at times, due to her lack of formal education was difficult. There were several works written in what she supposed was Latin that she had to guess about placement. But anything was better than the random 'toss where ye may' method the captain used to store his books.

The maps and charts were rolled neatly and stacked

beside his desk, which now proved her earlier assumption that it did indeed have a top.

She'd accomplished quite a lot actually, and the chore kept her from dwelling on the fact that Jamie MacQuaid turned the sloop toward New Providence. Not that she hadn't extended considerable thought on how to get him to change his mind.

But other than defying him and revealing her identity to the crew, she could think of nothing. And the captain had convinced her that was not a good idea.

Anne worried her bottom lip with her teeth. Another thought kept infringing upon her mind as she organized today. What made Stymie hurt Joe? She could only hope it had nothing to do with what Joe told the captain. Anne rocked back, grabbing her knees and pressing her chin forward. She needed to speak with the captain. She needed to speak with Joe.

But neither of them had seen fit to come below since the captain roared in earlier. No one had come. Which meant there'd been no food either. Anne sighed, twisting around till she could stretch out on the recently cleared bunk.

The captain didn't plan to starve her to death, did he? Anne fell asleep wondering.

And woke to a loud thump that made her jerk to sitting. Her heart jumped into her throat when she realized someone was in the room with her. Someone large, loud, and angry.

"Damnit it to hell, woman! I told ye not to mess with me things." Jamie bent to rub the knee he'd banged. "What?" he asked between clenched teeth, "is this?"

Waking up was never something Anne did easily . . . or well. A slow, gradual greeting of the morn was the one luxury she allowed herself. This arousal was sudden and abrasive . . . and it was hardly morning. Swinging her legs over the side of the bunk, she took a moment to steady herself. Her hat had come off while she slept and she swept her fingers back through her tumbled curls.

When she glanced up it was to see the captain, limned in moonlight, straightening to face her. She looked from him to the once neat stack of books, now tumbled helter-skelter on the floor. With a sigh she pushed to her feet. "Now see what you've done."

"What *I've* done?" Jamie grabbed her shoulder when she bent to pick up one of the books, pulling her to stand beside him. "What *I've* done," he repeated louder this time. "Seems to me, lass, 'tis you who've been doing more than ye should."

Her tone was exceedingly patient . . . to Anne's way of thinking. "I simply straightened your things."

"Ah." Jamie bent his face toward hers. "Then ye admit they are *my* things we're discussing here."

"Of course I do." She'd done him a favor, though that wasn't her motive by any means. "I couldn't live in such squalor."

"Squalor?" They were nearly nose to nose now. "Me cabin was the way I liked it."

"It was a disorderly mess."

"Mess or not, it be my mess, and the way I like it."

His eyes were so close that even in the near darkness she could see the prisms of blue and green that made them so intriguing. So mesmerizing. She forced herself to focus on the whole of him. "Little wonder."

"Aye, little won . . ." He paused. "Now what in the hell is that supposed to mean?"

Anne shrugged delicately. His hair, gilded silver by what moonlight filtered through the salt-encrusted transom windows waved wildly to his shoulders. She didn't have to look down to know his shirt flapped open. The warmth from his chest was proof enough.

Anne swallowed. "You have a pier glass, though it be barely more than a sliver. Surely you've looked in it." She knew he had. She'd watched him shave off the beard that had now returned as stubble shadowing his jaw shades darker than the sun-bleached mass on his head.

"If you're questioning my cleanliness I'd say it be a case of the pot calling the kettle black." With one finger he traced the curve of her cheek. A mistake he realized as soon as he felt the silky skin. He was almost thankful when she knocked his hand away.

"You know very well why I'm covered with dirt. And I hate it." Anne bit her bottom lip, wishing she hadn't said the last. It was too close to a crack in her defenses. She even thought she noticed an expression of sympathy glitter in his sea-colored eyes before he turned away.

"Well, that is your doing as I recall. All of this has been your doing. And ye are the one stuck with it until we reach New Providence."

His words gave her pause. They reminded her that her well-laid plan was failing and she hadn't been able to devise a new one. She took a deep breath. "I apologize."

"Of course ye do, but—" Jamie cut himself off, his eyes narrowing as he searched her delicate, blackened face.

She'd surprised him. Anne didn't wait for another word from him before pressing her advantage. "It was wrong of me to put your cabin in order. I realize now that you are a man who enjoys a certain amount of . . ." She searched her mind for a word to describe the muddle he lived in. A word that she could accept and that he wouldn't find insulting. She finally settled on, "Disarray. I imagine you find it comforting." She smiled up at him, hoping she'd assuaged his male pride.

Comforting, hell! He found it easier than cleaning. But he nodded anyway, wondering why the sudden urge to be accommodating struck her. He had a pretty good guess, of course, and it didn't take her long to confirm it.

"Well, at any rate, I shall mess it up for you again . . . I mean put it back to your comforting disarray in the morning." Anne felt her jaw tighten and she tried to relax.

"I thank ye for that."

"Of course, I don't wish to be any bother." Though she couldn't see his face well enough to discern his expression, Anne was sure his brow quirked. "Which is why I think you should forget this worry you have about returning me to New Providence right away."

" 'Tis no worry." Jamie moved away from her and settled on the bunk. He couldn't help noticing the blanket and sheets were tucked in. And there was a pillow. He couldn't remember the last time he'd slept on a bit of down softness. He wondered where she found it. But not as much as he wondered why she felt it necessary to help him off with his boots.

Anne knelt on the deck, her back to the captain and tugged. "I really wish you'd reconsider and just find d'Porteau. Having me along will make no difference." She clamped her teeth together when his other boot pressed into her backside and yanked. On the third try the boot flew free . . . and only Anne's elbows saved her from sprawling face first on the floor.

"All right, are ye?" came the mocking inquiry from the bunk and Anne could well imagine the wicked grin crinkling his eyes.

She pushed herself up and reached for the other boot. "I'm fine." This one came off easier, and she managed to stay upright on her knees. She stood, brushing at her breeches, a useless gesture given the state of their cleanliness. Turning to face him, she planted hands on her hips. "Well, what do you think?"

"Ye make a decent cabin boy," Jamie said, deliberately misunderstanding her.

"I mean about letting me stay aboard till you find d'Porteau." Her tone lost its accommodating edge.

"Ah, that." Jamie stretched his arms high above his head and yawned. "Perhaps I should think on it tonight." With that he stood, removed his shirt, reached for his breeches and thought better of it, then crawled beneath the sheets.

And Anne was left standing in the dark, holding his boots and wondering where she was supposed to sleep. Asking him didn't seem a good idea. For one thing she was trying not to cause any trouble. For another he was already snoring. But at least he said he'd think about letting her stay on board. Thinking of that made the floor seem a little softer as she lay down.

By morning it seemed almost comfortable.

Anne sighed and burrowed her body deeper into the softness, her eyes popping open when she remembered there was no way the deck could be soft.

She was in the bunk, thankfully alone, nestled between the clean sheets she found yesterday in one of the captain's sea chests. Her head resting on the pillow she discovered amidst a pile of dirty clothes. Yawning, Anne glanced about.

Sunlight poured through the windows, splashing across the cabin's shabby furnishings. There were no dark corners this morn. There was also no Captain MacQuaid. It appeared she would have to wait for his answer about keeping her with him.

Unless, he already made the decision and was heading back toward San Palma. Anne climbed out of the bunk slowly, wondering when the captain put her there, and went to the window. But try as she might, there was no way she could see the sun to figure which way they were heading.

When she turned back toward the room, she noticed something she'd missed before. On the desk was a wooden trencher piled high with a rice and fish mixture. Beside it was a pewter mug of rum. Without even considering it might be the captain's breakfast, Anne scraped the cabin's only chair to the desk and scooped up a bite.

She'd cleaned the plate, washing the sticky concoction down with the rum when the door opened. Realizing she forgot to yank the hat over her curls, Anne jumped up and dove for the bunk. The captain's voice stopped her.

" 'Tis no need to worry. I'm privy to your deception, remember?"

Anne just sent him a fulminating look over her shoulder, that changed to a smile when she recalled her new strategy. "I wasn't certain it was you. And I wouldn't want to do anything to jeopardize your position on your ship."

"How thoughtful." Jamie glanced at the empty platter, then back at Anne. She not only was without her hat, but her jacket was missing, draped over the back of the chair. Without its thick, camouflaging folds, there was no doubt of her sex. The shirt was loose, but threadbare. Beneath it she wore none of the female trappings. Her breasts were small, but standing in profile as she was, with the windows behind her, obviously womanly.

And he could recall their taste.

Jamie started flipping through the rolled pile of charts to get his mind going in another direction, hoping the stirring in his loins would subside. He found what he was looking for, and admittedly it took him less time than usual thanks to her arrangement, then turned to leave.

"By the by," he said when his hand rested on the door latch. "We should reach New Providence by tomorrow morning."

"Tomorrow?" Anne whirled around. "But I thought . . . You said . . ." He faced her, that cat-ate-the-cream grin on his face, and Anne lost her temper. Hands fisted she propelled herself toward him, striking first his chest then flailing for his chin.

"Ouch! Damnit, Annie. Watch where you're hitting."

He clutched her shoulders, making it difficult for her to aim high. So she aimed low. "You scoundrel. Rogue. Pirate!" Anne couldn't think of enough bad names to call him. She also could barely catch her breath. Rather than try to hold her away, the captain opted to draw her against him, pinning her arms to her side and her body to his.

She blew a tangle of curls from her eyes and glared at him. "You never were considering taking me with you," she accused."

Jamie shifted her away from his manhood, only to have her body slip back into the *V* between his legs. "You're damn right I'm not keeping ye aboard. 'Tis what I said since discovering ye."

"But you led me to believe—"

"Ye were so busy trying to smother me with attention, ye weren't paying any mind to what I said. Did ye think I couldn't see through your ruse, Annie?" Jamie tightened his grip. "Did ye?"

Anne's voice was little more than a whisper. "I don't know." She lifted her lashes, staring up at him, her eyes serious. "But you don't understand. I have to be there when you find his ship."

"Why, Annie? Why is it so important to ye?" When she didn't answer, he continued. "I told ye I'd search for him, and I will."

She couldn't tell him the jewels promised him were in d'Porteau's possession, not her own. No more than she could explain the guilt she felt over her cousin's kidnapping. All she could do was slowly shake her head.

" 'Tis not as bad as all that, Annie, girl. Once home on Libertia ye can take a good soak, then sit in the shade and wait for me to bring ye d'Porteau's head." Jamie grinned when her gaze flashed to meet his. " 'Tis but a manner of speech. I've no intention of severing his head for ye. But I will bring ye proof of his demise, and your cousin, be he—"

"Still alive?" Anne finished for him. "Of course, I've considered the possibility that d'Porteau killed him. And what that would do to Uncle Richard."

"Be that the case, and I'm not thinking 'tis, your uncle needs ye all the more safe and sound with him."

Anne smiled sadly. "I suppose you're right."

"Of course I am." Jamie was trying to be understanding, but it was difficult with her firm little body pressed against his. He wondered if she realized the effect she had on him. He supposed he should let her go. She seemed over her temper.

But Jamie was having a difficult time getting his arms to obey his mind's commands. Even his hands seemed to have a will of their own as they began rubbing the small of her back.

"What are you doing?" Anne tried to fight the heat flooding through her.

"What?"

"That." Wriggling away from his hands only plastered her more tightly to his hard chest and even harder lower body. "Stop it." Anne's upper arms were trapped in his embrace, but she could bend them at the elbows. She touched his hips to push him away and realized she wasn't.

His skin through the nanskin breeches was hot and erotic. Her fingers flexed.

"Annie. Look at me, Annie."

She couldn't seem to stop herself from lifting her face. He was smiling but it wasn't the devilish grin she was accustomed to. This smile was warm and seductive.

He lifted his hand to cup her cheek, using his thumb to wipe away a streak of dirt. "Ye can't hide your beauty from me, Annie. Not even with tar and oil."

As he slowly lowered his head Anne realized she was no longer his captive. Nothing but the slight pressure of his fingers caressing her face held her to him.

Chapter Eight

But there was more than one way to conquer. And the pirate, Jamie MacQuaid, ravisher of the Caribbean, was an expert in such matters.

His prismed eyes, so reminiscent of the sea itself, beguiled, seemed to suck you deep into their vortex. They summoned, challenged you to resist. And if you failed they promised all manner of erotic delights awaited.

Anne was no match for him.

Innocence rarely was.

Her heart pounded, a rhythmic beat that escalated as his head lowered toward hers. His scent was wild and free. His touch gentle. A most seductive tangle.

Anne's lips opened in welcome, greeting his in the age-old voice of surrender. Yet from defeat came sweet victory. Anne relished the firm mastery of his mouth. The conquering expertise of his tongue. Her head fell back and her arms reached up, encircling his strong neck, digging her fingers into the savage curls.

And all the while her body throbbed. Pressed to his, the heat first seeped, then exploded inside her till she writhed against him. The fasteners on her shirt lost their fragile hold.

When his hands cupped her bottom lifting her against his hardness, Anne knew instinctively 'twas what she needed to assuage the ache deep within her. She clutched at his shoulders, her fingers still tangled in the raw silk of his hair. She whimpered when his lips left hers. Cried out when that magical mouth clamped over her breast. Fire shot through her and she arched back to give him greater access.

Her nipples peaked painfully, their only relief coming with the carnal massage of his tongue. He nibbled. He suckled. And Anne thought she might lose her mind, if she didn't burn to a cinder first.

And then it was gone. All the heat and power. She stood on wobbly knees swaying toward him, wanting what had been taken from her so suddenly. Slowly she opened her eyes, to be greeted by the insufferable grin. Though this time it didn't seem as steady as usual. And it didn't reach his eyes. They stared at her with a mixture of passion and disdain.

" 'Tis tempting," he said, his voice a husky timbre.

"Tempting?" His meaning was lost in the smoky fog of her brain. Anne looked up, her expression full of question. She was beyond tempted.

"Aye." His jaw tightened. "But 'tis already promised me if ye recall. And a bargain is a bargain." He took a deep breath. "Even when made to naught but a pirate."

"I don't . . ." She was going to say understand, but unfortunately she was beginning to. At least with the distance he'd put between them her thought processes had returned. Along with a healthy dose of embarrassment and shame. Which only intensified with his next words.

"I appreciate how eager ye are to stay aboard." Jamie's gaze flicked down over her body, the rose-tipped breasts still damp from his mouth, the flush that slowly spread to pinken her neck and cheeks. "But this will not change my mind."

When he turned to leave Anne could do naught but stand as if her feet were rooted to the wide-planked decking. Temper flushed away all remnants of desire, all thoughts of self-reproach. She advanced on him not with punches and slaps, which he'd proved had no effect on him, but with words.

" 'Tis a bargain I shall never keep."

The quirk of his brow when he twisted his head to look at her spoke volumes. "We shall see, Annie. We shall see."

The door shut behind him. Though not slammed or even closed with excess force, the sound seemed to reverberate through her head. Slowly, for all the energy seemed to have drained from her body, Anne lifted her hands and began rebuttoning her shirt. When the first bit of moisture dampened her fingers she was perplexed. It wasn't until she reached up, tentatively touching her cheek that she realized she was crying.

It had been so many years since she allowed the tears to fall. Not since the sudden death of her parents when she was eleven. They had been festive, happy people, more childlike than their serious daughter ever was. Her father, the younger son of a marquis, married the love of his life, the beautiful enchantress Sophia, or so he had called her till his dying day. My beautiful enchantress.

Anne smiled now at the memory as she scrubbed knuckles across her cheek. Her mother was beautiful, blond, and willowy with blue eyes that rivaled the summer sky and a smile that lit up her husband's heart.

Her father had adored his wife, buying her jewels and gowns . . . spending more than they could afford. Anne sobbed, wishing she could stop these foolish tears. Wondering why now, after all these years she wept for her parents.

Or was it for herself?

The thought made Anne stiffen. It had come unbidden and unwanted into her mind, and she tried to push it aside. Gulping in a breath she grabbed up a shirt littering the floor and wiped at her face. Never one to give in to self-absorption, she wasn't about to begin now.

There was too much else to worry about. Besides, as soon as d'Porteau was found and her cousin returned to Libertia everything would be as it should. Her uncle would snap out of his despondency, or at least improve, Arthur could continue . . . being Arthur. And she would take care of things as she always had.

The pirate had given her a setback, but only a temporary one. She would find a way. She always did. With a determination she didn't quite feel, Anne wiped the shirt across her face, smearing it with grime. But there were no new tears.

Then she did what she always did when faced with a problem. Anne began to sort and straighten.

By the time she stood on tiptoe to check herself in the mirror, the captain's cabin was as clean and organized as she could make it. His clean or nearly clean clothes were folded and stacked in sea chests, the dirty ones on a pile waiting for water and scrub brush. She didn't care if he liked it or not. It was done.

Anne twisted her face, making certain she was thoroughly covered with soot from the lantern. Her hair was covered, the brimless hat pulled low over her forehead, and she'd shrugged back into the heavy coat. She looked like the boy she pretended to be.

And she was going on deck.

Joe was the first to notice her when she pushed herself through the hatch. He was lounging on deck, his back to the railing, his eyes wary. The bruises on his face had faded to a purplish green, but the swelling was gone. His expression didn't change as he watched Anne walk toward him.

"Joe," she said in greeting, then slid down beside him.

He didn't say a word, but Anne thought she noticed a slight shrinking away as her coat brushed against his arm. She decided to try again. "Your face is looking better. Does it still hurt?"

He merely shrugged, an offhand motion that could mean anything.

"What's wrong, Joe?"

"Where ye been, Andy?"

Anne hoped her blush didn't shine through the layers of dirt. "The captain had some work for me to do." She folded up her knees, wrapping her arms about them and turning her head so she could watch his profile. "I finished cleaning up his cabin." No response. " 'Twas a real mess. Clothes everywhere and books . . ."

When there was still no reaction from Joe, Anne reached out toward him. She didn't imagine his recoil this time. Anne let her hand drop to the deck. "Joe, what's wrong?"

"Ain't nothin' wrong." He pushed to his feet.

"Captain MacQuaid locked Stymie in the hold because

of what he did to you," Anne offered. She cupped her hands, shading her eyes from the blinding sunlight.

She couldn't see his expression, but imagined it was as flat as his voice. "Won't help," he mumbled before ambling off.

"What do you mean . . . ? Joe?" Anne stood up but before she could follow her friend a hand clamped around her arm. "Well, if it isn't *Andy*," a voice hissed in her ear. "Imagine my surprise when I glanced down from the quarterdeck to see ye here." Jamie effectively turned her toward the hatch as he spoke. "I thought ye were to stay below."

"I wanted some fresh air." Anne tried digging in her heels but it was no use.

"Well, you've had it." Jamie stopped near the gaping hole that led below. "Now can ye find your way back or must I escort ye?"

Anne jerked her arm from his grasp. "I know the way," she said, then softened her tone. "There's something wrong with Joe."

"No doubt. He was pummeled pretty bad."

Anne turned to face him. "I think it may be something beyond that. He won't even talk to me."

"One can hardly blame him for that."

Anne's lips thinned when she noticed the captain's grin. "I'm afraid this may be my fault."

"You can't be everyone's guardian." The words were gentle. "You're not to blame if Joe wandered off and aggravated Stymie."

"But you don't understand. Joe and I were watching him, because of what I heard about the mutiny."

"What *you* heard? I thought it was Joe who . . . Never mind. Get down to my cabin."

"But—"

"I shall be down directly." The captain turned and walked away, leaving Anne little else to do but follow his orders. She had no more than settled in the chair when he entered. Anne knew he noticed the cabin, but he said nothing as he turned and locked the door.

When he faced her again, his arms crossed over his wide, sun-burnished flesh, his expression was unreadable. "Explain yourself," was all he said.

Anne shrugged. "It's simple. It was I, not Joe, who overheard Stymie and his . . ." she hesitated, then used the words "friends" in place of anything more appropriate. "They spoke of taking over the ship."

"And?" His brow quirked.

"And what?" Anne paced toward the window, a much easier task without the litter of clothing and books on the floor.

"Is that all they said?" The captain's voice was tinged with annoyance.

"They don't like you," Anne tossed over her shoulder, then decided it only fair she explain. "Stymie has them convinced you're leading them on a wild-goose chase. He said the only way to stop you was to seize the weapons and eliminate you." A shiver ran down her spine as his crystalline eyes focused on her face. The window seemed a safer place to look. But the sea outside the grimy leaden panes was so near the color of his gaze she shut her own eyes when he began to speak.

"So, I have a possible mutiny on my hands?"

"You didn't know?" Anne whirled to face him. "Joe explained."

"He came to me with some jumbled story about hearing Stymie and some men grumbling about wanting me gone."

"And you didn't believe him?"

"There didn't seem much to believe or not believe. Questioning him led nowhere. He stammered, couldn't remember where he was when he heard the men speaking." Jamie dug fingers through his wind-tossed hair. "Hell, if I concerned myself with every pirate aboard who had a gripe, 'tis all I'd do."

"Surely you knew how Stymie feels about you? The way he defied you that morning when he grabbed me."

"Stymie's a mean son of a bitch. 'Tis a fool who'd deny that. But pirates are not choirboys."

"How can you stand being surrounded by them?"

"I'm no choirboy either, Annie."

She knew that only too well. Still, she wouldn't put him in the same category as some . . . Annie shook her head. This was hardly the point. He agreed to find d'Porteau, and she needed him. Needed him in control of the *Lost Cause.* "I think you should toss the lot of them in the hold."

"So now you've decided to help me run me ship, have ye, Mistress Cornwall?" He spread his legs in challenge. " 'Tisn't enough that ye take over me cabin and defy me."

"The *Lost Cause* is yours to control. Just as Styme is."

"Stymie's in the hold."

"And his friends are free, to do as they please."

His eyes narrowed as he strode across the room and back. He stopped near the desk, pounding the rough surface with his fist. "We are all bound to do as we chose. It is the way of freebooters. The reason we live the life we do."

He pivoted to face her, his body alive with raw

strength. An errant sun spray fired the burnished streaks in his hair, the twinkle of gold looped in his ear. Anne's mouth went dry. At that moment he looked every inch the wild, free pirate, savage in his intensity, passionate in his independence. Untamed. Powerful. Invincible.

She told herself he was human, and vulnerable in ways she had yet to understand. And then he spoke again, opening a tiny window to his soul.

"Do ye think I, any of us, could live under the yoke of oppression? Nay, we live as we choose. Do as we choose. And if there be those who disagree, they need only challenge me. There are rules." He jerked his head around, staring at a spot on the floor near his bunk. It was empty now and he kicked at the dust motes that swirled in his wake. "If you'd seen fit to leave things where they lay, I'd have shown ye the articles we sail under."

"Top drawer."

Hands on narrow hips, he twisted to pierce her with his stare.

"Your articles," Anne explained. "I put them in the top drawer of your desk." When he said nothing, only continued to glare, she rambled on, suddenly anxious to convince him she'd done him a service. "The drawers were empty and the floors so covered, you couldn't possibly find a thing. No one could. I only—"

"Interfered." His rough voice lowered. "Tried to control."

"No." Even to her the denial sounded hollow. Anne sighed, trying to lessen the uneasy feeling she had that perhaps he was right. Perhaps she should have left his cabin, his life the way she found it. He wasn't a man who needed or wanted her constraints.

But there was more at stake than what he wanted. And

perhaps he followed his bloody articles, but she'd heard the others. Heard the venom in their voices. They were not planning a vote, a free-will choice. Theirs was to be violent . . . deadly. And the man standing before her espousing noble ideals, worthy of John Locke himself, was their target.

"They spoke of stealing the weapons and using them against any crew member who defies them."

She'd captured his attention and continued before he could speak. "I heard them clearly. These were not men willing to risk a democratic vote or even a fair challenge. They are the kind of men you say you wish to be free of." Anne realized her voice had risen and tried to calm herself. "The kind of men who would pummel a child like Joe."

"Hell, Anne, I locked Stymie in the hold."

"But the others are just as dangerous. Don't you see?"

He didn't answer and at first Anne thought he was thinking, pondering what she said. But he cocked his head, listening. The alarm sounded again and this time Anne heard it, too.

"Sails ho!"

The cry started high above the deck in the cross trees occupied by the lookout and spread throughout the sloop. Jamie looked about, turning full circle before facing Anne, a questioning expression on his face. He opened his mouth to ask, but before he could she sprang forward, and knelt beside the bunk.

"I put them away." Wood scraped against wood as she pulled the mahogany box from beneath the bed. Quicker than she could Jamie reached down and threw open the box to reveal a brace of pistols. He checked them both, then tucked them in his waistband.

"What manner of ship do you think it is?" Anne followed him to the door, only to have him jerk around to face her.

"Stay here."

"But—"

"Do ye understand me, Annie?"

Of course she understood. She wasn't a dolt. But she felt like one as she slowly nodded. He didn't wait for anything else as he bolted from the cabin.

The vessel was much closer than Jamie expected.

When he reached the deck the schooner was no more than two miles away and closing fast. Whoever was on watch must have been asleep to miss giving the warning sooner. Jamie made a mental note to keelhaul the bastard when the danger was past.

Lurching forward he took the ladder to the quarterdeck three rungs at a time, and then rushed toward the railing where Deacon stood, watching the fast approaching vessel through the glass. "What do ye make of it?"

Jamie spared his silent quartermaster but a glance as he grabbed for the brass cylinder. Squinting, Jamie swept the spyglass over the cut of the hull, the sail, the black pennant snapping from the yardarm. A cold sweat broke out on his forehead. Despite the need for haste, Jamie lowered the glass slowly. "D'Porteau."

" 'Tis what I thought."

Those flatly spoken words spurred Jamie to action. "Set more sail," he yelled, his eyes flashing toward the yards of canvas spread blindingly white in the sun. The *French Whore* was approaching fast, to the windward side, leaving Jamie little room to jockey for position.

"Hell and damnation!" Whoever had failed to raise the alarm and made the *Lost Cause* so vulnerable would pay.

Jamie forced thoughts of what he'd do to the bastard from his mind and he tried to decide the best course of action.

Retreat seemed unacceptable. Besides, he didn't know if it was possible. D'Porteau's schooner was almost upon them. And Jamie knew from unhappy experience its speed could match the *Lost Cause*.

They would have to make a fight of it, despite the positions. Jamie glanced down toward the tars. Most of the men were huddled near the storehouse, surrounding Keena as he passed out the muskets and pikes. They were a sound lot, for the most part. Able to fight with the best of them.

"Look lively, lads!" he screamed down toward the main deck. "We've a French whore to screw!"

A burst of coarse cheering exploded from the wildly waving men, buoying Jamie's spirits. He snatched up the trumpet horn. "Topmen into the masts! Prepare to rake the decks!"

Jamie didn't have to worry about the cannons. Keena would have the gunwales open and the black snouts peering through the holes by now. Instead he turned his attention toward the helmsman who was clutching the wheel, his ruddy face sweating profusely.

"Hold her steady as ye can, Farley," Jamie said smoothly. Because of their leeward position they were forced to take the more sluggish windward tack. The situation was not one Jamie liked . . . or often found himself in. As soon as the *French Whore* came astride the *Lost Cause* was vulnerable. If the French gunners were accurate they could rake the sloop's hull below the water-line as the *Lost Cause* was heeled by the wind.

But Jamie tried not to think of that as his gaze flicked from the compass setting to the Frenchman's sail. "Stay with her now, Farley," Jamie warned. "Don't let her cross our stern." The wheel turned beneath gnarled, sun-browned hands and Jamie spread his legs against the swell. His gaze again flew to the pursuing ship, his grin spreading as he slapped Farley on his bent shoulder. "Ye be as good as they come, ye son of a bitch."

Below them on the deck tars pivoted the sails, hauling and releasing the sheet ropes and tack line. They worked in perfect symmetry, beautiful to see, despite their bare-chested, fierce appearance.

"All's ready with the guns," came the holler from Keena, and Jamie waved his arm in response. The *French Whore*, her black hull knifing through the turquoise water like a dagger from hell, was nearly alongside. Jamie expected to hear the thunderous roar of her swivel guns at any moment.

"Fire at your discretion, Master Keena," Jamie yelled down, lifting his hand in a smart salute. The blackamoor responded in kind, then turned on his bare feet. He tramped up and down the sandy deck, stopping at each of the four pounders, giving a word of advice here, a friendly nod there.

Jamie took a breath of salty air, letting it fill his lungs, and felt a quickening of excitement. What was he worried about? Luck still sat firmly upon his shoulder, as it had since the day he escaped the hangman's noose in London. Perhaps there had been a foul-up at the watch, but d'Porteau would need more than a favorable position to win the day.

The sloop heeled with the wind as they jockeyed for position, doing their best to keep the French pirate from crossing their stern.

"She's almost upon us, Cap'n."

Jamie gave Farley one more quick word before striding over to the rail. Deacon was right. There was no longer a need to look through the glass to see the *French Whore*'s shape looming to the east. Her tars were everywhere, mirroring the efforts of his own crew. Some monkeyed their way through the rigging, muskets slung over their shoulders. Others stood watch over their cannon, waiting as Jamie's men did, for the word to touch linstock to the powder in the base ring.

Jamie clutched the rail, watching the hated d'Porteau creep up his side. Counting the seconds by the pounding of his heart. Spray glistened like diamonds in the sunlight. The same wind that tangled his hair filled the sails giving them life, giving the *Lost Cause* life. Throwing back his head Jamie raised his face to the heavens. The moment was at hand.

His lips parted to signal the gunners but before a sound uttered, Jamie heard the order bellowed by Keena. Quicker than he could think how proud he was of his chief gunner's instincts, the thunderous roar of cannons shattered the peaceful paradise. His legs spread instinctively against the ship's recoil. Clouds of puffy smoke billowed from the guns, and filtered away to nothingness on the wind, but Jamie had eyes only for the *French Whore*. He watched for the fall of the shot, giving a whoop when he spotted the shattering wood on the Frenchman's deck.

But his joy was short-lived.

The answering salvo spewed from the facing black muzzles in a billow of orange-tongued fire. The *Lost Cause* trembled beneath the onslaught of bar and rope shot. Jamie peered through the smoke, trying to appraise the damage to the web of spars and rigging. The canvas still groaned, taut bellied against the wind, keeping the *Lost Cause* on pace with the French ship.

The firing was constant now, a steady pounding that shook the ship and turned the water between them into a boiling cauldron. Whenever the wind tore a curtain in the brimstone and saltpeter-laden smoke Jamie could see the gunners, grime covered and sweating, swabbing out the cannons' bores. They moved quickly, ramming the powder cartridge and ball home, before priming the touchhole.

"Take us closer, Farley!" Jamie shouted the command toward the helmsman, then turned back to watch the ever narrowing length of sea between the two vessels.

"Ye sure 'tis what ye want?" Deacon cupped his hands to be heard. "Moving closer to those guns . . ." He let the rest trail off. It was obvious what the consequences could be. On deck tars scurried around tossing buckets of water and sand on the myriad fires erupting there.

The pummeling was brutal.

Men screamed as splintered wood tore through the air. If there was a hell on earth, this was it. The smells, the sounds, the heat that seemed to cling to skin. And Jamie was pushing them closer into the jaws of Hades.

"Cap'n." Deacon turned toward Jamie tight-lipped, his good eye rolling wildly. "We be point-blank now."

"And holding our own." Twisting around, Jamie yelled to the helmsman. "Forward now. Steady." Looking back to Deacon Jamie latched on to his arm. "Prepare the men to board." His sweat- and grime-stained face split in a wide grin. "He missed his chance, Deacon. The Frenchman missed it."

"I don't under—" Deacon's words were cut off by the tearing of wood as the mizzenmast crumbled to the deck.

"He's after our spars." Jamie shook hair from his face. " 'Twould have been easy to tear open our belly, while we were heeled over in the wind." Jamie sucked in air. "But he went for our canvas. Now we're going to board her. Teach the lot of them how real pirates fight. Off with ye now."

As Deacon hurried down the ladder Jamie leaned over the rail, judging the distance, then calling back over his shoulder. "Farley, get us in hard alongside. That's it. Now hit the French bitch!"

The jolt sent tremors through the sloop. But before Jamie could give the order two pirates sprang from crouching to toss the multiclawed grappling over the side. The metal fingers caught in the shrouds, and more men leaped forward to tie off the ropes.

Yanking out his pistol Jamie vaulted off the quarterdeck. He was over the side before the smoke had cleared from the last sally. A tide of pirates swelled forward, following him onto the French vessel.

But there were those who held back . . . staying on board the *Lost Cause* and biding their time.

Jamie's saber arced, the sun gleaming off the steel as he slashed his way toward the quarterdeck and d'Porteau. He'd waited years for this without even realizing it, and the taste of victory was sweet on his lips.

All around him the battle surged, men screamed obscenities, but Jamie paid them no heed. His focus was fixed on the giant of a man standing by the wheel. He leaped over bodies and feinted from assaults. And all the while d'Porteau seemed to be drawing him forward.

When the blow struck his head, Jamie swerved, then turned to meet his assailant. The saber fight was short and bloody, the French pirate falling to his knees, before he toppled over.

Whirling around Jamie looked for d'Porteau, but the Frenchman no longer stood on the quarterdeck. Jamie scanned the deck and for the first time noticed what was happening. His men, what there were of them, were faring poorly. Bounding forward, Jamie emptied his pistol into a pirate lunging at Deacon with a boarding pike.

And then there were three sabers vying to cross his. Jamie never fought so hard . . . or was so overwhelmed. His gaze flew to Deacon, to Keena, to any of his men who might help him. But they were all as busy as he. Each fighting more men than they could handle.

What had happened? The question danced through his head as he thrust and parried. Thrust and parried. First one opponent, then another. Steel grazed off his shoulder but Jamie barely felt the sting. Where in the hell were all his men? Had they all been killed, or—

"They're striking colors!"

The heavily accented words penetrated his mind as none others could. Unbidden his gaze was drawn to the yardarm high above the *Lost Cause*. His flag was gone.

"What the hell?" Jamie whirled around in time to see d'Porteau aiming a pistol at his stomach. Then something exploded over his head and he hit the blood-smeared deck.

Chapter Nine

Anne slowly lifted her tearstained face from the hard pillow of her bent knees and listened. The quiet was eerie after the insufferable pounding. And the motion of the ship had calmed to a gentle sway. No more violent jerks, some so strong they threatened to toss her from the corner of the captain's bunk where she took refuge during the battle.

It was over.

And all she could do was wait.

Her hands tightened around her breech-covered legs, drawing her more tightly into herself. And she tried to fight the memories.

There had been quiet on the island, too. After d'Porteau's guns ceased their deadly pounding. Actually not quiet, Anne thought. Just not the noise of the cannons. The screams and crying had continued.

They still rang in her head.

But there was none of that now. Anne tilted her head, straining to hear. The timbers groaned, the sea slapped against the hull, but no other sound filtered down to her. It was as if she were drifting upon a ghost ship. A sliver of hysterical laughter slipped from her lips before she could clamp them together. She was going mad.

D'Porteau started the process when he dragged her down on the beach, and now alone in the middle of the ocean she would—

Heavy footfalls in the passageway proved her wrong. She wasn't alone. Her fingers tightened painfully about her legs, her eyes widened as she waited for the sound to come closer. Part of her mind screamed for her to do something . . . anything. Find a weapon. Hide.

But she couldn't make herself move.

When the door burst open revealing a half-naked savage she couldn't even scream.

Consciousness exploded upon him as water slapped his face. And with it came the realization of what happened. Jerking up, coughing, Jamie came face to face with d'Porteau. The Frenchman squatted in front of him on the deck, grinning his horrible gap-toothed grin.

"Well, we meet again, *mon ami.*" He just stood there, staring down at where Jamie sat. "But this time I think the circumstances are different, *oui?*"

"Ye damned son of the devil. I'll—" Jamie tried pushing to his feet, only to have someone jerk him down from behind. The slam he took to the wooden deck contained a painful reminder of the bleeding slash across his shoulder.

"You'll what, Jamie MacQuaid?"

D'Porteau's heeled boot stomped hard onto his gut, bringing Jamie waves of nausea.

"What? Nothing to say, *mon ami?*" He ground his foot. "But you always have something to say."

With every reserve of strength he had Jamie grabbed hold of d'Porteau's ankle and yanked. Caught off guard the hulk of a pirate faltered, then landed hard on his back.

If it was the last thing he did on this earth, Jamie wanted to follow through with his attack. To wrap his fingers around that whisker-covered neck and drag d'Porteau screaming and gasping for breath to hell with him. But the rough arms holding him down denied him the chance.

And when d'Porteau fumbled to his feet, his face contorted in a mask of rage, a pistol aimed at Jamie's chest, he knew he'd lost his opportunity.

The gun was cocked, and Jamie prepared to take his last breath. He expected hate and revenge to fill his mind, but it was Anne he thought of. Anne coming to him for help. Anne's sweet body. Annie in his cabin.

His head jerked toward the side where the *Lost Cause* was bound to the Frenchman's schooner. He couldn't tell what had become of his crew. What had become of Anne. Were they all dead? Was she dead?

An unexpected sadness engulfed him, and he shut his eyes, only to jerk them open when he heard the raucous laughter above him.

"A coward at the end," d'Porteau said, his voice full of contempt. "I always thought as much. You never came after me. And now . . ." He spit on the deck. "You must hide your eyes like a woman when I kill you."

Jamie strained against the arms that pinioned him down. "Get your scurvy crew off me." That earned him a twist of his wounded shoulder, but Jamie didn't care. "And I'll show you which of us is a coward."

D'Porteau snorted. "You had your chance, Jamie MacQuaid. And you have failed. I . . ." He pounded his gold-braided velvet waistcoat. ". . . am the victor today. I am the one to decide your fate." He released the hammer, sliding the pistol into one of the leather straps that crisscrossed his chest. "And I decree that a pistol shot is too fast and easy for the likes of you. You shall suffer as I did."

"Looky what I found snivelin' in the captain's cabin."

Anne stumbled onto the sand-strewn deck as the burly pirate shoved her forward. She blinked against the blinding light. Lifting her arm to shade her eyes she stared up at the figure looming over her. The sun radiated behind him, making his face indistinguishable.

But she knew who it was.

Spasms of terror clutched at her stomach and she wanted to just curl herself into a ball.

"Put him with the others," came the rough command and Anne grimaced when her arm was grabbed and she was hauled to her feet.

She looked around frantically trying to understand what had happened. There was obviously a battle, and judging by d'Porteau's presence it appeared the *Lost Cause* was defeated. Anne didn't even want to imagine what that meant to her. But she couldn't help wondering about Jamie MacQuaid. Where was he?

Her eyes scanned the deck as she was shoved along toward the forecastle. Shattered sparring rattled in the wind, and part of the mizzenmast lay twisted on the deck. She heard a scream and turned in time to see one of the crew, Farley, tossed overboard by two laughing pirates she didn't recognize. Her reward for turning toward the scene was a sharp poke between the shoulder blades.

"Get on with you, boy."

"But they . . ." Anne hesitated. "He'll die in the water."

"Die anyway," the pirate sniffed. "Ain't no sense hol-din' onto any man who can't pull his weight."

She wanted to tell him how barbaric he was, how thoughtless and cruel. But Anne knew it wouldn't do any good.

Besides, he just gave her another shove. This time toward a knot of men Anne recognized from the *Lost Cause*. They were sitting or slumped over ropes near the forecastle. Some seemed to be nursing wounds. Others just lulling the afternoon away. But all their faces showed a concern for their unknown fate.

Spotting Joe she slumped down on the deck beside him, waiting for the pirate to amble away before saying anything. "Where's Captain MacQuaid?" Anne realized how desperate her whispered question sounded and tried to calm herself. But her heart was thumping wildly and she didn't think she could bear to hear what she feared was coming. She swallowed when Joe didn't answer right away. "Is he . . . ?"

"There." Joe pointed his skinny arm toward larboard, where another ship was lashed to the *Lost Cause*. At first Anne could see nothing but the other ship and the peaceful blue sky beyond. The sails were doused but unfurled and though it must have been victorious, d'Porteau's ship had its share of damage.

But none of that told her a thing about the captain. She turned back toward Joe, a question on her face and he grunted, angling his sharp little chin up. Her eyes shot back to the other ship, her gaze lifting.

"Oh no." Anne bit back the cry that swelled in her throat as she caught sight of the man fettered to the ratlines spread-eagle. His golden head was slumped forward and matted with blood, his body limp. Manacles kept his wrists and ankles attached to the ropes.

It felt like someone punched her in the stomach. Anne tried to swallow but her mouth was too parched. Even when she spoke her words sounded dry. "Is he alive?" She couldn't take her eyes off the captain to see Joe's reaction to her question, but she thought he shrugged.

"He moved, maybe an hour ago. Maybe longer."

But he wasn't moving now. Anne watched until her head felt like it would explode, willing him to show some sign of life. But the wind rustling through his hair was the only sign of movement as the unmerciful sun beat down upon the scene.

"What happened, Joe?" Anne spared a quick look at the boy whose pinched features were even more drawn. He seemed reluctant to talk at first, but eventually shook his head.

"The *French Whore* done fought us, and we was winnin'." He sucked air through his teeth. "But when the cap'n went to board her, only some went with him. The others stayed on board."

"You mean they didn't follow?"

"Aye." Joe nodded. "They didn't do nothin'. Weren't shootin'. Weren't fightin'."

"But didn't they realize what would happen?"

"Don't know as if that weren't their intention. Leastways one of 'em struck the colors pretty quick."

"Leaving Captain MacQuaid and a few others on the enemy ship to fight it out alone." Anne wrapped her arms more tightly around her legs, then nestled her head to the side, her eyes on the figure hanging above the deck. She took a shattered breath. "Do you think they'll cut him down soon?"

"Don't know. Maybe they'll just leave him there as gull bait. Or for the rest of us to see what can happen."

"If we don't do what?"

"Join 'em, I guess. Seen Stymie and some of the others prancin' 'round. Seems like they already done it."

"Maybe they're the ones that struck the colors." Anne turned toward Joe. "Think about it. Think about what I heard that night. Their plans to take over the ship."

Joe shrugged in that way he had, that could mean he agreed or not. And Anne let it go. What difference did it make, really? How it happened wouldn't change anything. It simply gave her something to think about as the long afternoon wore on.

She should be trying to decide what to do. But was acutely aware the decision was not her own to make. At least all the pirates, friend and foe, still viewed her as a boy. She wouldn't receive the fate planned for her on the beach at Libertia.

But somehow it wasn't her own fate that concerned her, nor even her cousin's, though she'd seen no sign of him. It was the man hanging high in the shrouds that tormented her mind . . . and tore at her heart.

She watched him long after she thought there was a chance he still lived. She watched him until two pirates, one tall, with slumped shoulders and a scar sliced across his bare chest and the other young and almost pretty ambled toward the small group of prisoners.

"Captain d'Porteau wants the lot of ya on the *French Whore*." When no one moved, the shorter one whipped out a pistol and aimed it toward Joe. Scurrying to her feet, Anne grabbed the boy's arm and yanked him up. The rest followed, their bones cracking from their long stint on the hard deck.

Anne noticed now, what she hadn't before. Oh, she'd been aware the pirates were roaming around the *Lost Cause,* but she could see now the deck was clearer. Obviously some repairs had been made.

After she stumbled across the plank to the French ship it was clear the crew was busy here as well. But she gave the decks but a cursory glance before her gaze was drawn upward.

"What do ye think of yer mighty cap'n now, eh, boy?" The scarred pirate gave her a shove when she paused to stare, then laughed when she stumbled. Anne pulled her hat lower and trudged along. When the group was told to sit near the mainmast she did, then realized she'd lost sight of Joe in the transfer.

From what she could tell most everyone was assembled. Rum flowed freely, though none was offered the prisoners. Everyone else, however, seemed in a festive mood.

She feared a moment of truth was at hand.

When a wild huzzah rang out the hair on the back of her neck prickled. Twisting her head she saw d'Porteau strut toward the center of the deck. His burly figure was outlandishly clothed in the ornate fashion of an earlier era. Black velvet, liberally encrusted with tarnished gold braid and sea salt, draped over his protruding stomach, then flared out to skirt past his knees. His pantaloons were ruffled and drenched with tattered lace, dingy and soiled. And above it all, sitting atop the curled black hair was a huge plumed hat.

He struck a pose, preening on his heeled shoes, then turned with a flourish to plop his ample body upon a bench made of two upended barrels and a plank. While

Anne watched in amazement a snaggle-toothed boy draped a garish satin and ermine cape around his plump shoulders.

The pirates from the Frenchman's ship seemed to find this wondrous fun. Their cheers and bawdy laughter rippled through the sun-heated air. Once he'd settled himself sufficiently, d'Porteau lifted a ringed hand and the tall freebooter who'd brought Anne to the *French Whore* pounded the end of a boarding spike against the decking three times.

Quiet descended like a gossamer blanket.

"What say ye, Mister Attorney General?" D'Porteau's voice was high-pitched, and nasal.

The man he referred to as attorney general tried to straighten his rounded shoulders. "If it please yer Worship." His droopy-lidded eyes swerved to include the onlookers. "And ye gents, we got ourselves a real nasty one today."

"What be his crimes?" The jewels sparkled as d'Porteau swirled a dirty hand above his head.

"Crimes aplenty, Yer Most Reverent, crimes aplenty. He be a pirate of the worst kind." This brought a loud chorus of guffaws from the assemblage. "A charlatan and a rogue. A despoiler of innocent maids." He paused. "And 'tis rumored, a coward, the blackest of all."

D'Porteau stroked his chin. "Crimes such as these against mankind should not go unpunished." He snapped his fingers. "Bring the prisoner before me."

They were having a trial. A travesty of a trial to be sure, but one nonetheless. As royal governor of Libertia, Anne's uncle had presided over a few juries, acting as judge. The offenses were minor; most of Libertia's citizens lived together in peace and harmony. And of course Uncle Richard never put on such as show as this.

Anne wondered which of the group she huddled among would be brought to trial first, when a movement to her right caught her eye. Several agile tars had monkey'd up the rigging and were untangling Captain MacQuaid from the ropes. She gasped, surging to her feet as the binding went lax and he slumped forward. Only a rough hand on her shoulder restrained her from rushing toward the mast. She was jerked back abruptly, and before she could turn a voice hissed in her ear. "Don't make it harder on him."

Anne folded her legs and swallowed, nodding her head slightly as the blackamoor's fingers drifted from her jacket. It would do no good to run to Jamie's aid. She would probably be knocked aside before she reached him.

All she could do was sit, her back hunched over, her chin resting in the notch between her knees and try to keep the tears at bay.

At least he was alive.

His step was slow, shuffling, but he'd shouldered away the coarse hands of the tars once his feet hit the deck. Anne tried not to notice the raw and bloodied wrists, or the crusted, coppery blood on his upper arm. She tried. After all, thanks to d'Porteau she'd seen killing before, and suffering. People she'd lived with and liked. Innocent people.

So why did Captain MacQuaid's pain seem to tear at her insides and touch her soul?

"Ah, there is the prisoner. I thought he might have found some coward's way out of facing his accusers."

"Aye, here he be, Your Eminence. Though a more scurvy specimen of pirate blood, I've yet to see."

The *French Whore*'s captain found that amusing, the noise of his laugh rattled deep in his throat. "What say ye, Captain Coward. Be ye guilty as charged?"

Anne tensed as all eyes turned toward Jamie Mac-Quaid. He straightened his shoulders, though she could tell the effort it took. But he looked d'Porteau straight in the eye. "I'll not answer to the likes of a swine-nosed, blubbering idio—"

His last word was cut off when the pirate serving as attorney general brought his pike down over the back of Jamie's neck. He staggered, catching himself at the last moment before crashing to the deck. This, too, was greeted by loud guffaws and angry jeers. "Me thinks he be pronouncin' hisself guilty as charged, Your Most Wonderful Lordship."

It took a moment for the staff pounding to bring the pirates back to order. They were obviously tiring of pretending to be calm, law-abiding citizens. All except the men surrounding Anne. They had yet to utter a sound.

Crimson trickled down through the windswept curls at Jamie's nape. Anne watched the flow as if mesmerized, wishing she could do something to help him. Knowing she couldn't. So she willed him her strength . . . what was left of it. Shut her eyes and tried to send her thoughts to him.

Endure. Have courage. Survive. You are not alone.

It was all she could offer, and it was so inadequate. There were tears in Anne's eyes when she opened them. When they met his.

She couldn't explain it any more than she could change what was happening. But for one fleeting moment the captain turned his head. And stared straight at her. His sea-green eyes were bloodshot and strained. But there was no defeat in their depths. No despair.

He turned away so quickly, Anne could have imagined the whole of it . . . except she knew she hadn't.

D'Porteau was the next to speak. His expression was still puffed with rage, though he resumed his seat after jumping up when Jamie uttered his contempt. "Very well, Attorney General, sir, let us hear what the good men of this ship feel."

A loud swell of, "Guilty," filled the air.

"Be there a man among ye, who thinks otherwise?"

Anne felt the pressure of Keena's hand and bit her tongue. Silence reigned. The verdict appeared to be unanimous.

"Guilty, he be then." D'Porteau held up his hands for quiet. "But there be more to decide." His smile was sly. "What manner of punishment for the miscreant?"

There was a general demand for a hanging.

"From the yardarm," one yelled.

"Keep his body hangin' in the sun till his parts dry up and blow away," another shouted.

"Carve out his liver," came a call from a bloodthirsty tar.

"All very interesting suggestions," d'Porteau muttered after his attorney general had regained some semblance of calm. He stood and pranced toward Jamie, his gait awkward in the heeled shoes. "But I've another idea." He circled his prisoner, seemingly deep in thought. Again in front of Jamie he stepped closer, signaling for someone to pinion Jamie's arms.

"This man is a captain." He tilted his head. "Should he not have a boat?" A few of the Frenchmen's crew chanted their agreement. "And the wide open sea beneath him?" The outburst of agreement grew louder.

"Aye, Cap'n, give 'em the whole damn ocean!"

Confused, Anne glanced back toward Keena, who stared straight ahead, his black, tattooed expression unreadable. But he didn't seem relieved by this new form of punishment. And though it sounded preferable to hanging, Anne sensed it wasn't.

D'Porteau would never do anything that wasn't cruel and heartless.

Anne's head jerked up when d'Porteau moved toward the remainder of the *Lost Cause*'s crew. He stood less than a rod from her. So close she could smell the sweat seeping through the aged velvet. Sweeping his small eyes over the knot of men he pursed his lips.

"What of these wretches? What shall we do with 'em?"

"Let us join ye." Anne twisted her head to see a sandy-haired pirate she recognized from Captain MacQuaid's vessel. He stood, pulling another tar up by his sleeve.

"Aye, 'tis the way of it," the other adjoined, and more grumbled their acknowledgment as they stumbled to their feet.

Anne watched in awe as, like rebounding dominoes, each pirate stood. Until there were only a few including herself who still sat on the hard deck. Then there was movement behind her, and Anne felt a none too gentle tugging at her arm. Keena pushed up, bringing her with him. And everyone stood, ready to join ranks with the Frenchman.

Except, it wasn't d'Porteau's crew they were attaching themselves to.

"What do ye think, Captain Stymie?" d'Porteau called

toward the man leaning against the rail. "Will ye have these tars as your crew?"

Slowly, as if deciding upon a piece of prime horseflesh, Stymie pushed away from the belaying pins and ambled forward. The man who before the battle was imprisoned in the bowels of the *Lost Cause*, now swept his bulging eyes over the lot of them. Then more slowly, evaluating each man.

Anne tensed when his gaze settled on her. She saw the spark of remembrance before she looked down. Her life under *Captain* Stymie would not be easy. But then she didn't imagine anyone's would be.

He paraded around the group, some of whom called out his name in greeting, then turned back to the Frenchman. "They'll do," he announced and Anne could almost feel the general sigh of relief among the captives.

"Then 'tis agreed." D'Porteau took his time settling back on his rough-hewn throne. The boy who'd draped the dull satin cloak around his shoulders now jumped forward to arrange the folds. "Since the victory is in part yours, Captain Stymie, I award you the good vessel, *Lost Cause* and her crew."

Then with a sly grin nearly obliterating his eyes, the Frenchman twisted toward Jamie MacQuaid, who stood, surrounded by several guards. "Ah, do you hear that, poor captain? Your crew has deserted you for another." He made a "tsking" sound with his tongue and teeth. "Such a pity when I was bound to give you your own boat. Now ye shall be the captain of no one."

"I shall be his crew."

Anne didn't know she was going to say the words until they were out of her mouth. Then it was too late. She'd stepped forward, leaving the security of the group, to show herself. It was an impetuous act. No doubt a stupid act. Keena certainly must have thought so . . . Anne jerked free of the hasty grab he made for her coat. And saying it wasn't like anything she'd ever done before.

She sucked in her breath as all eyes seemed to rivet into her clothing. Were they seeing the woman beneath? Why hadn't she thought of that . . . thought this through? Sweat pooled between her breasts, riveting down into the waistband of the breeches she'd become used to wearing. And she waited.

D'Porteau was the first to overcome his surprise at her actions. He tilted his head, allowing the preposterously large feather in his hat to billow in the breeze. "What's this . . . a cabin boy for Captain Coward? Hmmm." His beady eyes swerved to Jamie. "What would elicit such loyalty in a youth, do you imagine?" Whether or not he expected an answer, he received none from the stoic, tight-jawed Captain MacQuaid. He soon lost interest in taunting his expressionless foe and turned back toward Anne.

"So ye wish to join your captain, do you, on his *cruise?*"

"Yes." There was no taking it back now.

His lips pursed. "Well, perhaps we should see what your new captain has to say about your desertion, though why he would want such a filthy urchin as yourself . . ." He let his lace-wristed hand flutter. "What say ye, Captain Stymie? Shall we hang the lad for treachery? His desire to leave you so soon smacks of it."

"Hang him for whatever ye choose," the thick-lipped Stymie responded. "I have no use for the dog." He wiped at his mouth with the back of his hand. "The pup's nothin' but trouble."

"Ah, trouble, is it?" The Frenchman seemed to roll the

word around on his tongue, savoring it. "Perhaps we should let him join his good captain's crew."

"I don't want him."

Anne's eyes shot toward Captain MacQuaid where he stood, bloodied and battered . . . and rejecting her sacrifice. Her utter foolishness in stepping forward was already blatantly apparent. She was to be hanged. Anne tried to swallow but couldn't get past the lump in her throat.

Yet to know that she had one option, to be sent with the captain, and he was refusing her that. . . . She wanted to bury her face in the palms of her dirty hands and weep. Instead she stood head bent and listened as the Frenchman continued this farce of a trial.

"Ah, the prisoner has a tongue in his head after all. And he uses it now to speak out against a boy, a poor *garçon*, who offered his services." D'Porteau shook his head and clumps of oily hair stuck to his cheek. "I think you have lost your right to make any demands. *I* . . ." He again pounded his chest. ". . . shall be the one who decides. *I* am the victor, this day." He paused and the pirates grew quiet. "Before the sun sets on another day we shall launch the captain and his crew of one, and wish them Godspeed."

The wave of jeering laughter swelled, seeming to surround yet separate her from everyone else on board the *French Whore*.

Everyone but Jamie MacQuaid.

Now that the decision was made, the judgment passed down, he stared at her. And as dangerous as she knew it was, Anne could not help being drawn to those eyes.

She made a terrible mistake, she knew. There was a joke here someplace. One she couldn't quite comprehend. But as she was grabbed from behind, she began to.

Rough hands jostled her, knocking her from side to side in an attempt to move her along toward d'Porteau. She looked around, but there was not a kind expression, a sympathetic tone. Even Keena seemed intent on doing her harm. He grabbed at her so roughly Anne thought her arm would pull free from its socket.

It wasn't until she slammed up against his solid strength that she realized his ploy. Dark fingers slipped into her pocket, but before she could discover what he gave her, his hand clamped over hers. Then he pushed her away.

Anne was moved and mauled across the deck to be joined by another, larger group bent on doing the same to Captain MacQuaid. With d'Porteau leading the procession they were both shoved to the rail.

One of the small boats was unlashed from its cradle. Blocks and tackles attached to the mainstay lifted the boat over the gunwale and sent it splashing to the sea below.

"There ye be, Captain MacQuaid," d'Porteau said with a flourish. "Your new boat awaits."

Afraid at first that she would be tossed overboard, Anne discovered as she was pushed over the side, that there was a ladder of sorts. She scurried down the webbing as quickly as she could . . . anything to escape the savage, angry faces above her.

Captain MacQuaid reached the boat first, but he didn't help her in. He simply sat there, his face as cold and hard as stone while on the *French Whore* and the *Lost Cause*, tars climbed into the rigging, turning the sails into the wind, bringing the great vessels to life.

Anne couldn't understand his attitude. They were free and well rid of the ruffians as far as she could tell. With a burst of energy she reached down, lugging one of the oars up and fitting it in the notch. If he was going to do nothing, only sit like a knot on a log, she would get them started.

"Which way do we row?" She asked what she thought the most obvious question. But her stomach sank with his response.

"Your guess, Annie, is as good as mine."

Chapter Ten

It took a moment for the captain's words to sink into her relief-drenched brain. Only minutes ago she thought it a very strong possibility she'd be hanging from the yardarm by now. Even without his cooperation Anne was able to pull and tug the second oar into place. Then she squared her body and faced him where he slumped, hands dangling between bent knees.

"Are you implying you don't know where we are?"

He lifted his head then, and Anne looked at him . . . really looked at him. The tears she'd kept at bay during the battle and mock trial sprang to her eyes. It was only the knowledge, intuitively gained, that he wouldn't appreciate her sympathy that kept her from slipping from her seat and cradling him in her arms.

Besides, both ships were still close enough that they could hear the raucous laughter. Occasionally one tar or another would jut his head over the side and wish them a speedy voyage . . . to hell.

Jamie took a deep breath. His arms still hadn't tingled to life from his stint hanging from the ratlines. Or perhaps it was more accurate to say they were tingling to life, and hurting like the devil. But he grabbed for the oars anyway, swallowing down the cry of pain that lodged in his throat.

He managed to speak between clenched teeth. "I'm implying nothing, *Andy*. 'Tis straight out I'm saying it." He swiped through the water, ineffectual strokes that at least moved them from the *French Whore*'s side. Fresh beads of sweat broke out on his brow, and he cursed the weakness in his arms.

Cursed the fate that had brought him to this.

"Let me help." Anne leaned forward, tentatively reaching for the oars, not surprised when his head shot up and he glared at her through red-rimmed eyes. His expression was enough to make her shrink back on her seat.

"All I'm about," he said, then had to stop and catch his breath, "is moving us from the bastard's wake. After that ye can toss the damn oars overboard for all I care."

"Toss them . . ." Anne's mouth gaped open. "But how would we row? How would we . . . ?"

"Escape?" The word was little more than a sneer. "Is that your well-laid plan, Mistress Anne? Is that why you foolishly volunteered to serve as my crew?"

"No." Her denial was immediate. And as quickly regretted. She didn't understand all the reasons why she did it, but she knew her own safety wasn't one of them. Yet she couldn't explain the unexplainable to him. Nor did she wish to try. Better he thought it a calculated "plan" to gain her freedom.

Except there was something in the depths of his eyes, when she finally returned hers to look at him, that made her wonder what he did believe. But then his expression hardened. " 'Twas a stupid thing to do."

The wound on his shoulder was bleeding again. Anne

steeled herself against his pain. "I'm well rid of the pirates." His laugh made her stiffen her spine.

"Annie, ye forget who you're talking to, lass. You're stuck on the high seas with a pirate." He sobered. "At least on one of yonder ships, you'd have had a chance of making port."

"We'll," she began but his angry voice cut her off.

"We'll do nothing, Annie." Jamie's rage seemed to swell, swamping him as surely as a tidal wave would their tiny boat. "When those pirates sail from sight, there will be nothing." He leaned forward to emphasize his point. "*Nothing,* do ye hear me? There will be only you and me and this poor excuse for a boat." He kicked at the side with his bare foot. "And water." His voice dropped. "Endless miles of water. By the time you die parched and sunbaked, you'll rue the moment you stepped forward. Rue the moment you ever heard the name Jamie MacQuaid."

He'd wanted to make her face reality and as soon as she did, felt like the most depraved of men. Her face, beneath the layers of dirt, grew still. Her eyes shadowed.

"I needn't wait for the moment of my death for that," she said with spirit, then wished she hadn't. Even in his weakened condition he could toss her overboard if he wished and she could do nothing. Despite his claim, valid she was sure, of being a bloodthirsty pirate, she'd seen evidence of his nature and didn't think him cruel. But then the situation was different.

But instead of grabbing for her, he threw back his head and laughed. "I'm sure ye do, Annie," he said when his chuckling ceased. "I'm sure ye do."

Then they were sitting in the boat staring at each other, quiet except for the lapping water and the occasional raucous pirate, a reminder of their solitude. Anne resisted the urge to twist around in the boat, to search out the wide expanse of horizon. For she knew he was right. Except for the two pirate ships that were now under sail and moving away from them, they were alone.

And though the area was dotted with islands, chartered and unchartered, unless one knew in which direction they were . . .

The late-afternoon sun beat down unmercifully as Anne tried to think rationally about their problem. Or more to the point their myriad problems. No amount of organization or careful planning seemed as if it would help. Events had gone awry and swept them along in their wake.

But did that mean she shouldn't try? The only place she was certain there was no land, was right where they were.

The captain had pulled the oars in, allowing the boat to bob and sway, following the lead of each rising swell. Though his eyes were closed, she didn't think him asleep . . . and she didn't care if he were.

"How far is it to the closest land you know of?"

One eye opened beneath a cocked brow. "Too far."

Anne tamped down her anger and frustration. "Yes, you've already made your opinions well known. However, I asked for a specific number. How far is it?"

He shrugged and Anne could see the lines of pain deepen around his mouth with the motion. "Fifty, maybe more, nautical miles." His other eye opened. "Farther than we can row in the . . ." He was going to say, "time we have left," but decided against it. "Farther than we can row," he repeated.

She did look around then, holding onto the seat as she

twisted her body first one way then the other. "Which way is it?"

Jamie squinted into the sun to get his bearing, then pointed in the direction behind him. "It be that way . . . more or less."

"More or less?" Now it was Anne's turn to raise her brow.

"Aye, more or less. In case ye hadn't noticed, the Frenchman didn't see fit to provide me with my quadrant and charts."

When she said nothing, only looked at him questioningly, Jamie explained. "*If* I had my charts to tell me where we were, and *if* I had a quadrant to take a reading, then I could use the tables in the *Nautical Almanack* to find our approximate latitude. That be *if* I had my *Nautical Almanack*."

Anne's jaw tightened. "And that's the only way?"

"Except to say that the sun rises in the east and New Providence is west, aye."

Lifting her hand to shade her eyes, Anne stared toward the low-slung golden orb. "Then I shall row that way," she announced, reaching for the oars.

His hands, warm and callused, covered hers. Anne's gaze traveled from his face, to where he touched her, then to the bloody rope burns on his wrists. Sympathy flooded her, but was quickly swept away by his words.

" 'Tis a waste of time."

"Which I appear to have plenty of," Anne countered.

"Nay, Annie, ye don't." His voice was as gentle as the pressure he now put on her hands. She wanted to cry. To fall across the boat, into his embrace and weep until there was nothing left inside her. She very nearly did, especially when her eyes lifted to meet his. Gone was the brash corsair, cocksure and roguish. Gone was the anger.

What was left when she looked into his eyes was a man, a man she cared about. The man she would die with.

Anne swallowed and shook her head. "I can't do nothing." She turned her hands over, palm to palm, clutching his. "I can't."

He linked their fingers, his long, and well-shaped, dwarfing hers. " 'Tis one of the differences between us, Annie. For I can."

And he proceeded to prove his contention to her as she unbraided their hands and reached for the oars.

He was still establishing his point when the sun touched the western horizon, spilling a golden carpet over the sea. Anne's shoulders ached. Her arms screamed and her back, she was certain, was broken in two. Each time she lifted the heavy oars and slapped them back into the cobalt-blue water her resentment of Captain MacQuaid grew.

He gave up his seat and now lounged in the bow, his long legs spread, his head back. He slept occasionally, she could tell by the deep resonance of his snores. But most of the time he was awake. And watching.

" 'Tis only making ye thirstier," he offered.

The oars slapped into the water once again and she tugged. "I'm already thirsty, thank you very much."

"Don't thank me, 'tis your own doing."

Though by this point she had to admit he was right, she was tired of hearing it. After giving him a scathing look, she pulled the dripping oars from the sea, wondering if her last effort had moved the boat at all. Deciding she was doing the best she could, Anne pushed them back into the water.

He was silent for so long Anne thought he'd fallen asleep again, but apparently he was only resting, thinking of new ways to torment her mind.

"Even if ye were rowing us due west, 'twouldn't be the right longitude."

Splash. Anne leaned into her pull. "And how would I determine that?"

"By a watch—"

I know, *if* we had one." Anne nearly grunted the words.

"Aye. Actually we'd need two. One set to Greenwich time, the other the actual time. Then by—"

"Why are you telling me this?" Anne set the oars and looked down at her palms. The blisters she'd felt forming were now bloody. Moving faster than she thought him capable of, he shifted, clambering over the seat. He latched onto her wrists before she could stick her hands into the water.

The boat swayed, sending seawater sloshing over the top. Anne sucked in her breath on a gasp, her eyes wide. He was so close she could see the fine squint lines where the sun was blocked from bronzing the skin. The lashes that framed his eyes, long and thick, made the blue-green color all the more dramatic and intriguing.

And she could smell him, that same musky scent that always had a weakening effect on her knees. But now her knees were already weak, and so were her arms and her soul. And she didn't know why he was tormenting her so.

With a flick of her wrists he turned her palms toward him. " 'Tis a shame you've bloodied yourself. But I doubt the sharks would care that these hands are attached to a beautiful woman." His gaze crept to the side, and Anne's followed. She stiffened when she saw the triangular fin slicing through the water.

"I . . . I didn't see it."

"Obviously not."

"Is it after us?"

Jamie grinned despite himself. "I doubt it. But give him a whiff of blood and he will be." With that he let loose her wrists.

Anne didn't have the strength to keep her hands from dropping onto her lap.

"And as for why I'm pointing out the problems of longitude to ye . . ." Jamie dug his hands back through the tangled curls of his hair. "By God, Annie, it should be obvious." His stare was penetrating. "Look at yourself. You're bloody and tired. Thirstier than even me, I'll warrant." His voice lowered. "And ye haven't changed a thing. Not one damn thing."

The realization that he might be right was more than Anne could handle.

Pressure seemed to build within her and she wanted to scream out her frustrations to the heavens. Instead she screamed at the pirate. "I can't be like you. I can't!" He settled back on his seat and she yelled all the louder. "You live your life doing nothing. If a ship crosses your bow you attack it. If not . . . Well, that's fine, too. You knew what kind of man Stymie was. Joe told you. I told you. Yet you did nothing because it was easier."

She'd run out of air and sucked in more. "And now look where we are." Though she didn't think their predicament entirely his doing, at the moment she wasn't going to quibble. "And you're still doing nothing."

"I'm doing nothing because 'tis not a damn thing I can do." Jamie sat up straighter on the wooden seat. He'd had enough for one day. He'd lost his ship, his crew, been hung in the shrouds to bake, and he was going to die. No doubt he deserved the latter. But it didn't make the reality of it any more palatable. And now he had to put up with this woman who'd been nothing but a thorn in his side, an unbelievable annoyance, from the moment he first set eyes on her.

Bossy. Domineering. So full of brass she'd probably sink to the bottom too fast for his friend, Master Shark, if Jamie should toss her overboard. Which was exactly what he felt like doing.

He clenched his fists because the urge was so strong he was afraid he might. Especially when he heard the part about his doing nothing because it was the easiest thing to do.

Jamie's jaw tightened until his teeth hurt. "Perhaps," he conceded, nearly spitting the word at her. "But I learned long ago 'tis not worth giving your all to something that's bound to fail regardless."

"But you can't know that before you try."

"I know how long we can exist without food, without water. I know how damn big this ocean is. And I know bending my back against the oars isn't going to get us anywhere, when there be nowhere to go." He bent forward as he spoke, moving closer with each word, until he was nearly nose to nose with her. He expected her to back away. Any reasonable woman would. But then he remembered he was dealing with Anne Cornwall.

"So that's it then." Anne refused to be cowed by him. "Your best advice is to give up. To implore God to take our lives mercifully. Why don't we simply end it ourselves then? Or would that be *doing* something?"

His eyes narrowed. "I'm not killing us, because in a typical showing of his merciless soul, d'Porteau didn't even leave us a pistol with shot enough to do it. That's right," Jamie continued when her eyes opened wider and she shied from him.

" 'Tis the custom followed by most of the brotherhood when marooning to leave the sorry bastard at least a way to end his suffering."

"But that's—"

"What?" Jamie straightened. "Barbaric? Did ye think ye were dealing with angels, Annie? I told ye from the beginning—"

"Yes, I know you did. And believe me I never thought d'Porteau anything but the lowest of creatures."

"But it isn't just d'Porteau. We all subscribe to our own code."

"Even you?"

"Especially me."

"Do you mean to tell me you've marooned someone? Done to them what d'Porteau did to us?" He didn't say anything at first, but he didn't need to. Anne could see the answer in his expression.

Jamie took a deep breath. " 'Tis one of the reasons d'Porteau despises me."

"You marooned him?"

"Don't look so shocked, Annie, or I might be tempted not to tell you who else was with him at the time."

"Who?"

"Your friend Israel Plowser."

Anne laughed. She couldn't help herself. "You're joking." When he shook his head, the gold earring twinkled, caught by the dying rays of the sun. "But Israel hates d'Porteau." Then a stranger thought came to her. "And he admires you."

Jamie just shrugged. "I can't help the way a man feels

about me. But I can tell ye they were both marooned, along with several others on an island . . . by me."

"But how did they get off?"

He shrugged again. "I haven't a clue. Picked up by a passing vessel perhaps. I thought them all dead." He paused. "They were given sufficient ammunition to choose the easier way to die. It was nearly a year later I started hearing tales of the Frenchman."

"And Israel?"

"Nay. When I saw him with ye was the first I knew he'd survived."

Anne rested her head in her chin, mulling over what she'd heard. It still surprised her that Israel and d'Porteau had been cohorts, and that the captain had punished them. She tried to remember all Israel had said about Captain MacQuaid, but she was too hungry, and tired and thirsty to concentrate.

Her mind kept swinging back to the captain's remark about ending their own lives. Was that indeed what they should do? Her gaze captured his. "If things were different. If d'Porteau had followed the code and left us with a pistol . . . ?"

"Aye," Jamie said when she didn't continue. "What about it?"

"Would you use it? Would you shoot me, then yourself?"

He didn't answer for so long, just sat, his hands dangling between his knees, his eyes glued to hers, Anne wasn't sure if he'd heard her. The boat bobbed, the sun sank farther into the western horizon, filling the sky with fuchsias and mauves, and still he said nothing.

"I said," Anne began only to have him interrupt her.

"I know what ye said. I also know 'tis not a question I

wish to ponder." He wiped both hands down over his face. "No good would come of it."

"I have a knife."

His head shot up. "What did ye say?"

"I have—"

"How did ye get that?"

Deliberately, Anne shifted, reaching her hand down the length of her breeches and slowly pulling out the short hunting knife that Israel gave her years ago. The blade caught the last rays of sun, glinting as no jewel could, as she held it out toward him. "I always carry it. If you recall on Libertia I used it—"

"I remember how ye used it, Annie." Shaking his head, Jamie laughed. "And not a one of the bastards thought to search ye." His sun-browned fingers closed around the hilt.

Anne swallowed as she gave up possession. "I know it isn't a pistol, but . . ."

Jamie paused in his examination of the weapon, and glanced up. "Ye think perhaps I should use it to slit your throat?"

Anne's fingers reached for the skin above her collar. She couldn't help herself. "I don't know. You said . . ."

He said a lot of things, Jamie realized, that he didn't always mean. He reached out and pulled off the woolen cap, freeing a tumble of brown curls. Angry with himself when she flinched at his touch. " 'Tis a decision that doesn't need made now." His hand tightened around the knife handle. "Besides, I think we can put this to better use than slicing through your throat. Unravel that cap of yours."

Anne looked down at her lap, then began doing what he asked. "What are you going to do?" He was busy rummaging around the bottom of the boat, making the sides dip and sway.

"This should do." He held up a piece of wood, no longer than his arm. "I, Mistress Cornwall, am going to see about our supper," he informed her, then proceeded to whittle matching notches at one end. He worked quickly, pausing several times to match up the knife handle with the grooves. Then he made deeper grooves at the other end.

"Rope," he commanded, reaching for the yarn Anne unwound. Then he carefully twisted and braided the knife around the wood, knotting and reknotting until he was confident it held securely. After cutting that off, he tied the rest of the yarn to the other end, then wound that around the seat and knotted it.

When he was finished, he held the weapon up for Anne to see, a grin brightening his face. "Well, what do ye think?"

She didn't know what to say. "I . . ."

" 'Tis a harpoon." With that he stood, bent over the side, peering into the indigo water. "Shark meat isn't too bad, but I think I'll forgo the pleasure of wrestling our friend tonight. Perhaps something small, though." As he spoke he kept his gaze trained on the swells.

The boat tilted and Anne grabbed for the sides, when he lurched forward, tossing his makeshift weapon overboard. The first few times he pulled the harpoon back empty.

The third time he gave a whoop and tugged it back, a bright yellow fish wriggling on the blade. Sliding it off, he twisted to try his luck again. By the time it was too dark to see anything beneath the clear surface, there were five fish, all small and brightly colored, on the bottom of the boat.

Without removing the knife from the stick, he began slicing and gutting the fish.

It tasted terrible.

Anne at first balked at the idea of eating raw fish, but given the alternative . . . Besides, the captain seemed to be wolfing down his share without any hesitation.

Using her front teeth Anne tore another piece of flesh from the scales and chewed. By now it was dark, the only light skimming across the waves came from the quarter moon. She felt all the more alone and defeated.

The captain, on the other hand, seemed to have gained a fighting spirit. After finishing his fish he reached for the oars and settled into a steady rhythm of rowing. At first Anne said nothing, thinking he might only wish to put some distance between the shark, who she hadn't been able to see since darkness fell, and themselves. But when it appeared that he planned to continue, she asked where he was going.

She could tell he glanced up, though it was too dark to see his expression. "Don't take too much to heart, Annie. 'Tis still a waste of me time and yours. But I'm feeling a bit revived, so . . ." He let the rest of his words trail off.

So he was rowing them . . . someplace. Though he denied knowing where, Anne noticed he occasionally tipped his head to study the heavens. The stars hung bright in the black velvet sky and Anne wondered if he gleaned some reading from them.

But she didn't ask, for she sensed he would deny it. And maybe he didn't. Or maybe he didn't want her to put false hope in something he couldn't provide. At any rate, she followed his suggestion that she settle into the bottom of the boat and get some rest. It was cooler now and Anne was glad for the coat, but though she tried, sleep would not come. Not even with the gentle sway rocking her and the hypnotic swish of the oars.

"What made you become a pirate?"

Jamie paused, braking the flow of his pull through the water when he heard her question, so unexpected in the darkness it seemed to come from his own mind. He thought her asleep, spared for a bit the reality of what was to come. Selfishly he was thankful she wasn't. For he was lonely to his soul. He'd been thinking, of the past . . . of his wasted life. And sitting on the cusp of oblivion, facing his own mortality, as he was, his thoughts were far short of comforting.

So he carved the oars through the swells and smiled. "What makes ye think I wasn't born one?"

"Because I doubt that's possible," came the voice from the darkness.

He decided to tell her the truth. What difference did it make? " 'Twas the hangman's noose that convinced me that piracy was my calling."

"If you don't wish to tell me, just say so."

"But 'tis true. I swear it. I'm surprised Israel didn't tell you the tale, he seemed so eager to have ye trust me."

"He didn't say. I thought perhaps he didn't know."

"He knew." Jamie pulled in the oars and stretched his back. "Israel was one of the first of his kind I encountered on my sordid voyage toward freebooting. 'Twas a ship he captained that captured one I'd booked passage on."

"Booked passage?" The tone was skeptical and Jamie could hardly blame her.

"Aye. Thoughts of staying in Scotland and hoping not to be recaptured held little appeal to me. I was a sad product of the defeat at Culledon. Caught I was, red-handed. The British brought the lot of us to trial and charged us with sedition. I barely knew what the word meant, except that being found guilty of it made one forfeit his life."

"How old were you?"

"Old enough to know better than to tangle myself with a lost cause," he answered cynically. "Seventeen," Jamie added more to himself than for her benefit. "Anyway, I managed to find a berth on a vessel heading for the colonies." He took up the oars again. "But the brig was attacked, those aboard were given the choice of joining the pirate crew or being killed." He paused. "I chose to live.

"Clever choice," Anne mumbled and heard him chuckle. But when he spoke again his voice lacked humor.

"Sometimes I wonder." He took a deep breath. "But what's done is done, and I'll not regret it."

"It would be a waste of time to do so."

"You've the right of it there, Annie."

After that neither said anything. The moon rose, the stars dimmed, and still Jamie rowed, wishing he knew why he bothered. He assumed, her curiosity quenched, Anne was asleep . . . that is until she spoke again.

"You think we're bound to die, don't you?"

Earlier he'd wanted her to stop her foolishness and face reality. Now he couldn't stand the thought. But he couldn't lie to her either. Instead he pulled in the oars and shifted off the seat to settle beside her in the bottom. Without a word he lifted her up against him.

His palm covered her cheek as he pressed it to his chest.

Chapter Eleven

It was the sun, bright and incessant, that woke them up.

Anne opened her eyes to find herself staring straight into his. At first, mesmerized as she was by the clear, sealike color, she forgot where they were. Finding herself in his arms was just a continuation of a most pleasant dream. One that had haunted her sleep. All she could do was smile.

He wanted to forget.

Fatigue and the constant draining of the tropical sun had been enough to allow Jamie to drift off to sleep. But though he'd appreciated the feel of Anne in his arms, frustrating as it was, his dreams were dominated by demons. Demons of his past.

But now, awake and looking into Anne's multifaceted brown eyes, feeling the gentle softness of her body pressed to his, the devils that haunted him, seemed more like ghosts, wispy figments fading away on a strong-edged sweep of desire.

The arm that pillowed her body tugged closer. The hand still molded to her cheek shifted, tilting her face. His thumb traced a smear of grease across the slant of her brow.

" 'Tis inconceivable to me that no one saw through your disguise."

"They saw what they wanted to see."

His mouth inched closer. "They were blind."

"Perhaps, but—" Anne's protest that she had fooled him for several days was cut off when his lips touched hers. Tremors of pleasure, stronger than she could control, shot through her, curling her toes. His mouth rubbed against hers, a delicious light friction. Then his tongue was there, dampening the sun-parched fullness, silently begging her to open to him.

She had no choice.

Anne accepted his kiss as she had on the beach at Libertia, with wonder that he could do so much to release her passions with so little effort.

Their positions were cramped, the wooden seats imprisoning them at the top, the slanting sides of the boat cradling their backs. But Jamie managed to shift, pressing his body tightly against hers. A wave of fevered desire quickened his loins.

He pulled away enough to read her expression. For there was no way she could know how much he wanted her. Under the circumstances it surprised . . . and embarrassed even him. His life was one of debauchery. But there was something about taking her, forcing her, while she had nowhere else to turn that he found unacceptable. Even as his body screamed for release.

He didn't want her to think badly of him.

Jamie spread his fingers back through her hair. "Annie?" Her name, the question, was barely more than a whisper, lifted and carried away by the soft morning breeze.

His mouth skimmed from her cheek to the tip of her nose, the abrasion of his whiskers sending shivers down her spine. She swallowed, sensing a hesitation that seemed foreign to him. She longed for the kisses that overwhelmed. Kisses that would stamp out reality . . . at least for the moment.

She tangled her fingers in his hair and drew his mouth back to hers.

And he was lost.

A moan escaped him as her lips opened, and then his tongue was inside, tasting. She was all sweetness and surrender. Kissing him back with an urgency that matched his own.

Jamie's legs tangled with hers, and he wished he had room to move, but he forced that thought from his mind. No use fancying something that couldn't be. Better to let erotic oblivion seize control.

Her jacket was coarse and bulky and Jamie longed to peel the fabric aside and rediscover the silken skin beneath. He faltered with the buttons, his fingers unwieldy, unwilling to break the seal of their lips to see what he was about. The jacket *V*ed open and he fumbled through the linen shirt.

When he finished exposing her to the sunlight and his eyes, Jamie bent down, nestling his face against her skin.

That's when something bumped the boat. Hard.

Anne screamed as it lurched to the side, then swished back to right itself.

There was a flurry of arms and legs as Anne and Jamie tried to extricate themselves from each other and the row of wooden seats.

They were banged again, this eliciting a string of curses from the captain as he bumped his head against the side.

"What is it?" Anne managed to pull her head high enough to look over the edge. What she saw made her cry out. "It's the shark!"

Jamie was desperate now to be free of the confining seats. Each time he knocked an elbow he berated himself for getting in such a bind. When he finally yanked his body from beneath the seats the boat was listing from side to side so violently that water sprayed over them. He grabbed for the makeshift harpoon, determined to kill the attacking shark or die trying.

Clambering to his knees, Jamie lifted his arm, the knife blade aimed toward the mass of grayish brown floating near the surface of the water. He blinked, ready to begin a downward thrust. And stopped.

"What is it?" Anne asked when he collapsed on a seat, his head thrown back in laughter. "Why aren't you killing it?" She managed to free herself from the bottom, but her coat was twisted and her hair tangled down in her face. With one hasty swipe she brushed it aside, trying to figure out what was so funny about being attacked.

" 'Tisn't a shark," Jamie managed to say. He stuck the harpoon under the seat and reached into the water, shacking his head when Anne gasped. " 'Tis but a dolphin."

"A dolphin?" Anne leaned forward cautiously at the same time the creature lifted its head. Diamondlike droplets dripped from the snoutish nose. No gaping mouth full of jagged teeth appeared. Instead Anne found herself staring into rather soulful eyes. And feeling foolish. "I saw the fin," she mumbled, annoyed when Jamie laughed all the harder.

Now he was actually petting the dolphin as if it were a lapdog, going so far as to scratch behind where its ears should be. Which seemed a bit reckless to Anne after what the creature did to their boat. The dolphin still had it bobbing in the wake of its playful antics.

"What does it want?" Anne settled on a seat and rested her chin in the cup of her palm.

"Some company, I'd wager."

Anne just rolled her eyes as the captain continued to talk to the dolphin as if it were a child. "But why was it attacking our boat?" Granted the animal seemed harmless enough now, but it had nearly swamped them earlier; things might have been different.

"I don't think we can call what Lucy did an attack."

"Lucy?" The dolphin seemed to glance around but Anne ignored it. "You named it Lucy?"

"Had to call her something," Jamie said, a grin forming.

"And what makes you so certain the dolphin is a girl?"

The grin was full-blown and wicked. "I know these things," he said as his gaze traveled down Anne's front.

Blushing Anne hastily yanked the edges of her clothing together, covering her breasts. Which only made him chuckle.

"No need to hide yourself. I know you're a woman, too."

Anne sent him a scathing look, as she buttoned the jacket. "I still don't understand what the dolphin—"

"Lucy."

Her lips clamped together. "Have it your way . . . What Lucy was doing if she wasn't attacking us."

"Signaling, perhaps."

Anne cocked her head in disbelief.

"Or getting our attention."

Anne wanted to tell him how foolish he sounded, but decided against it. If he wanted to think the dolphin was trying to get their attention, so be it. It did seem like a friendly creature and after several coaxings Anne reached over to touch the top of its head.

"She likes ye."

Anne shrugged. "I'd say she seems fonder of you."

"I do have a way about me, when it comes to the fairer sex," he responded and Anne felt the heated color rise all the way to her curls.

The captain continued to play with the dolphin as the sun rose higher in the east. Though she wanted to suggest he could make better use of his time . . . rowing perhaps, or catching something edible . . . Anne kept quiet. For one thing the light showed them surrounded by water just as yesterday. Even Anne was beginning to wonder if it was worth the effort to row.

And though she was hungry and thirsty, the idea of eating more raw fish made her nauseous. The only thing that held any appeal was settling back down on the boat bottom with Jamie MacQuaid, and she didn't think she should suggest that. So Anne sat, brushing her fingers back through her hair and waiting for the captain to tire of rubbing the sea creature pressed to the side of their boat.

As it happened, it was the dolphin who seemed to tire of the massage first. With a flip of its tail that sent a shower of salt water over Anne, the creature turned and dove beneath the surface. Moments later the dolphin shot into the air, gracefully executing an arc before again disappearing into the sea.

They both watched in awe as the dolphin performed

her water show, each time moving farther to the south. When the creature had all but disappeared, Jamie sighed. " 'Tis a sad thing we cannot swim like that."

"I can't swim at all."

He glanced at her, his dark brows raised. "Ye live on Libertia, surrounded by beaches and water so blue it hurts your eyes and ye don't swim?"

When he put it that way it did seem strange. But then she didn't spend her days lulling on the beach. *She* was the one everyone else depended upon to make certain the sugar was cut when it should, and boiled, and shipped. Anne lifted her chin. "I never had time for such pursuits."

He stared at her in earnest now, a quizzical expression on his bronzed face. Anne finally became so uncomfortable she crossed her arms and turned away, but not before she noticed the slight shake of his head. Well, he had a lot of nerve, disapproving of the way she spent her time. He who roamed the seas preying on innocent people. Robbing, and Lord knows what else.

A memory of what they were doing when the dolphin knocked into their boat sprang to her mind and Anne felt tingly all over. She also felt foolish. "Are you planning to catch us something to eat today?" Neither the question nor the tone was pleasant. Anne realized it as soon as the words blurted from her mouth. But she couldn't seem to help herself.

He shrugged in that noncommittal way he had, and reached for the harpoon. "I didn't know ye were so fond of raw fish."

"I'm not." Anne let out her breath. "But I am hungry . . . and thirsty." Parched was a more accurate term, and the tropical sun had barely begun its climb into the heavens. With nothing to shade them . . . Anne couldn't even finish the thought in her own mind. So she concentrated on watching the captain as he leaned over the side, make-shift spear held at the ready.

He seemed stronger today. The wound on his shoulder had scabbed over during the night, and his fall of un-bound, sun-bleached hair hid where they'd hit him.

Whereas Anne could feel the effects of the sun on her skin, and could only imagine how red she was, Jamie MacQuaid only grew a deeper brown from their expo-sure. He removed his shirt to fish, and his large body was covered only by a pair of breeches that clung to his lean hips. When he leaned forward and they slid lower, the skin was lighter, but still appeared darkened by the sun. She couldn't help wondering how far down one had to go to find untanned skin.

Her gaze dropped to his feet. They were wide and long toed, planted firmly on the boat's bottom. Of course they were as bronze as his face and hands. And like much of his body, spattered with burnished, curly hair.

"There 'tis a likely candidate to break our fast."

Anne's gaze leaped up from contemplating the muscles in his legs, to where he pointed. Just below the surface she spotted a large orange and turquoise fish. It was beautiful and she almost hated the fact that he would have to kill it.

He lifted his arm, balancing himself as the fish swam closer. Anne was so intent upon watching the grace of his movements she barely noticed the shape approaching from the other side. When what was happening did regis-ter it was too late. "Watch out, Jamie!"

Her warning came the same instant the dolphin slammed into the boat. Jamie lost his tenuous hold on stability and tumbled over the side. Anne screamed and jumped up as the boat rocked precariously.

He was only a blurred shape beneath the surface, seemingly going deeper. "Jamie! Oh God, Jamie." Anne wrung her hands not knowing what to do. In the meantime the dolphin batted his head against the side, splashing water.

He was coming up. Anne started breathing again as bubbles broke the surface, followed by his head. He shook wet hair from his face and laughed, and Anne, who felt on the verge of tears, could have taken an oar and knocked him over the head.

"I fail to see what you find so amusing." She reached out to help him aboard, glad to see he'd held onto the spear.

Ignoring her hand Jamie hiked himself onto the boat. "I'm afraid I let the fish get away."

"I shouldn't wonder."

He wiped both palms down his face, and grinned. "I see our friend is back."

"If that's what you wish to call her. She's the one who knocked you overboard."

"But ye didn't mean it, did ye, Lucy girl?" The dolphin seemed to nod her head in agreement, and Anne knew she'd been out in the sun too long to even imagine such a thing.

Again, the captain spent his time playing with the sea creature, seemingly forgetting about the need to find them food. He petted and talked, and Anne crossed her arms and watched with growing annoyance. She was thankful, though the captain obviously wasn't, when the dolphin swam away, again executing a series of swoops and dives.

"Now do you suppose—" Anne began only to have him hold up his hand to silence her.

Jamie shaded his eyes and squinted toward the south watching the porpoise. "What do ye make of it?"

"Make of what?" She was beginning to think longingly of the taste of raw fish, a testimony to how hungry she really was. She was also hot. Wishing she didn't feel quite so naked without it, Anne shed her jacket. When she looked up the captain was still watching the dolphin, who to Anne's consternation appeared to be swimming back toward them.

"Look what you've done. The poor creature is besotted." Anne folded her arms. "And we aren't in need of a pet."

"Nay." Jamie's eyes narrowed as he followed the dolphin's progress. " 'Tis more than that."

"More than what? What are you doing?" Anne watched as he pulled the oars off the bottom and settled them into the slots. "Don't you think we should find something to eat first?"

"Later." The captain started to row, pausing when the dolphin turned, as if he hadn't spent most of last evening preaching the uselessness of such an endeavor. When he noticed her expression, Jamie grinned. "I think Lucy wants us to follow her."

"Follow her?" Anne grabbed for the sides of the boat. "Are you mad? Lucy is a fish."

"Not precisely. Dolphins are animals much like a dog or horse, only they live in the ocean." He shook his head when her eyes opened wider. "I know it sounds like foolishness." Jamie bent into the oars, working hard to keep up. "But I've heard tales."

"Tales? What kind of tales?" Anne fell forward when he pulled up the oars.

"Where did she go?" Jamie scanned the swells, giving a whoop of joy when he spotted Lucy. "Be a good lass, Annie, and turn about. Keep an eye out for our friend."

It was ridiculous, absolutely ridiculous. But after sighing loudly Anne did it anyway. They might as well die following a dolphin as picking a random direction. And the dolphin was friendly. She played and splashed, swimming close to the boat, then diving deep only to surface and arc into the air. And she led them further and further south as the sun crept to its zenith.

She even stopped when they did.

" 'Tis sorry I am, Lucy, but I need a rest," Jamie called out as he pulled in the oars. "And something to eat." He grabbed up the spear and peered over the side. "Keep watch Annie and let me know if she deserts us."

Anne accepted the filleted fish with only a hint of distaste. She didn't eat hers nearly as fast as the captain did, but then she wasn't so sure that they needed to follow the dolphin. "Tell me about these tales," she reminded when they were again rowing south.

" 'Tis just pirate lore, or so I thought." Jamie grunted as the oars sliced down through the water. "Stories of sailors being saved from drowning by sea creatures." He shrugged.

"Dolphins?" Anne chanced a glance over her shoulder.

"Aye, dolphins usually." He paused. "Though occasionally the savior is a mermaid."

Anne's lips thinned when she heard his chuckle. "What exactly do these dolphins do?"

"I don't know exactly. I never paid that much heed. But I do recall that they befriended men."

"And saved them?"

"Aye."

Anne didn't need to ask if that's what the captain believed the dolphin was doing now. It was obvious he thought that. And Anne wanted to believe it, too. But the idea was so preposterous.

Still, as the afternoon dragged on, and the dolphin did seem to be leading them, a kernel of hope bloomed. And Anne began watching not only the antics of the porpoise, but the muted edge of horizon where the sky met the sea.

She saw nothing.

Even when the shadows turned the sea a deep cobalt, heralding the end of another day.

"We won't be able to see her once the sun sets." Anne voiced the worry that was nagging her mind.

" 'Tis all the more reason to hurry now," he responded. But Anne could read the exhaustion in his voice.

"You should rest," she said, turning toward him.

"And be accused of doing nothing?"

"You've done plenty today." In truth she didn't see how he was holding up as well as he was. She was weak from hunger and thirst and the constant exposure to the sun. And all she'd done was sit and watch the dolphin, while he rowed.

When darkness finally did shroud their world, making it seem smaller, there was nothing to do but stop. Jamie settled on the boat bottom, and was asleep before Anne had a chance to ask him anything.

She sat for a while staring out into the night, hoping for some sign that the dolphin hadn't deserted them. But she could see nothing, and soon settled into her own corner. But sleep didn't come as easily to her. She wanted to crawl over next to the captain and cuddle against his chest, but decided against it.

When she did sleep it was to dream of dolphins and mermaids and men of the sea who swam with them, their bronzed muscles gleaming in the water. It was a fantasy world, sparkling and erotic, making waking up all the more unpleasant.

The reality of her existence was skin that felt dry and burned, muscles sore and cramped and a mouth so parched her tongue felt swollen. Anne opened her eyes, only to close them again. There seemed little reason to even sit up.

It was the captain's voice that finally made her throw an arm across her eyes and struggle up. He appeared in equally poor spirits as he called out the dolphin's name.

"She isn't there," Anne said, after she twisted around, scanning the endless, endless expanse of sea.

He spared her a scathing look before calling out again. "Lucy, I'm ready to follow ye again."

"The dolphin can't hear you," Anne snapped. "And she never could understand you. So you might as well stop all your shouting."

His eyes met hers again, hard and narrowed, and this time they held. "I don't believe I need ye to tell me what to do."

"Well, you obviously need someone." Pent-up anger, at herself, at the situation, exploded.

"And ye think ye should be that someone, I suppose." Jamie sat forward on the seat facing her, hands clamping his knees. "Nay, I don't suppose. I know. You've been trying to order me about since the first time I laid eyes on ye."

"I merely asked—"

"Ha!" The boat rocked with the force of his delivery. "Ye never *merely* anything in your life. And ye certainly didn't ask. Ye demanded. And when I wouldn't listen ye drugged and kidnapped me."

Anne opened her mouth in rebuttal, then clamped it shut again. What he said was the truth. But she had her reasons. Reasons he didn't seem to care about.

"You're a bossy wench, Anne Cornwall. And 'tis nothing I hate more." The words poured from his mouth like venom from a snake. Once begun Jamie seemed unable to stop them. Not that he wanted to, he assured himself. Every syllable he uttered was true.

At least he thought it was until he saw her face. Her dirty, sunburned face. Her full mouth quivered and if he didn't already know that she wasn't a female prone to tears, he would swear she was going to cry. Not knowing what else to do, he reached out, grazing the tip of her chin with his finger.

Anne didn't think she had the strength to bat him away, but she did. Except he didn't stay away. Instead he lunged forward onto his knees, grabbing her shoulders and pinning her on the seat. The boat rocked, the sun glared and the heat from his hands burned through Anne's linen shirt.

"I shouldn't have called ye that."

Anne raised her chin. "Why not? It's what you think of me."

A grin played with the corners of his mouth. "Aye," he admitted. " 'Tis true in part." His grip tightened when she tried to squirm away. "But 'tis not all bad ye know."

"You're going to tell me now that you like bossy wenches?" Anne's brow lifted skeptically.

"Nay." He did grin now. "But ye do have a few other admirable traits."

At the moment Anne couldn't think of a thing about her that was appealing. "Such as?"

"Your courage."

"I'm not courageous." Anne sucked in air. "I'm really frightened."

He seemed to shrug that off. "Considering the circumstances anyone would be a fool not to to be scared."

"Are you?"

Jamie let his hands drift down her arms. "Aye." His eyes held hers for a long moment before he straightened and continued. "Do ye know what else I like about ye . . . other than your obvious feminine charms?" His gaze traveled over her as slowly and thoroughly as it had that first time they met.

Anne experienced the same tingling, the same flutter in her stomach. "Tell me."

"You're a woman of action. Ye don't just sit by and let someone else take care of ye."

"But you said you didn't like that."

"I know," he said, his grin wicked. " 'Tis a puzzle, isn't it?"

The breeze picked up, catching his hair and showing glimpses of the gold loop in his ear. He loomed before her looking every bit the pirate, and Anne couldn't seem to mind. Slowly her smile spread, until it was as wide and playful as his.

They were two people alone in their world. Destined to die, but somehow feeling a bit better.

Jamie slapped his knees. "Seems to me 'tis time I went fishing."

Though Anne protested the captain insisted he'd do better with the knife if he went over the side.

"Don't fret, I can swim." He carefully unwrapped the yarn holding the knife to its makeshift shaft.

"But what if there's a shark?"

"Then I'll be climbing aboard before ye can miss me." With a splash he was over the side.

Anne watched as he took a deep breath, then jack-knifed his body and dove under the water. The sea was so clear she could see him as he dipped and turned. When his head broke the surface he was streaming water and grinning. Tugging the boat to one side he slide a squirming fish off the blade.

Several more times he went under, and always he came up with a bright-colored catch. Anne was beginning to think he was right about going into the sea when she lost sight of him beneath the boat. She sat back, waiting for him to surface, growing more nervous by the second when he didn't.

"Captain." She leaned over the side, sticking her hand into the water and swirling it around. She could see nothing.

"Jamie!" She scurried to the other side searching the depths. Her heart pounded as she called again and again. But still there was nothing but endless sea, endless sky.

Suddenly the water's surface not two rods to her left exploded with a burst of streamline gray. Anne screamed and clutched the sides of the rocking boat, sure that some terrible sea monster had devoured the captain and would eat her in one gigantic bite.

But it wasn't a sea monster, but the dolphin, cavorting with its friend. The captain waved a hand. "Look who I found." He dove beneath the surface only to push up beside the boat. With a heave he pulled himself in, splashing water everywhere. His hands slicked the hair off his face and he braced himself on the seat.

Already the dolphin was by them, swimming and bounding its way south. Jamie watched a moment, then turned to face Anne. " 'Tis not just my decision." He continued when her expression registered bewilderment. "Do we follow the dolphin, or . . ."

Anne tilted her head. "Or stay where we are?"

The captain shrugged. "Rowing in another direction is an option."

Shifting around, Anne caught sight of the dolphin, then looked back toward the captain. "I suppose it can't hurt to follow Lucy."

But she was wrong, Anne thought later that day. It did hurt to follow the dolphin because they'd started out with hope, and now as the sun burned down to their right, that hope was fading.

Anne glanced around at the captain from her post in the front of the boat. He'd been rowing almost nonstop for hours, only pausing when a rain shower brought welcome relief from their thirst. They'd lifted their faces, drinking their fill, saving what fresh water they could in Anne's shoes.

And then he'd grabbed the oars and continued rowing. Now his strokes were more and shallow, moving them slower and slower toward some unseen and more than likely nonexistent destination. "You should rest," she said, lowering her eyes when he looked up.

"Later," was all he said.

"This is foolishness. You're so exhausted you can barely lift the oars."

He didn't respond, but Anne could see the tiny nerve jump in his cheek as he clenched his jaw.

"Captain MacQuaid . . ."

"What?" He splashed the oars into the water and yanked them back. "Now ye want me to stop. Make up your mind, woman. Before it was row here and there. Well, I've decided I'd rather die of fatigue than hunger and thirst."

"Fine." Anne turned back around in a huff. Let him row and row and row. He could follow the stupid dolphin to the ends of the earth for all she cared.

Anne shaded her eyes scanning the water. Where was the silly creature anyway? If she'd lost sight of it the captain would—

Anne blinked, then rubbed her eyes and blinked again. If she wasn't mistaken . . . "Captain MacQuaid. Captain."

"All right, Annie, I'll stop in a wee bit and do some fishing."

"No, no, it's not that." Anne took her eyes off the horizon long enough to spare him a look. "It's . . . I think I might see—"

"Land," he whooped as he shot to his feet.

Chapter Twelve

It took them longer to reach the island than Anne thought. She kept her vision focused on the gradually clearing specter of palm trees, afraid if she glanced away they might disappear, and be swallowed up by the sea. But she called out encouragement to the captain, who seemed to have a sudden spurt of renewed energy. The oars dipped and splashed in rhythm with the raucous song he sang under his breath. Anne wondered if he even realized what he was doing.

Her spirits were so high she didn't care if he crooned of loose women with breasts as large as melons. As long as he rowed.

Shadows darkened the landscape as they approached the embracing arms of the cay. The water within the outstretched semicircle of coral rocks was a cool turquoise that reminded Anne of the captain's eyes. But she didn't mention the comparison to him.

She was too busy pointing out features of the island and bombarding him with questions. Most of which he answered with a noncommittal grunt.

"Do you see the palm trees?" Anne hugged herself,

barely able to contain her happiness and relief. "Fresh coconut. Won't some coconut milk taste wonderful?"

"Aye." He no longer sang, now whistling the same tune through his teeth.

"Do you suppose there's fresh water? And something to eat? And people?" She did look around at him now. "What if the island is populated? With houses and beds and . . . Oh, wouldn't that be grand?"

But the closer they got the more obvious it was that this was one of the multitude of islands that dotted the Caribbean, uncharted and unpopulated. Beyond the stretch of white sand rimmed by palms was an interior of scrub pines and bushes, molded by their exposure to the constant trade winds. Not exactly hospitable surroundings, but after days at sea in a small boat, the island looked like heaven.

Anne's exuberance was such that when the bottom finally skimmed sand, she leaped from the boat, splashing through the surf to dance around on the shore. "What a beautiful island," she sang, throwing her arms out and twirling about. "What shall we name it do you think? Something magical. Camelot, perhaps? Or Heaven?"

"What about Dolphin Island?"

Anne stopped turning about and faced the captain. He still sat in the boat, hands wrapped around the oar handles, body slumped forward, as if his muscles had turned to stone when he finally reached shore. She took a step toward him. "You must be . . ." Anne hesitated, she couldn't think of a word to describe how tired he looked. "Come, let me help you."

"I can manage, Annie, thank ye." He moved then, slowly pulling in the oars and standing to survey the beach. Then he, too, leaped into the gentle waves and pulling the boat with him, stumbled onto the beach.

He barely cleared the froth of surf when he sank to the sand. He sprawled out, and before Anne's surprised eyes fell into a deep sleep.

"Captain?" Anne inched closer to him, at first worried that perhaps he died. But her hands settled at her waist when she heard his first deep snore. She bent down to shake his shoulder. "Don't you think we should look for water?" No response except his continued even breathing. "Or find something to eat?" Again nothing. "Or build some sort of shelter?" This time he mumbled something, but Anne couldn't make it out. And it was obvious he wasn't going to wake up.

So she stood and looked around herself. She was hungry, but not brave enough to explore the island's interior on her own. So she settled for sorting through the coconuts she found on the ground, shaking each in turn, and collecting three that sloshed with milk.

Using her knife she gouged out the holes and gulped down the milky liquid. Again she tried to wake the captain to offer him some, but he wouldn't budge. So she drank all three.

Then with a sigh she snuggled down on the beach beside the captain. She supposed building a shelter would have to wait until morning.

She awoke late and alone. Anne stretched, digging her hands into the sun-warmed sand to assure herself that finding the island wasn't just a dream. Taking a deep breath she sat up, annoyed with herself that she missed the captain's bulk beside her.

The sun was nearing its zenith, a fact that made Anne jump to her feet. She never slept this late. Never. And especially when there was work to be done. Twisting around she searched the area for the captain.

At first all she could see was blue sky, turquoise sea, white sand and when she looked behind her, the shadowy green of the interior. Just as Anne was ready to call out, she heard a splash near one of the curving arms of coral rock. Shading her eyes against the glaring sun, Anne made out the captain. And Lucy, the dolphin.

"So, they've found each other," she mumbled as she walked purposefully toward the shore. When the lapping surf licked over her toes Anne paused. Cupping her hands she shouted his name.

After the second time he heard her and threw up his hand. But he seemed in no particular hurry to return to shore. Anne stood, her patience growing thinner as he continued to swim and cavort with Lucy. By the time he finally began a leisurely paddle toward the island, Anne had worn a path in the sand with her pacing.

He emerged from the water, his body, the hard planes and muscles, the wide expanse of bronzed skin, sleek with moisture. He was wearing breeches, but they molded sensually to every part of him. Anne tried to swallow, but couldn't.

"Well, of course my mouth is dry," she said almost belligerently. "I'm thirsty." Being annoyed with the captain seemed preferable to swooning at his feet, which was what Anne thought she might do when he lifted his arms to rake the long hair back from his face. "You should have awakened me," was all Anne said before proceeding to tramp back and forth in her footprints.

"Ye seemed to need the rest." Jamie picked up his shirt where he'd tossed it on the beach and dried his face.

"Well, yes," Anne conceded. "I suppose I did." She angled him a look. "But I don't usually sleep so late. Especially when there's so much to be done."

The captain merely shrugged. "I caught some fish." He nodded toward a pile of seaweed farther down the beach. "But I didn't think they'd last long in this sun."

She was glad to see he'd done something besides play with the dolphin. Though she did expect the sea creature deserved their undying thanks. Not that she thought it purposely brought them here, but it was lucky that the captain believed in myths enough to head south.

"What about water?" Anne faced him again.

"What of it?" Jamie settled down in the sand and tilted his head to look up at her.

"Is there any fresh water on the island?" Anne tried to keep her exasperation from seeping into her voice. It was difficult when he merely shrugged. "Don't you think we should look?"

"Aye," he said but made no sign of getting up. "Though we might want to eat something first."

"I suppose you're right." Anne walked beside the captain as he ambled toward his stash of fish. "Then we can explore the island and see about building a shelter, and—"

With one finger pressed to her lips Jamie silenced her. "Let's just think about breaking our fast first."

All Anne could do was nod. What was it about him that made her feel so tingly all over? She stepped away from his touch, nearly tripping over her feet in the process. She needed to free her mind of this affliction. After all, they were stuck here alone on this island. "You're right, of course. We'll eat first."

"Actually, I had something else in mind to do."

"You did?" Anne's voice came out as a squeak because he reached forward and began unhooking her jacket.

"Now I know ye thought 'twas necessary to disguise yourself with dirt before. But we seem to be the only people here, and I know your little secret."

He was undressing her as a mother would a child, first one arm out of the coat, then the other. And Anne just stood there entranced, letting him.

"Ye have yourself a giant tub of warm water, there. Now I realize 'tisn't fresh, but I assure you 'tis better than nothing."

"You want me to bathe?"

"Aye, 'tis the general idea."

"But . . . there's no privacy."

His grin was naughty. "I'll turn me back."

She didn't believe him for one minute, but the idea of being clean was too tempting. Even if the water was salty and there was no soap.

But when he reached for the tie on her shirt, her hand covered his. "I think I can manage from here," she said, her smile sweet. Then she turned and walked toward the surf, leaving him holding her coat.

Wearing breeches, socks and shirt she stepped into the water.

He was right. It did feel good. Anne waded out until the gentle swells lapped about her waist, then leaned forward and splashed water onto her face.

"You'd get yourself cleaner with a few less clothes," she heard him call out, and laughed.

"I'm saving time by doing my laundry, too." Anne sank

down until her shoulders were submerged, and reached up beneath her shirt to wipe her hand over her skin. The warm water swirling around her body felt so good. She tingled all over. Anne's eyes closed and she sighed as her fingers skimmed down her stomach. This was wonderful.

Her head dropped back letting the water seep up through her curls and she realized the fantasy that engulfed her thoughts as her hand lifted over her taut breast.

Anne's eyes shot open and she jerked upright. My God, she was thinking about the captain. About him touching her, running his large hands over her body.

He was standing onshore yelling something and Anne whipped her head around, wet hair slapping her face. "I am not taking my clothes off."

"What did ye say?"

He appeared so bewildered that Anne had an uncomfortable feeling he hadn't been saying anything to her about clothing. He was holding something in his hand, but it was too small for her to see. She turned and sloshed through the water toward him.

"Why didn't ye tell me ye had a tinderbox," he was saying, and Anne could only shrug. "I didn't know."

"Well, ye must have put it in your pocket, and I'm thankful for it."

"I guess I must have," Anne began, then shook her head. "No. Keena put it there." She quickened her step. "When the pirates were pushing me toward you he bumped against me. I remember now that he slipped something into my pocket."

"He had more faith in us reaching land, than I did."

"I don't know about that. You did follow the dolphin."

The pirate's laugh mingled with the rattle of wind through the palm fronds. "Ye finish your bath, Mistress

Cornwall. Now that we have flint and steel I shall gather some wood and build a fire. Then we shall have a breakfast fit for a king."

He wasn't far from wrong.

The smell of roasting fish drifted over the beach, drawing Anne from the water. She'd managed to clean herself and her clothes pretty well, even without soap. Her hair hung down her back in streaming ribbons. There was no toweling, except her coat, but Anne couldn't bring herself to dry with the dirty fabric. Besides, the warm, tropical air would accomplish the same thing in no time.

"It smells wonderful. I can barely keep from—" Anne stopped, her mouth suddenly too dry to form words. The captain was squatting, his back to her, in front of the small fire he'd made on the beach. When she spoke he shifted to look at her. His stare seared her as surely as the flames danced around the stick-skewered fish.

He couldn't speak, and he couldn't look away. Jamie had seen his share, hell, more than his share of naked women. He'd even seen a fair amount of Anne, though his mind was so fogged by drugs, he couldn't remember clearly. But he'd never seen anything as erotic as the fully clothed woman before him.

If she only knew how the wet shirt molded to her breasts. How he could see the dusky circle of her firm nipples through the nearly transparent fabric. The breeches were fashioned of sturdier material, but the weight of the water pulled them low around her hips. He could see the curve of her body, the mysterious indentation of her navel.

It was all he could do not to leap toward her and strip away the barrier to her womanhood. He was hard and aching, ready to take her willing or not, on the sand.

It was only the memory of the man he'd once been, the civilized man, who would protect a lady's honor with his life, that kept him from doing it. Instead he jerked his head around toward the fire, gritting his teeth against the pressure in his loins.

He would have her.

There was no doubt in his mind about that. They were alone on a tropical island. Chances of anyone ever finding them was as remote as this tiny cay. He wanted her. There was no way they wouldn't become lovers. But he would not force her. He would wait. And then he wouldn't have to.

"Sit and grab yourself a leaf."

Anne glanced around, wondering why he suddenly seemed in such a foul mood. As far as she could tell their circumstances were definitely improving. Just the thought of eating cooked fish made her almost giddy. And being clean was wonderful.

She sat on the flattened surface of a small outcroping of rock, spreading one of the large palm fronds across her lap. He used her coat to shield his hand as he reached for the skewered fish.

They were hot, but that didn't stop Anne. Burned fingers seemed a small price to pay for such a succulent feast. "Mmmm." She sucked the tip of her thumb. "I never really cared for fish before. But these are delicious."

What was delicious was the way she ate. Jamie tried to concentrate on his food, but as hungry as he was, he realized he'd rather be kissing her lips than eating. Which was absolutely ridiculous.

"What do you think we should do first?" Anne wiped her hands down her damp breeches and leaned back. For the first time in three days her stomach was full.

"Explore the island, I suppose." Jamie took a swig of coconut milk.

"What of a signal fire?" Anne scooped out a shallow pit in the sand and slid her fish bones into the hole, glancing up when he questioned her.

"What about it?" His eyes narrowed. "What are ye doing?"

"Burying the bones." She patted the sand down after covering her garbage. "It makes it neater." Anne brushed her hands off. "Don't you think we should have a signal fire? I mean if a ship should come near us, we want them to know we're here, don't we?"

"It depends." Jamie tossed a fish skeleton over his shoulder.

"On what?" Her eyes followed the flying bones.

"On who's doing the rescuing." Jamie pushed to his feet. "Personally I'd as soon stay here as have the *French Whore* sail into sight."

"I hadn't thought of that."

Jamie shrugged. "I imagine they think we're dead, but . . ."

"No, you're right, of course." Anne took a deep breath. "Do you suppose anyone will ever find us? No." She held up her hand. "Don't answer that. I realize you don't know." Anne stood up. "We simply must make the best we can of the situation." She straightened her spine. "Let's see what we can find."

" 'Tis no need for you to come. I doubt this will be an easy trek."

"I'm coming with you." Anne slipped on her shoes.

Jamie slid the knife into his waistband, the tinderbox into his pocket and they started along the beach. When sand gave way to coral rocks, they climbed, still keeping to the shore. The west side of the cay, like what they could see of the interior was thickly vegetated with small scrub trees.

"Do you think any animals live here?" She accepted his help over a jagged rock; beneath them the ocean was much more energized than at the sheltered beach.

Jamie straightened and stared into the shadowed underbrush and trees. "I doubt it." He glanced down at her. "Sorry, no roast pork."

"I suppose that's what I was thinking. Pigs run wild over Libertia."

"Probably descendents of animals brought by some Spanish galleon."

"But you don't think a Spanish galleon ever found this place."

Hands on hips, Jamie stared out over the wide expanse of deep blue water. "It doesn't seem likely."

She knew he didn't say it but she felt he was answering her earlier question as well. Chances of anyone ever finding them were very remote. But Anne refused to dwell on that possibility. They were on land, with food to eat and hopefully fresh water to drink.

The captain spotted the small trickle of water seeping between the rocks. He dipped two fingers into the stream, and stuck them into his mouth, then smiled. "I think we've found it," he announced as he brushed away the dense underbrush that covered the water.

"It's cool." Anne cupped her hands, bringing the water to her lips. She sipped, then caught up in the feel of the clear liquid on her tongue, upended her hands splashing droplets over her face. Her laughter bubbled forth as sparkling as the small stream. It wasn't until she settled down on her haunches that she glanced up at the captain.

He stared at her, his eyes so intense and looking dark green in the shadowed light, that Anne sucked in her breath. She couldn't seem to break the pull of his gaze. The smile faded from her lips. Diamondlike droplets clung to her chin. In the background the ocean sang on, adding its eternal melody to the universe. And still they seemed caught in some mysterious trance.

It was Jamie who first broke away, releasing her. He let out a pent-up breath he hadn't even realized he held and gulped in another, then scrubbed both palms down across his face. "We best be on our way."

Scurrying to her feet, Anne rushed to catch up as he pushed forward, following the meander of the stream. He seemed impervious to the rough path, though he conquered it barefooted. Anne felt twinges of guilt wearing her shoes, when she wasn't engrossed in the more consuming question of what had happened between them. And why he hurried so now.

It seemed completely foreign to his nature, to tramp ahead so. It was all Anne could do to reach out and grab his naked arm. She pulled back the moment he turned. "Why did you stare at me like that?" She hadn't meant to ask that question. She simply wished to inquire why he was in such a hurry. But her mind obviously didn't have control over her speech.

After a moment he gave her a twisted smile. "Ye surprised me 'tis all."

"Surprised you?" He started walking again, eating up the ground with his long strides, and Anne darted after him. "You didn't think I would be excited about finding fresh water?" He stopped and turned so suddenly Anne almost plowed into his broad chest. She barely had time to back away.

"Nay, Annie. 'Tis that I didn't know ye could laugh." Or that the sight of her giggling in all innocent pleasure could affect him so.

She blinked. "Of all the ridiculous things to say! Of course I can laugh. Everyone can laugh. I do it all the time." Her eyes opened wider as he slowly shook his head.

Then with a shrug, Jamie forced himself to get back to the problem at hand. Finding the source of the water. From behind him he could hear Anne's occasional protest.

"I laugh all the time."

"In truth there has been very little to laugh about since I met you."

"Being marooned on a small boat in the middle of the ocean is not very amusing."

And then when he thought she was finished arguing with herself she yelled, "Constant grinning like some silly cat who lapped the cream is not a sign of good nature, you know." Because of her Jamie stepped into the clearing with that very grin plastered on his face.

"Looks as if we've found it," he announced, then stepped aside for Anne to get the full impact of the small pond of crystal-clear water. Trumpet-shaped scarlet flowers vined around the edge as if ready to herald their arrival.

"It's beautiful," Anne breathed, stepping forward into the shaded glade. "Where did the water come from?"

"An underground spring, I imagine." Jamie scooped some to his mouth, checking for potability.

"Well, I for one am thankful." Anne leaned forward and twirled her fingers in the cool liquid. "How far do you think we are from the beach?"

Standing, hands on lean hips, Jamie looked toward the

east. " 'Tis hard to say. We'll go back this way and find out."

"Yes, that's a good idea. Then we'll have to make a path. I suppose you can cut one out with the knife. And collect some sort of containers for the water." Anne wrinkled her brow. "Coconut shells will have to do at first until we can think of something else." Her expression brightened. "And a storage shed. We'll need something built near our shelter where we can store the water." She looked toward Jamie, obviously pleased with her suggestions. He merely stared back.

"We have storage for the water." He jerked a thumb toward the pond. "And there it be."

"Well, I . . ." Anne sucked in air that smelled exotic and mildly erotic. She ignored the scent. "I realize that's where the water is now. However, we need it closer."

"Why?"

Anne blinked. Few people ever questioned her orders. Partly because her ideas were usually correct, and partly because those around her didn't have the time or inclination to think of practical things. That task had fallen to her from the time she could remember. First with her parents, and then when she went to live with Uncle Richard and Arthur.

The citizens of Libertia, their minds full of lofty democratic ideals, had utilized Anne's talents to the fullest, putting her in charge of seeing that the island ran smoothly. While they lived their grand experiment.

With the exception of her parents' death and d'Porteau's devastating attack on Libertia, she'd never failed. She didn't intend to now.

Squaring her shoulders Anne faced the pirate. "If we

are to live here for any length of time, we need to behave like civilized people."

"Which means?"

"Building a storage shed for water." Anne turned and started to forge a path toward the beach. She heard him follow, imagined he shrugged in that offhand way he had. While she trudged, Anne tried to think of a foolproof argument for why they did need the water closer. Most of her reasons evaporated like smoke when after a short distance she broke through, stepping into the blinding sunlight onto the beach.

She didn't need to shift around to know the smug, self-satisfied expression on the captain's face. But she did anyway. Her chin notched up. "We shall need a path anyway."

"I've no problem with that."

"And some sort of shelter."

He shrugged and glanced around, squinting toward the treetops. "Nothing too fancy."

"Something sturdy enough to keep out the elements," Anne countered. My God, if he had his way they would sleep sprawled on the warm sand. An image sprang to her mind, of them lying, both naked to the night, gritty sand sticking to their entwined, sweat-slick bodies. She swallowed, forcing the thought aside. "I don't wish to sleep in the pouring rain."

"Nor do I."

"Good." Anne turned on her heel. "Then it's settled."

Except nothing was settled.

Jamie grimaced and clenched his jaw as she supervised the cutting of the palm fronds that would form their roof. Since he was near the top of a palm tree, having shimmied his way up, and she was giving unnecessary orders from the ground, he found it twice as annoying.

With a yelp she jumped out of the way just in time to avoid the broad leaf he let fall to the sand.

Construction of the shelter, which Jamie envisioned more as a lean-to type structure while Anne thought a square hut more the thing, was no easy task. By the time hunger drove Jamie to dive into the turquoise water, knife between his teeth, the roof he'd managed to fasten to the oars from the boat wasn't half the size of the plan she'd drawn in the sand.

"We need more room," Anne called after him as he disappeared beneath the water. With a sigh she glanced at the rough shelter he'd thrown together, a grimace darkening her face. There was barely room for both of them beneath the roof. And certainly no extra space between them. Which was fine, Anne assured herself, for she could sleep out under the stars. After all, she'd done it many times since going aboard the *Lost Cause*.

Just as long as it didn't rain.

While the captain fished for their supper, Anne set about making beds out of the dried seaweed that collected around the rock formations. She made certain to keep a strip of sand, no matter how narrow between the two mounds. When she was finished she looked around for something to use as a cover for the mattresses, but could find nothing.

"Tomorrow I'll start weaving mats," she mumbled, adding that to her mental list of things to do.

For now she gathered twigs and fallen branches, using some of the dried seaweed to catch the spark from the flint. She had a good fire going by the time the captain returned with a fish large enough to fed them both. To this main dish they added coconut meat, and crystal-clear water, each pronouncing their repast a feast.

If the captain noticed anything about the beds he didn't comment as he leaned back on his elbows and tilted his head to study the stars that came out while they ate. Anne sat stiff-backed watching the flicker of light and shadow from the fire play across him: the bold bone structure of his face; the plains and valleys of his body.

She'd always thought there was something savage about him, something wild, but never more so than now. He seemed to meld into his surroundings, the broad stretch of isolated beach, the untamed forest beyond. And the sea. Always the sea.

He shifted, the gold in his ear loop catching the light, and his eyes met hers. Even in the near darkness she could see their blue-green color, yet another link with the sea. Anne's heart thumped, and it was all she could do to breathe.

" 'Tis a good job ye did with the beds," he said, his voice low, blending with the eternal lap of the waves, the soft clatter of wind through the palms.

"Thank you." Anne's mouth was dry.

He pushed to his feet and without another word stretched out on one of the seaweed pallets. After he wriggled a bit to get comfortable he crossed his arms over his bare chest and shut his eyes. Within minutes his snores joined the symphony of night sounds.

Anne looked from him to the seaweed beside him, then back to him. True, there wasn't much space between, but then there didn't seem much need for any. After taking a deep breath Anne settled into her own bed. But it was a long time before she slept.

And even then her mind was filled with thoughts of the sinfully handsome pirate captain.

Chapter Thirteen

Sleeping late was becoming a habit Anne couldn't appear to break.

It didn't seem to matter how often she told herself that she would rise at first light, she still managed to wake to find the sun rising in the sky and the captain gone. On the third day on the island, like the other two, she found him swimming out by the rock formations. With the dolphin. Except for her stay-a-bed tendencies and the fact that she rose to the smell of fish cooking, Anne would have berated him for wasting time.

Not that he didn't work, Anne admitted to herself as she waded knee-deep into the water, scattering a covey of stiffly stepping herons. The previous day he hacked out a definite path to the pond. It wasn't as wide as Anne thought it might be, but there was a path. And since he only had her knife to work with, she gave him credit for an admirable job.

Anne splashed water onto her face and scrubbed down over her cheeks. By the time she finger-combed her hair and started back toward shore, Anne noticed the captain swimming her way. She braced herself for the sight of him emerging from the water. It still took her breath away. But at least she didn't let him know how much the sight of him dripping wet, his breeches clinging to him like a second skin, affected her.

As usual his spirits were good in the morning, a trait Anne found annoying.

"I think Lucy has decided to take up permanent residence here," he announced once onshore. He shook himself as thoroughly as any dog Anne had ever seen, then glanced out to where the dolphin arched out of the water.

"I imagine this is as good a place for her to stay as any," Anne responded without enthusiasm. She couldn't help thinking the captain spent too much time frolicking with the creature. Time he could use to accomplish something. She knew he credited the dolphin with saving their lives. Anne was less inclined to believe.

After pulling her jacket over her wet shirt Anne stepped into her shoes and followed the captain to their makeshift table. The fish was tasty; the water refreshing.

To keep her mind off the captain's bare chest, and the fact that the sun seemed to be bronzing it darker, and bleaching the hair lighter with each passing day, Anne started her mental list of things to do. It was growing to include such things as strengthening and expanding their shelter, which Anne still found too small, when the pirate leaned back and surprised her with his announcement.

"What do you mean today is a holiday?"

"I mean we should declare it one." He grinned at her. "Make it a day of thanksgiving."

Her brow arched. "You plan to spend time on your knees, thanking God?" Somehow she couldn't reconcile that vision with the pirate.

Apparently he couldn't either, for he leaned back and laughed, a sound that sent shivers down her spine.

"Nay," he chuckled. "Though I do believe today is the Sabbath, so if you're so inclined . . . He shrugged his powerful shoulders and left the rest unsaid.

"Is it Sunday?" A wave of sorrow passed through Anne when she realized she'd lost track of the days. From now on, she decided, she'd make a small mark on the largest palm each day.

"Aye." He smiled at her again after biting off a hunk of fish with his strong teeth. "A day of rest."

Anne didn't know whether to believe him or not about it being Sunday. But she didn't think they had time for a day of rest or a holiday, and told him so.

"And just what do ye think is so important that needs done?" He sat up and leaned toward her, his expression sober. "We have a shelter." Jamie ignored her mumbled, "of sorts." "A path to the pond." To Jamie's way of thinking, they'd taken care of the essentials.

"Well, for one thing, I thought we might begin drying fish today."

"Drying fish? What in hell for?"

His tone made Anne fold her arms. "Well, we have no salt to preserve them so . . . We do have sea salt. Do you think that would work?"

"I think 'tis foolish to bother. We have all the fresh fish we want."

What he said made sense. Except that Anne was a firm believer in squirreling things away in case of emergency. Experience had taught her that lesson. Her chin notched up. "What if something happens to you and you can't swim out to fish for us?" Anne thought her argument a good one and was gratified to see him nod slowly. She was confident there would be no more talk of taking the day to lie around on the beach.

" 'Tis a point ye have there, Annie." Jamie stood and stretched. "And one I've been remiss in ignoring."

"Good." Anne rose putting off cleaning the area for the moment in favor of explaining to him how she wanted the drying racks built. "I thought perhaps over there out of the way. We could dig a pit for the fire and then construct some sort of ledge where we could line up the fish. . . ." Anne stepped closer to him, her eyes narrowing. "Are you listening to me?"

His only response was to look down at her and grin.

"I don't think you heard a word I said."

"Ah, but that's where your wrong, Annie. You're worried I might be unable to bring in food, and ye be right in your concern. 'Tis possible that could happen. That's why it's time ye learn to swim."

"Swim?" Anne sputtered the word. "But I can't."

"And that's because ye've never been taught, I'll wager."

What was there to learn? You got into the water and either floated to the top, or as in Anne's case, sank to the bottom like a stone. She wasn't interested in swallowing choking amounts of salt water on such foolishness. "I haven't time," she told him, then turned to walk away.

But before she could take a step his hand clamped about her arm. "Now what are ye going to say needs doing?" His brow arched questioningly.

"Well there's . . . Anne began but stopped when he began shaking his head.

"There's plenty to eat. We've water to drink. A shelter's been built."

"Of sorts."

"Now, Annie, let's don't start denigrating me work."

"It isn't large enough . . . or sturdy enough." Anne glanced toward the roof on stilts because it was less disconcerting than staring into his sea-colored eyes.

Jamie studied the structure a moment, then shrugged. "Perhaps I could expand it a bit." He tightened his hold when she tried to slip away. "But not today." With one scooping motion he had a wriggling Anne in his arms.

"Put me down, you brute. No! What do you think you're doing?"

What he was doing was slowly walking into the surf. "Now, Annie," he said with a chuckle. "I don't believe ye want me putting ye down here."

He was right. Instinctively, as the water swirled higher and higher around his legs, Anne clung more tightly to his broad shoulders. "Take me back. Oh, please take me back."

"Now, Annie." Jamie slowed his pace when he stood waist-deep in the calm sea. "It seems to me that ye have an unnatural fear of the water."

"What's unnatural is swimming about like a fish." His laugh rumbled through his chest, vibrating into her body where she was pressed against him.

"I can see why ye might think so, but Annie, I assure ye it isn't true. Especially since, at least for a while we'll be living on this wee bit of land surrounded by water. Now try not to dig your fingernails quite so deeply into my arms."

"But you're trying to put me into the water."

"Aye, that I am." Jamie grimaced when her nails clawed deeper. "But ye can stand here with no trouble. And I won't let ye go till you're ready."

Since he was pulling her away from him, forcing her

feet into the water, it didn't appear Anne had any choice in the matter. Still, she persisted. "Do you swear?"

"Me word as a gentleman," he said with a grin.

The water crept up Anne's body. "You're no gentleman."

He seemed to take the insult good-naturedly, simply lifting a shoulder. "My word as a pirate then."

Hardly reassuring as pirates were notorious for not keeping their word, but it seemed the best Anne could do. Her feet were planted on the sandy bottom while warm water lapped at her breasts. The sensation was not unpleasant. Especially when the tall, powerful captain was close, his hands resting lightly on her shoulders.

They stood that way for so long with him grinning down at her that Anne wondered why she'd fought this so. That is until he suggested she dip her face into the water.

Her hands cupped, Anne decided to do the next best thing. Liquid dripped down her chin.

"Nay. Down under, like this." His hands skimmed lower on her arms as he squatted, plunging his head below the crystalline-green surface. He reemerged wet and blinking. "Just hold your breath and sink."

"I'd rather not."

"Now, Annie . . ."

Anne jerked her arms free. "I want no more of this foolishness," she said, taking a step toward shore.

"All right, ye don't have to stick your face under," Jamie conceded.

Anne hesitated. "We can just stand here?"

"For a bit." Jamie folded his arms. "Until ye feel comfortable."

"I'm perfectly comfortable." Anne started to cross her arms. "No, stop. What are you doing?" Again Anne was lifted off her feet, this time to be lowered until she lay on the water's surface. At least she would be lying if not for the arms that clung to the captain.

"I'm going to teach ye to float." Jamie unfastened her grip around his neck only to have her latch onto his arms. "Now ye have to trust me, Annie."

"But I don't," she insisted. "Put me down."

"Now, lass, you've hurt me feelings."

"What are you talking about? Oh!" Anne clutched his elbows tighter as he shifted, dipping her lower into the water.

"Saying ye don't trust me. After all we've been through." He actually did look as if his feelings were hurt. At least it seemed that way to Anne. "Who rowed day after day?"

"Following a dolphin."

"True enough. But it got us here, didn't it?"

"Yes," she finally admitted.

"Then to my way of thinking your trust is something I've already earned."

Anne took a deep breath, hoping it wouldn't be her last before plunging beneath the water. "What do you want me to do?"

"That's a good lass."

He smiled at her and Anne felt her toes curl under.

"Just relax." Jamie waited while she loosened her grip to lower her until she was nearly flat in the water, his arms cradling her body. She may have eased off her hold, but she was a long way from relaxing. Her arms and body were as stiff as a board. And each time the water lapped her shoulders she flinched.

Jamie had to admit to a bit of trouble relaxing himself. The water turned her shirt nearly transparent. Beneath the threadbare fabric, her breasts were rose-tipped, the nipples erect. His own body's reaction to holding her was intense.

But he'd asked her to trust him. And though her response fell short of complete confidence he didn't wish to shatter her faith in him.

So Jamie ignored his own desires and concentrated on her. "Pretend you're resting on the softest of feather beds."

Her eyes snapped to his. "There's but one difference between a mattress and the sea. I won't sink into a bed."

"The sea will hold ye up if ye let it." Jamie suppressed a moan as his gaze traveled down her body. "Now let yourself go limp." He waited a moment before complaining. "Do ye call that limp?"

"No, actually I call this entire exercise ridiculous." Anne struggled to get upright, but the captain countered her efforts.

"I've an idea," he said when she was again spread out on top the water, his arms supporting her. "Look up at the clouds and tell me what ye see."

She did as he said, her brows beetled in concentration. "Why, I see clouds," she finally said.

"Aye, they're clouds." Jamie tried to keep the frustration from his voice. "But what are they shaped like?"

"Clouds." Anne tried again to push her feet to the bottom, but with little success. The pirate seemed determined that she should lie atop the swells. He seemed equally determined that she find some mysterious shape in the clouds.

"Annie, haven't ye ever stared up at the sky and imagined ye saw a dragon, or a whale?"

"Of course not." Anne's lips thinned. "If there are

clouds, I wonder when it will rain, and how it will affect the sugarcane. I haven't time to pretend I see fish swimming toward the sun."

Jamie shook his head. "Poor Annie."

Anne flapped her arms, annoyed with his assessment of her. Annoyed period. "This is foolishness."

"Nay, Annie, that's where you've the wrong of it. 'Tis never a waste of time to see the beauty in things." Jamie let his gaze drift upward. "Now do ye see that cloud over to the east?" He waited for her eyes to obey. "It looks to me as if a trim-lined frigate is sailing across the heavens. Do ye see it, Annie? Do ye see the sails, unfurled and catching the breeze?"

"I see a cloud."

"Ah, but Annie, you're only looking with your eyes. Open your mind to see what is really there."

"May I go back to shore if I do?"

Jamie let his breath out slowly. "Aye," he finally said. "Spend some time really looking and I'll take ye back to shore."

Anne didn't bother to ask for his word. Not that she didn't trust it. That wasn't the case at all. Actually to her surprise she did believe him.

She also wanted to see the ship. To see the cloud as he saw it. Anne tilted her head, letting the warm water flow around her ears. And she studied the cloud. Its shape. The way it drifted like a giant cotton ball across the sky. But she didn't see sails, nor a hull, or anything else that remotely resembled a frigate.

Anne was just about to tell him so when something caught her eye. Her body relaxed as she looked more closely. "It isn't a ship," she announced. "It's a cow."

"A cow?"

"Yes, yes, look." Anne lifted her hand and droplets of water showered off her arm. "There's the head, and the body." She traced the shape with one wet finger. "There are even legs and a tail. Don't you see it?"

Jamie grinned broadly, though when she turned her head to look at him, his expression was sober and his attention riveted to the cloud in question. "Well now, lass, I do believe I can make out the shape you're describing."

"Of course you can." Anne stretched out more comfortably in his arms. "And over there," she said as the gentle swells soothed her body. "That's an angel. See her wings?"

"Aye, a beautiful angel," Jamie agreed, though he never lifted his eyes to the sky.

"Now over there's a ship. It looks something like the *Lost Cause,* don't you think?" Anne shifted slightly when the captain didn't answer and was surprised to see him standing nearly a rod away from her, his arms folded across his chest. Panic swept over her and she jerked and would have sunk if the pirate hadn't grabbed her. As it was water splashed over her face and she swallowed enough to send her into a coughing spasm.

"You said you'd hold onto me," Anne said when she could. "Are you trying to drown me?"

"Aye," Jamie agreed, standing her on her feet. " 'Tis my goal for all of this. I drown ye in four feet of water and then feast on your carcass. A steady diet of fish can be so boring."

Anne merely narrowed her eyes at his sarcasm. "You let go of me and I sank."

"You'd been floating on your own since ye started describing the cow."

"I . . ." Anne started to take issue with his statement,

but stopped. There was something about the way she'd felt, free and unrestrained, that changed her mind. Instead she tilted her head to the side, staring up at him, her eyes open wide. "How did you do that?"

" 'Twasn't me. Ye did it yourself." Jamie's brow lifted. "I told ye 'twas just a matter of relaxing."

"Yes, I know what you said, but . . ." A smile played with the corners of Anne's mouth. "Show me how to do it again."

After a few tries Anne was able to simply lower her head, let herself go and her feet drifted to the surface, her toes peeking out into the sunlight.

She made such a delectable picture, with her hair floating out around her face and the expression of contentment on her sweet face that Jamie could barely stand the temptation. Deciding he was better off staring at the clouds than frustrating himself, he lay back. Soon they were both floating on their backs, comparing different cloud formations.

"I don't understand how you can think that's a lamb," Anne said. "Where's the head? And what about a tail?"

"He's lost his head."

"What?"

"Aye, that's it. The poor lamb lost his head. That's why he's racing across the sky, trying to find it"

Anne giggled. "How did he lose it? A head is attached."

"Ah, but this one was removed by a wizard who cast a savage spell on the poor mite of a lamb, turning him into a headless beast."

"You're the beast to make up such gruesome tales." Anne laughed. But she listened avidly as he spun the tale, thinking that she could almost distinguish the wizard and headless lamb drift across the sky.

It was a hungry rumbling in her stomach that finally made Anne push her feet to the bottom and stand, breaking the spell. "My goodness, how long have we been floating about?"

Jamie twisted and dove beneath the water. When he surfaced he glanced toward the sun. "Most of the morning, I imagine."

"That's what I feared." Anne began trudging back toward shore. "We've wasted so much time."

"We've plenty of it," Jamie mumbled, not sure she even heard him until she stopped and turned about.

"That's true, isn't it? We'll never leave this island so we have every day for the rest of our lives."

"Now that's not what I was meaning." Jamie lifted her chin with a wet thumb.

"But it's true, isn't it? I'll never see my uncle again, or anyone else for that matter." He didn't answer, but then Anne didn't expect one. She didn't know what she wanted until the space between them seemed to evaporate. Anne wasn't sure how she ended up in his embrace, his strong arms wrapped around her. And she didn't really care.

His strength was what she needed. What she craved. When his mouth touched hers, she met it eagerly.

The cloud fantasy had offered some release from reality, but this, this exquisite madness, was so much more consuming. Anne snuggled closer, wrapping her arms about the strong pillar of his neck. Water lapped around their thighs, a sensual tease. And still the kiss deepened. His tongue mated with hers. Hot, wet, tempting beyond reason.

She wanted him. Wanted the oblivion. And what was stopping her? It wasn't as if they'd ever leave this island.

"Please." Anne twisted her head, separating their lips.

At the same time she pushed at his shoulders. "Please stop," she managed, and out of obedience or surprise, his arms dropped away from her body.

"This isn't what I want," she insisted, and wondered if he knew how much she lied. But he didn't say anything, just stood there as Anne splashed to shore.

That evening dinner was quiet . . . and uncomfortable.

Anne had built the fire and gathered coconuts while Jamie fished. When he returned she took the path to fill the shells they'd found with water. They'd both stayed busy avoiding each other as best they could on the small island. But now they sat with the flames flickering between them and the soft tropical night closing in.

And her gaze kept sliding toward his.

"I should apologize," Anne finally said when the silence became suffocating.

"Why?" He didn't even glance up.

Anne took a deep breath. "I made it seem this afternoon as if you . . . as if I . . ." Pushing to her feet Anne turned toward the whisper of the sea. She couldn't do this. "Never mind." Before she could take a step her arm was grabbed from behind and she was jerked around toward the pirate.

"Ye are going to have to face this sooner or later, Annie."

"I don't know—"

"Don't be trying to fool me or yourself." His fingers tightened. "I want ye. I've made no secret of it. And I'm wagering ye want me, too."

Anne started to deny it, but couldn't. He was staring

down at her, his eyes intense, and she could barely breathe.

"I'm not a patient man, Annie. But I won't be forcing ye either."

His hands fell away from her shoulders, and Anne missed his warmth. He was waiting for her to say something . . . anything. When she didn't he turned and stalked away.

He took the path leading across the island, and Anne told herself she was glad to have some time alone. She cleaned up their eating area, then settled down to stare out toward the sea.

"I'm not used to having someone always underfoot," she murmured to herself, then drew her knees up to her chin. "Now I can think."

But there was but one thing that filled her mind.

Jamie MacQuaid.

She was obsessed with him. His smell. His voice. The feel of his touch. Even his taste was vivid and strong in her mind. They were alone on a tropical island. Would most likely stay that way for the rest of their lives.

And he wanted her.

Anne hugged her legs, resting her cheek against the rough fabric of her breeches. Around her the night enveloped her like an obsidian cloak, making her feel alone and lonely. She tilted her head, wondering what he would do if she followed him. Knowing she wouldn't.

So she waited, listening for any sound that might herald his return. But there was nothing except the hypnotic ebb and flow of the sea and the occasional rattle of palms.

*   *   *

Glowing embers were all that was left of the fire when Jamie returned to the beach. He was foolish to leave. But he said he wouldn't force her, and leaving was the only way to assure that. So he walked and tried to think of something other than Anne Cornwall. An impossible task.

Now it was late, after midnight by the look of the stars. Jamie crept to the lean-to, hoping he was tired enough to lie beside her without dying of frustration.

She wasn't there.

Jamie's heart skipped a beat and he straightened, looking around and wondering where she could be. Damning himself for selfishly leaving her alone all evening. He didn't think at the time that anything could happen to her. But now that's all he could think of.

What if she decided to wade into the water and drowned? Or hell, there could be wild animals on the cay. Just because he hadn't seen any didn't mean none existed.

Jamie paced to the fire, then back, not knowing exactly what to do. He glanced toward the path. Had she followed him and gotten lost on the other side of the island? He took several steps that way, then hesitated and turned toward the beach.

At first he thought the dark shape was a piece of coral. Then he recognized Anne, snuggled up on her side. When he bent down and realized she was sleeping, he let out his breath.

She looked so small and defenseless, Jamie had another surge of guilt for leaving her alone. "Poor little princess," he whispered as he dropped to his knees by her side. The moonlight caressed her cheek, the straight line of her nose, and Jamie forced himself not to do the same.

He leaned forward to scoop her up . . . and realized her

eyes were open. In the near darkness they studied each other.

Then she reached up, wrapping her arm around his neck, and Jamie felt the blood pounding in his ears.

"You're right," she whispered.

"About what?"

Anne tugged him closer. "I do want you."

Chapter Fourteen

And oh, how he wanted her.

Jamie swallowed, staring down at her tumble of curls sugared by the sand, her sweet face, now tight with desire. Her body was enveloped in the voluminous shirt and rough breeches, but the sea and his imagination had revealed the sumptuous beauty beneath.

Oh yes, he wanted. His own breeches were full and heavy with that need. A need made more urgent by his earlier fear for her.

He'd wanted and he'd dreamed and he'd waited for this moment. So why did he hesitate? Why, when she slid her cool fingers against his burning skin did he pull back?

A pirate took what he wanted, after all.

"Captain?" The question, the uncertainty in her voice, made him look away.

"Why did you change your mind?" he asked when she propped herself to sitting.

"Change my . . ." Anne shook her head, not truly understanding the question or even why he asked. "I didn't, not really. You were right this afternoon. I wanted you then." Anne took a deep breath. "You must have known that."

His only response was to stare at her, stare at her so boldly, that even in the dim light, Anne could feel the intensity in those sea-green eyes. She tucked up her legs, hugging them to her.

When he still said nothing, Anne broke the silence. "I don't understand. I thought you . . . I thought this is what you desired."

"It is. It has been since the first time I saw you."

Warmth flowed through Anne at his admission.

"Ye stood before me all cool beauty and passion for your cause, and you reminded me of . . ." His voice drifted off and a wry smile touched his lips. He wouldn't dwell on his other life. On the man he used to be. "When I saw you in the street, when you seduced me, I thought I'd been given a glimpse of heaven."

"And I drugged you."

"I'd have done the same, Annie," he said with a bit of his usual aplomb.

"So I don't understand."

"Why I haven't stripped those ridiculous breeches from your wondrous body by now?"

Anne couldn't see his expression but she imagined the cocky lift of his brow, the grin. "Yes, I suppose that's what I mean."

With a grunt he settled onto the sand beside her. "I don't know for certain myself." He laughed then. "Mayhap the tropical sun has finally fried me brain." His voice sobered. " 'Tis just that we may be here for a very long time, and I want ye to be sure. I shouldn't have wandered off tonight and left ye alone. Don't think it was some punishment for rejecting me."

"You think that's why I said that I wanted you? So you wouldn't leave me alone again?"

Jamie stretched out, elbow bent, chin cupped in his palm. "It did cross my mind."

"It's not the reason." Anne was glad for the intimacy of the night. Without its concealing curtain she might not be able to speak so freely. "I admit to being a bit angry when you left. But being alone gave me a chance to think."

"About me?" He sounded almost hopeful and Anne smiled.

"Yes . . . and about me. You were right about the path to the water, and the storage. We don't need it."

"That's what ye thought about?"

Anne's laugh drifted out to sea on a gust of wind. "Not entirely. I also remembered how you taught me to float and look at the clouds. I'd never done that before. . . . I never thought I had time."

Jamie filtered sand through his fingers and waited for her to continue. It didn't take long.

"On Libertia it was important that someone be in charge of the daily activities. The sugar works. Assigning duties in the fields." She shrugged. "Everything. Uncle Richard had more important things to think about. And Arthur, well, Arthur is like his father in some ways."

"So ye did it all."

"I'm not complaining. Actually, I enjoy making certain that everything works well. But it does take a great deal of time." Her tone softened. "Thank you for showing me the clouds."

" 'Twas my pleasure, Mistress Cornwall."

Anne leaned forward, feeling very bold, but unable to

stop herself. He lay perfectly still as she brushed her lips across his.

"Have ye thought about the possibility of our being rescued?"

"Yes." Her breath mingled with his, and though he tried to seem aloof, Anne could hear the proof that he wasn't immune to her in the strained timbre of his voice.

"Next week, hell, tomorrow, a vessel could come sailing into the bay. And what if 'tis a British ship of the line? You'd be saved, and I'd be hanged, and ye'd be sorrier than ye know that ye let me have my way with ye."

Anne pulled away only enough to see the glitter of his eyes. To wish she were closer to him. "What you say is possible, I assume." Anne sighed. "So perhaps I should have my way with you instead." That said Anne pressed against him, wrapping her arm around his neck and touching her tongue to the seal of his lips.

He tried, but couldn't resist such sweet torture. Jamie's groan vibrated through his hard chest into hers. He opened his mouth, kissing her now as he had before, with passion and wanting and delicious desire.

They rolled together onto the beach, Anne welcoming the captain's heavy weight. His tongue thrust deep in her mouth, the sensation spiraling through her body, pooling heavy and molton at the juncture of her thighs. She could barely breathe, and found she didn't care.

It wasn't until he pulled away, resting his forehead on hers that she could suck in a ragged breath. "Oh, my," she gasped. "Oh, my."

"Oh, my, 'tis right." His own voice was as raspy as hers.

He flattened his palm over her breast, shaping it, abrading the sensitive nipple against the rough linen. And her legs spread, allowing him to slide between. Allowing his hard maleness to slide over her.

His mouth skimmed over her jaw, biting, soothing. Anne arched back, giving him greater access to her neck, loving the feel of his beard, of his mouth on her skin. Everywhere he touched her she burned.

When the coarse fabric of her shirt blocked his progress he ignored it, wetting the linen, clamping his mouth over her nipple.

Anne's fingers dug onto the raw silk of his hair, holding him to her. Her mind, her body, was swamped with sensation and she couldn't stay still. She writhed and whimpered, wordlessly begging for something she didn't understand.

Then his hands were at her waist, his long, clever fingers untying the length of rope holding up her breeches. Soft island breezes caressed her stomach, the skin covering her hips as he inched down her pants. When his hand covered the tight curls guarding her woman-hood, Anne gasped with pleasure.

"So pretty," he murmured. Two fingers slid through the down, touching, igniting a spark that made Anne cry out.

"Did I . . . ?" Jamie could barely catch his breath. And forming words seemed an impossible task. "Are ye hurt?"

"No." Anne grabbed for his hand, pressing it back where it had been. "You didn't hurt me."

"But I will." Jamie bent down to brush his whiskered chin across her belly. "The first time, I can't help it." The scent of her body drew him lower. "Oh, Annie." He drew his mouth across the smooth skin of her stomach, caught in the spell of her.

Jamie pulled away long enough to tug off her breeches,

and then his own. Her shirt was next to go, leaving her naked and wanting as he lowered her gently back to the gritty sand.

Ah, Annie," he said as his palm skimmed down her body. "I want to be slow with ye, and gentle." He caught his breath when she arched into his hand. "But I don't know that I can."

"Then take me as you will." Anne's hands rode the crest of his brawny shoulders as he lowered himself between her legs. She could feel the heat and power where his hardness throbbed against her inner thigh. It frightened her. It excited her.

And then it was his mouth inching up as it had that night when she drugged him. But tonight there was nothing to stop him and she moaned, deep in her throat when his tongue found the tight bud of sensation. "Oh, Captain," she managed, only to have him lift his head.

" 'Tis Jamie," he rasped, his breath fanning her tight curls.

"Jamie," she said, repeating the name until the exquisite torture made speech impossible. Her breathing came between exquisite moans and still he tormented, spearing her with a rhythm that opened a dam of pleasure, bursting forth in wave after wave. She writhed, unable to keep her thighs from spreading for him.

Jamie poised above her, allowing himself a moment of anticipation. She was hot and wet, the tremors still racking her body. He thrust forward until he met the barrier of her maidenhood, then arched, impaling her. She stiffened and he stopped, holding himself on bent arms.

"There was nothing I could do to keep from hurting ye," he whispered into the soft skin beneath her ear.

"It's all right . . . really." The pain had been sharp, but

quickly gone. Now Anne felt only a fullness that was not unpleasant. She tilted her hips, and the anticipation of erotic sensation was fulfilled. His hands dug beneath her buttocks, lifting them, lifting sand, and instinctively she wrapped her legs around his muscular thighs.

He drove deeper, rocking her body, sending her higher as each thrust set off a shower of sparks behind her closed eyes.

The ecstasy built, white hot and frantic, until Anne wondered if she could stand it longer without fragmenting into a thousand pieces, like the sand that covered the shore. She could no longer think, no longer control the cries that passed her lips. Her fingers opened and closed, alternately clutching his tautly muscled shoulders and thin air. She was consumed. And still he drove her higher.

When his mouth locked with hers, the explosion came. Overwhelming in its power, blinding in its intensity. Anne could do naught as the surge of pleasure swept her up, shattering her.

Her body convulsed around his staff, snapping his hard-won control. Jamie's thrusts became frenzied and he erupted within her with a ferocity that he wasn't prepared for. With a wild cry he collapsed, his face buried in the sweep of soft, sweet-smelling curls.

Reality returned slowly. Gone was the urgency of moments before. Now Anne felt complete and satiated like never before. His fullness still filled her. His chest and shoulders flattened her, grinding her deeper into the unyielding sand. She should have been uncomfortable. But she wasn't. Even though her breathing was shallow, she didn't want him to leave her. She lifted her arms, languidly wrapping them around his shoulders. His skin was slick with sweat, and smooth.

She could stay like this forever.

But the captain . . . Jamie had different ideas. Anne keened in protest when he rolled off her, but her dissatisfaction was short-lived as he took her in his arms, cuddling her close.

They slept then, caressed by the tropical breezes, canopied by the stars.

It was the strong feeling that someone watched her that made Anne slit her eyes open. Her smile was slow and sensual as memory and the expression on Jamie's face brought her to full awakening. His chin was propped up on bent elbow and he watched her with something akin to fascination.

Anne reached up and touched his cheek above the line of whiskers.

"I've a mind to teach ye to swim," he said before turning his face and kissing the tender underside of her wrist.

Her skin tingled where his mouth touched and for a moment, what he said didn't register. When it did, Anne sat up, knocking him away in the process. "I can't swim. I don't even like being in the water."

"Ye enjoyed floating." He was back feasting on her skin, this time the sweet line of her neck. "Ye told me so last night."

She would have told him the sky was green last night, though he was right, floating was wonderful. But it also didn't involve sticking her face into the water. And she'd watched the way he dove beneath the surface, moving his body like a fish.

"I can't do it," was all she said, as the soft whisper of his whiskers trailed lower along her collarbone.

"Which is why we shall start our lessons."

"Now?" Anne's head fell back, her hair, sprinkled with sand, tickled the base of her spine.

"Soon," Jamie promised as his mouth clamped over the already distended crest of her bosom.

His tongue teased the tip, then he pulled away, his thumb taking up the delicious swirling. "You're sandy," he said. "And so am I."

What did something as insignificant as sand have to do with anything? Anne's body arched toward his touch.

But he stopped the sensual movements of his hands and mouth and stood, reaching down to pull her to her feet. Anne didn't understand his intent. His arousal was thick and heavy, the burning desire in his green eyes, obvious. But he was pulling her toward the water.

"No, Jamie," Anne protested but he wouldn't stop until their feet splashed into the gentle surf. "Please."

"Ye need to be cleaned off, Annie. And as much as I'd like to explore every inch of your sand-covered body, I don't think 'tis a good idea. You'll be sore enough after last night without adding sand to your misery."

"I'm not sore . . ." Anne insisted, but as she walked, she admitted to herself at least that there was slight discomfort between her legs.

He pulled her deeper, the water teasing her knees, then her hips. But it didn't cool the desire, the heat he'd sparked with his touch. It did soothe. Warm water against naked skin. She didn't resist at all when he tugged her away from shore. When the turquoise liquid lapped about her breasts.

He stopped then, cupping his hands and trickling water over her shoulders, watching the droplets, his eyes smoky with desire as they rolled down her skin. He skimmed gentle fingers down her body, washing away the encrusted sand, igniting the flames. His touch lingered on her nipples, his thumbs beading the tips until Anne moaned.

"Bend your head back."

His voice was husky and deep and Anne obeyed, letting her hair float out around her face. He stepped between her legs, pressing his hard staff against her womanhood as he reached around and finger-combed the sand from her curls.

Anne's back arched, her toes barely found purchase in the sandy bottom. If not for his arms holding her, his muscular thighs anchoring her body, she would have floated to the surface. As it was her breasts lifted, wet and thrusting above the water.

Jamie couldn't resist licking the salty brine from her nipples.

"Perhaps my suggestion of a bath wasn't as unselfish as I thought," he murmured as he drew her lower body against his.

Anne instinctively spread her legs wider, wrapping them securely around his. The hands that moments before tangled in her hair, now moved down to support her back, lifting her up toward him. Her breasts skimmed the damp fur on his chest. He held her high, her thighs around his, his swollen manhood pressed to her stomach. He was hot and hard, and Anne clung to his shoulders as her hair dripped water down her back.

"Are ye sore, tell me true, Annie. For I want no part in hurting ye again."

She could barely think with his staff throbbing between them, but she knew the ache she felt would not go away until he was deep inside her. She told him as much, her voice muffled by the kisses she rained over his eyes and nose. "But how?" she asked, grabbing onto his shoulders when he laughed, a deep booming sound that vibrated through her body.

"We shall find a way, my practical Annie. We shall find a way."

He lifted her then, his muscles bulging from the strain, until he could reach out and take a nipping bite at her breast. Anne squealed and wriggled closer, following his urgent commands to spread her legs further.

"Around like this. Ah, Annie. Ye feel so good."

"Mmmm." Anne could only moan her agreement as she settled onto his impaling hardness.

His open mouth tasted her skin, the sweet curve of her breast and Jamie thought he might keel over from the pleasure of it. "I've had fantasies of this," he admitted, clamping his hands around her hips and lifting her. Gravity brought her back until she accepted all of him. He shifted her again, and this time Anne wriggled down, eliciting a deep, heartfelt moan from the captain.

"Annie, lass, you're a fast learner, ye are."

"I . . . I do my best." By now Anne had discovered she could help pull herself up along his hair-roughened chest. The slippery feel of him was so intoxicating she barely noticed when he told her to hold her breath. The order registered as he bent his knees, plunging them both beneath the warm, caressing water.

Anne sputtered as they shot up, still intimately joined, to continue their sensual dance among the swells. His hands moved lower, clutching her buttocks and separating them for his aggressive thrusts. They dipped beneath the water again, but this time Anne barely noticed, so wild was she with wanting, so close to the maelstrom he'd shown her last night.

She sank down hard and his fingers reached lower, dancing across flesh sensitized by his invasion. And Anne lost her hold on reality. Spasms of pleasure seized her, tightening her thighs, raking her with pure sensual sensations.

His body stiffened, then as he exploded inside her, his knees buckled and they both sank into the water. When they reemerged, his lips were sealed to hers. They broke off the kiss when the need to breathe became too great. As they each sucked in air, their eyes met. Their laughter burst out simultaneously and so hard that their limbs grew weak.

"Did you really have fantasies about . . . about that?" Anne asked as Jamie set her down, holding onto her shoulders while she got her footing.

"Aye. But in my daydreams it wasn't so hard on my knees." He grinned. "Not that I'm complaining, mind ye."

"No, I didn't think you were."

"Actually, I think with a bit of practice we can master this technique."

"I've no doubt about your abilities," Anne said with as serious an expression as she could. But again when their gazes locked, sobriety gave way to mirth.

"Well, practice we may need, but it won't be now that we're getting it." Jamie took her hand and started wading back toward shore.

"Why not?" Anne stuck out her lower lip in a pout. A pout he quickly took advantage of as he bent around and gave her a hard, fast kiss.

"For one thing, my apt student, ye really will be sore if we don't take a bit of a rest."

"How long?"

Anne smiled as his face whipped around toward hers. She actually shocked him.

"I should think a day would do it."

Anne let out her breath on a sigh. "Well, I suppose if you insist."

"I do." The water played around their ankles now and she stood before him naked in the sunlight. The skin usually covered by her clothes was pale, like ivory silk, and slightly puckered from their stay in the water. Her breasts were small but full, with the most delectable pink-tipped nipples that tasted as luscious as they looked.

Jamie caught himself as his gaze roamed lower to the swell of her womanly hips and the tight curls that shielded her sex. With a jerk he raised his head, realizing his own sex was swelling and that there was nothing to stop her from noticing.

Actually she seemed quite taken by the phenomenon, watching him, her eyes wide, her delectable mouth open.

"No more today," he said, catching her chin with his thumb and lifting her face toward his. She merely smiled, a smile he didn't know her capable of smiling. The tip of her tongue peeked out, licking her lips and Jamie nearly dropped to his knees.

It was all he could do to turn and walk toward the spot where they slept last night. With jerky motions he yanked on his breeches, then moved to their shelter to find the knife. Without looking her way he raced toward the surf. "I'll catch us some breakfast," he called back, before splashing face first into the water.

He just hoped to goodness she did something to cover herself before he returned.

* * *

By a week later, August seventh to be exact, for Anne still kept a series of carved notches on the largest palm tree, they'd settled into a routine of sorts. By unspoken agreement Jamie fished and cleaned whatever he caught. Anne started the fire with the wood they both gathered, and she fetched the water. Obtaining coconuts was no problem. And cooking seemed to be a "whoever was near the fire" chore.

Anne complained that he roasted his catch too quickly, searing the outside and leaving the inside not evenly done. "It takes patience and an orderly turning of the spit to cook the fish correctly," she told him one evening. But her argument lost its appeal when he laid the fish aside on the palm frond they uses as a plate.

"Aye, and 'tis true," he said advancing on her step by deliberate step as she sat watching his approach. "But how can I linger over a dead-eyed fish when 'tis ye I want most to devour?"

Proper cooking, the fish, dinner, were all forgotten as he showed her how thoroughly he meant what he said.

Anne no longer nagged about their shelter. It appeared he was right anyway. They needed only the minimal roofing, certainly nothing wider then their entwined bodies . . . and often not even that. Many nights they fell asleep under the stars, satiated and happy. With Anne's head resting on Jamie's shoulder, his voice as he pointed out different constellations, vibrating in her ears.

They'd slept that way last night and Anne woke in a bed of dried seaweed to stretch her hands high above her head. It was late, by the position of the sun, she guessed nearly ten, but Anne no longer chastised herself for her stay-a-bed tendencies. As Jamie said, "There was plenty of time left in the day to do whatever needed doing."

Leaning up on her elbows she squinted out over the diamond-splattered water, searching for Jamie. He was by nature an early riser, and spent his mornings swimming, frolicking with Lucy, and occasionally fishing.

Anne decided the dolphin was the pet he never had, and though her own parents never kept dogs or even cats, she didn't feel the pull to connect with Lucy. That wasn't why she planned to swim out to the end of the rocks today.

Anne pushed to her feet and lifted her hands lazily over her head. Then with a quick motion she yanked off the captain's shirt, and ran naked toward the surf. Warm water tickled up over her feet, then calves as she splashed forward, diving under when it reached her waist.

He taught her to swim with a patience he didn't give to cooking. Slowly, lovingly, he showed her how to hold her breath, then blow out through her nose. How to open her eyes to the beauty beneath the surface, and to sweep her arms forward, and undulate her legs to propel herself through the water.

As in most things she did, Anne was an adept student. She could now dive and float about, holding her breath, then popping her head above the surface to gulp air and laugh. But she hadn't gone past the security of the shoreline.

The pirate hadn't tried to force her, though she knew he wished her to swim out farther with him. He would come back from his daily excursions with tales of the wondrous, rainbow-colored fish he saw. Or describe Lucy's antics in such vivid detail, that she knew he embellished, trying to make the adventure seem more tantalizing. More unmissable.

But it wasn't the adventure that lured Anne toward the

coral rocks. It was the pirate captain himself. As odd as it seemed. As incomprehensible as it was a mere fortnight ago, Anne wanted to please him. To witness his smile of pride when she reached him.

Anne paddled her way to the surface and worked her arms and feet the way he taught her to stay up. She'd been practicing, inching her way out beyond where she could touch bottom. Not far beyond. But far enough to know she could do it . . . for long periods of time, if necessary.

Anne's toes twitched with the desire to feel sand beneath them. And she wondered just how far down she'd have to drop to find solid ground. But she didn't attempt to find out. Instead she slowly moved in a circle, quickly shading her eyes, then windmilling her hands back into the water when she felt herself sinking.

The glare made it difficult to see, so she squinted her eyes. But she still couldn't find Jamie. Yelling for him was an option, but Anne dismissed it as silly. She could swim further. She could swim to the rocks. Then wouldn't he be surprised when he saw her there.

Diving back beneath the surface Anne struck out toward the formation that formed the boundary of what she thought of as their harbor. Lucy swam around the area. Anne often sat onshore and watched the dolphin arc into the air and land with a playful splash. Jamie most often was with her, especially in the morning.

The next time Anne surfaced it took her longer to catch her breath. Her arms were beginning to feel as if she were dragging several cannonballs with her. And she had to concentrate on keeping her leg motions slow. Flailing about would only make her sink. She didn't want to sink.

Anne swallowed down the panic, along with a dose of seawater that sent her into a coughing spasm.

Stay calm. She could almost hear the captain's voice giving her the advice.

She could do it. But first she would rest. Leaning her head back, Anne allowed her body to float to the surface. Relax. She studied the clouds, wondering why she couldn't find a single discernible shape to any of them, then twisted around to swim some more.

She sank lower than she wished, then frantically shoved her way to the surface, gulping air and more seawater. She jerked around to look toward the shore, then the rocks, trying to decide which was closer.

The rocks won.

Wishing it weren't so, Anne took a deep breath and headed toward the formation. She thought of the captain as she forced her arms to pull through the water. Of the way he looked. His smell. His taste. Of where he might be this very moment.

But though she pulled herself up often to look, there was no sign of him.

Still, the coral rocks loomed larger and with a sob of victory Anne lowered her head and body and surged forward.

It was then she saw the gray shape swimming toward her. Lucy, she thought, and experienced a shiver of relief mixed with fear. The dolphin for all her fun-loving ways did not know Anne. It was Jamie she doted on. Jamie she protected.

Would she even care what happened to Anne?

The question became moot, and the twinge of fear

became overpowering when Anne realized her mistake. It wasn't Lucy at all undulating its way toward her.

She opened her mouth to scream and choked on seawater.

Chapter Fifteen

The jacket slung over his shoulder to form a pouch was bulging with conch shells to make Anne's dinner. Jamie whistled as he sauntered along the sandy path toward what he was beginning to think of as home. He woke earlier than usual this morning and wandered off toward the far side of the island, deciding to dive for the savory mollusks.

Because Annie was fond of them. He brought them several times before, and each time she relished their meat roasted in the coals. The last time, day before yesterday, she admitted, the conch was her favorite island meal. She liked it even better than the green turtle soup they made.

Enough incentive to send him diving into the rougher waters off the rock-littered western coast.

Jamie stopped whistling the Scottish folksong as this last thought caught hold. He was growing fond of her . . . more than fond. Jamie didn't give a name to the feelings that swelled within him at the thought of Annie, but he knew they were strong enough to send him foraging around the sea bottom for these large snails he didn't even like.

Strong enough, too, to make him hope she was awake. Or wonder if she'd mind if he brought her into the day with a kiss or so. The thought brought a smile to his face and a stirring to his groin as Jamie stepped into the early-morning sunshine.

One glance told him the beach was deserted. Good, she was up. As someone who'd always enjoyed his first view of day early, Jamie found it amusing how Anne preferred to ease into it. She'd stretch her delectable body, yawn, and slowly open those big, golden brown eyes.

Jamie sighed. His arousal was more than a mere twitch, now, and since she was already awake they might as well make the most of it. He set the jacket pouch on the sand near the burned-out fire, then glanced toward the forest as she liked to call the stretch of dense vegetation that formed the island's interior.

Anne now considered it her job to collect wood each day. She chose only dead limbs she found on the ground and brought them back, stacking them neatly beneath the overhang of the lean-to. To keep them dry, she informed him one day in that no-nonsense way she sometimes had. Jamie's chuckle scattered a gull who showed too keen an interest in what lay beneath Anne's ragged jacket. Jamie was even beginning to like the woman's bossy ways . . . as long as he kept them in check, he added to himself.

"Annie," he called, losing patience. "There be a pirate waiting for ye with a powerful hunger for the taste of your lips." He listened for the sound of her laughter to drift to him on the breeze that always swept the cay.

His first inkling that something was amiss came when he heard nothing but the squawking gulls and the rattle of palm fronds over the backdrop of surf. She never wandered far from the beach when she collected firewood. He called again, this time cupping his hands to his mouth. He was used to yelling loud enough to be heard over the din of battle. There was no way she couldn't know he called her.

Jamie turned full circle. Looking. Stopping, his jaw dropping when he caught sight of her, her head barely above water, near the rocks.

Before his mind could begin to comprehend what she was doing out there, by herself, Jamie was splashing into the surf. He dove beneath the surface, driving his hands through the water and pulling back with all his strength. She wasn't a strong swimmer, by God. He pushed to the surface to take a breath and get his bearings. Then kicked back under.

What in the hell did she think she was doing? Jamie's heart pounded, and he knew it wasn't all from exertion. If anything happened to her . . . Jamie wouldn't allow himself to complete that thought as he knifed smoothly through the clear swells.

She'd be all right. He repeated the thought again and again in his mind, like a litany. She'd float until he could reach her. Jamie lifted his head to yell for her to do just that.

And saw the dorsal fin slice through the water between them.

His hand clamped over the knife handle tied to his waist. His fingers shook so out of fear for her that they slipped, and he almost dropped the weapon. But he managed to hold on. Ducking beneath the water he wove around behind the shark, hoping he could get close enough before it was too late.

Before the predator tired of stalking Anne and moved in for the kill.

* * *

Anne's arms felt like lead and her legs could barely move. It seemed with each second that passed her head slipped a bit further into the water.

And still the shark circled her.

Anne took her eyes off the sleek gray shape to gaze longingly at the rocks to her right. If she could just strike out and swim there, perhaps she could climb. . . . The notion lingered just out of reach as she jerked her sights back to the shark.

What if she tried to leave the swirling prison and it attacked? Or what if she swam into its path as she made her escape? Or what if she couldn't make it at all, and . . . ? There were so many ifs, they seemed to paralyze her.

And then from the corner of her eyes she sensed a movement. Her heart lifted only to plummet lower than the sea floor.

"Go back, Jamie," she yelled, coughing when water splashed into her mouth. "There's a shark!"

"Be still." Jamie stopped worrying about sneaking up on the mammoth fish and surged forward.

"No, Jamie." Tears poured from Anne's eyes, mingling with the salt water already dripping from her hair. "No. . . ."

He was perhaps five rods from Anne and the shark when Jamie ventured another look. What he saw made his blood run cold. With a frenzy Jamie began slapping the water and kicking. Anything to make a distraction.

He was coming at her. Anne held her breath, her eyes wide as she saw the giant mouth gaping open, showing row upon row of sharp jagged teeth. Closer and closer it came until the sight of the yawning aperture consumed her full vision.

So this was how her life was to end. Anne sucked in her breath wishing she'd had more time with the pirate, wishing many things. Most of all that he didn't sacrifice himself for a lost cause. That he would swim back to shore as quickly as he could.

Anne shut her eyes unable to face the awful truth. The monster mouth. And she waited. And waited.

Water surged around her and Anne's eyes popped open in time to see another shape, this one brownish with elongated spots shoot toward the shark.

Lucy.

The dolphin emitted a shrill whistle as she plunged full-force toward Anne's attacker. The dolphin's prominent snout bashed into the predator's side, knocking it off its course . . . and gaining Lucy the shark's attention. The sun shone off its teeth as the shark turned toward Lucy. Anne thought the dolphin would pay with its life as the shark lunged toward her. But before teeth could connect with flesh the dolphin dipped, contorting itself about and swimming beneath the charging shark.

But the shark was also an agile swimmer, and it was in a feeding frenzy. This time when the dolphin attacked, the shark twisted, meeting her head-on. There was a loud thump as their bodies hit, and then the sound of Jamie yelling for her to get away.

Frantic now, Anne flailed her arms, moving as quickly as she could toward the outcroping of coral. The thrashing of the shark and dolphin sent the water boiling, the swells higher. Anne arched her neck trying to see above the foam, trying to find Jamie. She'd lost sight of him, and hoped he was on the rocks by now. But just as that thought caught her imagination she heard a loud roar.

Twisting her head she saw him, arm raised, body poised beside the shark. Anne screamed, but it did no good. The captain slashed at the sea monster, slicing into the shark's back with the knife.

Crimson stained the turquoise.

When the mighty fish plunged beneath the surface, Jamie followed it.

Anne could see nothing now. Not Jamie, nor the shark, nor the dolphin. It was as if suddenly they all decided to leave her in peace. Yet there was no peace. Not knowing what else to do Anne continued toward the rocks. When she was close she kicked. Catching her foot on a sharp protrusion, but ignoring the pain she scurried up the outcrop and turned to scan the water.

Where was he? Why didn't the captain resurface? Anne didn't want to think of the reasons. She didn't want to think at all.

Then from her position above the water she spotted them. Jamie faced the counterattacking shark, which was unmistakably trailing blood. As before Lucy propelled herself at the shark's flank when it made a rush at the captain.

The force of the dolphin's headlong impact left the shark slow and listless in the water. But more importantly, again facing Lucy. Jamie didn't need an invitation to seize the moment. He lunged with the knife, driving the blade deeply behind the shark's gills, then pulled smartly to open a long, deep wound. This roused the large shark from its doldrums and it swam haltingly out to sea, blood gushing from its wounds.

"Jamie! Jamie!"

He appeared dazed, but her cries finally seemed to register and he moved her way.

"Are ye all right, Annie?" he called, his voice breathless. He stopped abruptly as he climbed onto the rocks. "My God, did it bite ye?"

At first Anne didn't know what he meant, then she glanced down at her foot and saw the blood. The sight surprised her because she honestly didn't feel anything. But she did remember kicking the sharp coral. "It's just a scratch, from the rocks," she told him, wincing when he scrambled up the jagged rocks to grab her foot. Now she could feel it. "It's nothing, really," Anne insisted. "Are you . . . ?" Emotion clogged her throat and she couldn't continue. She reached down, her fingers skimming his water-slick hair.

When he looked up Anne thought she might drown in the blue-green depths of his eyes. Her fingers traced down his cheek and he turned, pressing his mouth against her salty skin.

"We have to get back to the cay," he said.

Anne couldn't help it. She glanced toward the water, then shook her head. Her voice was small. "I can't."

"Ye must." He reached up grabbing her chin when she would have shaken her head again. "Ye must and ye can, Annie." His gaze caught her and it was as if he imbued her with his strength.

"I can help ye, but ye must help yourself, too."

Anne took a deep breath, trying to stave off the tears that lay just beneath the surface. He was so strong and intrepid, and she wouldn't appear the coward in front of him. She wouldn't. Anne swallowed. "All right," she said, forcing her voice to be steady. "I can do it."

"That's my lass," he said and smiled.

And Anne thought her heart would burst.

In that moment she realized she'd do anything for him . . . or die trying.

But making herself slide back into the water was harder than she thought it would be. The memory of the shark, its jagged-toothed mouth, tore at her confidence. When she caught sight of a dark shape undulating through the water, Anne gasped.

" 'Tis but Lucy."

Other memories flooded back. Of the dolphin attacking the shark, giving her time to escape. "Is she all right?"

"Aye." Jamie grinned as he reached out a hand to help her into the sea. "She's a tough old bird," he said. As if the dolphin heard the compliment and the warmth behind the words, she lifted her long snouted head above the water and emitted a series of clicking noises.

Pushing away from the rocks, Anne laughed nervously. "It's almost as if she's talking to us."

"Perhaps she is."

There were times during the swim back to shore that Anne wondered if she could go on. Fatigue washed over her as steadily as the swells of warm water. But whenever she thought her arms couldn't move, or her feet couldn't kick, the captain was there with something amusing to say. Besides, she knew after his battle with the shark, he must be as weary as she. So she kept going.

They were both breathless as they stumbled ashore, collapsing to their knees, then rolling face up onto the sand. Side by side they lay, waiting for their hearts to stop pounding.

Jamie twisted his head to look at her, and Anne did the same. For a moment they simply stared, then as if a dam broke, began laughing. After jerking the knife from his waistband and tossing it aside, Jamie shifted toward her, leaning on his elbow.

"Just what were ye doing out there, by yourself?" His question might have seemed harsh except for the gentle expression on his face and the caress of his fingertip.

"I . . . I wanted to surprise you."

"Well, ye sure as hell did that."

"I know it was foolish, but I'd been practicing and I wanted to show you how well I could swim, but you weren't there." Anne gulped air after delivering that speech.

"I was on the lee side of the island, diving for conch."

"But you don't like conch."

He grinned. "Ye do." Jamie's palm curved around her cheek. "But we were talking about ye."

"I've told you most everything. I swam out, and got very tired. And then the shark came, and it seemed like forever that it circled me. Almost as if it knew my fear and toyed with me." Anne's eyes narrowed. "Do you think that's possible?"

Jamie's shrug was noncommittal. "I can't say, Annie, but I do know this." He let his breath out slowly, deliberately. " 'Tis glad I am that you're safe." Jamie lowered his head, anticipating the moment when their lips would meet. He tasted her surrender, and the remnants of fear, and the kiss deepened.

Anne's arms locked around his neck, holding on as if she'd never let him go. She thought of this, of the strong feel of him when the shark imprisoned her. And she feared she'd never know the sweet oblivion of his touch again. But now he was here, warm and sturdy, and real.

His mouth left hers to feast on the tender skin of her neck. She wore his shirt, but it was soaked and nearly transparent, molded to her body enticingly. And Jamie already knew he couldn't resist her.

She was arching and wriggling beneath him when he clamped his mouth over her straining nipple. Jamie was so aroused he almost didn't notice her flinch. He lifted his head, his breath rasping. " 'Tis something wrong?"

Though she shook her head, Jamie could see the lines of pain around her mouth. "What . . . ?" In that instant he remembered her foot, and glanced down. The jagged cut was bleeding and bruised, and Jamie felt like a fool for not tending it earlier.

She protested when he carried her back to their pallet. "I'm perfectly fine. It's just a little scratch."

Ignoring her words Jamie set her down and preceded to examine her foot. He cleansed it with clear water from the pond, then wrapped it with the lining from her coat.

Despite the stinging pain Anne smiled when she looked down at the golden tangle of Jamie's head as he bent over her foot. His expression was so serious, and she doubted a surgeon could do a better job of bandaging.

"That should keep the sand out, at least," he said, glancing up. "What's so amusing?"

"You." Anne leaned back on her arms.

"Me?"

"Yes." She was grinning from ear to ear now. "Despite your gold ear loop, you don't look very much like a pirate now."

His brow arched. "No?"

"No," Anne said emphatically.

"What, pray tell, do I look like then?"

Anne thought for a moment, finally shrugging her hair off her shoulders. "A nice man, I suppose."

"*Nice?*" He spat out the word like it was insulting.

Anne decided to taunt him further. "Yes, and sweet, caring . . . kind." His eyes widened with each word, until he was staring at her in disbelief.

"Hasn't anyone ever called you those things before?" When he shook his head, Anne simply laughed. "Well, they obviously don't know you as I do."

The expression on his face changed. "Few people know me as well as ye, Annie," he said as his gaze raked her body. "But then no one knows *ye* like I do either."

The gleam in his eyes personified buccaneers but his touch was gentle as he lowered Anne onto the dried seaweed. His kisses were light, butterfly wings that flitted from her cheek to her ear then lower. His tongue flicked out, dampening the skin at the base of her throat, and Anne moaned.

But though she burned for him, he took his time, kissing her fingers and toes, mindful of the bandaged cut as he softly pressed his mouth there.

By the time he entered her, Anne was wet and aching. She clung to his shoulders, reveling in the slow, steady rhythm of his thrusts. Feeling the pleasure build until she threw back her head, crying out as he brought her to a consuming release.

" 'Tis best if ye get some rest now," he whispered into her damp hair.

"But I'm not tired in the least." Anne's yawn belied her words. "Well, perhaps just a little." It seemed decadent to sleep in the daytime, to stretch and shut her eyes and feel him beside her. But it felt so wonderful.

Anne wasn't sure how long she slept, but she awoke to a pounding sound that made her sit up and look around. "What are you doing?"

Jamie paused, the rock he used to knock the boards off

the rowboat stilled in midair. "I'm making us a proper shelter," was all he said before going back to work.

"A proper . . . ?" Anne pushed to her feet, wincing a bit when she put weight on her cut. "We have a proper shelter." She motioned over her shoulder toward the thatched roof held up by oars. She may have complained about it before, but he was right. It had served them perfectly well for a fortnight. That's why his sudden contention that it wouldn't do seemed all the more strange.

He stopped what he was doing to backhand sweat off his brow, then looked over and gave Anne a wry smile. "You were right. It isn't much of a shelter."

Had she said that? Of course she had. But that was before . . . Before what, she wasn't sure. Except that now she knew better. She glanced back at the cozy, drooping roof, and the pallet underneath, then back at Jamie. "It seems perfectly fine to me."

He shook his head, and Anne noticed he'd tied his hair back with a bit of yarn from her hat. She noticed something else, too. "You've shaved." She reached up to touch his cheek. The skin there was fairer than on the rest of him. It also sported a nick or two. "How . . . ?"

He shrugged again and his face turned crimson. "The beard was getting straggly," he mumbled before bending back to his task of dismantling the boat.

"But I still don't understand how." Anne's eyes opened wide. "The knife? You shaved with the knife?"

"I told ye, it was getting straggly. Now haven't we something better to talk about?"

"Yes." Anne settled on the sand, pulling his shirt down over her drawn-up knees. "Perhaps you can tell me why you're doing all this."

"All what?" He pried a board loose and carefully

stacked it with the others. Then he worked the peg free and placed it in his pocket.

Anne simply folded her arms and waited until he finished. When he looked up she arched a brow in question.

"It came to me today," he said, carefully choosing his words. "How vulnerable we are . . . ye are." He seemed embarrassed as he squatted in front of her. "There's not much I can do. . . ." He shrugged. "But I thought ye might feel more secure with walls."

"Is all this because of what happened today?" Anne bit her lip. "That's it, isn't it?" She hurried on without waiting for his reply. "It was my fault, my foolishness that the shark attacked me." Anne grabbed his hands.

"I want to protect ye."

She bent her head, resting her forehead against his, love for him burning in her heart. "I don't need a fanciful house." All she needed was his strong arms, Anne thought, and almost said. But his next words stopped her. And made her sit back.

" 'Tis another consideration. One I hadn't thought of till today, though Lord knows why not."

"What is it?" Anne couldn't imagine what could make him so serious.

"There could be a child," he said simply and Anne's lashes drifted down, blocking her gaze from his. "Is there . . . ?" Jamie swallowed. "Are ye enceinte already?"

"No." Her eyes shot open to meet his, then lowered again. "At least not that I'm aware." With one finger she drew circles in the sand. She may have been an innocent before the pirate captain, but she did know how babies were made. Anne took a deep breath. "What do you suggest we do?"

His shrug reminded her of the pirate she knew.

Anne tried to think of a solution to this problem. Only one came to mind. "Should we . . . ? Do you wish to stop . . . ?"

"Nay." He lowered his voice. "Do ye?"

Anne had to smile at his response. First vehement denial, then consideration of her feelings. She shook her head slowly. "I doubt we could, even if we thought it best."

"And do ye think it best?"

He seemed to her at that moment very vulnerable. Not like the arrogant pirate captain at all. Anne reached out, touching the cheek he'd taken pains to shave. "I can't imagine not sleeping in your arms. Or kissing you. Or feeling your strength inside me." Or loving you, Anne thought, but didn't say. She couldn't imagine what his reaction to a declaration like that might be.

He turned into her hand, pressing his lips to her palm. "I'm of the same mind." He carefully lowered her hand, linking his fingers with hers.

So she helped him make improvements to their island. It amazed Anne how their roles had changed. Now it was Jamie who hollowed out a log to fill with rainwater. Who experimented with and discarded a drying rack to smoke fish. The gulls didn't seem to realize he hadn't built the contraption for their convenience.

"We have plenty of fish in the sea," Anne pointed out, nearly repeating the words he said to her when they first arrived on the island.

He merely nodded his agreement.

The house building proceeded slowly. But he managed to work on it a bit each day. Actually after discussing the design they decided walls were not a good idea. They impeded the cooling trade winds. But he did expand the roof, making the columns holding it up sturdier.

Anne's monthly menses came and went, opening again the question of abstinence. They were dealing with a clean slate, so to speak, and they both knew it. She wasn't with child. Should they risk conception?

At first neither spoke of the problem. But Anne noticed days passed and still he made no move to touch her beyond holding her as they slept. That he still desired her was evident. They could not live in such close proximity, and wear such little clothing without Anne noticing his obvious state of arousal.

But he just turned away and either plunged into the water or worked at improving their shelter.

On the third day Anne stripped off his shirt and waded into the surf after him. Her foot was nearly healed, and she'd been back in the water before. But only to bathe close to shore. Now she dove smoothly beneath the water and surfaced near him. He looked around, surprise stamping his features. Desire darkened his eyes until they were the color of the sea beyond the rocks.

"You promised to take me to see Lucy," she said. The water skimmed over the swell of her breasts and Anne smiled as his gaze held there.

"Are ye certain you're up to it?" When he'd offered to take her into the deeper water, Anne hesitated, not sure she wished to risk another encounter with a shark.

But now she nodded, and jackknifed her body, sliding cleanly through the clear, warm water. He did the same, pulling alongside her and touching her shoulder. When she looked toward him, he motioned for her to follow.

Anne stayed below until she thought her lungs might

explode, then surged to the surface to gulp air. He emerged almost immediately.

"Don't wait until ye can't stand it to breathe."

"But . . ." Anne gasped. "But you were still down there, too."

"I'm more used to it than ye are." He kicked forward, brushing hair from her temple. "Signal when ye need to come up."

After that they took their time, floating, and weaving through the water. Jamie pointed out a rainbow array of fish to her in colors so bright and beautiful they reminded her of the flowers in her parents' garden back in England.

Being with him like this almost made Anne forget her fear, though she did jerk around, her heart pounding when the dolphin approached. But Lucy only nudged Anne gently with her nose, then swam to Jamie and did the same thing. Then she whistled excitedly and dove to the bottom, turning and shooting toward the surface to leap through the air.

"I think she's happy to see you," Anne told a grinning Jamie.

"It does seem that way, doesn't it?" Jamie gave her a self-conscious smile. "Ye know, I've often thought . . ." He shook his head and chuckled. "Never mind."

"No, tell me." Anne floated closer.

"You'll think I'm daft, but I wonder if she's not trying to talk to me."

Anne only stared at him a moment while her hands made lazy circles in the water. When she spoke her expression was serious. "I would have thought you mad to suggest such a thing. But that was before." She grinned. "I know Lucy attacked the shark so I could get away. And I believe she led us to this island. So . . ." Anne spread the word out. "Is it that unbelievable that she tries to communicate with you?" She moved closer to him. "I know that would be my goal were I a dolphin."

With a deliberate swish of her body Anne let her breast skim his chest. The contact of naked, water-slick skin made them both moan.

"Now, Annie, what are ye doing?"

"I should think that obvious." With one swirling motion she brought her foot up his inner thigh.

The dolphin floated by, undulating its body side to side, but Jamie paid it no heed until a flipper slapped against his arm.

"I believe she wishes to play," Anne said, then sank beneath the water with a sweep of her arms. To her amazement Lucy seemed to do the same thing. When Anne spun around, so did the dolphin. She even shot to the surface when Anne did.

But though she enjoyed her romp with the dolphin, Anne kept her eyes on Jamie. And he certainly did the same with her. She wasn't surprised when he soon suggested they return to the beach.

They glided through the water side by side, rarely touching, but their movements becoming more and more sensual. The sea seemed to flow around them in a warm caress of anticipation.

When they reached the shallows his arms wrapped around her, and he rolled her over in the gentle swells. "Ye know this is madness, don't ye?" His lips forged a burning trail down her neck before he stood, dragging her up in his arms.

He sank to his knees in front of her on the beach, cupping her bottom, shaping her wet legs. His mouth was on level with her tight delta of curls and Anne moved closer, crying out when his tongue found the heart of her sexuality.

"Jamie." She dug her fingers through his thick wet hair, pulling him deeper into the web of her love. Her thighs spread and she arched her head back, her eyes mere slits as drugging pleasure swept through her.

Anne writhed, squirming and clutching his head as the dam burst and the waves of erotic shudders spiraled through her body. She thrust forward, crying out, her knees going weak as he held her suspended above reason.

He pulled away, jerking at the ties on his breeches. Released, his staff swelled forward as he grabbed her hips. But though her body was still flushed and wet with desire, she held herself rigid.

"Annie." Jamie pushed to his feet when he saw her tense face. "What's wrong?"

She didn't answer, simply pointed to the horizon beyond the rocks.

Chapter Sixteen

" 'Tis the *Lost Cause*," Jamie muttered before grabbing Anne's hand. The sensual fog evaporated and reflexes took over. He became the pirate he was, his mind focused on survival. With barely a thought he scooped up the knife, motioning for Anne to gather her clothing before leading them both into the thick underbrush.

He never told Anne, he hadn't wanted to worry her, but he planned for this eventuality. The hiding place he'd found was deep within the tangle of windblown trees. Jamie had further camouflaged the spot with palm fronds and brush. Inside he stored coconut shells full of water and the dried fish he managed to save from the squawking gulls.

Jamie ushered Anne in, following her and pulling the blind across the entrance. Inside it was crowded, with barely room for them both to sit on the sandy floor. The surrounding foliage stifled the air, filtering it a dusky green.

"Do . . . do you think they saw us?" Anne tried to control her breathing, but her heart pounded so fast it was near impossible.

The pirate didn't answer at first just motioned for her to get dressed. "The breeches and everything," he said.

It was a struggle but Anne finally managed to don her boy garb. "The hat is gone," she whispered, and he reached out to touch her hair.

"It doesn't matter, Annie."

Which was tantamount to admitting the truth. Discovery would mean death.

Which was why Anne was so surprised later when the captain stated he was leaving their nest.

"Why?" Anne clamped his arm, trying to hold him. "They might not find us here."

"D'Porteau and Stymie are not fools. He'll see what's left of the boat. Our fire is still warm. He'll know we're here." Jamie wrapped his arm about her, pulling her close and burying his face in her damp hair.

For long moments he said nothing, but Anne could feel his shoulders tremble.

"Annie," he whispered at last, his breath fluttering the curls near her ear. "Stay here for a day and night . . . and till you'd normally wake the next day. Then listen very carefully. If ye haven't heard anything in all that time ye can come out. But be careful." He stilled her shaking head with a hand cupped to her cheek. "Aye, Annie. Do as I say. There be food and water enough for ye and—"

"What about you?" Anne's question ended on a sob.

"I'll be about." He paused a moment as they both listened to the far-off voices. The pirates were on the island. "There may be only a few who came ashore. I plan to catch them off guard one at a time. "If I can capture a musket or two—"

"And what if it's you who is captured?" She couldn't disguise the panic in her tone.

"I'll be—"

"I won't let you go." Anne's fingers tightened on his warm skin. "I won't."

"Don't, Annie." He shifted, bringing his mouth to hers, skimming her lips before touching his forehead to hers. "Don't make this harder than already 'tis."

"But I don't understand." Tears were streaming down her face faster than he could brush away with his thumb.

"We both knew this could happen." Jamie swallowed. "This . . . our island, was just a fantasy."

"It doesn't have to be that way. Stay with me," Anne begged, but he was already pulling away. "Jam—" His mouth, hard and unrelenting, cut off the rest of his name. His kiss was fierce and savage. Then he jerked away, wriggling through a small hole in the underbrush.

It wasn't until he was gone that Anne noticed the knife. He'd forgotten the knife. She grabbed up the handle. How could he hope to fight any of the pirates without a weapon? And then the awful truth dawned on her. He wasn't planning to capture anyone. He was leading them away from her hiding place. And he didn't forget the knife. He left it to her on purpose.

Anne drew up her knees, burying her face in the rough fabric of her breeches as sobs wracked her body.

Jamie hid behind the thicket of stunted trees, listening to the men approach. He guessed there to be three, though he couldn't tell for certain. None of them spoke, but they did nothing to muffle their footsteps, which meant they didn't suspect that he intended to leap out at them.

He hadn't lied to Anne . . . not completely. He did

intend to try and capture some weapons. To try and defend their island. But if worse came to worst, he would lead them away from her.

They drew nearer, and sweat rolled down to the hollow of Jamie's back. His muscles tensed. When they were directly in front of him Jamie gave a yell and pounced. He had the blackamoor pinned to the sandy ground before Jamie noticed who it was.

"Cap'n?"

"Keena?" Jamie jerked his head around to where Deacon stood, his pistol cocked. "What in the hell are ye doing here? Where's d'Porteau? Stymie?" After climbing off his chief gunner, Jamie offered his hand.

"We left them in Kingston," Keena said, brushing off his jacket. "Stymie made the mistake of leaving the *Lost Cause* unguarded while he went into town."

Jamie's grin was slow to form. "So ye stole her?"

"Since the vessel was ours to begin with I'd hardly call it that."

"Right ye are, Deacon." Jamie draped his arms around the two men, laughing despite himself when Keena inquired about the lad, Andy.

"Ye didn't throw him overboard, did ye?"

"Ah, nay. I didn't do that. And *Andy* is well and good, though probably anxious to know what's going on about now." Jamie paused. "How did ye find this place?"

"Just happened upon it, though to be truthful we been lookin' for ye, Cap'n. Didn't think the Frenchman could get rid of ye so easy like."

"Easy?" Jamie shook his head. "I wouldn't be calling it that. But at any rate, 'tis glad I am to see ye. Who else be with ye?"

The list included many of Jamie's old crew. Good pirates and seamen all, but not a saint among them, except maybe for Deacon.

Jamie stopped walking and rubbed his chin. "I have a bit of a dilemma." He sucked in his bottom lip. There was no way Anne could pass as a boy now.

"What is it, Cap'n? Ye know we'll help ye out."

He shrugged and then called out, deciding one look was better than any lengthy explanation. Anne stuck her head from beneath the palm curtain immediately. "Come on down here, Annie. 'Tis all right."

Watching his friends' faces, their eyes growing wide, their mouths dropping open as Anne emerged was almost worth the trouble he was going to have.

"Why he . . . she's a woman."

"Very perceptive, Deacon."

"How . . . ?" The black-garbed man rubbed his good eye as if he needed to put things back in focus.

"Hot damn." Keena slapped his knee. "I knew I wasn't seeing things. I told ye. Didn't I tell ye, Deacon, that I saw a man and woman on the beach."

Anne's face turned scarlet, but Jamie only chuckled. "That would have been Mistress Cornwall and myself," he said, reaching out his hand for her. "Now as ye can see I might have a bit of a problem with the rest of the crew. I'm counting on ye to help me . . . to help Mistress Cornwall."

Anne stared out the stern windows as the island, their island, slowly disappeared from sight. For all it had been their home for nearly a month there was very little fanfare upon leaving. They had nothing tangible of value except what they brought with them . . . a knife and tinderbox.

Memories weren't something one packed up and carried off.

They left the island quickly after Keena and Deacon promised their support. Jamie had greeted the remaining crew members who'd come ashore looking after the crude hut was spotted. They all seemed glad to find him alive . . . as glad as pirates could be about anything.

Then he brought her forward, introducing her as the niece of the governor of Libertia. Not a hostage exactly, still he implied she was untouchable if they wished the coin she'd promised.

There had been some grumbling, but Jamie was adept at making people see things his way. And then there were the jewels.

Anne sighed, wondering where her jewels were at this moment. Did d'Porteau still have them or had he sold them, squandering the money on women and drink by now. And what would Jamie do when he found out she lied about having them?

Anne pressed her forehead to the cool glass, an overwhelming wash of sadness seeping over her. Despite the problems caused by d'Porteau, she should be pleased about their rescue from the island. No more sleeping on dried seaweed. No more diet of fish and coconut. Her eyes swept toward the bowl that contained her uneaten meal. She should be thrilled to sup on salt pork and beans.

Anne sighed. She missed Jamie. It was as simple as that. She'd grown used to him on the island. His company. His wicked humor. His touch.

She cared about him. Her heart nearly broke when she heard Lucy's shrill whistles as they rowed to the waiting *Lost Cause*. Jamie hadn't made any move of recognition, but Anne could tell by the tightening of his features that he heard Lucy's goodbye. And how much it moved him.

Anne pulled her legs up beneath the borrowed skirts found in one of the captain's sea chests. They were bright red, and too long, and she'd decided never to ask why he had them, though her curiosity, and some other emotion she couldn't name was sorely strained.

She was sitting like that, cheek resting on her knees, when Jamie walked in. He didn't knock, deciding it was his cabin. And after all, he'd lived with her intimately for nearly a month.

But it amazed him how different someone could seem when wrapped in the silks of civilization. Despite the bright garish color and cut she looked every bit the lady she was. And he felt every inch the pirate. It almost seemed as if the past month never happened. As if it were nothing but a sailor's dream.

He cleared his throat. "The food wasn't to your liking?" He nodded toward the full trencher where broth congealed around bits of pork and beans.

Anne stared at him wide-eyed, wondering why he didn't come closer, wishing he would. But he stood near the open door, arms crossed, and booted feet spread. He looked more the pirate, less the free savage he'd seemed on the island. Anne sighed heavily. "I found myself missing roasted fish," she said wistfully, wondering if he could guess all the other things she missed as well.

He looked at her a moment, his expression softening. But he didn't step toward her, and after a moment Anne wondered if she hadn't imagined the change. For now he stared at her with barely a hint of recognition.

"D'Porteau plans to return to Libertia."

"What?" Anne stretched out her legs and jumped to her feet. "How do you know?"

The pirate shrugged and leaned back against the door. "The *French Whore* and the *Lost Cause* sailed together for a while. Some of my crew was with him. He even seemed to trust or at least tolerate a few. Keena. Deacon amused him."

"And he told them about Libertia?"

"He mentioned it."

"Then we must do something." Anne clasped her hands together and paced to the small mirror and back, glancing over her shoulder only when she heard his mocking, "We?"

She whirled around to face him. "You can't mean 'tis your plan to let him do it. To sit by while he does?"

"I wonder, Annie, why ye find that so difficult to believe." Jamie shook his head. "But as it happens you've the right of it this time."

Bottled-up air rushed from Anne. "Then you are going to do something?"

"Aye. 'Tis personal at this point."

Anne wanted to believe he meant personal because of her, but she didn't. Not the way he acted toward her. And his next words only convinced her more.

"After what he did, I think d'Porteau deserves my revenge."

It shouldn't bother her why Captain MacQuaid chose to fight d'Porteau, only that he did. At least that's what Anne tried to tell herself. She straightened her shoulders. "What are you going to do?"

"I haven't decided yet." He hesitated, not sure if he should tell her everything, finally deciding she should know. "To be honest, 'tis possible we are too late."

"Too late?" Anne's eyes sought his, but he refused to look at her.

"The *Lost Cause* didn't find us right away."

"So d'Porteau might already have attacked Libertia?"

Jamie tried not to be affected by her stricken expression. But he felt a tightening around his heart, and a desire to drop to his knees and swear to protect her always. " 'Tis doubtful," Jamie said and hoped he spoke the truth. "D'Porteau lost more than a few men when my crew commandeered the *Lost Cause*. He probably needs to recruit more sailors."

"How will he do that?"

"There be several ways." Jamie pushed away from the doorjamb and crossed to the window. Their island was little more than a wavering speck on the horizon. He turned back to face Anne. "Knowing d'Porteau I imagine he'll attack a merchant vessel and kill half the crew, thus convincing the other half they'd be fools not to go a pirating."

"He really is a despicable wretch, isn't he?"

"Aye." The grin was back. "He gives pirates a bad name."

Despite her fears for Libertia and her uncle, Anne smiled. "I doubt he's the only one."

Jamie moved closer, caught by the spell of her smile. "And what are ye implying by that, Mistress Cornwall?" he asked, his tone playful.

"Not a thing, Captain MacQuaid." Anne's pulse quickened. He was so overpoweringly masculine and sensual, she could barely breathe. It was with great effort she didn't throw herself into his strong arms.

What was he thinking? Jamie stopped himself before he reached out to her. Another few moments and he would have her shed of scarlet silks and stretched out beneath him.

And the door to the passageway wide open, where any jack-tar could walk by and see them.

And get ideas of his own.

Jamie was having a hard enough time convincing the crew that Anne Cornwall was of no use to them deflowered. Convincing them he hadn't already plucked her for himself.

Turning on his heel, Jamie strode back toward the door. When he'd put a safe distance between them, he glanced her way. "We should be in Libertia day after next. Until then I suggest ye stay below." That said he left his cabin shutting the door behind him.

She didn't see him again.

Anne spent the first night tossing and turning, tangled in the sheet, wondering why he didn't come. It was the first time she'd slept alone in almost a month and she didn't like it. Longing for his touch kept her awake the next night, too, but by now Anne was resigned to his absence. For whatever reason the pirate had decided to forget their relationship on the island. To forget her.

By the time the *Lost Cause* sailed into the harbor at Libertia, Anne was convinced it was for the best. She would forget him as well. Of course, it would be easier once she was back home, off his ship and out of his cabin. Who wouldn't think of him constantly surrounded by his things! Sleeping on his bed, where even the pillow carried his scent.

Besides, she had much more important things to occupy her thoughts.

As soon as she was summoned Anne hurried on deck. Squinting, she studied the shoreline, searching for any sign that d'Porteau had made good on his threat to return.

"I'd say we beat him here," came a deep, masculine voice behind her. Anne's hands tightened on the splintery rail.

"We can thank heaven for that, I suppose."

"Aye." Jamie lifted his hand to touch her shoulder, then let it drop. "I've been waiting to talk with ye about the colonists on Libertia."

"Really?" Anne turned to face him, backing up until the rail pressed into the small of her back. "I wasn't difficult to find."

Ignoring her barb, knowing he deserved it, Jamie stared out toward the island. "How committed do ye think they are to defeating d'Porteau?"

"They hate him. Many lost friends or relatives the first time he came."

"But are they willing to fight?"

"Fight?" She said the word as if its meaning were lost on her. "But I thought you were going to do that."

"Perfectly willing to sacrifice tainted pirate blood, are ye?"

Anne's jaw dropped open. "That's not what I meant at all. It's just . . . well, you know how to do battle. And these people." Anne let her arm swing about to indicate the islanders. "They're farmers and scholars. They haven't a clue how to defeat a man like d'Porteau. I thought that was obvious."

"Well, they shall have to learn, and learn quickly. I haven't enough men to do it myself. Besides, since they have such a stake in the outcome—"

"Im sure every citizen of Libertia will fight to the

death," Anne said, squaring her shoulders somewhat indignantly.

"Let's hope it doesn't come to that."

Hoisting the too-long skirts up with one hand, Anne balanced herself with the other as she crossed the narrow board that served as a gangplank. Getting about on the pirate ship was much easier garbed as a boy. But that adventure was definitely over. Now she must face her uncle and explain her long absence.

He waited on the beach with several other men, Mort Tatum, Matthew Baxter, Dugald Miller . . . and Israel. Anne had a wild, totally uncharacteristic urge to turn and flee back onto the *Lost Cause*. And she might have except that Captain MacQuaid was right behind her.

"Uncle Richard." Anne stepped into his waiting embrace. "I'm so glad to see you. I can explain," she added, whispering softly into his ear.

"No need of that, Annie. Israel already told us where you were. How was your shopping trip? I see you found a pretty new gown." He held her at arm's length and Anne's gaze shot to Israel who merely shrugged. "And I see you've brought our friend with you. Captain Mac-Quaid, isn't it?"

"Aye." Jamie stepped forward and bowed. His hair was trimmed and tied back neatly in a queue. The suit of clothing, made for him by a tailor once captured off a packet, fit well and distinguished him as a gentleman, deceiving though it was. " 'Tis my honor to see ye again. I wonder if we might have a word? Perhaps a general meeting of your colonists?"

Richard's face beamed. "Ah, Captain, you've decided

to join us after all. And how many new converts to John Locke's thinking do you bring?"

Jamie looked at Anne, then back toward the *Lost Cause*. Richard's madness wasn't the same as his mother's, but being around him unleashed a maelstrom of emotions that Jamie preferred to keep locked up inside. A cold sweat broke out on his upper lip. He didn't know what to say.

"Captain MacQuaid will tell you everything at the meeting, Uncle," Anne said as she led him up the path toward their cottage.

Fewer men assembled in the common area than Anne expected. There was a platform built of whitewashed boards on which her uncle and several of the elected Headmen sat. Captain Jamie MacQuaid was also there, looking handsome, but uncomfortable in his civilized clothing.

Turning to Israel who stood beside her on the edge of the group standing in the shade of circling palms, Anne looked him over. "What exactly did you tell my uncle?"

"Damn little." Israel rubbed a gnarled hand over his grizzled head. "Ye knows yer uncle. He wanted to believe ye went to New Providence to order supplies. Was as simple as agreeing with 'im."

"But I was gone so long."

Israel's eyes narrowed until there were nothing more than glistening slits in the wrinkles of his dark face. "That reminds me. Where was ye all this time?"

Anne could feel the heated blush creep up her face, but she refused to look away. "I imagine Captain MacQuaid will answer part of your question," she said, thankful that

Lester Perdue had risen to call the mumbling colonists to quiet.

Then her uncle spoke . . . a mixed-up rambling speech about more colonists coming and how successful the grand experiment was, a true democracy in action. He didn't seem to notice the disenchanted mumbling from his audience. When he introduced Jamie, the griping grew louder.

It didn't stop until Jamie pulled out his pistol, slammed it down on the table and leaned forward.

"Now some of ye might have a . . ." He paused and glanced down at Richard Cornwall. ". . . a slightly misconceived idea of why I'm here. I do believe in the teachings of John Locke . . . at least those that I know. Why even the *Lost Cause* has a set of articles that every pir— sailor votes on." He cleared his throat, deciding it best he didn't go too deeply into philosophy. "But that's not why I'm here."

"Then tell us and be off with you so we can get about our jobs," someone yelled from the assemblage and others grumbled their agreement.

Anne's jaw dropped in surprise. Though the other women weren't included in the grand experiment's democratic meeting, she, as her uncle's assistant, was often included. In the past there were disagreements, of course, but no one ever spoke so rudely as Dugald Miller just did. She had half a mind to tell him so, and actually took a few steps forward before Jamie's announcement stopped her, and the undercurrent of voices.

"Willet d'Porteau is on his way here."

The silence was so complete, Anne could hear the pounding of the sugar works on the lee side of the island.

But when the astonishment wore off the questions began.

"How do you come of this information?"

"What else can he take from us?"

"How many can you squeeze on that sloop in the harbor?"

Jamie held up his hand, and answered each in turn. "I know because some of my men heard the Frenchman say he was coming here. And how they came into his company isn't important, except to say he attacked my vessel and took some of the crew hostage."

"Did you hear him yourself? What of you, Anne Cornwell? What do you have to say for yourself?"

"I didn't hear him nor did Mistress Cornwall, but you can be sure—"

"Be sure of what?" It was Dugald Miller again. "Rumor has it you're a pirate yourself. How do we know you ain't here to steal what your friend d'Porteau left behind?"

This time Anne did start forward, but the rapier cut of Jamie's eyes brought her to a standstill. He then faced the crowd, the same expression on his face.

"If I was after your riches, this island would be flattened by now by my cannon. Your gold and women would be locked in my cabin." His gaze momentarily caught Anne's. "And most of you," he said, pointing out toward the group, "would be dead."

Jamie took a deep breath. "Now, I'm not saying that won't happen. I'm just saying it will be d'Porteau who does it, not me."

"Then we've got to get off Libertia. We've got to leave."

"No!" Richard stood, shaking his head and lifting his

fists high. "We can't abandon our ideals. Remember John Locke. We must prove that his grand design will work. We must—"

"Nothing to be proved by getting us all killed!"

"Yea, sit down, old man. You haven't known what was what for a long time now!"

She couldn't get to her uncle quickly enough. The group grew ugly, yelling at the man they once revered, and jostling Anne around as she tried to make her way to the platform. Ahead of her she could see her uncle's stricken expression as he tried to understand what was happening.

The loud explosion caught everyone off guard.

All eyes turned on the captain who held a smoking pistol pointed toward the heavens. "Now we can all try to run-tail," he yelled, his voice booming off the palm trees. "But there be no guarantee we can all get aboard the *Lost Cause* without it sinking to the bottom. And even if we do get her under sail d'Porteau might attack us on the high seas."

"What else can we do?"

"Yea, there's no other choice."

Jamie lowered the pistol and leaned forward, fanning the group with his gaze. "Ye can stand up like men, by damn. Ye can fight for what ye believe in!"

Chapter Seventeen

Enthusiasm does not a soldier make.

Jamie sensed the truth of those words often as he tried to train the Libertia militia. After his call to arms, which many on the island called stirring, the Libertians volunteered to a man. Their vehement war cries filled the air, drifting off to sea on the trade wind.

"Down with tyrants!"

"Long live Libertia!"

"Death to all pirates!"

While this last slogan made Jamie cringe, Anne seemed to find it amusing. "They don't know what they're saying," she said with a chuckle as she listed each man's name beside the weapon he was given. The pistols and boarding pikes came from the *Lost Cause*'s arsenal.

"I'm not so sure about that." Jamie hoisted a barrel of powder onto his shoulder. " 'Tis Dugald Miller I hear screaming that particular phrase the loudest." He glanced down as he passed by. "What are ye writing all that down for?"

"So we'll have a record." Anne stared up at him wide-eyed.

"A record for what?"

"Well for . . ." Now that he asked Anne wasn't sure why she did it. But she always kept records, lists of crops planted and sugar harvested, and sugar cones shipped. Perhaps it wasn't necessary for her to record everything. But it made her feel useful, and right now Anne needed to perceive herself that way.

With a wave of her hand and a mumbled, "It needs to be done," Anne dismissed his inquiry. But before he left she offered an observation. "Don't let Dugald bother you. He's always been puffed with hot air."

Jamie's grin and thoughts of Anne stayed with him as he started drilling the men in proper use of the muskets. The grin quickly faded. A passion for defending their freedom didn't alter the fact that most of the colonists were tradesmen and farmers. Not a one had been in the military. Not a one knew more than the rudiments of loading and firing a musket.

So they drilled. Practicing speed. Wasting more powder than Jamie thought prudent. But he couldn't ask these people to go into battle against d'Porteau unprepared.

And he refused to think this was a lost cause.

Refused to dwell on the similarities between this ragtag group facing d'Porteau, and the followers of the Young Pretender defying the better-equipped army of Duke of Cumberland.

"Load."

"Ram."

"Fire!"

Over and over they practiced, until their muscles screamed and Jamie's voice grew hoarse.

The strategy was simple.

When d'Porteau sailed into the harbor, there was to be

no resistance. "Let him think his task an easy one," Jamie told the group. "Lure him into our trap with acquiescence."

Only after the Frenchman came ashore would he know of the settlers hidden behind the blinds that bracketed the beach—the blinds now being built of toppled palms and underbrush. Too late to retreat, the pirates would know the carnage of being caught in a cross fire.

"What of their cannon?" one man, a wheelwright asked. "Won't the pirates left on board his ship know d'Porteau's distress and fire on us?"

"Which is exactly what they might do," Jamie answered the newly appointed sergeant. "Except that by this time sailors on board will be too busy battling the *Lost Cause*, which will have sailed around the spit yonder where it hides to bottle them into the harbor."

"Do you think it will work?" Anne asked as evening shaded the island in gentle tones of mauve. She and Jamie had been on Libertia a sennight, and there had barely been time for more than a casual word between them. Even now, while most islanders were eating a simple repast, Anne expected the captain to be surrounded by people. She was pleased to find him alone, studying the camouflaged earthworks.

However, he didn't appear pleased to see her. The lengthening shadows didn't keep Anne from noticing his expression when he turned to stare at her.

Jamie took a deep breath, feeling compelled to speak the truth. "Let us pray it does, or we shall all pay dearly." Jamie turned away, continuing his inspection, not surprised that she followed. He should turn back toward the village. Each step took them farther away from the only protection he had from her. The protection offered by civilization.

He had to remember they were no longer the only two people in their world, unfettered by what others thought. By their histories.

But when he was near her like this, when he could catch the sweet scent of her on the tropical air, hear her voice, reality seemed to fade.

"I've wanted to talk with you," Anne began, wondering how honest she should be about her feelings and finally settling for a half truth. "To thank you for all you're doing. It can't be easy." They'd reached the point where the thick growth of trees met the sea. "I . . . my uncle and I appreciate—"

"How is he doing?" Jamie stood, his feet spread, hands clasped behind him, staring out toward the bay and ocean beyond.

"Fine . . . at times." Anne paused. "Actually he's confused by all the goings-on, the gunfire. Israel's with him now."

"And does Israel know where ye are? That you're here with me?" He turned his head to look at her and Anne resisted the urge to retreat a step.

"I . . . I don't see where that's any of Israel's concern."

"It should be someone's care. Damnit, Annie, 'tisn't right for ye to be down here with me alone."

"And why not?" Anne was tired of speaking to his back and stepped in front of him. "Because you're a pirate?"

"Aye," Jamie agreed with a nod of his head. " 'Tis a good enough reason."

"We spent nearly a month alone together on our island."

"A fact I hope you've the sense to keep to yourself."

Anne lowered her lashes. "I haven't told anyone here, no." Raising her eyes she caught his gaze. "But that doesn't mean it didn't happen."

"Ye'd be best off forgetting it did."

"I can't."

Her simple declaration seemed to splinter Jamie's resolve. Reaching out he gave in to temptation and grasped her shoulders. She felt warm and soft beneath the simple dark bodice. "Ye are making a mistake, Annie Cornwall. One you'll live to regret."

She didn't have a chance to disagree. His mouth assaulted hers, driving all but her need for him from Anne's mind. With the pounding surf as a backdrop he pulled her body tightly to his.

His tongue sought hers, deepening the kiss, till there seemed to be no more Anne, no more pirate, only the whole they formed together.

He inched them toward the curtain of trees, reluctant to break the spell of their kiss. Shadows deepened and the breezes slowed as they stepped beneath the sheltering palms. But as Jamie pulled his lips from hers he knew they could still be seen. If someone were to walk onto the beach, there would be no more question of their relationship.

At first Anne clung to him as he pulled away, not knowing the reason. Caring only that she was losing him again. Then she saw his eyes nervously cut toward the beach.

"Come with me." She took his hand leading him through the tangle of trees toward the interior of the island. There was no trail, but Anne knew her way unerringly. When the pirate questioned where they were going she silenced him with a fleeting kiss, then twisted away and pulled him along, laughing.

When they stepped from the overhang of leaves onto a beach bathed in the last subtle glow of the sun, Anne looked up at him. "I found this once when I was searching for a new place to locate the mill. At the time I thought it wasn't much good for anything." Her brown eyes twinkled. "I was wrong. It's hidden and no one knows of it but me."

Jamie glanced around. They stood on a curved crescent of sand surrounded by thick foliage. To the left and right coral rocks reached into the sea. The surf splashed over them noisily, hypnotically. It was a spot for lovers. It reminded him of—

"I know we no longer are on our island. We have other things to consider now besides ourselves," Jamie heard her say . . . as if she could read his thoughts. "But for this one night can't we just pretend nothing else exists?"

She stepped into his embrace then, smiling when his arms tightened about her.

"Ye know I want ye."

But she could still sense his resistance. "And I want you." Standing on tiptoe Anne brushed a string of kisses along his chiseled jaw. His eyes closed, the gold-tipped lashes fanning his cheekbones, and his body quickened.

"Ah, Annie, I can't resist ye." His open mouth melded with hers.

And Anne was lost.

When he lowered her to the sand, still warm from its afternoon sunbath, she sighed. Her tongue met his in a dance as old as time, a thrust and parry, a forecast of what was to come.

Then his lips trailed hungrily down her neck, nibbling

at her tender skin. "Annie. Annie." Jamie faced her, knee to knee, chest to chest. He couldn't seem to get enough of saying her name. Of tasting her. Her head fell back giving him greater access.

Jamie reached up, tangling his fingers in her curls, dragging the lace cap and pins down into the sand. Pulling away enough to see her in the ever dimming light, Jamie spread the tangle of hair over her shoulders, smiling at the picture she made. "Ye are so lovely," he whispered as his hands curved around to the front.

Her breasts strained against the linen fabric and she moaned when he brought his palms down over her bodice. "So lovely," he said again as he slowly unlaced the ties holding her simple gown shut.

Like peeling away the petals of the most sensual flower, he pushed aside her gown, then plucked at the ribbon on her shift. Her breasts were full, thrusting forward, their crests hard and irresistible. Rarely one to resist temptation, Jamie leaned forward, flicking his tongue provocatively over each torrid rose-colored tip.

Then with a growl he pulled one nipple into his mouth, sucking, and biting, and sending fingers of sensation burning through Anne.

"Oh, please." Anne grasped his golden head, pulling him closer. His hair was thick and curled around her fingers as she held on to him. And inside her an ache grew until she was trembling.

Didn't he know what he did to her?

Anne's fingers loosened their grip and she let her palms slide sensually down over his shoulders and chest. Lower and lower she went, twisting her hands around until his mouth left her body with his quick intake of breath. His forehead pressed between her breasts and his breath tingled the moist tips as he sighed. "Be ye angel or devil, Annie?"

"Neither." Anne's fingers continued to explore and measure the rock-hard ridge beneath his breeches. "A mere woman, Jamie." A woman who loves you, she wanted to say, but didn't. With shaking fingers she unfastened one, then another button, spreading the fabric until his flesh thrust out into her waiting hands.

"Oh, God, Annie, you'll be the death of me yet." Jamie bit his bottom lip as she brushed her fingertips up and across the top of his manhood. His breath was harsh and rasping as he tried to absorb the pleasure without completely losing control.

When she bent forward, touching him oh so gently with her lips, he knew the battle was lost. He grabbed her shoulders, jerking her up and against him, clenching his jaw and trying to calm himself.

"Did I hurt you?" Anne's words were muffled into the warm skin of his chest.

"Nay." Jamie sucked in humid, salty air. "Nay, Annie. Ye could never do that. But 'tis been awhile since we made love and I don't think I can withstand such sweet torture as that." He tilted her chin up, kissing her lips hungrily. Then he gently lowered her back onto the sand.

Jamie forced himself to undress her slowly, pressing his mouth to her sun-kissed skin. She writhed beneath him as he skimmed the dimple of her navel, crying out as his mouth searched for and found the tiny bud of her womanhood. Anne was swept up over the brink, chasing stars that exploded, swirling around her in the colors of the rainbow. And then he was leaning over her, blocking out the little light left in the sky with his broad shoulders.

Between them his staff throbbed as he lowered himself

between Anne's thighs. His first thrust was like coming home. Like the pleasure of a feast after a long stretch of hunger. The first drink of clear, cold water to a parched man.

Jamie sank into her body, fighting the strong urge to move, and simply relished the feel of her, tight as a sheath gloving his flesh. She was hot and slick and on a grunt of pure male satisfaction he retreated only to drive deeper.

Her slender legs wrapped up and around his hips, locking him to her as he rocked them back and forth with each powerful thrust. Jamie's hands plunged beneath her buttocks, lifting her against him. And this time when she cried out, when her body soared helplessly into ecstatic oblivion, he joined her, pumping his seed deep into her womb.

They collapsed together onto the sand, Jamie turning and pulling her into his arms. They lay still waiting for their breathing to quiet, for their heartbeats to return to normal.

Jamie pulled her close, resting Anne's head on his shoulder, twisting down to plant a soft kiss on her hair. "Ye make me forget my wits, Annie."

"Mmmm."

Her agreement, a mere sigh of contentment, made Jamie smile. He hugged her to him, tightening his hold . . . wishing he never had to let her go.

"I should probably get ye back to your cottage."

"Must we go now?" Anne squirmed against his side, draping her arm across his chest and tangling her fingers in the thick mat of golden hair. "I've missed you."

Craning his neck, Jamie tired to catch sight of her face, but all he could see was a sweep of tangled, sand-sugared hair. Jamie bent his free arm, pillowing his head, and shut his eyes. "I've missed ye, too."

"You have?" Anne twisted around, lying partially on top of him, her chin cupped in her palm. "I know it's silly because we were stranded there, but sometimes I wish we could go back to our island, just the two of us."

"The thought has crossed my mind."

Anne smiled at that, then rested her cheek against the warm, hair-roughened skin of his chest. "Everything seemed so simple there. No worry beyond where our next meal would come from."

"I kept us in fish."

"That you did." Anne drew lazy circles along the ridge of muscle.

"Besides, I think you're forgetting we also feared d'Porteau. The shark. We had our problems there, too."

"You're right. I suppose it just seemed easier because you were there."

"I'm here now." Jamie drew his hand down over her silky curls, letting his fingers caress the smooth skin of her cheek. He wished there was something else he could do . . . something to ease her mind.

But he could offer her nothing but the heat of his body and his protection against d'Porteau. And for all the anguish the French pirate caused, Jamie didn't think he was Anne's main concern as she lay in his arms.

She confirmed his belief moments later.

Her voice was soft and low. "Uncle Richard appears to grow more . . ." Anne hesitated. "Disoriented." She shifted to search the shadows for his expression. "Have you noticed?"

He'd noticed. When Jamie first came to Libertia, Richard's confusion was, for the most part, harmless. He forgot who you were, and misplaced time, but there wasn't the underlying anger Jamie sensed now. It was as if the constant befuddlement was becoming more than he could handle.

"Mayhap when there is no more worry over the Frenchman. . . ."

"Yes . . . I suppose that will help." But Anne didn't think so. She sighed, dropping her cheek back down to his chest when he spoke again.

"My mother was mad." The fingers that were gently stroking his skin stilled. "She wasn't like your uncle . . . at least I don't think she was." Jamie took a deep breath, hoping it would calm him. It didn't. He'd never spoken to anyone about this, not even his father. Especially not his father.

He wasn't certain why he felt compelled to share this private torment with Anne, but he knew he couldn't stop now. "She cried . . . nearly all the time. And she would scream and throw things. Dishes . . . anything."

"At you?" Anne braced her arm around his arm, holding him.

"Nay, never at me. She was always very kind and gentle to me. She called me her spot of sunshine." Jamie's voice grew gruff and he cleared his throat. "At least that's as I recall it. I was very young. But I remember hearing the shattering glass, the screaming. Then being called into the drawing room by my father and shown the mess." Jamie shut his eyes. "He wouldn't allow the servants to clear away the broken shards. He said it was best to remind everyone of just how mad she was."

Anne swallowed. "What happened to her?"

"He sent her away."

"Away?"

"Aye, to a place where madwomen were kept. . . . That's what he told me." His voice caught. "I never saw her again. He told me she died."

Anne pushed herself up until she could see the outline of his face. Her hand cupped around his cheek. Gently she wiped at the moisture there. "I'm so sorry."

Jamie turned his face away, embarrassed by his show of emotion. "It happened a long time ago. And as my father often said, perhaps it was for the best. She was of no use to us."

"You can't believe that."

"Nay." Jamie took a shattered breath. "I never believed him. Never. I loved her."

Anne pulled his head around. The moon had risen, gilding his strong features with a silvery light. Love for him swelled her heart and made it difficult for her to speak. She swallowed. "How old were you, Jamie?"

At first she didn't think he would answer. He seemed embarrassed by his tears. Sitting up, he backhanded the wetness from his face, but he didn't turn away. He picked up the hand she'd used to caress his face and linked it with his own. "I was six when she went away. As I told ye, 'twas long ago."

"I won't send Uncle Richard away."

His smile was sad. "I never thought ye would. But I worry about ye. He's angry."

"Not at me. I think 'tis more himself, his inability to remember. That frightens him."

Jamie shrugged. "Just be careful, Annie." His thumb tilted her face up toward his. "I wouldn't want anything to happen to ye."

Then he pushed to his feet, pulling Anne along with

him. " 'Tis a moonlight swim we need to get rid of the sand, and then I'll take ye back."

But after the swim they both had other ideas. This time when they made love it was slow and bittersweet, for they both knew there probably would never be another chance for them to be together.

Afterward Jamie led Anne back into the water, stopping when it pooled around her waist. With infinite care he cupped his hands, drizzling water down over her, washing away the sand caked to her body.

The sensation of warm water and warmer fingers brushing against her skin made Anne close her eyes dreamily. "Don't leave me," she whispered, then froze, realizing she said aloud the thought running through her head.

His hands stilled as well, though diamondlike droplets of water skimmed over her skin. "Ye don't know what you're saying, Annie. I'm a pirate."

"But not as evil as you pretend."

"Ah, so ye want to reform me, do ye?" His smile was endearing.

"I really don't think ye need reforming, Jamie Mac-Quaid."

"Well, the British Admiralty might have a different opinion on that." Jamie took a deep breath, wishing this wasn't so hard to do. Wishing he didn't have to do it. "Annie, lass, there's a mighty attraction between us to be sure. But don't go getting that mixed up with feelings ye should be having for some worthy gentleman."

"But—"

Two fingers pressed to her lips silenced Anne's rebuttal.

"I'm a no-account, Annie. A rogue who can't even keep the one promise he made to himself." He shook his head, a wry smile lifting one corner of his mouth. "Two, actually. Don't get entangled in lost causes. And steer clear of beautiful gentlewomen."

"You said we could defeat d'Porteau." Anne lifted her brow. "If so, 'tisn't a lost cause."

"Mayhap not now, but it will be, Anne. Libertia will fall prey to some other scoundrel, mark me words. Lofty ideas always do."

"So then you don't want to stay and be part of the grand experiment?"

"You're not listening to me, Annie. I can't. Not for ye. Not for myself."

"I see." Slowly Anne turned and started walking toward shore. The water swirled around her hips, then thighs, then—

Jamie's arm clamped around her upper arm and he swirled her around to face him.

"Now why are ye acting like this? You've known from the beginning what I am. What kind of life I've led. Hell, my own father disowned me, left me for dead."

"From what you told me earlier, your father doesn't sound like an exemplary man."

"He wasn't, or isn't, if he's still alive. He was a heartless curr, and that's the God's truth. He treated my stepbrother as vilely as he did my mother and me. But that doesn't change a thing." His hands lifted to cup her shoulders. "If anything it should make ye more leery of me."

Anne opened her mouth to speak, but again Jamie stopped her.

"Ye don't want me, Annie."

Oh, but she did. Anne saw no sense in arguing the point now. She would wait, but she wasn't giving up on him no matter what he said.

They dressed slowly, then neither anxious to leave sat, their backs to a palm tree. It was only when they woke, ribbons of light light teasing their eyes, that Jamie and Anne realized they'd fallen asleep.

"Damn it to hell, I didn't want to give rise to any talk about ye." Jamie helped Anne to her feet, then proceeded to brush sand from her gown.

"It's all right." Anne twisted about to help. "Uncle Richard won't even know I was—"

Anne's words stopped abruptly as her eyes focused on the horizon. Lifting her hand she pointed to the ship heading full sail for Libertia's harbor.

She didn't have to ask whose vessel it was. One look at Jamie's expression was proof enough.

He grabbed her hand as they raced toward the settlement.

Chapter Eighteen

"Hold your fire."

Devon crouched among the men scattered behind palm trunks, waiting, their sweating hands gripping the muskets. He could smell their fear . . . or was it his own?

The sound of shelling still rang in his ears. A sound he hadn't expected. But leave it to d'Porteau to pound the seemingly defenseless island with cannon before coming ashore. It was all Jamie could do to keep the men he trained from racing for the far side of the island when the first mortar exploded on the beach. A well-aimed pistol and a harsh reminder of what the Frenchman would do to their women and children kept them steady . . . or at least at their posts.

Luckily d'Porteau's aim was no better than his character. He'd pockmarked the sand and shattered a section of wharf, but luckily no one was hurt. At least not on Jamie's side. He wished he could run across to the other side of the trap and see for himself how those men fared.

But that might give away the surprise. He had to content himself with yelling a brief inquiry, to which Mort

Tatum responded in a high-pitched, nervous voice that all was well.

So they waited. Waited beneath the unforgiving tropical sun. Waited with hearts pounding and sweat pouring down their backs for the pirates to reach the island.

Jamie swallowed, listening as the boats grew closer. He could hear the pirates calling back and forth, hear the swish of oars.

Come on, ye bastard, Jamie prayed. Step right into our trap.

The man beside him, a printer by trade, jerked, and Jamie lay a steadying hand upon his shoulder. "Not much longer, now," he whispered. " 'Twill be over soon."

But how would it end? The nervous anticipation of waiting sent his mind hurtling back in time to another battle. Culledon. A world, a lifetime away, and yet it seemed so close he could still taste the wild expectancy of youth, the bitterness of defeat.

The slide of wood over sand as they pulled the longboats onto the beach reverberated through the air. First one, then another. For better or worse the Frenchman seemed unaware of the welcoming committee.

"Are they all gone?"

Jamie wasn't sure who asked the question but it was d'Portreau who answered. He'd recognize that nasal-toned voice from here to hell.

"Perhaps they've all scurried away like a litter of scared rabbits. Is that the case, *mon ami?*" The last he bellowed so that anyone on this end of the island could hear him.

"I think they all did run away, Cap'n."

The voices grew nearer. The pirates were far enough up the beach to be between the two camouflaged blinds.

Jamie pulled his pistols from the holders crossing his chest, then lifted one hand high above his head.

"So what we gonna do now, Cap'n d'Porteau?"

The Frenchman's laugh was sinister. "We'll steal what they didn't take with them, of course."

Jamie's hand whipped down through the air. Gunshots exploded, and were answered by the islanders across the beach.

For an instant the pirates, as if caught in a painting, stood still, their mouths gaping open.

Then as one they sprang to life, scampering, barely taking the time to shoot, back toward the boats. Some didn't make it. The screams of those hit in the cross fire rent the air.

With a roared command Jamie leaped over the palm logs. Saber in hand he led the attack against the retreating pirates.

D'Porteau.

Jamie saw him farther down the beach, pushing aside a swarthy-looking pirate to jump into the first boat. Ignoring the carnage around him, Jamie rushed toward the shore. His boots sank in the wet sand, then splashed in the surf as he grabbed hold of the boat.

But d'Porteau wasn't the only one trying to get back to the *French Whore*.

"Damn." Jamie sucked in his breath as a cutlass ripped down across his shoulder. Crimson swelled up, staining his shirt, mixing with the sweat and splashed salt water. Fighting had erupted all around him as the islanders caught up with the fleeing pirates.

Turning, Jamie faced Stymie.

"Well, if it ain't Cap'n MacQuaid, back from the dead." The giant of a man lunged, forcing Jamie back against the side of the boat. "But ye ain't gonna escape this time, Cap'n."

He thrust again but this time Jamie feinted to the right, then sliced his own cutlers down across his nemesis's arm. Blood spattered. With an angry roar, Stymie leaped toward Jamie, knocking them both off balance and into the surf.

Arms and legs went flying as they both tried to gain a foothold in the swirling eddy of water. Jamie rolled to his knees, sputtering water. He grabbed Stymie's shirtfront and brought his fist down hard onto his jaw. Again and again, he slammed his knuckles into the pirate's face, while holding him under the surf with the other hand. When Jamie finally yanked Stymie up, the former crew member was coughing and hacking for breath.

By this time Israel and the other islanders had either killed or subdued the remaining pirates. Except for . . .

When Jamie jerked his head around he saw that one of the longboats was gone. D'Porteau and several others were rowing frantically toward the *French Whore*.

"It be all right, Cap'n." Israel came up behind Jamie. "The *Lost Cause* be out there ready to do battle."

Israel was right. As Jamie scanned the dancing waves he saw his ship bearing down hard on the French pirate's vessel. But Jamie had wanted to capture d'Porteau himself. To know the satisfaction of grinding his flesh beneath his boot. Of revenging his treatment upon the *French Whore*.

Shoving Stymie toward shore, Jamie followed, pleased to see that the few pirates left onshore had surrendered and were now being tied together, their hands behind their backs. Stymie was pushed into the group, and Jamie turned back to watch the progress of his vessel.

He wished now that he'd stayed aboard the *Lost Cause*. It would seem strange watching a sea battle from this perspective. His skin itched to be on the quarterdeck shouting commands.

"They aren't going to get away, are they?"

Jamie twisted his head. "What in the hell are ye doing here?" Wrapping his arm around her, Jamie hustled Anne away from the cursing group of pirates. "Didn't I tell ye to stay back with the other women in the cabins?"

Anne's lips thinned. She been through too much to sit on her hands now. "I heard the shooting," she began.

"Which should have been enough to tell ye how dangerous 'twas here."

For the first time since she came up behind him Anne really looked at the captain. What she saw made her skin grow pale. "You're wounded."

Jamie twisted his head to see the cut on his upper arm, then grimaced. " 'Tis nothing but a scratch."

"But it's bleeding." Bending over Anne flipped up her skirts and proceeded to tear a wide strip off her petticoat. Before she could tie the bandage around his arm a loud boom sounded, pulling both their attentions back to the two vessels in the harbor. Clouds of puffy smoke hung above the facing gunwales of each ship.

"The *Lost Cause* is going to win, isn't she?"

Jamie had answered Anne's question with a resounding "aye," a mere half hour before. But he wasn't so confident now. From what he could tell the battle raging between the *French Whore* and his ship was pretty nearly a standoff.

And what was worse, if he didn't miss his guess, the Frenchman had decided enough was enough.

"Damn, I wish I had my glass." Jamie shaded his eyes, then shook his head. With long strides he paced back and forth along the beach, not slowing his stride until Anne grabbed at his arm. Then he winced and cursed again.

"I'm sorry, but can you please tell me what is happening?"

"I can't be sure, but it looks as if d'Porteau is sailing away."

"Sailing away! But he can't. Wait, where are you going?"

But Jamie didn't take the time to answer. He ran toward the remaining longboat, signaling to several of the men guarding the pirates to follow. He had shoved the hull into the water by the time they reached his side. They all splashed through the surf, then leaped over the side and started rowing.

Anne, hands planted firmly on hips, watched from shore wondering what the captain thought he would accomplish by his actions.

As it turned out, nothing.

By the time he reached the spot where the two vessels had been they were sailing out into the Caribbean, the *French Whore* trying to distance itself, the *Lost Cause* close behind.

Anne met the longboat when it rowed back to shore. She waited, saying nothing while Jamie climbed out and helped pull the boat onto the sand. "It wasn't your fault, you know." She fell into step beside him as he headed toward the village.

He only glanced down at her, not saying anything.

"You did your best."

"Damnation, Annie. I had the Frenchman in me grasp, and I let him go."

"Perhaps the *Lost Cause* will catch him."

"Not with Deacon at the helm. He's a fine quartermaster but he's not a sailor like d'Porteau." Jamie turned his head away in disgust. "I should have stayed onboard."

"You couldn't be in two places at once. And the islanders needed you here."

"For God's sake, Annie, will ye stop making excuses for me. I can recognize another failure. I've had enough practice with it."

"Jamie. . . ." Anne reached for his hand. She expected him to pull away, but he didn't. Instead he stopped and turned toward her. His fingers were gentle as they curved around her cheek.

"Don't concern yourself, Annie. 'Tis but fatigue and frustration talking."

"And pain?" Anne nodded toward the cut on his arm that was bleeding through the bandage she wrapped about it.

"Aye." His grin flashed white in his grime-smeared face. " 'Tis that, too." He draped his good arm around her shoulders. "Come, help a poor wounded pirate to his bed."

But when they entered the small settlement it was obvious Jamie wouldn't get any rest. The Libertians were jubilant. Anne had never seen them in such a mood.

Most every man had escaped from the battle unharmed. Mort Tatum did twist his ankle and now hobbled around with a crudely fashioned crutch propped under his arm. And of course, Captain MacQuaid suffered a minor wound, but compared to the last time d'Porteau visited Libertia, it was nothing.

And they'd driven him away.

"He's learned his lesson good."

"True enough. We won't be seeing him in these waters again."

"Huzzahs for Captain MacQuaid!"

The villagers celebrated long into the night. It was like a holiday. Despite Anne's initial reluctance, knowing Jamie's state of mind, she was caught up in the excitement as well.

Lester Perdue tuned up his violin for the first time since d'Porteau's initial raid. The women who could only sit nervously wringing their hands during the battle now came to life, cooking a feast of thanksgiving.

By unspoken agreement everyone ate together, pulling tables and chairs into the palm-shaded common area. A pit was dug and one of the wild pigs that roamed the island was roasted, filling the air with mouthwatering aromas.

While the plates were heaped with pork Jamie was called upon to speak. Anne, knowing his mood, feared he would dampen the villagers enthusiasm. But he had nothing but praise for the Libertians accomplishments.

Lifting a mug kept routinely topped off by a bevy of adoring women, he toasted the island's bravery. "Ye should all be proud of yourselves."

"We showed the cowardly pirate what to expect if he ever shows his face in these parts again," one of the equally inebriated warriors yelled, and Jamie nodded his agreement.

"Aye. Ye showed yourselves proud. Every Jack man of ye." This was followed by a cheer as Jamie downed the rum, coming up for air only when the last drop was drained.

Even Richard Cornwall joined in the mood of the day, his mind seemingly clear. He sat beside Anne exalting the great victory. But he never mentioned the other time d'Porteau visited the island. And he never mentioned his son.

Anne was certainly glad for her uncle's rational mind, be it only temporary, but she was more concerned about Jamie at the moment. He drank too much . . . more than he had since the first time she met him. And though he said nothing of his wound, brushing any comment aside with a wave of his strong, long-fingered hand, she could see the white lines of pain etched around his mouth.

But any suggestion she made that he seek out his bed or simply rest were met with a negative shake of his head. "Come now, Annie, don't ye wish to have a good time?" He draped an arm around her shoulders, leaning his face down close to hers. "Ye heard them, Annie mine, I'm the hero of the moment. The savior of Libertia." He pulled her closer. "No longer the prince of lost causes."

When everyone had eaten their fill, the tables were pulled aside and the dancing began. Lester Perdue's violin flowed from one tune to another as the villagers tapped their toes and swung their partners about.

Anne was sitting with her uncle, Israel, and Jamie when Matthew Baxter asked her to dance. "It's the Cheshire Rounds," he said as if that would somehow make her more willing to join him. It didn't, of course. She wanted to stay as close to Jamie as she could.

He worried her.

Ever since the *Lost Cause* disappeared on the horizon he and Israel had downed mug after mug of rum. She glanced his way, hoping he'd say something about needing her to stay by his side . . . needing her at all.

But he simply lifted his mug in silent toast, then turned back to Israel and downed his drink. Anne felt heat sweep over her cheeks, and she pushed to her feet, taking Matthew's proffered hand. She didn't look back as he led her to the center of the common area.

"She ain't a lass to hide her feelings be they good or bad." Israel leaned back on his stool and crossed his ankles.

"What are ye rambling on about, old man?"

"Mistress Anne, as if ye didn't know."

Jamie knew. He knew every move she made. He narrowed his eyes and watched as the thick-necked young man took her hands and circled her back to the right. He was taller than her by a head, not hard to look at, if you cared for thick necks, and just the type of man she should be with.

He lifted his mug, growling deep in his throat when he found it empty. Anne Cornwall wasn't for the likes of him, and he needed to remember that. Forget her. Forget about d'Porteau while he was at it.

Hell, the good citizens of Libertia were right. The Frenchman probably wouldn't show his face around here again. That was if Keena and Deacon didn't catch him and bring him back.

But the more he tried to forget, the more he tried to wash away memories under a flood of rum, the more his gaze was drawn to her.

"Gawd, lad, but you've got it bad."

Jamie's gaze whipped around toward Israel. He opened his mouth to protest, then snapped it shut again. Flattening his hands on the rough-hewn table he wobbled to his feet. "I'm goin' where I don't have to listen to your jaw flappin'."

Israel's laughter mingled with the strident strains of the violin as Jamie stumbled toward the beach.

Anne saw him go. She missed her quick turn to the left, standing still and pumping into Matthew when he made the correct move. Being the sweet man he was Matthew steadied her, then set about apologizing profusely.

"No, really. It was entirely my fault." Anne took a deep breath. "Do you suppose I could sit for a while? I seem to be more tired than I thought."

"Of course. Let me see if I can find your uncle."

"That's quite all right. Please." Anne placed her hand on his sleeve. "Don't bother yourself."

As she hurried out of the glow of the bonfire and burning brands, Anne heard Israel calling her. She stopped and turned to face him. He was puffing for breath as he approached her, but it didn't stop him from getting right to the point.

"Do ye know what yer about, Mistress Anne?"

"I think I do." Anne lifted her chin.

"And I'm just as sure ye don't."

"I really don't see that this is—"

"Now don't go tellin' me 'tis none of me business 'cause it is. This whole crazy scheme for ye to bring Jamie MacQuaid into this only occurred to ye because of what I told ye about him." His voice lowered. "And I don't like the thought of ye getting hurt."

For a long moment Anne could only stare at Israel. Backdropped by the flickering light of the village, he seemed an odd one to be giving her advice, a retired pirate with grizzled hair hanging loose around his gaunt face, and a pipe stuck in his mouth. It crossed Anne's mind that she should be angered by his interference, but she wasn't.

She lifted her hand slowly, and though she couldn't see his features, Anne knew they registered surprise when she touched his cheek. "I thank you for your concern, Israel. For all you've done over the years for Uncle Richard . . . for me." Anne sighed in her breath. "But it's too late. I already love him, you see."

Saying the words aloud seemed to make it real, bringing all her emotions glaringly into focus. Not waiting for him to say anything, Anne turned and started toward the beach. Her step didn't waver when she heard Israel. He apparently recovered from his shock.

"He's a pirate, Mistress Anne. He'll break yer heart."

"He already has," Anne whispered to herself. "He already has."

She found him standing in the surf, the water splashing onto his boots, his face turned toward the sea. Moonlight limed his broad shoulders and narrow hips, the long muscular legs. Anne resisted the urge to wrap her arms around him, to lean against his strong back. He didn't turn around when she spoke.

"Are you planning to swim out to find your ship?"

She heard his deep intake of breath. "I don't belong here, Annie."

"Really?" Anne walked to his side, feeling the tug of warm water as it seeped through her shoes. "What brought you to that conclusion?"

He looked down at her then, the moonlight sparkling on the gold hoop in his ear. He smelled of rum and the sea, but despite the swell of incoming waves his stance was firm. Anne wondered just how drunk he was.

"I just don't, is all," he said before resuming his study of the endless darkness of sea.

"The good citizens of Libertia seem to think you do."

"They be fools."

"What of me, Jamie? Am I a fool, too?"

His head whipped around. Anne could feel the intensity of his stare. It warmed her in all the places she'd learned to crave his touch.

"Aye, Annie. Ye be the biggest fool of all . . . except for me."

"I don't want to believe that." Her words were spoken softly and carried on a gust of wind toward the breakers.

"Ye have no choice."

Anne's spine stiffened. Jamie MacQuaid created a problem to be sure, but problems had solutions. "There are always choices, Jamie," she insisted. "We simply need to find a way."

His laugh was sharp and without mirth. "Ye haven't changed even a wee bit, have ye, Annie?" His tone was without rancor. " 'Tis still your contention that a solution is there if only ye look hard enough." He shook his head slowly. "Life, my dear Annie, doesn't work that way. I'd have thought your brief acquaintance with me would have taught ye that."

"I want you to stay." There, she'd said it. "With me."

"Here, on Libertia?"

"Yes, why not? 'Tis a lovely island, and the people seem to like you. They—"

"Tolerate me, Anne. They tolerate me. And that's only because they don't know who I really am." He paused, and then tried to change the tone of his denial. "Besides, I don't think I have it in me to be a follower of the great philosopher, John Locke."

"That's not true. You ran your ship by his doctrines. I saw it for myself."

"Ye saw what ye wanted to see."

"Does that include you? Am I only imagining the feelings I have for you? Imagining that you care for me? Tell me I am. Tell me true and I'll leave you in peace to stare into nothingness."

She gave him the perfect out. The perfect opportunity to take the easy road. He could lie to her. Lying was one of the things he did best. Part and parcel of the scoundrel he was. Then why couldn't he do it?

His fingers fisted. "My feelings for ye are not the issue." Jamie strained to make out her features in the silver glow from the moon. "I'd lay down me life for ye, Annie." He heard her swallow. "But I won't stay and sacrifice it."

"But—"

"Annie. Annie." Jamie gave into desire and laid his hands on her shoulders. It seemed only natural to pull her into his arms. To soften the reality. "I've a price on me head. A noose awaiting me if I'm caught." He tugged in a breath but his lungs still seemed starved for air. "How much time do ye think we might have? A sennight? A year, perhaps? Though part of me . . . a strong part is willing to take the risk, I won't."

"I'm not asking you to sacrifice yourself. I'd never want that."

"But it's not meself I'm thinking of, Annie. 'Tis ye." He tangled his fingers in her hair, loving the feel of it, the way it curled around his fingers.

"You needn't worry about me." Anne wrapped her arms around him. Water seeped up her skirts and petticoats. But she didn't care. She didn't care about anything but him. She held on as tightly as she could, but in the end it wasn't tight enough.

Gently, as if he feared she might shatter at his touch, Jamie separated them. "But I do worry about ye, Annie. And that's why as soon as the *Lost Cause* returns, I must leave."

Yet he hesitated, putting off his departure. The *Lost Cause* had sailed back to Libertia . . . without the *French Whore*, as Jamie predicted.

"We lost sight of her on the third day," Deacon explained. "Off the coast of Jamaica." He stared at Jamie soberly, fixing him with his good eye. "I don't think d'Porteau wants to risk this island again.

"Let us hope not," Jamie said before rowing back to Libertia. He'd suggested that his crew would be better off staying aboard. They'd been less than pleased, but he promised they'd sail into New Providence soon and with jewels in their pockets.

Which was all the more reason for him to finish his business here and be gone, Jamie decided as he sat across the table from several of Libertia's leaders. Richard Cornwall was there. But as his mind kept losing focus, Jamie imagined his presence was requested out of respect.

Anne was not present. He hadn't seen more than a passing glimpse of her since he left her on the beach the night of the celebration. He planned it that way, purposely staying away from any place she was likely to be.

And it was breaking his damn heart.

"I don't understand why you won't transport these vile creatures to New Providence for us. We are willing to pay you well for your trouble."

Matthew Baxter's words interrupted Jamie's thoughts and he shifted his attention to the man who'd danced with Anne. Jamie knew it was stupid, but he couldn't get past his dislike for the young man. He tried to hide it as he again gave his excuses . . . not the real reason he couldn't sail into a British port with a brig full of pirates, but the one he'd come up with when first asked.

"I'd like to help ye, Matthew. But I can't. We've tarried too long in these waters as it is. We've cargo bound for the New World that we must see to."

"But New Providence is but a few hours out of your—"

"And I told ye I can't do it." Why wouldn't the man just take no for an answer? He'd probably pursue Anne with the same dogged persistence, finally breaking down her resistance and wedding her. Jamie's jaw clenched, and he flattened his hands on the tabletop, pushing to his feet. He had to get off this island before he lost his mind.

"But what are we to do with them?"

Jamie had no answer except to hang them all from the highest tree, but he knew the good citizens of Libertia didn't want to hear that. Hell, he'd suggested it once and most of them had turned pale with shock. They were law-abiding people, who let the court system take care of their criminals. Even if it meant feeding and keeping the pirates prisoners in a makeshift jail until they could be transported to New Providence . . . where they would undoubtedly be hung.

And where he'd most likely join them in their swing from the gallows if he took them there. As it was Jamie couldn't imagine why some of the pirates hadn't filled their jailor's ears with stories about Jamie.

Another reason for him to leave this island as quickly as he could.

Which he would do. Today.

That decision made, Jamie went in search of Anne. He found her in a cane field standing among the tall grassy plants.

"Looks as if 'tis doing well," he said, holding her stare when she whirled around.

She hesitated a moment, then sighed. "I hope we can get one more good crop this year." She turned back to survey the sweep of green.

"I came to tell ye I was leaving."

Anne picked a leaf and twirled it between her fingers, but she said nothing.

"Did ye not hear me?"

"I heard you." Anne tossed the leaf aside and turned to face him, anger and pain warring with her features. "What do you want from me? A goodbye kiss? A wish for a good voyage?"

"Must we part like this?"

"Yes, Jamie, I think we must, for you're the one forcing the parting." Crossing her arms Anne twisted away from him.

" 'Tis not me, but circumstances, as ye damn well know."

"Then take your circumstances and leave. Just don't expect me to be happy about it."

"If it helps any, I'm not pleased by the prospect of never seeing ye again, either."

"That surprises me." Anne slanted him a look over her shoulder. "As much care as you've taken to avoid me."

Jamie reached out but dropped his hand when she flinched away. " 'Twas for your own good, and ye know it."

Time passed with only the chatter of birds and the eternal wind breaking the silence.

"There be something else."

"What?"

"I don't like asking, Annie. And if it were just me, I wouldn't. But ye know how things be run on me ship." He shuffled his feet, hating his reluctance to ask, and finally blurted it out. "I'll be collecting those jewels now, if ye don't mind."

But she did mind. His request at least temporarily blotted the pain of his leavetaking from her mind. "But I . . . I . . ."

"It be true we didn't capture d'Porteau, but it weren't for lack of trying. And most everyone agrees he'll not be coming here again, and—"

"I don't have them." She blurted out the truth.

"Well now, of course, I knew ye wouldn't be carrying them around with ye but—"

"No." Anne sighed and wrung her hands. "You don't understand. I really don't have them."

Realization of what she was saying spread across his face. "Ye mean ye lied to me?"

"No," she blurted out. "Not exactly. I had the jewels, every one I offered you. But they're gone. Stolen by d'Porteau. That's why I wanted to go with you so I could find them when we captured his ship." Anne couldn't tell by his expression whether or not he planned to give in to his desire to wring her neck. She stepped toward him ready to plead for understanding when they both turned toward the boy running their way. He was yelling at the top of his lungs.

"What's he saying?" Jamie asked when he saw how pale Anne had become.

"Arthur is back," she murmured before taking off at a run. "My cousin has returned!"

Chapter Nineteen

"How did you escape him? Wherever have you been?" Anne hugged her cousin closer. "Oh, never mind all that. I'm so happy you're home.

"You just can't imagine how upsetting this has been for Uncle Richard. Have you seen your father yet? Oh," Anne pushed away with a laugh, "of course you haven't! I've kept you as much a prisoner as d'Porteau ever did."

Despite her words Anne wrapped her arms tighter and buried her face in his shoulder, unaware that the man she was holding, and the man she loved were staring at each other. And that their expressions were anything but friendly.

They stood on the dock. The small schooner that brought Arthur to the island bobbed at anchor, the handful of sailors still busied themselves furling the sails.

"Come. Come. We must go find Uncle Richard. Arthur, he just hasn't been the same since you left. But I'm sure now that you're—" Anne paused, catching her breath and realizing that though she had Arthur by the arm and was doing her best to pull him toward the settlement, he didn't move.

"What . . . ?" she began and swallowed as she caught sight of her cousin's face . . . and the direction of his stare. She whirled toward Jamie and the chill in his eyes made gooseflesh pepper her skin. "I don't under—"

"What is this . . . this *man* doing here?"

Anne stepped away from Arthur, unconsciously placing herself between the two men. A few other settlers had come down to the dock when Arthur arrived, but most of them had wandered back to the village to spread the word.

"Arthur," Anne began. "I don't think you realize what has happened here. This is—"

"I know who he is." Arthur's hard gaze left Jamie to focus on his cousin. "The question is, do you?"

Anne let out a breath of amazement. She couldn't believe the way her cousin was acting. "Yes, yes, I know. I also know he saved us from—"

"What he has or hasn't done is immaterial. This is Jamie MacQuaid." His jaw jutted out defiantly. "And he's a pirate. No doubt he's part of some deadly plot with his friend d'Porteau to destroy us."

"No, don't . . . please." Anne's hand pressed against Jamie's chest; the pleading look in her eyes, stayed him from grabbing Arthur. And Anne had no doubt what the outcome of any altercation between the two would mean to her cousin. But there were more ways to be hurt than being beaten to a pulp. She meant to protect Jamie as well. "Let me talk to him."

"Talk all ye want, Annie. Will do no good."

"Annie, is it?" Arthur raked his gaze over his cousin. "How well do you know this blackguard? Did I save you from rape at the hands of one pirate only to have you become the whore of another?"

She couldn't stop him this time. Jamie was around her, his hands buried deep in the bunched-up fabric of Arthur's jacket before Anne could do anything. She'd never seen Jamie look so fierce as he did now, the tendons in his neck standing out in bold relief, his eyes no more than shards of blue-green glass. He lifted Arthur up so that his toes barely touched the sand.

"If I ever hear ye talk about Anne like that again you'll think the time ye spent on d'Porteau's ship a stroll on the beach." His knuckles tightened until Arthur struggled to get loose. "And ye have the word of Captain James Mac-Quaid on that."

"Jamie, don't. Please."

Anne's pleas finally penetrated Jamie's fury and he dropped Arthur, sorry to see he didn't fall on his arse when he landed. But Anne clutched at his arm, helping to steady him. Jamie didn't think he liked Anne very much at that moment. He definitely felt the full impact of her displeasure when she looked at him.

"I asked you both to stop." Her voice softened. "For my sake, please."

Jamie fisted his fingers, and his jaw ached from clenching it, but he kept his hands to himself, though he felt the need to point out what she obviously missed. " 'Tisn't me going about calling ye names, Annie."

"I know that." Her eyes flashed to Arthur, who stood trying to straighten his rumpled clothing and resurrect his dignity. "Arthur, I won't ever forget the sacrifice you made for me. D'Porteau would have ravished me, killed me more than likely, if not for you." Her shoulders straightened. "But that does not give you the right to say what you did. About me, or about Jamie MacQuaid."

"If you're expecting an apology, don't." He swallowed

nervously when Jamie shifted his feet. "Not that I blame you, Anne. It's just I know what kind of man this is. And I know he has no business being on Libertia. I demand he leave immediately."

"No, Arthur, I—"

"As it were, Annie. I believe 'tis finally something your cousin and I agree upon. I shall leave this island . . . immediately."

"Jamie, don't." Anne tried to catch his arm but he was already moving away from her toward the shore. She turned to Arthur, but there was no help there. He stood, his narrow shoulders squared, a smug expression on his thin face. "Oh!" She was so exasperated with the both of them she could hardly stand it. With Arthur for being the pompous fool she always thought he was. And with Jamie for allowing Arthur to have his way.

Grabbing up her skirts Anne raced after Jamie, catching him just as he approached a group of men gathered on shore. They appeared curious as to what was happening between Arthur and the captain. Mort Tatum was there and Matthew Baxter, and to Anne's relief Israel. If anyone could talk sense into Jamie it was the old pirate.

"I'll be leaving," Jamie announced to the group. "It was a pleasure knowing ye and . . . well, I hope you've no more trouble from d'Porteau."

"Ye wants me to gather up your stuff, Cap'n?" this from Israel whom she'd hoped to solicit as an ally. Anne couldn't believe it.

"Thank ye, Israel."

"No, wait," Anne called, but the grizzled old man was already hurrying off toward the village. So she turned to the men who in her uncle's stead were Libertia's leaders.

"Surely you aren't going to allow Captain MacQuaid to be forced off Libertia after all he's done for us?"

"No one be forcing me, Mistress Cornwall. I made my thoughts clear on that earlier." His eyes held hers and Anne felt the sting of tears.

"Yes, I know what you said, but—"

"I mean it, Annie. 'Tis no good can come of this."

She was going to cry. She was going to break down and fall to her knees in front of everyone, begging him to stay if she didn't get away. Turning on her heel she began walking toward the bank of trees to her right. She didn't stop until she felt the gentle pressure of Jamie's hand on her arm.

He'd followed her, leaving the other men staring after them in bewilderment. Not caring except for what they might think of Anne after he left.

"Anne, ye must know this is for the best."

She just shook her head, refusing to face him, not wanting him to see the tears wetting her cheeks.

"Annie. . . ." The pain in his voice seemed as genuine as her own.

"How can it be right, when it feels so terribly wrong?"

She heard him swallow. "I won't touch ye, Annie. Kiss ye as I'd like." He hesitated and when he spoke again Anne thought she heard heartbreak to match her own. "But, Annie, I have to leave ye. Please understand."

She did. Anne shut her eyes, letting out her breath on a deep sigh. She hated that he was leaving, but she did understand. And knowing why made everything seem all the more hopeless.

He broke his own rules by lifting his hand and cupping her shoulder. But Anne never knew what he was going to say for at that moment Israel yelled from the pathway.

"Got yer stuff, Cap'n, and me own."

It took a moment for the words to register with Jamie. Then he looked around, annoyed by the interruption . . . glad for it. "What are ye talking about, old man?"

"Goin' with ye," Israel yelled. "I've got seawater runnin' in me veins and it be time I answered its call."

"Take me." Her voice was so low Anne wasn't sure if Jamie heard her until his fingers folded over hers.

"I love ye too much to do that to ye," he said and then he was gone.

Anne jerked her head around but he was already striding toward the wharf, his powerful gait eating up the distance quickly. Israel jumped into a rowboat, unlashing the oars as Jamie shoved the hull into the foaming surf . . . and Anne could watch no more.

But she did make her way to the secluded beach where they'd made love and she waited for the *Lost Cause* to sail by. She could almost hear the song of billowing sails, feel the wind hard in her face, taste the salt, and know the freedom.

Almost.

She didn't die of a broken heart.

Though Anne thought that a definite possibility at the time, as the weeks went by, she knew it wasn't going to happen. At first she wasn't sure it was necessarily a good thing . . . but at times death seemed preferable to the longing that swept over her . . . now she was glad to be alive. Someone had to talk with Arthur, and it appeared she was the one to do it.

Anne knocked on the door of the office that used to be hers, opening it when her cousin bid her enter. He was seated in a winged chair he had brought from Richard's house, his feet resting on a stool, a glass of wine in his hand.

"Yes, Anne." He eyed her over the goblet's rim as he took a sip of amber liquid. "What did you want?"

He offered no seat, nor did Anne want one. She paced the length of the small room, then turned to face him. "Uncle Richard seems to be worse."

"Oh?" Arthur took another sip of wine. "In what way?"

"Perhaps if you visited your father you would know." To Anne's surprise, Arthur had moved into a cottage left vacant by a family who'd quit the island after d'Porteau's first raid killed their son. Arthur said at the time he needed some time to himself after the horrors of imprisonment aboard the Frenchman's ship, and Anne had sympathized. Even without his frequent reminders that his capture had been a result of saving her.

But now, nearly two months after his return to Libertia, after his escape from d'Porteau, Anne wondered about his reasons for ignoring his father. Actually she wondered about quite a few things regarding Arthur. Her fingers tightened around the brooch in her pocket. She barely listened as Arthur listed his excuses.

"Besides," he said. "I know you will come here every day with reports and recriminations." He stretched out his legs. "What is your complaint today?"

"You mean other than your neglect of your father?" Anne raised her chin, then continued when her cousin merely glared at her. "Actually I have several."

"Well, make them quickly. I am busy."

"Really?" Anne arched her brow. "Then perhaps you can explain why there has been nothing done about arranging for a vessel to transport our sugar cones? A meeting should have been called—"

"For what reason?" Arthur rubbed his prominent nose. "All those gatherings to decide who does what and when, are a waste of time."

"They are one of the foundations that Libertia was built upon." One of the cornerstones her cousin was slowly chipping away, at least according to all the citizens who came to her with complaints.

"He makes all the decisions himself, without a by your leave," Matthew Baxter remarked.

" 'Tis true," Lester Perdue agreed. "Why just yesterday Arthur had Elmer Dodd thrown into jail without so much as a trial. When I questioned him about it, he told me to mind my own concerns or I'd be joining old Elmer."

Arthur simply shrugged his narrow shoulders now. "Perhaps we should rethink the way things are handled around here." He waved his hand in dismissal. "Now if there's nothing else."

"Actually there is." Anne took a step closer. "I mentioned your father." She ignored the thinning of his already narrow lips. "He's taken to roaming about. He wanders everywhere on the island seemingly unaware of his destination. Besides my concern for his safety—"

"A lock and key might be in order."

"Perhaps you think we should jail him as you did Elmer?" Anne said, then hurried on. "But that isn't the point at the moment."

"Then pray get on with it and leave."

"This morning I found Uncle Richard wandering along the beach. He was clutching this." Anne pulled the ruby-encrusted brooch from her pocket, holding it in front of her for Arthur to see. "You do recognize it, don't you?"

"Yes." He fluttered his hand. "It's yours, I believe. You really should take more care with your belongings."

"It hasn't been in my *care* for quite a while, Arthur. Not since d'Porteau stole it, along with the rest of my mother's jewels." When her cousin made no comment, Anne continued. "Naturally I was curious as to where Uncle Richard found the brooch." She paused. "He told me it was in your cottage."

"And you believed him. The old man is madder than a rabid dog."

Anne's spine stiffened in response to Arthur's description of her beloved uncle but she reminded herself that arguing over Richard's condition was not her goal. "I did have my doubts, but when he led me back to your cottage and showed me—"

"You entered my home uninvited?" Arthur yelled, jumping to his feet. "I shall have the both of you jailed for thievery."

" 'Tis more you who should bear the name thief. Arthur, several of the jewels are hidden in your chest. My mother's diamond necklace, the emerald ring. Where did you get them?"

"I don't answer to you." He took a menacing step forward. "I don't answer to anyone."

Though frightened Anne held her ground. "Tell me how my jewels came to be in your possession. Did you take them from d'Porteau when you escaped?" That had been the only logical explanation . . . the only explanation that put Arthur in a favorable light . . . that Anne had come up with. And she expected him to embrace it readily.

But he didn't. He simply stared at her, his pale blue eyes narrowed, his gaunt cheeks sucked in. "I suppose you might as well know. The secret will be out soon."

"What secret?" Anne did take a step toward the door now. His quiet tone, the hard expression on his face frightened her more than his explosive anger.

"You tell *me*, Anne. You were always the clever one. The one my father turned to for guidance."

"That's not true. He always looked toward you. Losing you was the reason his mind went."

"Oh, don't tell me that." Arthur stalked closer. "He never cared a fig for me except where I could help him with his beloved 'Grand Experiment'. That's all either of us ever were to him. Bodies he could use to populate this godforsaken island."

Anne swallowed down fear. "If you feel that way why don't you leave?"

"Exactly what I intend to do, my clever little cousin." His hand snaked out, manacling Anne's wrist. "But I'm not going empty-handed."

"You're hurting me." Anne tried to wriggle free, but he was a lot stronger than he looked. In a panic she reached through the slit in her skirt, grabbing for the knife she kept lashed to her thigh. But Arthur was quicker, knocking her aside. Anne stumbled and grasped for the arm of his chair to break her fall, but she missed. In a tumble of petticoats and skirts she fell to the planked floor.

He was looming over her before she could scramble to her feet.

And now he had a pistol aimed her way.

"You know I'm rather glad you came to visit me today, Anne." He cocked the hammer. "I suppose I have much to thank you for. If not for your penchant for taking charge, Father might actually have expected me to do something around here. And of course, I'm quite appreciative of your jewels."

"How did you get them?" Anne inched away from him until she felt the solid wall press into her back.

He stepped closer. "Why I took them, of course." He smiled benignly. "While everyone else was in a dither over d'Porteau's visit, I simply broke into the chest where you kept them."

"But d'Porteau, surely he—"

"What? Took them from me?" Arthur shook his head and laughed. "You really don't understand yet, do you? It's too bad Father is so mad, I'd love to show him how his doltish son outsmarted the great Mistress Anne. Outsmarted everyone else on Libertia as well."

He nudged the stool toward him with the toe of his silver-buckled shoes, then sat down. "You see, the Frenchman came to Libertia at my suggestion. Oh, I see I've shocked you." Arthur made a "tsking" sound with his mouth sending a fine spray of saliva over his chin. "But I assure you it's true. Our scheme was simple. And it worked like a charm."

"But you saved me from him."

"It may have appeared that way to you, but it was a mere coincidence, I assure you. One that Willet was less than pleased about. He apparently took a liking to you, Annie, and didn't care for my interruption. But he shall forgive me I'm sure when I hand you over to him."

"Oh, no you won't." Anne pushed herself forward, barreling into her cousin and knocking him off the stool. As she scurried to her feet she heard his surprised "umph" when he hit the floor. Balling up her skirts she rushed forward. Her hand was on the latch before the pain exploded in her head.

Then everything went black.

The fog in her mind lifted slowly. At first Anne couldn't separate the pounding on the door with that in her head. She tried to move, but it was as if her limbs were weighted. Her tongue suffered the same malady. She opened her mouth . . . or at least tried to . . . but no sound came out.

The only function of her body that worked was her hearing. The pounding was incessant. The screams a cruel taunt. "D'Porteau is coming! D'Porteau is coming! D'Porteau is here!"

Anne struggled to think, to do *something*. Until the dark veil of oblivion settled back over her.

Nightmares, torturous nightmares, plagued her sleep. Anne woke with a start and this time a howling roared in her ears. She opened her eyes, unable to tell if it was night or day. She lay on a bed. On her back. Her hands were tied in front of her and an experimental twitch of her legs showed they were bound as well.

Panic seized her and Anne forced herself to lie still and take a deep breath. The nightmares hadn't been nightmares at all, but the sting of a cruel reality.

Her memory opened slowly like petals of a hateful flower. Finding the brooch. Confronting Arthur. His admission of guilt and his association with d'Porteau. D'Porteau. Was she still dreaming or could she hear his high-pitched, nasal voice over the keening of the wind?

Anne concentrated on listening, a cold sweat breaking out on her skin when she recognized his hated voice. She was in the bedroom of Arthur's cottage. Her eyes were accustomed enough to the eerie light to recognize the chest where she found her mother's jewels. The sound of the voices . . . D'Porteau, her cousin, and several others she didn't recognize . . . came from the parlor.

She tried but could not understand what they said, that is until the door slammed open and Arthur and d'Porteau stepped into the room.

"Ah, there is our little flower." D'Porteau leaned over her, his oily black curls grazing her cheek. "Awake at last." He chuckled at Anne's futile struggles, then turned toward Arthur, who stood beside him. "I'd begun to fear you'd given her too much laudanum."

"What difference does it make? I don't like the idea of tarrying here."

D'Porteau shrugged. "You worry too much, *mon ami*. There is nothing these cowardly villagers can do now. You saw the way they practically welcomed me with open arms."

Arthur stopped his pacing. "Don't forget that was my doing."

"Non, non, do not fear. I shall remember it was you who told them all was lost and their best chance was to surrender."

"It saved you a fight," Arthur said with a nod of his head.

"One I would have won." D'Porteau lifted a black velvet-draped shoulder. "But *oui*, you are correct." He turned his attention back toward Anne, tracing beringed fingers down the center of her chest, smiling when she tried to shrink away. "Besides, there is nothing we can do in this weather, but allow ourselves a bit of pleasure."

The smacking of something against the outside wall of the cottage caught d'Porteau and Arthur's notice. Anne's cousin moved to the shuttered window and tried to peer out between the louvers. "This isn't some little storm," he said, twisting around toward d'Porteau. Seeing the other's eyes focused back on the woman on the bed, he gave a deep sigh.

"Take her and be done with it, by God."

D'Porteau's laugh was as nasal as his voice. "Ah, but that would ruin the anticipation." He caught Anne's eye. "For the both of us." Then with an evil sneer he turned and pranced from the room, his stout body balancing tenuously on the high-heeled shoes.

Arthur stepped to the side of the bed and looked down at Anne, his expression full of contempt. Then he, too, left her alone.

As soon as the door latched behind them Anne spread her hands as wide as the constricting rope would allow and clutched fabric. Slowly she pulled upward, bunching her skirt and petticoat, revealing an inch of ankle. Again and again she repeated her movements, trying to hurry, ignoring the pain as the rope tore into the skin of her wrists.

Outside the rumble of the storm grew louder. Lightening flashed, spearing the room with hot, white light, and thunder roared, vying with the fury of the wind to be heard.

Inside, too, the noise increased. She could hear their voices. It was only her cousin and the Frenchman who talked now. They were arguing about something. And drinking. She heard the clinking of glasses as their words became louder and more insistent.

Anne had almost bared the leather sheath that held her knife to her thigh when she heard the gunshot. There was only one and it came from the next room. Her heart pounded faster, and her fingers no longer remembered to be cautious lest she knock down her skirts, undoing all her tiresome effort. She grabbed at the ruffles, pulling them as best she could, lifting her head to keep a wary eye on the door.

She had no idea what happened but she expected the door to burst open any moment. When her hand clamped around the bone handle she gave a small cry of relief, muffled by the gag stuffed in her mouth. She yanked it up, careful, despite her haste not to let the knife slip from her fingers.

Leaning forward she hacked at the rope binding her feet, nearly dropping the knife when the blade sliced through the rope. Freeing her hands was more difficult. She wedged the handle between her feet, then sat up, sawing rope binding her wrists back and forth over the honed surface.

There was still no sound from the other room . . . there hadn't been since the gunshot, but Anne's eyes still strayed to the door often as she slowly hacked through the rope. When her hands broke free she pulled the gag down, gulping air in through her sore mouth, then leaped from the bed.

Her knife was poised as she slipped to the door, placing her ear against the paneled wood and listening. Then carefully she lifted the latch and peeked through the small wedge of space. She couldn't help the gasp that escaped

her when she saw Arthur sprawled on the floor, an ever
blossoming flower of crimson blood on his chest.

Anne quickly looked around the room, but d'Porteau
was nowhere to be seen. Avoiding the blindly staring eyes
of her cousin Anne raced across the room and yanked
open the door. Before she stepped outside her hair and
clothing were soaked by the torrential rain. The wind
blew so hard it was difficult to get her bearings. The
murky, yellow-tinged sky and the howling wind seemed
like a part of her earlier nightmares.

But Anne had no time for fantasies. She had to do
something. Get help somewhere. She clutched her knife
and raced toward her uncle's cottage.

"Uncle Richard!" Anne screamed his name as she ran
inside. But the rooms were empty. Back outside she
dashed toward Matthew Baxter's, her head bowed by the
storm.

She let out a piercing scream when she plowed into the
hard body. In the dim light it was difficult to recognize
Israel until he spoke.

"Oh my God!" Anne dropped her knife in the mud as
she reached up to grab the old man's shoulders. "Jamie,"
she yelled. "Is he with you?"

Israel gathered his wits, cupping his hands and calling
to a dark shape farther up the path. Anne was barreling
toward him before Jamie was turned around. She flew
into his arms, burying herself against his soaked chest as
his arms wrapped around her.

The wind tore at her skirts and hair, whistled about her
ears, but for this brief moment he was her safe harbor
against the storm. Anne reveled in his strength, dreading
the moment when reality pulled them apart. It came
sooner than she anticipated. His hands cupped her shoul-

ders, drawing her back, until she could make out the anxious expression on his face. Water streamed from his hair, down the hollows of his cheeks.

"What are you doing out in this weather?"

Anne could tell by his expression that he was yelling, but such was the intensity of the storm that she could barely hear him. "D'Porteau," was all she answered as the horror of the past hours surged back to her.

"I know." Jamie tucked her under his arm, protecting her as much as he could from the elements and head down trudged toward the nearest cabin, Richard Cornwall's. He fought the wind to open the door and push them both inside.

His hands bracketed her face, brushing away the wet strands of hair from her forehead and cheeks. "I kept close to Libertia. I just didn't trust that d'Porteau wouldn't return. When he did, I followed," Jamie said after his lips touched hers. "The *Lost Cause* is hidden in a cove on the lee side of the island. When the Frenchman lands we'll be ready for him. What is it, Annie?"

"He's already here." Words tumbled from her mouth so quickly Anne wasn't sure she made any sense. "Uncle Richard found my mother's brooch and I confronted Arthur. He was in on it, Jamie. He helped plan d'Porteau's raid on Libertia. And he grabbed me and drugged me, I think. Then I heard them talking and d'Porteau shot him. He's dead."

"Who's dead? Annie, tell me." He shook her shoulders, until she looked back up at him, crystal droplets tipping her lashes.

"Arthur. D'Porteau shot him."

Jamie let his hands drift down her arms. "Ye stay here. I'm going to find him."

"But I want to come with you."

"Nay. There's a hurricane blowing out there, Annie."

Anne's eyes widened and she grasped his forearms. "Uncle Richard's missing. He's begun to wander around the island of late and this is his cottage and he's not here."

"He's probably a hell of a lot drier than we are, huddled safely in someone else's house."

"No." Anne shook her head. "No, I just know he's out there."

"Anne, listen to me." He shook her again. "There be nothing ye can do now. Where's d'Porteau?"

"I don't know. I saw only him once, when he came in the bedroom and threatened me. That was at Arthur's cabin, but he's not there now." Anne sucked in her breath, trying to regain her composure. She knew Jamie was right about her uncle. There was no way she could find him in this weather. And d'Porteau was a threat to everyone's safety.

"He could be anywhere. No, wait." Anne clutched his shirt. "I heard him say something about the sugar mill. He said his men were there, and the prisoners."

"What prisoners?

"I don't know. That's all I heard."

"That's enough, sweetheart." Jamie hugged her to his body quickly, then reluctantly let her go. "Now pay me heed this time and stay here. I'll be back for ye as soon as I can." With that he turned and shoved the door open, allowing rain and debris to blow into the room. He slammed it behind him and was gone.

And Anne, heedless of her wet clothes, and the thunderous roar of the storm, began to pace the small room.

Chapter Twenty

Their pistols and muskets were useless.

Jamie stared down at the wet firearm in his hand, then stuck it back in the sash across his chest. There was no way the powder would catch the spark. Unfortunately, d'Porteau's crew, languishing snug and dry inside the sugar works didn't suffer the same malady. Jamie imagined their guns would fire just fine.

He and the few men with him would discover that sad truth the moment they broke through the door.

"What we gonna do, Cap'n?"

Jamie glanced over at Israel. The wily old man was barely holding his own against the wind. Besides him, he had five other men, and a supply of knives and pikes from the *Lost Cause*.

Jamie cupped his hands so Israel could hear. "Be there a back door to this place?"

When Israel nodded, Jamie signaled him to lead him to it. Before they left the rest of the men in the dubious shelter of some rocks, Jamie lashed a sword and several knives around his waist, clamping an extra between his teeth.

After they fought the wind and blinding rain around to the back, Jamie struggled with the hook of one of the shutters covering a rear window. As soon as it was loose, the louvered wood began flailing back and forth, knocking against the building.

It wasn't long before the door slivered open. Cursing a stream of obscenities worthy of his calling, a pirate inched through the door. Huddled over against the storm he looked left and right, then spotting the loose shutter, started toward it. He didn't notice anyone until Jamie tapped him on the shoulder.

One punch had him sprawled in the mud.

Jamie signaled for Israel to fix the shutter, then he opened the door and slipped inside. He quickly settled behind some barrels and wiped the water from his eyes. A light was glowing toward the front of the building, and it was from there that Jamie could hear voices. Loud voices, muffled by the wild fury of the storm, but clear enough to recognize the slur of heavy drinking.

Jamie worked his way from barrel to barrel, wondering how long it would take before d'Porteau would miss the pirate he sent to fix the shutter. He could distinguish the Frenchman's nasal twang now, and Jamie honed in on it as he crept silently forward.

He was so intent upon his foe that Jamie almost missed the shuffle of sound behind him. He jerked around, expecting an attack from the rear, only to see a half-dozen men crouched down and tied together. Matthew Baxter and Mort Tatum. Jamie recognized the leaders of the settlement. The young men likely to give d'Porteau the most trouble. They stared at him above their gags with imploring eyes.

Circling back behind, Jamie worked quickly to slice

through the ropes, passing out all the knives. He pressed a finger to his lips, then directed three to the left, three to the right, and motioned for the rest to follow him.

Candlelight showed perhaps twenty pirates sprawled on kegs, benches, and the floor. A few had tin cups, but most simply drank from bottles and jugs. By their sound and posture, they'd been imbibing the rum for quite a while.

Which was to Jamie's advantage. That and surprise. But he couldn't help noticing the loaded pistols within reach of most of the pirates.

His fingers tightened on the knife handle and he watched, waiting for the other men to position themselves around the group of revelers. Then he pushed to the balls of his feet and leaped forward.

The pirates twisted around awkwardly, their faces contorted in a grotesque mask of surprise. But drunk though they were, these men were fighters. Jamie heard the first explosion of gunfire as he grappled d'Porteau to the ground. Air left the Frenchman in a loud *whoomph*. For all his drunkenness and effeminate ways d'Porteau had not gained his success as a pirate by chance. He was strong and tough and ruthless, curving his fingers toward Jamie's eyes like a cornered panther.

But there was too much at stake, and Jamie was in no mood for defeat. He pummeled his fist into the sagging jowls again and again. D'Porteau grasped for his pistol, yanking it from his jacket and swinging it forward. The barrel caught Jamie's temple. Blood spurted out, the pain blinding him for the costly few seconds d'Porteau needed to stagger to his feet and aim the gun.

A shot reverberated through the building, and Jamie waited for the darkness to follow. But it was d'Porteau who fell back. His burly shoulder knocked against the table, jarring the candle from the shallow dish where it swam in a pool of hot tallow.

Jamie's head whipped around in time to see Israel standing over d'Porteau, a smoking pistol gripped in his hand.

"I alway's did want to kill the bastard," he said before dropping the spent gun and whipping out his knife as another adversary rushed toward him.

Jamie pushed to his feet, joining the melee. Confusion reigned, made more hauntingly eerie by the ribbons of smoke filtering up from the floor. The pirates had not been neat drinkers. Flames leapfrogged from one bit of rum-soaked timber to the next, feeding on anything flammable. When the fire reached the kegs of rum they exploded into an inferno, sucking oxygen from the air and shooting flames toward the roof.

"Let's get out of here!"

It was Lester Perdue yelling, and Jamie turned as Israel grabbed his arm. The old man doubled over coughing, but his fingers didn't lose their grip on Jamie's arm. "Come on, Cap'n," he managed to sputter before his legs folded under him.

Jamie caught him before he hit the floor, tossing him over his shoulder. Lowering his head, Jamie pushed through the smoke toward the front.

"Is anyone else inside?" Jamie yelled as he stumbled through the doorway. The rain had all but stopped and the wind stilled. But the sky held a strange light beyond what the fire gave it. Jamie dropped to his knees in the mud a few rods from the sugar works. He propped Israel against a tree trunk, then sucked in breaths of clean, clear air. A small knot of men stood, silently watching the flames eat up the building. Some of them turned toward him when Jamie repeated his question.

"It appears we all got out," Mort answered. "Except the pirates, and Les Milkens, but he had a hole in his chest. Wait, Captain MacQuaid." He stepped between Jamie and the fiery inferno. "He was dead. And that's what you'll be if you go back in there." At that moment the roof collapsed in silent agreement, sending a glitter of sparks spraying into the sky.

The storm was over . . . at least for the moment.

Anne had lived in the Caribbean long enough to know the respite was temporary, that the backside of a hurricane was often more deadly. But she had time, especially if she hurried. And she didn't think she could bear any more pacing back and forth across the floor, wondering what had happened. She needed to find Jamie. She needed to find Uncle Richard.

Anne hurried along the path, picking her way around the debris. She knew the storm was bad, but she hadn't anticipated this much damage to the island.

In the distance she could see smoke—the sugar works—and rushed toward it as quickly as she could. It wasn't until she was almost past the upended tree before she caught sight of something beneath the fronds. Her breath coming in painful gasps, Anne rushed forward, somehow knowing what she would find before she fought her way through the sharp-edged greenery.

He wasn't dead. Anne could see the shallow rise and fall of her uncle's chest beneath the wet waistcoat. But his color was bad, contrasting white to the streaks of brown-gray mud covering his face.

"Uncle Richard!" Anne tried to wake him, but her frantic calls didn't elicit so much as a flutter of his stubby lashes.

And moving him was impossible. When Anne tried she discovered his legs were pinned beneath the uprooted palm. Though she shoved and pulled, she couldn't budge it an inch. Anne scrambled to her feet, determined to run for help. But before she could her face was pelted with a fresh torrent of rain. The wind and rain resumed in earnest and she squatted down, shielding her uncle's head with her body least he drown in the downpour.

She was gone.

"Damnation!" Jamie thumped his palm against the door after checking the small cottage for Anne. He left Israel and the others at the church, where most of the citizens had congregated to wait out the storm. And he'd come to fetch Anne and take her there, too, arriving here just as the fury of the hurricane broke free again. Only to find her gone.

But where?

She wasn't at the church or sugar works. And it made no sense for her to go to another cottage. This one seemed to have weathered the first half of the storm as well as any.

Which only meant one thing. Jamie shoved through the door and into the howling tempest, not sure where he was going, only knowing he couldn't leave her out there. Not without trying to find her.

He would later think of it as a miracle, but for now he only called it blind luck as he stumbled over the tree where she sat bent over her uncle's still form.

"My God, Anne." Jamie hugged her sodden body to

his. She clung to him but when he tried to pull her up, resisted.

"I can't move him. He's trapped," she cried, her words immediately whipped away by the wind.

And nearly dead, Jamie thought but didn't say. "Ye get on back to the cottage. I'll bring him."

"No."

She shook her head frantically and Jamie decided he didn't have time to argue. He worked his way through the mud down the trunk until he could get a good hold. Then he wrapped his arms around the smooth bark and with a grunt lifted. The tree was heavier than he thought but he finally managed to shift its weight.

"Pull him, now!" he yelled into the storm.

She knew she must be hurting him as she tugged at his body. But she had no choice. When his legs were clear she called to Jamie. The tree trunk sank into marshy soil.

Gathering the older man in his arms, Jamie bent his head against the howling wind and followed Anne toward the shelter of the nearest cabin.

He knew he'd find her here.

Jamie stood watching Anne a moment, feeling her pain, before he walked toward the burial plot. The islanders had surrounded the simple graves with a fence of unpainted pickets, as if they could somehow protect those who lay beneath the ground. Or perhaps it was a reminder that civilization had once survived and flourished on Libertia.

Bending down Jamie twisted off a tangle of vines already encroaching under the fence.

She glanced around, giving him a sad smile and brushing a strand of hair beneath her bonnet. "It's time to go, I suppose."

"Aye." Jamie tossed the leaves toward the undergrowth. "We'll miss the tide if we don't sail soon."

Anne folded her hands, though she didn't turn away from the small cross that marked her uncle's grave. "Perhaps it's best he didn't live to see his dream destroyed."

She turned the full force of her dark eyes on him, and Jamie could only shrug. He felt like a cad for taking her away, yet there was nothing here for her. The hurricane destroyed what was left of the sugar crop after the fire at the mill.

And the settlers, the believers in Richard Cornwall's dream, wanted to leave. Jamie was taking them to the New World. The morning after the storm, when the sun rose in a clear Caribbean sky they'd surveyed the damage. Then they'd buried the dead, including their leader, and the pirates . . . and Arthur. After the funerals they held a meeting and voted . . . to abandon the colony.

For the sennight since, Jamie and his crew had worked making repairs on the *Lost Cause*. It had survived the storm better than the French ship. The morning after the hurricane all that could be seen of the *French Whore* was the tip of its mainmast. Debris from the wreckage still washed ashore.

Jamie followed Anne as she walked to the crest of the hill. From where they stood, the island lay below, a crazy quilt of downed trees and windswept fields. Beyond, on the turquoise bay, was the *Lost Cause*.

"I know ye don't want to leave, but—"

"What made you think that?" Anne looked up at the captain. The incessant wind streamed burnished hair back from his face, showing the glitter of gold in his ear.

He looked every inch the pirate, but his expression was gentle as his eyes met hers. "Libertia was my uncle's dream, not mine. Oh, I wanted to see it succeed . . . for him. But I will not mind quitting this place." Her lashes lowered. "At least I wouldn't if we were together."

"Annie." His voice was raw with pain.

"I love you, Jamie. Nothing can change that. Not the fact that you're a pirate . . ." Her words trailed off. "Not anything."

"Why do we have to discuss this now?"

"When would you prefer? When you leave me in Charles Town? Or perhaps you'd rather we never talked about it at all. It would be easier that way, wouldn't it?"

"Damnation, Anne. I think I've shown I'm not always willing to take the easiest course. And you're mad if ye think that's what I'm doing now." He turned away from her. "I've explained to ye why it would never work."

"Because you're a pirate."

"Aye. Nothing's changed there."

"But what if you weren't?"

He turned on her slowly, his expression sad. "Annie, don't do this."

"I want an answer." Anne stepped away from his hand when he would have touched her. "I think you owe me that much." She ignored the brows he raised at her last comment. "All right, perhaps you owe me nothing. But I'd like an answer just the same. If you weren't a pirate what would you do?" Lifting her chin she challenged him to answer.

He hesitated only a moment. "I'd marry ye, Annie, if you'd have me," he said simply, and Anne was filled with so much love for him she vaulted into his embrace, snuggling against his wide chest. He smelled of wind and salt and freedom, and she was wont to let him go, even when his hands gently pushed her away.

"What I want, and what I shall have are two entirely different things. 'Twas a lesson hard learned, but not easily forgotten." With that he turned and slowly walked down the hill. Not stopping until she caught up with him and forced a rolled parchment into his hands.

His gaze fell on the document, then raised to meet hers in question.

"Read it," was all she said. Anne watched his face as he untied the bit of twine and spread the paper out in his hands. He scanned the words written in her uncle's meticulous script, then read them more carefully before looking up again at Anne.

"Don't you know what it is? What it means?"

" 'Tis a Letter of Marque . . . made out to me. But why . . . ? How . . . ?"

Anne let out a breath she didn't realize she held. "The 'why' I don't know for certain, but the how is easy. Uncle Richard founded Libertia on a royal grant, which made him the governor, equal in standing and importance with other royal governors."

"Capable of soliciting privateers?"

"Exactly. England is at war with France. I suppose Uncle Richard felt that since d'Porteau was a French pirate, you were helping England." She paused. "Uncle Richard had vice-admiralty powers. Actually as royal governor, he had many powers, but in keeping with John Locke's philosophy he rarely used them."

"But he did this. . . . By official decree he made me and my crew privateers rather than pirates." Jamie could barely contain the excitement in his voice as he stared down at the parchment, then back at Anne.

"He was fond of you, Jamie, and he believed in you. As I do."

Anne no sooner had the words out of her mouth when she was drawn into his hard embrace. They were both laughing and crying and holding on to each other.

"Did you notice at the bottom where he gave you a pardon for past crimes?"

"I did. But I can still hardly believe it. 'Tis like a second chance at life." His thumb brushed along her cheek. She looked up at him, her eyes bright with love. Slowly his lips brushed hers. "A second chance for us, Annie, love."

Epilogue

Charles Town, South Carolina
Spring 1764

As soon as the crew had the gangplank in place Anne rushed onto the *Lost Cause*. She'd watched from the docks in Charles Town as the sloop sailed into port, shading her eyes and trying to catch a glimpse of Jamie. She waved now as he leaped from the quarterdeck. The sight of him took her breath away, even dressed as he was in the more subdued garb of a respected sea captain.

He wore his hair brushed back in a queue with nary a glimmer of gold showing at his ear. And his jacket covered a shirt fastened at the throat. But there was something about him that conjured up images of making love with the trade winds drifting over her naked skin and the tide tickling her toes.

Her body quickened at the thought, and her cheeks were a rosy pink when he lifted her into a sweeping embrace. His kiss was deep and hungry, and Anne's knees could barely support her when he lifted his head.

"Captain . . . please," she whispered, as she grabbed for the hat tilting off her head.

"Please what, Annie?" His grin was wicked. A pirate's grin. "Isn't this a proper greeting for my wife?"

"Well, yes." Anne smiled. "I suppose it will do . . . for a start. But it's not as your wife I've come aboard." His brow arched and Anne hurried on. "I've come as your business partner."

"I see." His expression sobered. "Then I suppose if it's business we're to be discussing, my cabin be the place for it." He grabbed her hand, before she could say a word and led her through the maze of sailors, toward the hatch. He yelled something to Deacon about needing a private discussion with his partner before hustling her down the ladder.

He pulled her through the door, kicking it shut and backing her against it. Anne found herself wedged between the hard wood and his equally hard body in one fluid motion.

His mouth trailed a path down her neck, not stopping when he encountered the border of ruffled lace. Anne arched her back as he bit at her nipple through the binding silk.

"Now," he teased, glancing up at her through gold-tipped lashes. "What did ye want to speak with me about?"

She had no idea. And the more he fondled her breasts the less she cared. Anne moaned when his hands skimmed off her hips to search through the layers of petticoats.

"Oh, Jamie." Her fingers tangled in his hair. "I've missed you so much."

"And I ye, Annie." His palm splayed the tight curls between her legs. "Lord help me, but you're soft." His voice caught as she fumbled with the front packet of his breeches. "And wet."

His mouth fused with hers as his manhood surged into her hands.

And then he was filling her, deep and complete.

Anne buried her hands beneath his jacket, clinging to his hot skin as he lifted her legs, wrapping them around his waist.

Jamie thrust, and Anne melted around him, neither able to stop the explosive release that gripped them. They both trembled, clutching each other as the sky opened to reveal love's tempting peek at heaven.

He was staring at her, his forehead pressed to hers, when Anne finally floated back to earth. She couldn't help the tiny giggle that burst forth. "Two months is a long time," she said, sighing.

"Too long, Annie," Jamie agreed. "I do not like leaving ye."

"I don't like it either. While we were at war with the French there was no choice. But now . . ." Anne let the rest of the sentence fade away as he settled her feet onto the floor. Taking her hand Jamie led her to his bunk. She didn't say anything as he brushed the charts and rumpled clothing to the deck.

When they were comfortably settled, lying side by side, Jamie spoke again. "I wish there was another way to live other than this." He shifted to look down at her upturned face. "Not that I'm not especially fond of the homecomings, but living apart is hard on us both."

"What if there was a way to be together?"

"Now, Annie, we've been through this before. I don't care if ye have gotten over your seasickness, I won't be taking ye with me. It's too dangerous."

"I don't want to go."

"Ye don't?" He lifted her around until she faced him.

"No. I'll be too busy to go off on sea voyages."

"Doing what?"

"I'll tell you in a moment. First of all, I want to know how important captaining a ship is to you. I know how long you've done it and how you enjoy the wind in your face and the freedom, and—"

"Are ye asking as me wife or business partner?"

Anne settled on his chest, her breasts flattened against his hard chest. "Both."

"Then I'll answer as both your husband and partner. I'd rather be home with ye." He drew in a breath "I know that's not possible."

"But it is." Anne hurried on when he looked at her. "You've made a great deal of money, Jamie."

"We've made it."

"Well, you've been the one to risk your life going after French ships; all I did was sell some jewels to make some repairs on your sloop." Even so, he'd called her his partner from the beginning. "Anyway, I've been going over the books and we have enough money to expand. Buy a schooner. And there's more business than we can handle now that peace has come."

" 'Tis a good idea, but I don't see how it will help me stay in port."

"We'll need someone to handle the business end, arrange for shipping the rice and the like. And I won't have time to do it anymore."

"A merchant. Me?" Jamie scrunched higher against his pillow. "I think I like the notion." He hesitated, realizing what else she said. His eyes narrowed. "But what are ye going to be doing, Annie?"

"Well." Anne stretched the word out. "I'm speaking as your wife now."

"So tell me, wife, what's goin' on here?"

"We're going to have a baby."

Anne didn't think she'd ever see the pirate speechless, but as he pulled himself to sitting, Anne across his lap, he was.

"Aren't you going to say something?"

He hugged her to him, burying his face in her hair. "A child," he murmured. "I love ye, Annie."

They spent some time just holding each other, speaking of their future and the love they shared, before straightening their clothing and going above deck. Arm in arm they walked to their house on Tradd Street.

"Oh," Annie said, as they climbed the steps toward the door. "I almost forgot in all the excitement. Last Sunday at Saint Philips I met a woman with the last name of MacQuaid. She's married to the Indian agent and lives to the west on the frontier. She was very nice and terribly interesting to talk with. Do you think she could be a relative?"

"What was her husband's name?" Jamie scooted his wife through the door and toward the steps leading to the second floor.

"Raff."

"Nay, I've but a half-brother named Logan, and he's far away in Scotland."

"Mmmm." Her pirate scooped her into his arms and Anne had no more time to think of anything but him.

To My Readers

I hope you enjoyed *My Seaswept Heart*. The love story of the handsome pirate, Captain Jamie MacQuaid and his Annie, is one of my favorites. Perhaps one reason is that I adore men of the sea. And I seem destined to reform pirates. It's a tough job, but I suppose someone has to do it.

My Seaswept Heart is the second book in the MacQuaid Brothers trilogy. Thanks to all who helped make the first book, *My Savage Heart,* such a success. And now the trilogy continues.

In May 1995, I hope you'll look for *My Heavenly Heart,* Logan MacQuaid's story. Logan was introduced in *My Savage Heart* and he'd just lost his wife and infant daughter in the Cherokee uprising. The sinfully handsome Logan is tortured by guilt and the last thing he wants is a blue-eyed angel to care for. But Logan needs love . . . and perhaps a bit of magic . . . in his life.

Thanks so much for taking the time to write to me. I really appreciate all your letters, and I'm so happy you enjoy my characters and their love stories. I read every letter and answer it personally. You'll never know how much your kind words mean to me.

For a bookmark and newsletter write me care of:

Zebra Books
850 Third Avenue
New York, NY 10022
SASE appreciated

To Happy Endings,

Christine Dorsey

Please turn the page for an exciting
sneak preview of Christine Dorsey's
next enchanting historical romance
My Heavenly Heart
to be published by Zebra Books
in May 1995

Prologue

"Blast Elizabeth and her confounded romantic notion of love."

A grimace accompanied her words as evening dew seeped through Lady Rachel Elliott's satin slippers. They were blue, encrusted with silver lace, and they matched her gown of silk taffeta. "All celestial blue and star glow," Prince William, the king's brother said, when he saw her earlier. "You look like an angel."

"Perhaps, but that was before I overheard Lord Bingham demand to know his wife's whereabouts," Rachel grumbled to herself as she shifted the wide skirts of her gown to avoid a flowerless rosebush. Despite her effort a bit of lace caught on a thorn. She gave the fabric a yank feeling more devil than angel now. Rachel imagined she looked it, too. Neither the shoes nor the gown were meant for tramping along overgrown garden paths and for all the care she took while hurrying through the arbor, Rachel could tell her carefully arranged and powdered wig was askew as well.

No doubt about it, her evening was ruined. And all because her cousin and friend, Lady Elizabeth Bingham insisted upon continuing her dalliance with Sir Geoffrey . . . even though her husband was newly arrived at court.

Rachel paused to get her bearings. Behind her, aglow with candlelight and warmth was Queen's House. If she listened intently, Rachel could hear the melodious strains played by Queen Charlotte's band. There was laughter and fun, and scores of swains, their lips nigh dripping with flattery, awaiting her. The tug to return was strong.

"Oh . . ." The sound started deep in Rachel's corseted chest and gritted through her clenched teeth as she forced herself to turn away and tramp down the grass-covered slope toward the lake. Wait until she found Liz. She would show no mercy in reproving her cousin. And if Sir Geoffrey spoke up . . . well, he would feel the sharp edge of her tongue as well. Rachel didn't care if he was broad of shoulder and handsome of face. *She* didn't even care that his very smile sent Liz into a swoon. There was a time and place for such affairs. And from the expression on Lord Bingham's face when he stormed from the ballroom, it was obvious this wasn't one of them.

There were fewer lanterns now that she'd left the formal gardens. They offered little light and Rachel hoped she'd be able to find Liz and Geoffrey. "Don't let them have gone off to his lodgings," she pleaded to no one in particular. But Rachel didn't think they'd risk leaving the palace this evening.

"Rachel, I must go to Geoff and explain," Liz insisted earlier in the evening after guiding them both into a small private alcove.

All around them music played, gaiety abounded, and Rachel's mind was still on her flirtation with the king's brother. It took a moment for Liz's words to register. "Explain what?" Rachel asked, but Liz had simply looked at her with that dreamy expression on her face as if to say Rachel wouldn't understand.

And she didn't. If this was what love did to a person, Rachel was glad not to be afflicted with the emotion.

Rachel paused when she heard voices over the gentle swishing of the lake lapping the shore. With a sigh she set off toward the sound. The grass was taller here, wetting the hem of her gown even though she lifted it. Why couldn't the lovers find somewhere more civilized to meet, for goodness sakes?

"There you are." Rachel marched toward the couple when she spotted them standing near the end of the pier that jutted out into the lake. It was too dark to see the expressions on Liz and Geoffrey's faces but Rachel imagined they both were surprised when she spoke. They separated quickly, though Sir Geoffrey kept his arm about her cousin's shoulders.

"What . . . what on earth are you doing here, Rachel?" Liz sounded thoroughly flustered.

"I should think that obvious." Rachel gave an unladylike snort. "I've come to fetch you back." Rachel addressed Liz. She decided she didn't give a fig what Geoffrey thought or did. And it wasn't because he monopolized her cousin's time . . . time usually spent with her . . . since his arrival at court.

"But, Rachel, I told you where I was going. . . ."

"Yes, you did. And though I thought at the time it utter foolishness—"

"I fail to see why Elizabeth and my whereabouts are your concern, Lady Rachel."

Rachel opened her mouth to tell him what she thought of men like him but before she could Liz stepped between them. "Please." She touched Geoffrey's sleeve with one hand, Rachel's with the other. "Please don't argue. You're the two people I love most in the world."

Geoffrey seemed to think this admission called for him to step closer to his beloved.

Rachel only sighed.

"I thought you should know," Rachel began, "that your husband is looking for you."

"Albert stopped gaming long enough to realize I was gone?" Liz seemed to sink back into Geoffrey's embrace. "Do you think he suspects?"

"I haven't a clue." Rachel softened her voice and reached for her cousin's hands. They were cold. "I think we should go back to Queen's House. He seemed angry and—" Rachel paused when Liz made a low, whimpering sound. "Elizabeth, it's the only way. I'll say we were together."

"You don't understand." Elizabeth's fingers linked with Rachel's. "You don't know what he's like. If he suspects something he'll—"

The rest of Elizabeth's words were cut off when a shot rang out sending a flock of ducks exploding into the night sky. It also sent Geoffrey crumbling to his knees.

Rachel's head whipped round toward the shore in time to see the man standing there, a pistol in each hand. "Arthur." His name escaped her on a gasp as another report sounded. Rachel felt the jolt of the ball slamming into her cousin through their linked hands. Then Liz fell forward, the weight of her body sending Rachel plummeting off the pier into the lake.

Panic seized Rachel the instant she hit the frigid water. The lake embraced her as surely as if it had tentaclelike arms, dragging her down. She fought, struggling in its grip until her limbs grew weak. Screams for help thundered in her ears but succeeded only in filling her mouth with the foul taste of death.

She tried to think. It was the heavy gown that caused her to sink, the silver lace and metal hoops. If she could only rid herself of her clothing. But it had taken three maids nearly an hour to dress her and no amount of wriggling could undo their accomplishment.

She was dying. Her chest burned, the pain near unbearable. Then suddenly it was gone. So was the frigid water and the awful fear. All that remained was a slightly dizzying spin, spiraling her upward. And calm. Blessed calm.

"You've done it now. You are an idiot."

"But how was I to know she'd go after her cousin? It wasn't at all like her."

"Haven't you learned anything since you've been here? Mortals are full of surprises."

"Especially this one."

How annoying they were, Rachel thought as she tried to ignore the argument. They threatened to ruin an otherwise wonderful experience. The dark that surrounded her was soft and soothing. And up ahead a white light shone so blindingly pure and warm that it should have hurt her eyes. Except that she had no eyes, or body either.

She simply existed.

Never before had she felt so accepted, so cared for. Love surrounded her, flowed through her as she drifted about. Content, though anxious to move toward the light. At peace except—

"What are we to do?"

"Would you cease your whining? And what do you mean we?"

"Surely you plan to help me."

"I shall remind you again. It was your mistake."

"But I'm merely an apprentice. You were to guide me. And I only glanced away for a moment."

"Stop it!" She'd had enough of their bickering. Of them disturbing her. But Rachel hadn't meant to yell at them. Actually she hadn't yelled. It was as if she communicated with them on some plane other than the spoken word. Whatever it was, they both seemed stunned by her scolding. At least they were silent for a moment. That is until the whiner started again.

"See, I told you she was trouble."

"You didn't say trouble, merely unpredictable, and that I will readily concede." He sighed "The question is what is to be done."

"Done about what?" Rachel decided she must help them solve their dilemma if she was to have any peace.

"About you, of course."

"Yes," the whiner agreed in an accusing tone. "It wasn't your time to die."

"Die? But I'm not d—" Rachel couldn't complete her denial. For as difficult as it was to accept . . . she didn't feel dead . . . in her heart she knew it was true. But where were the things she'd been led to expect? The host of heavenly angels? Or, God forbid, the fiery brimstone? And Rachel had another question. "What happened to Liz?"

"She's gone on, as has her soulmate Geoffrey."

Rachel knew instinctively the spirit meant gone on toward the light. The radiant light that shimmered just out of reach. "Then send me on," Rachel insisted. "I'm ready to go."

"If only it were that simple."

For the first time Rachel felt an inkling of fear. "You can't mean I'm destined for . . . for hell?" At that moment her soul seemed awash with memories of her life. To Rachel's discomfort, some shone less than sterling in the pure light of the afterworld. There was the time she lied to her mother about how she scraped her knee. And then there was gossip. She was quite fond of court intrigue and never hesitated to pass any crumb of information along to Liz. And she wasn't very pious. Or charitable. Just last week she passed by an alms seeker pretending not to see the wretched man. And then there was—

"Oh, do stop your reminiscing. I don't care to review all your misdeeds. Besides, you're not destined to eternal damnation."

Thank God, Rachel thought with a sigh of relief.

"Precisely. But never mind that now. Didn't you hear what Ebenezer said? It wasn't your time to die."

Ebenezer? The spirits had names? Rachel pushed that thought aside. The answer to the problem seemed simple enough. It wasn't her time to die, so. . . . "Send me back to life."

"It isn't that easy."

Ebenezer agreed. "You've passed over."

"But it was a mistake. You said so yourself. Your mistake." Her temper . . . another of her faults if she were honest . . . was upon her.

"I'm only an apprentice."

Rachel was preparing her next argument, after all, none of this was *her* fault, when the other spirit interrupted.

"There is something we might do." He paused just long enough to garner Rachel and Ebenezer's attention. "Perhaps if she earned her way back."

"Of course." Ebenezer sounded relieved. But then the whiny edge returned to his thoughts. "Do you think He will agree to it?"

"We shall see. There are precedents, of course. We must speak with Him straightaway."

Rachel felt the force of the two spirits leaving her. "Wait!" She wasn't sure she liked this turn of events any more than she liked the ones that brought her here. "What do you mean precedents? What must I do to earn my way back?"

Off in the distance near the light she felt the spirits pause. Then the one who seemed to be in charge answered. "It's very simple, actually. You need only save the life of another lost soul."